DARKENING SONG

DARKENING SONG

DELPHINE SEDDON

This is a work of fiction. All of the names, characters, organizations, places, and events portrayed in this work are either products of the author's imagination or are used fictitiously.

DARKENING SONG. Copyright © 2026 by Delphine Seddon. All rights reserved.
The right of Delphine Seddon to be identified as the author of this work has been asserted by her in accordance with the Copyright, Designs and Patents Act 1988.

First published in the USA and Canada in 2026 by Saturday Books,
an imprint of Macmillan USA.
www.saturdaybooks.com

First published in Great Britain in 2026 by Blue Neon Books Limited.
www.blueneonbooks.com

Interior designed by Michelle McMillian

Cover design by Delphine Seddon

Lips: Shutterstock

A catalogue record for this book is available on request from the British Library.

Paperback ISBN: 978-1-9194284-0-6
Ebook ISBN: 978-1-9194284-1-3

The publisher of this book does not authorize the use or reproduction of any part of this book in any manner for the purpose of training artificial intelligence technologies or systems. The publisher of this book expressly reserves this book from the Text and Data Mining exception in accordance with Article 4(3) of the European Union Digital Single Market Directive 2019/790.

First Edition: 2026
Printed and bound in Great Britain by Clays Ltd, Elcograf S.p.A.

This novel is dedicated to all women in music—past, present and future.

Dear Reader,

For a long time I worked in the music business. I have many treasured memories from those years and met some incredible people, a lot of whom remain friends. But it was (and remains) a boys' club, so even back in the days when this book was nothing but a seed of an idea in my brain and heart, I knew I wanted to drop a partnership between two young women into that male-dominated environment and watch them navigate it on their own terms.

I have occasionally included a named famous person in the book's fictional setting, but all other characters are entirely fictional and figments of my imagination and any similarities between any character and any real person, dead or alive, is pure coincidence. The fact that this is a work of fiction does not, however, detract from the very real nature and gravity of some of the topics in *Darkening Song*. So please do be aware that the following sensitive subjects are discussed in the book: anxiety, substance abuse, sexual assault and an off-page attempted suicide. When they are described it is through the characters' own words. I have made every effort to handle these sensitive subjects carefully and responsibly, but please be aware if they are personally challenging. Please also be aware that you are not alone. Help and support are available—I will include a list of resources on my website at delphineseddon.com on publication.

Thank you so much for reading.

All my love,
Delphine x

DARKENING SONG

ALORA

I WRAP THE CURTAIN AROUND MY BODY. It's blush-pink velvet, soft like the skin of a peach. A repetitive triangular pattern is woven through the fabric in fine gold thread. The penthouse lights are off and I'm lurking in the shadows, watching *them* for once, tiny black dots in the street below. They carry their cameras on straps across their shoulders. I carry their presence around my neck. They surge back and forth in relentless anticipation of a sighting, a dark tsunami. I've heard that shots of me go for a hundred grand, that one of me crying or yelling or allowing any semblance of emotion to seep through the stone-faced tolerance will go for two—my face, my tears, for sale to the highest bidder.

I step away from the balcony, de-cocooning myself from the curtain, and lie down on the chaise longue which stands on bronze lion's paws. There's a point when luxury becomes plain silly and an even further point when you stop seeing it altogether, when you're ushered through the lobby of the five-star hotel in the middle of a scrum of bodyguards and all you see is the toes of your Fendi boots. I passed that point at sixteen years old when my first album went to number one in fifteen countries. I flick the switch and stare up into the chandelier, at the dappled patterns it paints on the ornate ceiling, a mesmerising kaleidoscope of light, a temporary distraction.

I stand quickly, my eyes misting over as the blood rushes to my head, and make my way to the bathroom. My bare feet sink into the plush cream carpet and I count each footstep, as though every one of them is significant. The silk of my gown whispers around me—a strapless bodice blooming out into a full floor-length skirt, red as rage, as a massacre. I've dressed for the occasion. The bathtub is already full, steam rising from the hot water like escaping dreams. I wipe a face-shaped porthole in the condensation clinging to the mirror and apply lipstick, electric-green eyeliner, mascara, a little blush, painting myself into the person they expect me to be. My eyes stare back at me, green and solemn beneath the numbing glaze of a tumbler of tequila. I'm buried at the bottom of the ocean, watching a distorted reflection of real life pass by above me with the clouds whilst the diamonds layered across my knuckles and cascading from my earlobes wink like tiny flashbulbs. I climb into the bath fully clothed, my dress floating up and rippling with the surface of the water, and open up the z-pix app, then I position my phone behind the gold taps. I've got 207 million followers on this platform alone. The owner of z-pix, Jared Brisk, boasts about his no-censorship approach to social media like he's liberating humanity. Politicians rant, lobby groups rave, whilst Brisk counts his billions. I click on Livestream and perfect the angle so I'm centre shot.

Tomorrow night the stadium will be full. My second album is at number one in the charts. My world tour has sold out. But I'm about to give the most unforgettable performance of my life.

EVA

TWO YEARS EARLIER...

I SAT DOWN AT MY DESK in Low Slang Records and began typing out the invite list to the MD's exclusive summer party at Soho House, delegated to me by his PA seemingly so she could free up more time to paint her fingernails a lurid shade of pink and gossip with Jeff from the post room. At moments like this it was difficult not to think about food. I tried to muster up the willpower not to sabotage the eternal diet and make a second midmorning trip to the vending machine. Roxanne, the head of marketing at the record label, stopped by and asked if I fancied doing the coffee run. She was tall and glamorous with glossy brown hair which hung to her shoulders in a professional blow-dry, reeking of Le Labo perfume like she'd marinated herself in the stuff overnight. She was wearing multiple gold necklaces and a tight, white angora sweater which clung, fluffy and rabbit-like, to her significant breasts. She'd worked for the MD for fourteen years. According to the rumours, their relationship wasn't entirely professional, I'd been told some private things about her at after-work drinks which sometimes made it difficult to meet her eye. I always did the coffee run. It was a detail about my day which, when my friends asked how the internship at the record label was going, assuming it to be a chic, star-studded, rock-and-roll existence, I routinely omitted to mention.

The day Aunty Liz took Katerina and me to see Adele at the Shepherd's Bush Empire, I decided I wanted to work in the music business. Before then I'd had zero career ambitions to speak of, and when asked by cooing grandmas at family gatherings that age-old question, 'What do you want to be when you grow up?' I always answered honestly, much to their apparent dismay: 'I don't know.' I wasn't even a particular fan of Adele, or anyone else that I remember. At thirteen years old my twenty-one-year-old sister was my idol. Katerina—a grunge kid who wore ripped jeans and Pearl Jam T-shirts and listened to Nirvana and Sonic Youth with the volume turned up so loud that she developed mild tinnitus in her right ear. Every band Katerina liked, I insisted I liked too. And when Aunty Liz presented us with the Adele tickets across the dinner table one evening, thinking we'd be thrilled, Katerina said she was busy that night so I—somewhat comically since I had zero social life—said the same. Mum was livid. She immediately marched us up to our rooms and much yelling ensued with some door slamming by Katerina, and soon we were back downstairs apologising to Aunty Liz, thanking her profusely for the tickets and saying we'd love to go.

The show was sold out, the venue packed. Aunty Liz bought

branded T-shirts from the merch stand and insisted we put them on over our clothes. Even before Adele walked out I could feel the anticipation in the air, like static. Then she appeared, and the crowd went berserk. With her enormous eyes which held the entire universe within them and her golden hair she looked otherworldly, a goddess from an ancient fable. But when she began to sing, I was floored. Her words seemed to be written just for me, despite the fact that back then my greatest romantic heartbreak was my unrequited crush, Alistair Greenwood, kissing Victoria Lawson at the school disco. Her voice was like all of my favourite foods—tiramisu and morello-cherry ice cream and profiteroles with chocolate sauce—blended together and poured into my ears in one delicious soup of sound. I myself had no musical talent whatsoever, as had been confirmed by my violin teacher who, after three tortuous lessons, told Mum that her hard-earned cash would be better spent elsewhere. But that day, standing in the middle of a crowd of adoring Adele fans, some of whom were actually weeping, the music wrapped its arms around me and embraced me. It sucked out the stresses of my tiny life and filled me with hope. I now understood its power, and a few Google searches later—how do you work with musicians when (to quote my former violin teacher) you've got no rhythm and you're tone-deaf—I'd found my calling. So if traipsing up and down to Starbucks every day, pandering to the demands of Roxanne and the rest of the Low Slang Records staff gave me an in, then I'd do it with gumption.

I smiled sweetly and said, 'Sure, I'll get the coffees, no problem.' I would have probably removed her socks and kissed her feet if she'd asked me to.

The head of A&R, Jason—second-in-command to the MD

in deciding what artists the label signed—had lost his wallet on a night out and was waiting for new cash cards to arrive, so I said I'd shout him, the words leaving my lips before I'd had chance to lament the disastrous state of my bank balance. Ray—the other intern who got special privileges because his dad was high up at the BBC—changed his mind about ten times, seemingly oblivious to the possibility that he could actually come with me and help, and Levi insisted I read his order back to him to ensure I didn't 'fuck it up like last time' (his exact words). I returned with two cardboard trays slotted full of coffee and distributed the drinks, but just as I walked into Jason's office with his double macchiato, I knocked into the corner of his desk and sloshed coffee all over my sweater. It soaked right through to my bra. Jason was sitting on his minimalist Scandinavian-style sofa wearing headphones, nodding and tapping one large-tongued trainer in time to whatever potential hit record was playing. He pulled a half-hearted impression of a sympathetic face and slid a headphone off one ear.

'Hey, don't worry about it, Eva,' he said. 'Just nip back down to Starbucks and fetch me another.'

After I'd maxed out my account on a second four-pound-fifty cup of coffee, made it back into the glass lift, up to the top floor and into Jason's office without a second spillage, after I'd returned from the loos where I'd scrubbed my sweater in the sink and attempted to dry it under the hand dryer without removing it from my bikini-unready body, I finally sat down at my desk and realised I'd forgotten to buy a coffee for myself.

'Shit,' I muttered under my breath, but not loud enough that anyone else could hear me.

Then I closed the MD's invite list, unlocked my phone, and

dully resumed swiping through endless grainy videos online, trying to discover 'the next big thing'. Jason had set this task for Ray and me at the start of the summer. When I'd asked for some guidance as to what kind of artist Jason thought 'the next big thing' might be he'd wafted a dismissive hand at me and said, 'I'll know it when I hear it.' He'd been mildly interested in some indie band from Liverpool which Ray had come across on SoundCloud—five young lads with messy bed hair singing about their mums—but Jason said everything I'd found was 'too derivative' or 'too early' or was seemingly unworthy of any feedback whatsoever when he simply ignored my emails.

But that morning, careening from one video to the next, ingesting wannabes as mindlessly as shoving handfuls of peanut M&M's into my mouth whilst watching repeats of *Love Island*, I found her.

Sitting alone, centre stage in her high-school auditorium, the angle of the camera—probably someone's phone—was looking down on her. She had long white-blonde hair with a blunt wedge of a fringe, red lips and electric-green eyeliner which flicked up at the corners. I would later realise how beautiful she was, how delicate her elfin features were with huge sea-green bedtime-story eyes. But from a distance, in platform DM boots with ribbon for laces and an oversized hoodie dress which reached her knees and swamped her slight frame, it seemed like her existence was something she wanted to disguise. She didn't introduce herself, made no attempt to silence the murmuring voices, sniggering or shuffling of feet. She simply picked up the acoustic guitar, positioned it on her lap and began to sing. The room hushed. I was transfixed from the very first note:

I've forgotten how to live
Or maybe I just never knew
Convince the shrink I'm doing fine
When I'm drowning in the blue

Kill me with your kindness
Suffocate me in belief
Don't know how to love myself
So how could he love me?

That voice, powerful and pure, swelling effortlessly from deep within the gut. The cryptic darkness of the lyrics. Someone in the background whispered, 'Wow.' There was no other word for it.

ALORA

I HEAR VOICES, URGENT AND INSISTENT. I try to resist, but the pull of consciousness is too powerful a force. I open my eyes into bright white lights, the obnoxious glare of life. Doctors surround me, five solemn faces peering into mine.

'She's okay,' one of them says. 'She's with us.' And I know that I have failed.

They wheel me to a private room where nurses fuss and gossip to the soundscape of incessant bleeping, checking my vital signs and scribbling on charts. Julia and Eva appear at my bedside. Julia's sobbing, her makeup congealing in the creases beneath her eyes.

'How could you do this to me?' she wails.

She leans over the bed and presses her cheek against mine. Her skin feels cold and unfamiliar and I want her to stop.

I glance at Eva. Her face is gaunt and pale and she's biting her bottom lip hard enough to sever it in two. 'Julia, maybe give her some space?' she says, her voice quivering with emotion, like she's trying not to cry. She touches Julia's arm and my mother steps back, too involved in her own dramatic performance to object.

My wrists are concealed by white dressings, but I know what lies beneath. I watch the movement in my own fingers with morbid fascination, as though they don't belong to me. Clearly I didn't damage any nerves or tendons—a pathetic attempt at ending it all. 'What's in this?' I say to the nurse, gesturing to the tube puncturing the back of my hand. She glances up from her clipboard and says something about replenishing lost fluids. 'But I don't want them replenished,' I say, or maybe I say nothing at all. The TV on the wall is showing an all-female chat show with the sound muted. The presenters and guests are wearing pastel colours and seem impossibly happy. I ask Eva to switch it off and she hurries over to do my bidding. I close my eyes and sink into a deep, dark morbidity which feigns as sleep.

I'm standing in the doorway. It looks like any other hotel room; a double bed to my right, shelving lined with the coloured spines of hardback books, polished wooden floorboards, and a copper bathtub with a selection of shampoos and body lotions in tiny bottles, white labels fashionably embossed with typewriter print. The back wall is made of glass and looks out onto fields, miles of undulating green beneath an oppressive mass of bleak grey sky. I'm on a private island somewhere off the Scottish coast, accessible only by chartered boat or helicopter. But this is no hotel—it's a rehab clinic.

I don't particularly want to talk about what happened, but talking is how we're supposed to pass the time in this place. I completed the form, told them my age, weight, a vague sliver of my family background. I hovered the Biro over the neat little boxes that gave everything a label, made it all sound so simple. I don't want to be here. I don't want to be out there either. I just want to be a blank empty space where a person used to be. I follow the woman into the room. She introduces herself as my 'carer'. She's talking and Julia and Eva are nodding like plastic dogs off that insurance advert they used to show on TV. I can see her lips forming the shape of words but it's impossible for my brain to decipher the meaning and they merge together as one continuous garble of sound. Eva looks tired and Julia's curls are intrusively large and buoyant, taking over the room. I can see the lace of her bra where her shirt hangs open at the neck. My mother. She pouts like a child's doll.

I sit down on the edge of the bed whilst Eva and Julia talk to the woman. She's wearing navy-blue trousers and a matching tunic which is tapered at her thick waist, her name embroidered at her chest—MAUREEN. Despite everything I start to think about *him*. I can't help it. Pathetic I know.

'Alora?' I look up. Maureen's smiling. Her skin is brown and her eyes are optimistically bright, brimming with false promises about how they're going to fix me here. 'Do you want to say goodbye to Julia and Eva?' She speaks to me in a slow, pronounced tone, rolling the vowels and consonants around her mouth as though I'm hard of hearing or a toddler being dropped off at day care.

'Where are they going?' I hear myself say, but my voice is faint and seems to be coming from somewhere outside my body.

'We have to leave now,' Eva says. 'We can come back and visit you in a month.'

The clinic is owned by some revolutionary psychiatrist called Max Beaumont. It's the only one of its kind in the world. He developed a form of therapy he humbly named the Beaumont

Method, which took off when some big Hollywood actor talked about it on *Oprah*—he said it saved his life—but everyone just calls it the Method. I know a few people who've done it for addiction issues and got clean to the point of death by boredom. From what they've told me, it involves sitting around in a circle with other unhinged rich people, acting out weird role-plays and collectively wallowing in your own problems, all for the bargain price of thirty grand a month. No wonder Max Beaumont could afford to buy the whole island. I stand up and endure my mother's arms around me, then Eva's. Her touch is light and tentative, like she's worried I might snap in two beneath the pressure of a hug. She smells of the perfume I bought her last Christmas, custom made in Paris, musky and floral and rich.

'Take care,' she whispers. 'I'm sure you'll feel better soon.' I almost laugh out loud.

Once they've left I slip off my trainers and walk towards the window. The complex consists of a series of chalets in a courtyard formation, one for each patient, a canopied walkway which protects its clients' privacy from photographers hovering in the sky. The therapy centre sits to the left in a stone building with the restaurant, freshwater swimming pool, health spa and shop to the right. I trail my fingertips around the edge of the glass, searching for an opening where there's none. I press my nose against it and feel the damp warmth of my own breath as it condenses into fog. The view makes me feel anxious, the vast expanse of nothingness. An entire SWAT team on reception searched my body and bags when I arrived. I leaned against the wall and closed my eyes as they confiscated a Gucci belt, a packet of Xanax, a long silk Hermès scarf. Eva pulled out my phone which I'd left balanced on the taps at the Edinburgh

Grand Hotel, streaming it all live on z-pix, and they locked it away. I've got no means of communication with the outside world, no way of finding out what *they're* saying about me or what *he's* doing. Panic rises in my throat like bile. I don't want to care, but I still do. I see an eagle swooping low on the horizon and squint into the sunlight, then I realise it's a crow. It cries out with its ugly voice like it's laughing.

EVA

I PRACTICALLY RAN INTO JASON'S OFFICE. I had visions of him jumping up from his seat, summoning the MD, Roxanne and the rest of the team to tell them what an incredible artist I'd found, how they needed to sign her immediately and offer me a job at Low Slang Records finding new talent—the ultimate dream when I'd applied for a place on the intern scheme. What actually happened was I knocked on Jason's door, he looked up irritably, said he was busy and told me to come back later. Then he left the office for lunch and didn't come back for the rest of the day. So I emailed him a link to the video and he replied saying he'd watch it when he had a spare minute, which was apparently never, because a week went by, and then another, and he said nothing more about it. I finally plucked up the courage to insist I play it for him. But this time when I walked into his room he was on the phone, puffing on a cigarette despite the building's impenetrably unopenable windows and no-smoking policy and gesticulating with his free hand. I waited until he ended the call which concluded with him yelling 'Tell Jordan he can go fuck himself!' Then I somewhat timidly asked if I could play him something. 'Play me what?' he barked, and when I told him, voice trembling, at first he looked confused to see me standing there in the middle of his rug in my baggy jeans, Glass Animals T-shirt and battered Adidas trainers. Then his cheeks flushed and his eyes seemed to bulge out of his skull. I wondered if he was about to have an aneurysm. He asked me who the fuck I thought I was, waltzing in here telling him how to do his job. He said I needed to get back in my box.

'So fucking uncool,' Ade said when I told him about the whole mortifying incident later that day, reliving it in the process and going blotchy all over. We were at Mimi's parents' place, hanging out in the pool house which Mimi had commandeered as her own private residence for the summer. It was a warm summer evening, the sun slowly fading from the sky in a haze of lilac, the air lapping gently against my skin. The glass doors were opened out onto the terrace where Petra, Mimi and Mairead were lounging in the shallow end of the pool wearing minuscule bikinis and drinking frozen margaritas. I'd decided not to change into my swimming costume, which had a high neck and special tummy-control panels, but Ade was in his swim shorts. He had the body of an athlete even though the extent of his exercise regime was the occasional game of five-a-side football with his mates. He scratched his chest and took a sip of margarita as Mimi positioned her glass on the side of the pool and rolled over onto her stomach. I looked away but I could still feel her eyes burning into me, which I tried to ignore.

Ade was my best friend, my favourite person in the entire world. He was incredibly non-judgemental, chill and positive and always found the silver lining in whatever cloud of doom I chucked his way. With Ade, everything was either 'cool' or 'uncool', and he always took both scenarios perfectly within his stride.

'Seriously, Eva, don't waste your time on losers like that. You found her on z-pix right?' I had found her, the handle was @darkeningsong and the profile pic was definitely her, and I'd been surprised to see that she had nearly twenty thousand followers—more than some of the development acts signed to Low Slang—who wrote comments like—

Hit me up dark sis ☺
U speakin str8t to my soul no lie!!!

—beneath posts of her lyrics and video clips of her singing, sitting on a single mattress with a guitar in her arms, the wall behind her covered in posters for classic dystopian movies (the originals, not the remakes)—*1984, Mad Max, Westworld, Battle Royale*. She had, I'd discovered, also self-released a couple of songs. The quality of the recordings wasn't great, like she'd possibly just recorded them on a phone, but the streaming numbers on Spotify and Apple Music were decent—just shy of a million per track. She'd obviously got some initiative, because as far as I could tell there was no team around her, she was just getting on with it all by herself.

'Just DM her,' Ade said.

'And say what? Low Slang is never going to sign her if I can't even get Jason to listen to one song. He's the only person who's got the MD's ear and I'm hardly going to walk into the MD's office and play it to him myself.'

'Why not?'

'Because he's terrifying and I'm an intern, a complete nobody! I doubt he even knows I exist.' I looked up to see Mimi whispering something to Petra. She stopped when I met her eye.

'Hey, do you remember when I got that summer job in Espresso Yourself on Mare Street?'

'Uh-hum. You told them in the interview you knew how to work the coffee machine and make a leaf pattern in the milk when you barely knew how to boil a kettle.'

'Exactly! And that worked out all right, didn't it? Okay, apart from a few minor customer complaints until I got the hang of it.'

Mimi climbed out of the pool and made her way to the deep end, bikini bottoms conveniently riding up between her cellulite-free ass cheeks. She stood poised on the side for a moment, flexing her sinewy body, and I, with a certain degree of repressed jealousy, watched Ade watching her. Then she stretched her arms above her head and dived in. The water barely rippled. 'What's your point?' I said.

Ade returned his gaze to me. 'I just followed one of life's basic principles.'

'Which is?'

He drained his glass and smiled. 'Sometimes you've just got to fake it 'til you make it.'

ALORA

MAUREEN SAYS I SHOULD EAT SOME lunch before my first therapy session begins. I tell her I'm not hungry and she arches one eyebrow. She says that it's obligatory for me to eat three meals a day. I ask if they do room service.

The restaurant is in the same building as the swimming pool and spa. The windows are tinted like the windows of all of my cars. Maureen walks by my side, swinging her sturdy arms in an enthusiastic manner. A blonde woman is standing outside the door smoking a cigarette. Her straw-coloured hair is set into a rigid bouffant cloud. She's thin, painfully so. The skin of her forehead is taut, her eyes lift at the corners like everything's been pulled back and up and her lips are grossly plump, that bee-stung look everybody wants these days but she must've been attacked by the whole hive. Her age is apparent despite all of this, which is tragic really. Her hand trembles as she takes a last drag before throwing the cigarette to the ground. Maureen tuts. The woman ignores her. She casts her eyes over me as though I'm an object in a shop that she has no interest in buying, pulls open the door to the restaurant and struts in ahead of us.

'I'll leave you here,' Maureen says, picking the burning cigarette butt up off the ground and holding it disapprovingly between her thumb and index finger.

'Can't I just eat in my room?' At eighteen years old I'm whining like a child. I've already asked this question twice and Maureen regurgitates the same answer with unfathomable patience.

'We don't insist that our clients interact with each other, but we do find that it's beneficial to the Method if they dine communally.' I roll my eyes in an exaggerated manner. She smiles into my petulance and says that she'll collect me in an hour.

Some diners sit alone, others congregate in clusters, chatting amicably as though they're old friends holidaying together in the Algarve, all of them wearing the same clinically white uniform complete with gold trim like they've just escaped from a luxury mental asylum. I attract a few glances as I weave my way through the tables but people quickly divert their eyes. One of the many rules of this place is no staring at other guests, no questions about their lives unless expressly invited to ask or in the context of an open discussion in therapy sessions, and we've all signed contracts with confidentiality clauses as long as my arm. I choose a seat as far away from everyone else as is possible. The internal window looks out onto the pool and the surface of the water is still. Palm trees erupt from terracotta pots and the ceiling is covered in lush green vines with a tropical feel although the air-con is turned up so high it's like they're trying to cryogenically freeze us all. A waiter darts towards me. He's wearing jeans and trainers with a crisp blue shirt. 'I'm professional but relaxed,' his clothing screams. He introduces himself as Jacob and asks if I'd like still or sparkling water. The clinic is dry. How am I even supposed to get through the day? I shrug in a non-committal way and he returns with a bottle of each, asks what he can get me to eat. He looks disappointed when I tell him that I'm not hungry, like he's been trained to pretend he genuinely cares.

'We've got some small plates.' He picks up the menu, points to a section at the top which lists a few fussy-sounding dishes, all jus and foam and caramelised air.

'I said, I'm not hungry.' I say it firmly, probably a little louder than necessary.

He walks away looking defeated and I notice the blonde woman is staring at me from across the room. She's sitting alone, holding a glass of thick green juice which looks like blended grass cuttings, which she's stirring absentmindedly with a straw. With her eyes yanked back like that she looks more feline than human but not in a cute Instagrammable way. I stare back, opening my eyes as wide as I can to make the point that she's staring, but she doesn't get it, she doesn't look away and I wonder if she's going to walk over and ask for my autograph. I stand up and make my way towards the door. Jacob gets there before me.

'You're leaving?'

'I'm going for a walk.'

'But you can't, not by yourself.'

'Seriously?' He's standing in the doorway, blocking my path. 'This is ridiculous.'

'Please.'

I sit back down. The woman isn't staring anymore and I relax a little, turn towards the pool. A middle-aged man with flabby jowls and a super-hairy chest is swimming now. He's doing front crawl, slowly and methodically. He seems oblivious to the diners observing him as he lifts one fleshy arm after another and slices his way through the water in his Speedos, enough to put anyone off their food. He duck-dives as he reaches the side before commencing another lap. Back and forth, left to right, these small repetitions which formulate a life, getting older and weaker until we finally sink to the bottom.

A few minutes later Jacob appears with two plates and places them down on the table in front of me with a flourish. He announces, 'Avocado salad with pine nuts and mushroom risotto with cashew cheese. I know you're vegan.' He seems proud of this knowledge, which he probably acquired from the columns of a gossip magazine.

'But I didn't order...'

He starts to look nervous and I suddenly realise that I'm going to cry. He can obviously tell. He asks if he should take the food away and I nod, because it's all that I can do, because I can already feel the water leaking from my eyes. He points to the toilet and touches my back lightly as I stand, which seems like a kind gesture but one he's probably not permitted to make. I rush towards it, heart thudding as though invisible paparazzi are pursuing me. I lock myself in the cubicle, slide down the back of the door and sob into my palms. I can still smell the hospital on my skin, the unmistakable fragrance of disinfectant and death. I tip my head back and emit a long, anguished howl. 'Please!' I cry towards the ceiling. 'Please, please, please!' But I don't know who I hope is listening or what exactly I'm begging for. Eventually, I scrub at my face with a wad of toilet tissue, unlock the door and emerge. I stare at the girl who greets me in the mirror. She's thin and scrawny with an excessive amount of hair. Her face is red and swollen like a beef tomato. Julia's right, I've always been an ugly crier, she says it's genetic. I hear a knock and Maureen appears. She doesn't blanch at my appearance.

'Come on, you,' she says, with a sense of familiarity that I find slightly shocking. She links her arm through mine and walks me back to my chalet where she gestures for me to take a seat in the armchair. She perches her ample ass on the edge of the bed, then reaches over and covers my hand with her own. Her hand is plump and matronly, mine a shrivelled weed beneath it. 'You're here to heal,' she says.

I emit a loud gasping sob. 'I wish I was dead,' I say, and she clucks her tongue.

'Maybe you do, but we might be able to change that. This is a good place, good people. Be kind to your body. Eat the nourishing food. Open your heart to the possibility that we might be able to help you.'

I narrow my eyes and her outline blurs through my tears. 'There's no helping me,' I say. 'You're all wasting your time.'

EVA

I ADMIT THAT I FOUND HER intimidating, this cool, aloof sixteen-year-old girl—the polar opposite of me at that age—sitting in the front room of a dingy flat on the outskirts of Manchester. The flat was above a café and the air smelled of rancid chip fat. It was incredibly stuffy in there and when I asked if we could possibly open a window, please, I was told they were painted shut. I could feel sweat patches forming at my armpits beneath my denim jacket. I smiled at Alora. She stared back at me blankly. She had that trendily malnourished look about her, razor-sharp cheekbones and grey half-moons beneath her eyes. And the mum was not what I'd expected at all.

Julia had the appearance and physique of a Barbie: large, bulbous breasts sloping into an impossibly tiny waist, dark hair which swept across her back in lustrous curls and long, false eyelashes. Everything about her was tight; her vest top, her jeans, her smile as she said to me, 'I didn't expect someone so young. You must be what, the same age as Alora?'

'I'm eighteen,' I said.

'Hmm, you don't look it. And you work at a record label, you say?'

I felt my cheeks colour, my body's betrayal of the lie. What had I been thinking, coming here alone on a Sunday afternoon on the pretence of officially representing Low Slang? 'Yeah, I do... I mean, sort of.'

'Well, do you or don't you?' she snapped.

'Yeah, yeah I do.' She leaned forwards in her seat and asked me if I'd met any famous people. I told her I'd once got in the lift with Chris Martin and she asked what he was like and whether I knew if he was single.

'So can you get me a record deal, or what?' Alora said. It was the first time she'd actually spoken to me other than a grunted hello when I first walked through the door. Her startlingly green eyes seemed to be searching mine as though she would soon find the truth and use it as a sharp implement with which to bore into my soul. The temperature in the room suddenly seemed to reach boiling point, the walls appeared to be moving inwards and the various objects—the record player and shelves full of vinyl, the strange assortment of pottery figurines lined up across the mantelpiece and the many framed photographs of a much younger version of Julia, the soft-focus kind where the backstreet photographer tells you he'll make you a model then charges you five hundred quid for the privilege—seemingly multiplied and threatened to avalanche. 'Is that what you want?' I managed to say. 'A record deal?'

Alora tucked her hair behind her ears. She was wearing tiny gold-hoop earrings, two in each earlobe, and a ring on her index finger in the shape of a bird in flight. 'No,' she said. 'I don't *just* want a record deal. I want to be an icon.'

And I heard myself say, 'I can make that happen.'
'How?'

I'd heard about artist management. I'd seen managers wandering around Low Slang Records with their clients, off to the MD's office in search of the holy grail of a record deal. I knew that they worked independently from the record labels, outside of the confines of 'the machine', that they looked after the artists' careers, representing them, guiding them, advising them, with seemingly no formal qualifications whatsoever necessary. If Jason wouldn't listen, I would do it without him. In a voice brimming with conviction which surprised even me, I said, 'Let me be your manager, and I'll show you.'

ALORA

THE FIRST THERAPY SESSION TAKES PLACE that afternoon. There are six of us in the group. We sit in a circle on hard wooden chairs, facing each other. I recognise two of them, I think. Maybe I've kissed the air above their cheeks at an awards ceremony, maybe I've seen them on TV. I instinctively hang my head so that my hair falls across my face, the best disguise I can muster in the circumstances. I'm wearing the white tunic, trousers and soft lace-less pumps which Maureen brought into my room and laid out on the bed.

'All of our guests wear these,' she said, before adding, 'Everybody is the same in here,' like she expected me to object, to demand something custom-made or haute couture. At least the sleeves are long, so no one will be able to stare at my wrists.

The therapy centre has a high ceiling with wooden beams running across it like a rib cage with resonant, cathedral-like acoustics. Particles of dust float like cotton through the narrow shafts of light falling in quivering oblongs onto the floorboards.

Our 'Method Teacher' is called Elijah and I'm positioned next to him, so when he says, 'Let's start by introducing ourselves,' he turns to me first.

I realise with a stab of irritation that the woman sitting opposite me is the staring blonde from the dining room—just my luck. I smile at her insincerely. She does not reciprocate, insincerely or otherwise. I already know that we don't have to use our real names during these sessions, that we can refer to ourselves as anything we like—an animal, a flower, simply as a number. Slowly, so as not to draw attention to my movements, I take hold of my left wrist with my right hand and search for the wound. The hospital removed the stitches, but it's nowhere near healed, the incision so much deeper than the skin. I press into it with my thumb. A sharp pain ricochets up my arm and into my shoulder and my eyes smart reassuringly.

I exhale, clear my throat and say, 'My name is Nobody.'

Somebody coughs. Elijah purses his lips. But if he's thinking of objecting he thinks better of it because he presses his palms together, bows his head like a sensei and says, 'Pleasure to meet you, Nobody.'

And I sit and feign attention as the others do the same—the skinny old blonde, the steroid-pumped muscleman, the blandly pretty woman with auburn hair and instantly forgettable facial features, the lanky teenager with a million-dollar smile and a cheerful-looking guy with a bulging stomach and swollen sausage fingers whose rosy cheeks deflect from the misery in his eyes. I realise as Elijah returns to me that I haven't listened to a single name of the other members of the group. But what does it matter? As soon as I've done the obligatory minimum one-month stint I'll check myself out of this hellhole and get back to the task at hand.

EVA

I WAS WINGING IT, BULLSHITTING MY way through the meeting, and yet I'd never been more certain of anything in my life. She had the inner torment and anguish of Amy Winehouse or Kurt Cobain, the sincerity and captivating presence of Adele or Taylor Swift, and the raw, honest punk defiance of Debbie Harry or Patti Smith. She looked like she was shining, and I kept switching positions in my seat thinking it was the sunlight refracting weirdly through the window. I later realised that she always looked like this—the talent inside of her was coming out through the surface.

Julia stood up and said she needed to make dinner and Alora started scrolling through her phone. I knew it was my cue to leave, that I'd totally blown it and was now overstaying my welcome. But even though it was becoming increasingly awkward, I couldn't quite bring myself to go. I asked her if she'd play me a song. She shrugged as though she could barely be bothered and reached for her acoustic guitar, which was propped up against the wall. She played what became her first single, 'Faker.'

I'm just a faker just a pretender
Been like this so long don't know who I am

Got to peel back the layers and start again
But how do I do that where do I begin?
Would you still like me would you recognise me
If I lose this disguise I've been wearing to hide me?

And it was such a privilege to see her perform in the intimate setting of her own front room, looking back on it now, it's one of my most treasured memories. When the song ended I clapped and a slight smile snagged at her lips. I said she was an incredible performer, a natural. She said she'd just had a lot of practise, that she'd been performing since she was nine, that from the age of thirteen she'd been lugging her guitar around Manchester to gigs, sometimes catching the coach to Liverpool or Birmingham where she'd play her set, sleep rough in the bus depot until morning then catch the first coach back.

'You're kidding?' I said. 'You were doing that when you were thirteen? All by yourself?'

'I wanted it,' she said. 'I knew I had to work hard for it.' I was still feeling slightly in awe of her ambition when she dropped the bombshell question I'd been dreading from the moment I rang the doorbell.

'Do you really work at a record label?'

I opened my mouth but no sound came out. She stared at me and I stared back at her. And I found myself babbling my way through the truth. That I was an intern, that I'd found her YouTube channel and thought she was amazing but the head of

A&R wouldn't listen to me, that I knew she and I could achieve great things together if she'd only give me a chance.

Ten minutes later I was sitting in the café beneath the flat, commiserating my failure with an iced bun. It was stale and dry, the icing setting around my tongue like cement, but I took huge bites and gobbled it down anyway where it sat heavy in my stomach, layered over my disappointment like a new formation of sedimentary rock.

'Oh,' she'd said, her tone of voice flat and parched of feeling. Then she'd simply flicked her hair over one shoulder and said, 'I'll think about it and let you know.'

And I saw in her eyes that she didn't need me, that I was just an intern and she was destined for great things. So when the café door swung open and I looked up, enveloped in a gust of exhaust fume–tinged air, I wasn't expecting to see her there.

She strode over in a determined manner, dropped down into the plastic seat in front of me and said, 'Okay . . . so I've thought about it.'

I swallowed hard. 'And?'

'I want you to be my manager.'

When I look back on it now, it felt like something in the universe shifted in that moment, some higher power picked me up and plonked me down on destiny's path. 'Seriously?'

'Uh-hum.'

'Are you sure?'

'Yes! Now quit asking me before I change my mind.'

ALORA

I KNOW ELIJAH WILL ASK ABOUT my parents, it's always where these people start. But he throws me completely when he says, 'I'd like you to describe a significant moment in your life.'

I can imagine what he thinks I'll say: the day my debut album slid straight into the number one spot in the charts, or the morning I woke up to find my z-pix following had hit a hundred million, or when I bought my first house—a seven-bedroom turreted mansion in North London—or maybe when I bought my fourth, or my back-to-back shows at Madison Square Garden selling out in seconds. But if any of these moments felt significant at the time, the memory of them leaves me cold. Because when it comes down to it, none of the stuff you think matters, which you spend every day and night struggling and striving for, ever touches the sides of the dark void of human existence. Life is just about pretending to be fine when all you want to do is crawl into the foetal position and cry.

There is one moment that felt significant though. I sometimes find myself thinking about it late at night when I can't sleep, alone in a hotel room in some strange city. I was maybe eight years old. Dad had taken me into Manchester with him as he sometimes did after he'd had a fight with Julia, to a bar in the Northern Quarter where he liked to hang out with his friends, painters and poets and musicians, genuine bohemian types who lived in squats and caravans and who sometimes wouldn't eat for days so they could afford to buy new brushes or guitar strings. When we arrived a group of them were already there, sitting around a low wooden table at the back of the room, supping pints and drinking whisky, knocking it back from short glass tumblers. They cleared a space for Dad, they pulled out a stool from underneath the table and Dad sat down. Someone poured him a drink. I loitered behind him. I rested one small hand on his shoulder, seeking reassurance from the warmth of his body through his shirt. And at first, he seemed to forget I was there. Conversation flared up, cigarettes were rolled, one of Dad's bandmates, Kev, slotted a couple of coins into the jukebox and 'London Calling' by the Clash began to play over the crackly speakers. I knew the song, Dad had all of their albums, and we'd sometimes listen to them together on lazy Sunday afternoons when sheets of rain were sliding down the window and the world was just the living room. So after a few bars I began to sing along, very softly under my breath.

Then I remember Jonny, the drummer in Dad's band, suddenly looked up from his beer and said, 'Fuck me, Billy, your girl can sing. Will you listen to that voice?'

All talk silenced. Everybody at the table, Dad included, turned and stared at me. I immediately stopped singing and covered my mouth with my hand.

But Dad hooked his arm around my waist and pulled me towards him. 'Let's hear it then,' he said.

I was a shy kid, not confident at all. I spent most weekends alone in my bedroom listening to music with headphones on, trying to block out the intensity of the world. But I did as I was told—I began to sing, concentrating furiously on the floor, hitting all the notes with ease. And I remember a delirious light emanating from everyone's eyes as they stared, so obviously enchanted by my voice, by me, and that light dissolved into my skin and lit me up inside. I felt my chin lift and my shoulders move back of their own accord. For the first time in my life, I wasn't invisible.

But this is not a moment I care to share with a group of strangers. So instead, I tell them about meeting my manager. I explain how she DM'd me and said she worked at a record label. She asked whether we could hang out. 'Sure,' I replied, barely able to hit the letters on my phone with my trembling fingers. I was so nervous the night before that I couldn't sleep and by morning I was tired and pale and looked like I'd been drained of blood. I'd self-released a couple of tracks and had a small but loyal following on socials by then, but I was chomping at the bit for more. I was certain she was the gatekeeper to my dreams. I was certain I was going to mess it all up. I'd heard stories from Dad about these record label executive types, all swagger and cigars. So when she turned up at the flat with her mousy brown hair and sweet little moon face, not much older than me, wearing scuffed Adidas trainers with one lace untied, my heart sank. She sat on the battered, rust-coloured couch, crossing and uncrossing her legs and fidgeting with her hands, fingernails bitten down to the cuticles and I knew that I'd been had. Turns out she'd lied. Because being an intern definitely isn't the same as full-time employment. I felt like an idiot for getting so excited and performing the whole charade in front of my mum, Julia, who was deeply cynical at the best of times. So when Eva offered to be my manager instead, I didn't exactly bite her hand off.

After the meeting was over I wandered into the kitchen, feeling embarrassed and deflated. Julia was in there slicing carrots and listening to *Desert Island Discs* on Radio 4. She looked up from the chopping board and asked whether Eva had gone. I said that she had. 'Good,' she said firmly. 'Because she was a complete time waster. Maybe now you'll take my advice and focus on getting a proper job instead of all this daydreaming.'

I'd just left high school. I'd flunked my exams and Julia kept emailing me links to vacancies at supermarkets, call centres and the local council. Making music was the only thing I'd ever wanted to do; it was the only way the world made any sense to me. So if that was a daydream, then daydreaming was all I had. And I realised in that moment that Eva was my only connection, however spurious, to the people who could get me quickly to where I wanted to be, the elusive record label executives drinking champagne in their ivory towers. How could I have been so stupid—I couldn't let her leave. So without saying another word to Julia I flung open the kitchen door and ran downstairs into the street. I scanned the road, which was empty apart from a passing car honking its horn at a wobbly cyclist. I thought it was too late. But I turned and there she was, sitting in the café, looking forlorn beyond the condensation-smeared window. I walked straight up to her and told her that I wanted her to be my manager and as I said the words, the sun seemed to rise up through her body with her smile.

'I guess that was the beginning of everything,' I say to the group. 'But in a funny way, it was also the end.'

EVA

'NOW WHAT?' I SAID.

We were at Ade's parents' place in Clapton, sitting in the kitchen. Their flat was colourful and eclectic, chaotically filled with various artefacts from his parents' home country of Nigeria: a feathered headdress on the wall, a carved wooden statue on the shelf, glorious coloured throws tossed haphazardly across the furniture rendering every mundane item a thing of great beauty. A pan of jollof rice was simmering on the stove and the kitchen windows were all steamed up. At eighteen years old both of us still lived with our parents—me on a gap year doing the internship and Ade embarking on a two-year diploma in music production—and faced with skyrocketing London rents, that didn't seem about to change anytime soon. Ade and I were supposed to be celebrating my exciting new job as Alora's manager—he'd bought a bottle of Cava especially—but instead I was freaking out.

'I'm serious! I don't know the first thing about artist management. I mean, what on earth was I even thinking? Is there some kind of manual I can read? Or online crash course I can go on?' I grabbed my phone and started frantically Googling. Ade took hold of my phone, placed it down on the kitchen table and rested his hands on my shoulders, a companionable platonic gesture but I still felt like I was melting into the floor.

We'd met at a warehouse party when I was sixteen, not long after my parents moved to London and I enrolled at sixth-form college. New life, fresh start, and I was determined to be a completely different person. I deleted all of my old social media accounts, cut my hair, saved up my allowance and splurged on new clothes from Urban Outfitters. I even had my tragus pierced, which for a while turned septic and looked like a green bean sprouting out of my ear. He was standing next to me at the makeshift bar—a wooden door balanced across a couple of oil drums—the dance music pounding, the bass seemingly emanating from within my own skull. He was tall and Black with a shaved head and a tiny silver hoop piercing one perfect nostril. He was talking to a lanky, freckly white guy with ginger curtains and a mermaid tattoo on his neck who I'd later learn was his best mate, Warren. I'd clocked Ade before, he'd been on the decks for the past few hours and if artists can be described as having stage presence, Ade had his own force field; I found myself pulled inside and trapped within it. It seemed to have the same effect on the barman too, because despite the fact that I'd been waiting for a good twenty minutes the guy went over to Ade first.

But Ade said, 'Mate, this girl's been standing here longer than everybody. Serve her next, will you?' The guy nodded in acknowledgement of my existence. Ade introduced himself. I offered to buy him a drink and blushed like a maniac when he said, 'Ah, I can't, the girl I'm seeing's just over there, but thanks.'

'No, I...' But I didn't finish my sentence, so the words 'don't think for one second someone who looks like you would ever be interested in me' never made it into the sweat-dripping, marijuana-infused air between us. I followed the line of Ade's finger as he pointed and the crowd seemed to part like the Red Sea for Moses, revealing my new college pal, Mimi, the same Mimi who had just the previous week told me it was okay that I looked a bit fat in my new jeans because I was funny so it 'complemented my personal brand'.

'Hey, babe,' she said, prowling towards Ade in leather hot pants and mesh bra top. She wrapped her arms around his neck and claimed him as her own.

After that night Ade and I bumped into each other regularly at parties and gigs. He always said hey, we always ended up talking. He was an aspiring house DJ and was teaching himself how to produce music on what he referred to as his 'shitty old laptop'. He wanted to work in the music business.

'Me too!' I said. 'Maybe we're kindred spirits.' And instantly wished I could reverse time and unsay it.

But Ade just smiled kindly and said, 'Maybe we are.'

He told me he loved Black Coffee, Miss Kittin and Carl Cox. At the time, I'd never heard of any of them but I pretended that I had. I looked them up on Spotify as soon as I got home and listened to their music well into the night until it became the soundtrack to my dreams. He started emailing me SoundCloud links to some of his own music, and I always replied with encouraging words. He kept saying he was going to self-release one of the tracks, but he never seemed to get round to doing anything about it. One day, when Ade had tickets to see Drake at the O2 and Mimi had the flu, it was me he invited to go along with him instead. He waited for me outside with Warren and some girl Warren was seeing at the time whose name I forget. Warren made a joke about it being a double date and I must've looked super-awkward but Ade just laughed and said, 'Yeah, don't tell Mimi.' We bought beers at the bar with fake IDs and danced side by side standing on our seats until one of the security guards told us to get down. Occasionally our arms brushed up against each other, which sent tiny electrical currents sparking through my entire body, but Ade didn't seem to notice.

A few weeks later Mimi and Ade broke up, something to do with him feeling they didn't have enough in common. She was seriously pissed off (but pretended she wasn't) when not long afterwards he got together with an aspiring model, a stunning Swedish girl called Astrid who Mimi went round telling everyone was bulimic and threw up in her handbag after lunch. After Astrid he dated the lead singer in a band which was booked to play the John Peel tent at Glastonbury. Michelle—she was intimidatingly confident, I was hands-down terrified of her and barely uttered a word in her presence—but Ade ended it because he said she was self-obsessed. The girlfriends came and went whilst I remained a constant; reliable, stoic, sexually invisible. Ade was the one who suggested I apply for the internship at Low Slang Records. He applied too, he said that it was our foot in the door. And when they picked me and not him he seemed so genuinely happy for me, not in the least bit resentful, it almost made me want to cry. Because Ade was one of the nicest, coolest and most caring people you could ever hope to meet. He was also completely unattainable, I had come to terms with this fact. So I made do with friendship, the consolation prize.

That day, sitting in his parents' kitchen, swigging Cava

straight from the bottle because ingesting large quantities of cheap fizzy alcohol seemed like the most sensible solution to having promised the world to Alora with no means of delivery, Ade took hold of me by the shoulders and looked into my eyes.

'Eva,' he said. 'It's going to be okay. Because I have a brilliant plan.'

ALORA

I TRY TO FEIGN ATTENTION WHILST the others are describing their significant moments. The blandly pretty woman whose features are a tepid blur of inoffensive nothingness talks about the day she won a BAFTA for best supporting actress in some TV drama I've never heard of. Rosy-cheeks-but-sad-eyes guy who turns out to be a politician talks about getting a double first in politics and economics at Cambridge at the same college his father attended. Million-Dollar Smile says the most significant moment of his life was the day his dad bought him a Lamborghini—gross. Muscleman is now referring to himself in the third person as Python which is probably a deluded reference to his dick. He bangs on about the birth of his son, and I find my mind starts to exit the room entirely just as the skinny old blonde leans back in her chair, crosses her twiglet legs and proclaims, 'Doll, if you were the one who'd had your body ripped apart by some creature growing inside you like a parasite, you really wouldn't say that.'

Python reddens a little and Elijah swiftly reminds the blonde that none of us are here to judge each other's significant moments, that critique and criticism is not the purpose of the exercise, and subsequently invites her to share her own. She says that the most significant moment of her life was when she appeared on the front cover of American *Vogue*. She sent a copy to her mum, dad and sisters, all of whom were still living in Ohio on the family poultry farm and had told her she'd never make it as a model and should be content with shovelling chicken shit for the rest of her life, accompanied by a handwritten note which read simply:

FUCK YOU ALL.

EVA

I DON'T KNOW WHAT I WAS THINKING. I don't know why I let him talk me into it. But I was a young and inexperienced manager, barely a manager at all, and to be fair to Ade I didn't exactly have any better ideas. I invited Alora down to London. Before I booked her train ticket on my card I texted her:

Hey, is this all ok with your mum?

She texted back:

Julia prefers it when I'm not home so she can
pretend to guys she brings back she doesn't have
a daughter

I met her in McDonald's on Kensington High Street. We sat at a sticky plastic table next to a toddler and his harangued-looking au pair. The toddler was eating a Happy Meal and I noticed Alora staring longingly at his podgy fingers reaching down into the cardboard container before shoving fries into his mouth along with his entire fist.

'You hungry?' I asked. 'I can buy you some food, if you want?' She shook her head, then continued to stare at the toddler like she might eat him as well.

I admit that I was completely in awe of her. I felt like I was sitting opposite a magical creature from another realm, a fairy or a woodland elf, and I was trying so desperately not to say the wrong thing that I probably came across like a blithering idiot. In every awkward silence which fell between us, of which there were quite a few, I took it upon myself to monologue about her songs—my favourite lyrics, her influences, the melodies which were already firmly wedged in my brain from listening to them on repeat.

I said I'd probably racked up thousands of streams. 'I must be your number one fan!' I declared, then curled up my toes in my trainers as I cringed at myself.

She frowned and tilted her head to one side. 'You're strange,' she said. Then after a pause. 'I like it.'

'Thanks, I think.' I smiled and she smiled back and I finally began to relax. 'Your friends must think you're so cool,' I said.

She glanced down at the bird ring and looked slightly wounded and in that moment, for the first time, I saw the vulnerability she hid so well. 'I don't have any friends.'

I sat up a little straighter in my chair. The hard plastic back dug into my spine. 'I'm sorry, I know what that's like.'

'Do you?'

'Yeah, I do.' I glanced around us to check no one was listening—it wasn't something I talked about, ever, I'd never even told Ade. But the au pair was packing her bag whilst trying to appease the child who was demanding another Happy Meal, an old man was settling down at an adjacent table to enjoy his Big Mac with a copy of the *Daily Express* and a posse of tracksuit-wearing youths were commandeering the stools—the exclusive clientele of McDonald's didn't seem remotely interested in anything I might have to say. 'I had a hard time in high school. Some girls in my year were kind of awful to me.'

She shook her head gravely. 'Girls can be such bitches.'

'Tell me about it. What about you?'

'I don't know, I'm just a bit of a loner I guess. Sometimes I think trying to fit in's more hassle than it's worth.'

A few minutes later we were making our way over to the mirrored-glass monstrosity which was the Low Slang Records building. Alora followed me through the tunnel of TV screens in reception showing muted music videos, various bootylicious ladies twerking their asses at the camera. Even now, looking back, I can't pinpoint the exact moment when I realised Ade's idea was a terrible one, destined to end in complete disaster. Maybe it was when I lied to the receptionist and pretended Alora was a guest of the MD's so she'd swipe her though the electronic barrier. Maybe it was when I ushered Alora up the stairs and into the central glass atrium which housed the office canteen and opened up onto each of Low Slang's five floors, told her to climb onto one of the tables with her guitar and sing—the perfect platform from which to canvas her talent to Jason and the rest of the A&R team. Or maybe it was when, a verse into 'Faker', two uniformed security guards strode up behind her, grabbed hold of her under the arms and carried her kicking and screaming out of the record label, one of them muttering to the other, 'We've got a live one here, Trev,' as junior members of the facilities team waiting in line at the salad bar filmed it on their phones. I'd definitely realised it by the time I was sitting in HR, being told that my internship was terminated with immediate effect.

'That's just not how we do things around here,' the HR lady said primly, brushing a piece of lint off her oddly tapered lilac trousers. 'If you want the A&R team to listen to some music you can send a link along with the rest of the world.'

I was surprised to find Alora waiting for me outside, sitting on the kerb cradling her guitar between her legs with her ankles sticking out in the road, smoking a cigarette and being yelled at by passing cab drivers who were having to swerve to avoid running over her feet. I'd cleared out my desk and was carrying beneath one arm the potted lily my sister had bought me, which had already begun to wilt.

'Huh,' she said. 'That went well.' I apologised and she shrugged. I asked if she wanted to head over to Euston Station to catch her train home. It went without saying that I was sacked. 'Let's grab a drink,' she said.

I glanced at her sideways. 'But you're sixteen years old.' She shot me a withering look and stubbed out her cigarette in the gutter.

We went to a bar round the back of the Tube station. It had dim lighting, mud-brown carpet and a wall of slot machines which interchangeably lit up and played a mishmash of sonically clashing jingles. Alora ordered a pint of snakebite and black and I did the same. The bar woman asked to see my ID but not Alora's which would've been humiliating had my levels of humiliation not already surpassed their peak. We sat side by side on high stools and sipped our drinks in silence. A Fleetwood Mac song was playing over the speakers, the one about going your own way. Ade messaged me and asked how it went. I sent him the disaster face and two exploding-head emojis.

Eventually Alora said, 'Those security guards were such wankers. They could've at least let me finish the song.'

I took a deep, intent-filled breath. 'Alora,' I said. 'I'm so sorry, I messed up, but it won't happen again, I promise.'

She glanced over her shoulder. 'Dad always used to say the music business is a graveyard for broken promises, but maybe you'll prove him wrong.'

It was the first time I'd heard her mention him—Billy Storm-Jones. I'd assumed from that first meeting—the absence of male presence in the flat, no photographs on the walls, no shoes by the doormat—that her parents weren't together anymore, but I didn't know the details. I'd done a bit of online sleuthing and had come across a few pictures on Julia's Facebook of a man I'd deduced to be Alora's dad. He looked a bit like Tim Burgess from the Charlatans crossed with a poor Liam Gallagher impersonator. His arm was invariably slung around Julia's shoulders, occasionally a small, much less peroxide-blonde child hovering somewhere in the corner like an afterthought. 'Do you see him much?' I ventured.

She stared into her half-drunk pint. 'Not really. He lives in Melbourne now.'

'Wow, that's a long way away. When did your mum and dad split up?'

'He left when I was twelve.' I said that must've been tough and she visibly flinched at my sympathy. 'It wasn't his fault,' she said.

Three pints of snakebite and two shots of sambuca later, me and Alora were standing in the middle of the bar, which was now packed with the after-work-drinks crowd, arms wrapped around each other, swaying from side to side whilst singing along to 'Dancing on My Own' by Robyn at the top of our voices, admittedly Alora significantly more tunefully than me. At one point we lost our balance and crashed sideways into a table, sending the drinks flying, much to the irritation of the three male suit-wearing punters who demanded we buy them a replacement round of pints.

It was then that Alora grabbed hold of my hand and commanded, 'Run!'

We sprinted outside into the street. The sky was dark with clouds and it had started to rain and we laughed joyfully and drunkenly as we wove in and out of the other pedestrians, splashing through the puddles. We ran until our limbs ached, we were breathless and our hair and clothes were completely soaked. And we didn't let go of each other's hands—she clung to me, and I in turn clung to her.

Of course we hadn't been checking the time and of course Alora missed the last train back to Manchester. So we caught an Uber to mine.

I remember she stood out in the street, looking up at the house with wide astonished eyes and said, 'You actually live here?'

My parents' place was a Victorian terrace in Stoke Newington, two storeys, four bedrooms, a forest-green front door with a brass knocker, interior designed into a uniform shade of beige. I'd never thought it to be anything particularly extraordinary or grand, but with Alora next to me, I witnessed my own privilege. She sat at the kitchen table sipping a glass of water which I'd forced upon her whilst I fetched her a pair of my pyjamas and a towel. When I came back she was standing in front of the fridge, peering at an old photograph of me and Katerina which was stuck to the door with a magnet. The photograph accurately depicted reality, as photographs tend to do—Katerina as an elegant grown-up with a sleek black bob and me an awkward spotty teenager by her side. My sister was, by then, a midwife, professionally peering between rich women's legs in an expensive hospital in Marylebone in which Victoria Beckham had once given birth by caesarean, being too posh to push as the tabloid press reported. She'd ditched the Pearl Jam T-shirts and ripped jeans for floaty blouses and high-waisted trousers and had acquired herself a trainee doctor boyfriend called Arif. She and I were sitting in a restaurant eating ice cream, both of us digging long silver spoons into tall sundae glasses. I remembered the occasion—Mum's birthday meal at her favourite Italian. Katerina had ordered pistachio flavour and I'd insisted on ordering the same even though Mum said I wouldn't like it and should stick to something 'less adventurous'. Katerina was looking directly into the camera smiling confidently, and I was looking at Katerina with an expression of bewildered awe.

'How old were you here?' Alora asked, tapping the photo with one black fingernail.

'Not sure, fifteen maybe?'

'That your sister?'

'Uh-hum.'

'You don't look much like her.'

'That's what everyone says.' With Katerina, it was as though Mum's uterus had exhausted itself creating a physically perfect being and by the time it got round to me, it simply did what it could with what energy it could muster. Quietly I said, 'She's beautiful, isn't she?'

'I think she looks a bit scary.'

'Do you reckon? She's actually really nice.'
'You look lovely though.'
'I look terrible, a right old pizza face.'
'No, you look cute.'

I walked towards her and handed her the pyjamas. 'I was such a loser back then. I wore awful clothes, I was terrible at sport and I couldn't flirt with boys to save my life. I mean, if a boy so much as looked at me I went bright red. I spent every lunch break at school sitting by myself in a toilet cubicle, drawing comic strips.'

Alora ran her finger along the photo where it was curling up at the edge. 'What were the comic strips about?'

'Argh, it's embarrassing. They were so babyish.'

'Oh go on, tell me.'

I rocked back onto my heels. 'They were about this girl who finds a secret tunnel under her bed which leads to a magical world. It's so dumb, I know.'

'And what was this magical world like?' she asked, with what seemed like genuine interest.

I rubbed the back of my neck, embarrassed to be talking about it. 'Well, it didn't look all too different to this one, I guess, but there weren't any humans and all the animals could talk. This tawny owl was one of the main characters and she made the girl some wings out of her own feathers and taught the girl how to fly.'

Alora smiled in a slightly whimsical way and said, 'That sounds nice. I'd love to be able to fly.'

'You know,' I said, 'you're pretty different to first impressions.'

She turned towards me, surprised. 'Really? In what way?'

'I just found you a bit... I don't know... aloof maybe, and intimidating.'

She laughed then. 'No way! Seriously? I'm just really awkward, I'm probably, like, the most introverted person I know. The only time that feeling ever really goes away is when I'm onstage.'

The next day I woke up feeling groggy. Through the floorboards I could hear Dad shuffling around downstairs, opening kitchen cupboard doors and closing them again, the whirr of the coffee machine as he ground fresh beans, the small insignificant tasks which seemed to happily compose his life. For a brief blissful moment my memory remained blank and I wriggled down beneath the quilt in comfortable ignorance. Then I remembered and groaned out loud. I'd been kicked off the internship scheme at Low Slang Records. Alora—who was presumably still passed out in the guest bedroom—had been forcefully ejected from the building without even a sniff of a record deal. And to top it all off, I'd posted a drunken selfie on z-pix of me and her sticking two fingers up to the camera and tagging everybody I followed who worked at Low Slang including Roxanne, Jason and the MD—the sentiment was clear. I reached for my phone on the bedside cabinet, intending to swiftly delete the post before anyone else saw it. But as I squinted into my phone screen, I stopped, confused. The screen was congested with missed calls and texts, from Ade, Mimi, Petra and a number I didn't recognise. And before I could open any of the messages or call anyone back, the number rang again.

I sat up in bed and answered. 'Hello?'

A deep, resonant voice at the end of the line said, 'Eleonor?'

'It's Eva, actually.'

'Of course. I'd like you to meet me at the office today, if you can find time in your busy schedule.'

It was Doug Malone, the MD of Low Slang Records.

ALORA

IT'S INEVITABLE THAT THE TOPIC OF Julia will come up and I'm anticipating, almost looking forwards to the release of venom as I say her name. But Elijah doesn't ask a thing about her, even as the session is drawing to a close. Instead he explains how we'll wrap up by asking a question of the person to our left, omitting him for the purpose of the exercise. I'm to the left of the actress Elijah addresses as Jane. I wonder if it's her real name and if not, why she would pick something so ordinary, although perhaps fitting for a woman on the wrong side of thirty who's only won a BAFTA for a supporting role.

'Nobody?' She interrupts my critical thoughts, the whiff of huffiness in her tone indicating that I've missed her question entirely.

'Yeah?'

'I *said*, you haven't mentioned your mum at all. Are you close to her?'

A small gloating bubble of resentment forms in my chest. I

hold it there, not wanting it to burst. 'No,' I say. 'I barely even feel like we're related.'

I expect her to ask me to elaborate, but she doesn't. Instead she says, 'What about your dad?'

And I feel the word in my heart. 'My dad's my idol.'

Dad's a local legend up in Manchester, I say. If you ask anybody about him they'll all have some story to tell, from watching him steal the show from Radiohead at the Academy with his band, The Lightnings, when they were just the support, to dancing on the bar with him at Ravello's whilst he played one of his famous guitar solos. He dated Justine Frischmann before she was in Elastica and hung out with the Stone Roses, he even wrote one of the singles off their second album. He was signed to a super-cool independent label, Hi-go Records. Everyone said he was destined for great things.

I remember the first time he took me to one of his gigs. I was just a kid, six years old. The venue—Ravello's—was packed, shoulder to shoulder, a mob of spilled beer and floppy bowl haircuts. Dad sat me on the bar and ordered me a pineapple juice. The bartender was wearing a tight leopard-print vest with a matching neckerchief. Dad asked her to keep an eye on me and she replied in a sultry voice that she'd do anything he wanted her to. I stared at my dad up on that stage, grabbing hold of the mic, strutting back and forth like he owned the joint and suddenly, I felt afraid.

'Why?' Python asks. 'Why did you feel afraid?'

I felt afraid because I knew that one day he'd be taken away from me, because he was too enigmatic, too talented, his star shone too brightly to be confined to a tiny backstreet venue in a northern city where the carpet stuck to your feet when you walked. He was the candle's flame, drawing all of the dust-brown moths. I drank the pineapple juice he'd bought me and crunched my way through the ice until my brain froze. After the gig was over we went backstage and I sat on the floor at his feet whilst he analysed the set with his bandmates, Rich, Kev and Jonny. And when I was shy and didn't want to tell them how old I was or where I went to school, Dad tickled me until I screamed the answers.

I reach for my neck and work the thin gold chain out from beneath the collar of my tunic. 'This is his,' I say.

Everyone simultaneously leans forwards in their seats. 'What is it?' Best Supporting Actress asks.

Million-Dollar Smile pulls a face. 'Gross,' he says. 'It's a fucking tooth.'

Julia and Dad had fought badly that night, over what I don't remember—it was usually money or Julia's insane jealousy. The fight concluded with Julia chucking the brass mantel clock—a wedding gift from my nana—at Dad. He ducked and it narrowly missed his head, leaving a dent in the living-room wall that's still there to this day. In response, Dad grabbed his guitar with one hand, me with the other and stormed out of the house.

'And don't you dare come to the show!' he yelled behind him, as he slammed the front door.

And Julia respected Dad's wishes. She didn't come to the show. But she turned up after it had finished. Ravello's was officially shut for the evening, it was nearly two AM. She demanded to be let inside and the doorman knew who she was and obliged. We were all still in the dressing room. Kev and Jonny were playing cards and Dad was perched up on the windowsill talking to the singer in the band who'd been on the bill before them, a dark-haired nymph-like creature with an intense, drug-induced stare. Dad jumped down as soon as Julia marched in. She threw her head back and began to cackle and not for the first time, my mother reminded me of the Wicked Witch of the West.

'Oh, here we go again,' she said.

Dad raised his palms in surrender. 'We were just talking,' he said softly, cautiously, the tone he often used with his wife as though trying to soothe a dangerous animal that somebody needed to tranquilise and cage. 'She's just starting out, she was asking for tips.'

Julia stepped towards Dad. He took an equal step backwards. 'Oh, I bet she was. Well, here's a tip for you, love. Stay away from my husband!'

Julia lunged towards the window. The girl screamed and scrambled against it, pressing herself against the glass as though her body might miraculously pass through like a ghostly apparition. Dad stepped in between the two of them just as Julia raised her fist and swung. An impressively powerful right hook made impact with Dad's jaw.

He clutched at his cheek and lifted his eyes to meet hers. 'Jesus Christ, Julia,' he said. 'I think you knocked my fucking tooth out!'

Jonny grabbed hold of Julia to prevent a second swing. Dad spat the tooth out onto the floor. Julia was by this time yelling her usual repertoire of obscenities. The singer from the other band jumped down from the windowsill and legged it out of the fire exit with Dad close behind her. I crawled under the table, picked up the bloody tooth and slipped it into the front pocket of my dungarees.

EVA

AS IT TURNED OUT, SOME GUY from facilities who'd been standing in the queue for the salad bar filmed everything and uploaded the footage onto z-pix. The video, which went from Alora standing on the table singing to her forced extraction by the security guys, went viral. The artist community was up in arms. KAZY-K reposted it across her socials to all two hundred million followers. Rock legend Jed Lacy publicly declared he wanted to terminate his record deal with Low Slang if this was the kind of welcome the label gave to unsigned talent.

'It's disgusting,' he said to NME.com. 'Initiative should be encouraged not shut down. And what makes it even worse is the girl's incredible. I mean, did you hear that voice?'

Lazy Lover said it was a classic example of the patriarchy silencing young women—she was quoted on *Good Morning Britain*.

I ran into the guest bedroom where Alora was still in bed, wearing my pyjamas, propped up against the headboard staring at the phone in her hand. She turned the screen towards me. 'What's going on?' she said. 'My z-pix following's gone up by like, a hundred thousand. I've got a million DMs asking me when I'm going to release "Faker" as a single.' She was talking at double speed, stumbling over her words. I could tell she was excited.

'A million DMs?'

'Maybe not that many, I'm exaggerating, but still loads.'

I told her what the MD had said and she stared at me for a long time. 'What the . . . ? I mean how . . . ? This is crazy!'

'He wants to meet us.'

'Me and you?'

'Yeah.'

'When?'

'Like, now.'

'What do you think he wants?' I said I didn't know, but secretly I was hoping, wishing, dreaming . . .

She looked down at herself. 'But I'm completely hanging and I don't even have any clean clothes!'

As soon as we walked through the revolving glass doors at Low Slang, there was Jason, sitting on the white-leather sofa in reception. He was wearing a baseball cap backwards with his legs splayed wide, the ultimate in manspreading. He sprang up and scuttled towards us with open arms.

'Eva, so good to see you! We've missed you!'

'I've been gone for a day.'

'Yeah? Well, it felt like a year. And this must be Alora Storm-Jones. What an absolute pleasure.'

He kissed Alora's hand like she was a princess at court and proceeded to do the same to mine, which left me feeling slightly queasy and like I urgently needed some antibacterial hand gel. He escorted us to the lift, all the time babbling about Alora like she wasn't there in a manic, too-many-double-macchiatos-for-one-lifetime manner.

'She's an absolute star,' he kept saying. 'That track's a hit, guaranteed.' When the lift doors pinged open on the fifth floor he stepped out before us, elbowing me to the side and announced to everyone sitting in the open-plan area, 'Hey, you guys, look who's here!' I lifted my hand and gave a pathetic little wiggle of my fingers. Alora stared out into the room, unsmiling, with that cold aloofness that I'd encountered myself the first time we met, and not for the first time, I wished that I could be more like her. Then Jason's phone rang and his attention switched. He shoved his earphones into his ears and mouthed, 'I'll call you,' over his shoulder before launching into, 'Hi, Tom! Love the new mix!'

'You don't have my number,' I said weakly, but he was already striding away down the corridor.

We took seats outside the MD's office. Alora was wearing the same outfit as the previous day—a frayed denim skirt and platform DM boots—with one of my T-shirts knotted at her waist, exposing her concave stomach. I was in jeans and a vest top that I'd hastily fished out of the linen basket. Neither of us were exactly dressed for the occasion and both of us were horrifically hungover—I'd only minutes earlier thrown up in a dustbin by the entrance to the Tube. Alora was playing with her hair, twizzling it around one finger before releasing it again. I picked up a copy of *Rolling Stone*. Lana Del Rey was on the front cover looking unbelievably beautiful in a black one-piece with cutout panels. I opened it and scanned my eyes across the paragraphs of text without reading a word.

'You okay?' I said to her.

'I'm so nervous I think I might piss my pants.'

Roxanne came over and made a big show of saying hi, doled out air-kisses and more talk of missing me. She asked if I'd had my hair done. I hadn't. I'd barely even brushed it in my rush to get to the meeting on time. 'Well, it looks amazing anyway,' she said. Ray said we should go to a gig together soon, then gave me a hug. He introduced himself to Alora as one of my 'besties'. It was all very weird and I was relieved when the MD's PA said that he was ready to see us.

I had never stepped foot in the MD's office before, I'd never been invited. It occupied the far corner of the building, the windows looking out onto pigeons congregating on grey-slate rooftops and other people's less exciting lives. The MD was sitting in a leather swivel chair behind a large mahogany desk, suspiciously dark hair slicked back against his scalp, smile veneered and gleaming. On the desk was a single framed photograph of a model type with two matching miniature versions, presumably his wife, Marianne, and twin girls. Behind him was a cabinet filled with industry awards, BRITs and Grammys and the occasional Emmy. There were platinum discs all over the walls and an electric guitar in a glass presentation case which according to the plaque had once belonged to Jimi Hendrix. The MD shook both of our hands with a vice-like grip, then gestured to the sofa where Alora and I sat down, side by side. I was trying hard not to fidget or bite my fingernails but the truth was, I felt like I was in the presence of some kind of deity—the MD was revered and more than a little feared. He cleared his throat, ordered his PA to fetch us drinks and then he began.

There had been a little misunderstanding, a mountain-out-of-molehill-type situation, a storm in a teacup. The actions of the security team and the HR lady with the peculiar fashion sense did not reflect the ethos and culture of Low Slang Records nor the business's approach to finding new talent, and those members of staff had, just that morning, been given their marching orders.

'It goes without saying that we'll reinstate your internship, Elise, with immediate effect. And you,' he said, turning towards Alora, his eyes practically lighting up with dollar signs. 'I'd be delighted to offer you a record deal.'

But if the MD had expected excitement or even a little gratitude from Alora, then he was left disappointed. Because she narrowed her eyes and said, 'Thanks, but I don't *just* want a record deal.'

And I watched the MD falter, revealing a flash of irritation before resuming suave composure. 'Then what can I do for you, dear girl?'

'I want to be an icon.'

At this the MD tipped his head back and positively roared with laughter, tears streaming down his cheeks. 'That's what I like to hear!' he boomed, clapping his hands together. 'Ambition! Well, let me tell you, Alora, you've come to the right place. But every icon needs a premier-league manager, so first of all let me introduce you to Kenny Dodson. He's one of the best in the business, me and him go way back. He manages KAZY-K and he's got big balls on him, that man, a fierce negotiator and that's saying something coming from me. I'll give him a call right this second.'

KAZY-K was one of Low Slang's most successful signings, a talentless sex bomb who jilted robotically through coordinated dance routines in all of her music videos. She had a powerful, distinctive voice which relied heavily on auto-tune to bring it into key. The story goes that the MD had discovered her at eighteen, sourced the most mindlessly catchy songs for her to sing and hired a team of stylists to dress her every time she stepped outside her front door. He told her he'd make her a star as long as she did exactly as she was told. He was fond of saying to his A&R team that KAZY-K was living proof that you can't polish a turd but you can roll it in glitter and go on to sell fifty million albums worldwide.

Alora frowned. 'But I've already got a manager.'

'S-sorry if there's been some confusion,' I stuttered. 'But *I'm* Alora's manager.'

The MD sat back in his chair and proceeded to crack his knuckles one by one. 'Girls,' he said, 'let's get real for a minute. The music industry's a slippery business and you're playing with the big boys now. Alora, you're an exceptional talent but you need experienced representation. Eliza, promising as you may very well be, you're just an intern and no offence, but you look younger than your client. It would be in Alora's best interests, for the sake of her career, for you to step aside and let Kenny take over from here.'

And he was right, of course. He was right and in that moment I opened my mouth to say so. I was ready to acquiesce to his chauvinistic opinions and relinquish Alora to big-balled Kenny, to revert to being an intern with my proverbial tail between my legs. And I turned and looked out through the glass door of the MD's office into the open-plan area where Ray was flirting with one of the junior marketing girls, Jason was shouting at the video commissioner and Roxanne was yanking at her scoop-necked top to greater reveal the magnificence of her tits to the professional environment. It was a room filled with ruthless ambition, sex and ego, not one artist in sight. It was Alora who stepped in and stopped me from making the biggest mistake of my life: not believing in myself.

'If you want to sign me, then Eva's my manager, she's part of the deal. And if you don't, there's plenty of other record labels that will.' Okay, so she wasn't *completely* bluffing. For the past hour, as we made our way over to Low Slang, our phones had been blowing up with messages and calls from other A&R executives wanting to meet up and hear more music. We could've paraded around town and got Alora a record deal ten times over, not that either of us knew it back then. Her words were defiant but in her eyes, I saw the uncertainty. She was gambling with her future, her dreams, and all for me.

The MD glared in my direction as though he was seriously contemplating an act of violence. I think Alora and I were both holding our breath. But then he smiled and said, 'Very well.' He picked up a Montblanc fountain pen and started scribbling something on a pad of paper, before tearing off the top sheet and sliding it across his desk. My heart was, by this point, doing an Irish jig inside my chest, but I tried to maintain a façade of composure and sat on my hands to stop them from shaking. 'Go on then, take a look,' he instructed. We both peered forwards at the same time. On the paper was a number, a sum of money large enough to make your eyes water. I stared at Alora. I stared at the MD. I very nearly asked, *Are you being serious?* 'And if the deal's signed within twenty-four hours,' he said. 'I'll double it.'

ALORA

AFTER GROUP THERAPY MAUREEN COLLECTS ME and takes me to the restaurant for dinner. A few of the others are already there, sitting together—Best Supporting Actress, Python, Politician. Python is holding court and the others are laughing and I wonder why they're wasting their money on this place if they're all so fucking happy. They don't acknowledge me as I walk past their table nor do they invite me to join them. The skinny old blonde is notably absent, which isn't surprising: she looks like she doesn't eat at all. I take a seat alone in the corner and suddenly, I'm back in the high-school canteen on that very first day.

The summer's over and I'm wearing the regulation pleated grey skirt, which itches like the fabric's infested with lice, a burgundy-and-royal-blue-striped tie strangling me. My hair's longer than before and I've bleached it twice, stripped it of colour, my eyelashes so caked in mascara that I can see them fluttering in my peripheral vision like spider-legged butterflies. Jess is sitting at a table by the door with some of the others. In front of them is a calorific buffet of chips and gravy, chocolate muffins and cans of full-fat Coke, teenage culinary rebellions facilitated by a few pounds' lunch money and absent parents. I occasionally hear her laugh, a sweet familiar sound which makes me want to cry. I pick at my side salad, which consists of a few limp strips of wilted iceberg lettuce, flaccid tomato and the occasional hunk of cucumber. It's almost entirely devoid of flavour but it's cheap and I'm on a tight budget—Julia's been holed up in her bedroom for weeks and my piggy bank's nearly empty.

I didn't see anyone from school over the holidays. Whilst other kids my age cycled to the park or went to the latest blockbuster movie at the Odeon, I lay on my bed beneath the quilted darkness and watched back-to-back videos on YouTube: Blondie's 'Atomic', Joni Mitchell performing 'Coyote' live in 1979, Taylor Swift, Adele, Nico, Billie Holiday. I studied each performance with more obsessive attention to detail than any homework assignment I'd ever been given at school. My mission: find the common thread between all these incredible artists, the seam of gold in an otherwise idyllic landscape, so that I could find it in myself. And it came to me at two AM one morning, when my phone battery was nearly dead and my eyes were stinging with tiredness—these women didn't just perform with their words and voices and the movement of their bodies, they performed with the very essence of their beings. They revealed every part of themselves to the audience, publicly bared to the bone for their art. I immediately jumped out of bed, switched on the light and positioned myself in front of my full-length mirror with my guitar in my arms. I began to play, and with Julia out as she so often was, there was no one around to complain about the noise. I rehearsed throughout every remaining night and day of the summer holidays, until my eyes could no longer see my own reflection in the mirror and the tips of my fingers were calloused at the neck of my guitar. I made my preparations to walk out onto that stage for the very first time.

I know Jess is coming over before I look up from my plate, I can smell her vanilla-scented body spray. We scratched each other's names on our pencil tins with compasses in year six. Now, her eyes are wary and tentative.

'Hey,' she says. She doesn't sit down, she hovers in an awkward, obligatory manner. I imagine this was all her mum's idea.

'Hey,' I reply stiffly.

'Did you have a good summer?' I nod and make a gruff, nondescript sound at the back of my throat. 'You didn't text me back.'

'I was busy.' I spear a piece of cucumber with my fork.

'How are you feeling about... you know... your dad?' My body tenses, I clench my jaw.

'Fine. He'll be in touch soon, once he's settled into his new place.'

She glances over her shoulder at the others, as though she's subliminally willing one of them to come over and rescue her. 'A few of us are heading over to the diner after school, if you fancy it?' The diner's on the high street. It's got red-leather booths and a chrome-rimmed counter, milkshakes served in silver shakers with candy-striped straws and cookies in glass jars. Jess's mum used to take us sometimes. I love it there.

'I can't,' I say, and Jess nods like she already knew the answer, and I hate her concern and I hate that I know she's relieved that I won't come. She says we should hang out soon and I say sure thing and then she walks away, back to her friends who were once mine too. We pass each other in the school corridors many times after that day, eyes dropped low to the laminated flooring which squeaks beneath the soles of our shoes, avoiding the unsaid, before truancy becomes a way of life for me.

Jacob skids towards me and I shake my head, snap out of the past and into the disconcerting present. He smiles. 'Hello again,' he says.

'Sorry about... you know,' I say, meaning the dramatic waterworks without actually saying so. He says it happens all the time and it's no big deal.

I order, then slump as low as possible in my chair and pick at my split ends. My food arrives quickly—wholemeal tortellini in a creamy-looking sauce with a garnish of fried courgette. I nibble at it with minimal enthusiasm for sustenance, which Jacob, the undercover spy posing as my pal, secretly counting my every mouthful, must message through to Maureen, because the first thing she says to me when she collects me to take me back to my chalet is 'You need to eat! It's the first step towards enrichment of the soul.'

This lecture of woo-woo nonsense continues for a good few minutes. I nod along like I'm listening, then ask if she can get hold of any tequila. I offer her money, enough to buy a new car. I know I won't sleep without it or at least half a Valium, that by morning I'll still be pacing back and forth, wearing tread marks into the rug of my luxury cell.

Maureen folds her arms across her chest, tips her head back and stares at me down her nose. 'I don't really think I need to answer that, do you?'

That night, my first at the centre, I toss and turn in bed for what feels like all eternity. I move my head across the pillows searching for a cool spot, my insomnia raging in all its infuriating glory. But I must eventually fall asleep because I wake in the darkness with silence thrumming in my ears. I instinctively reach across the bed for *him*, but of course he isn't there and hasn't been for a long time. I sit up, pull back the sheets and walk to the window. I lift the blackout blind, yet on the other side there's simply more black. I'm wearing the white-cotton pyjamas Maureen provided, which are almost identical to the shapeless clothes we wear by day, all outfits merging into one with the hours. I'm itching for my phone, I can practically feel the montage of comments and threads multiplying beneath my skin. I slip into my jacket, unlock the door and step outside beneath the canopy into the cool night air.

A guard is sitting at his station at one end of the walkway, presumably on the lookout for escapees like me. He stands when he sees me and approaches.

'Please return to your room.'

He says it calmly but with authority. He's broad with muscular arms and thighs—I definitely wouldn't win if he decides to restrain me and I have no idea if I've signed away my right to object to such things—but his eyes are gentle. The name embroidered into his shirt is DAVID and I think of Goliath but then the roles are the wrong way round, playing out in reverse, back to front and upside down like all my thoughts. I say I can't sleep, that I need some fresh air and my window won't open. He says he knows this, that it's intentional.

'Can I get my phone?' I say. 'There's this meditation app I like, white noise, running water, you know the kind of thing.' He shakes his head as though he's disappointed in me for lying and

I stop short of dropping to my knees and begging. 'Okay then. Just a walk. I'll go for a little walk. Tire myself out.'

'Miss, please.' He gestures in the direction of my chalet. It's then that I start to cry and I have no idea if the tears are real or whether this is all some great act of manipulation, but either way it has the same effect because he nods and says, 'Five minutes.'

She's sitting on the steps of the therapy centre, smoking a cigarette. I don't realise that it's her at first, I see only the fiery orange tip moving through the darkness of its own accord like a magic trick and the expulsion of misty white breath. As I approach the silhouette takes shape, the minuscule limbs, the skeletal frame—it's the old blonde, the woman who sent the note to her family saying FUCK YOU ALL in the face of her modelling success. I'm at a dead end but I can't bear to return to my chalet so I walk past her without acknowledgement and try the door of the therapy centre. It's locked.

'It's locked,' she says, like I need her confirmation.

Her gravelly voice is accented—American but with more hick in the vowels than New York or LA, she'd mentioned she was from Ohio I think—rising up from the throat of a dedicated smoker. She cranes her neck to look at me but she's more than looking, I'm familiar with stares of this nature. She's judging, critiquing, comparing. Yes I'm younger but she was more beautiful once. I imagine her concluding this with satisfaction, I can practically see the thoughts swimming beneath the surface of her liquid blue eyes. Despite the time she's wearing a full face of makeup—thick lines of kohl in a winged style and bright-pink lipstick—and even in the dim light emanating through the glass doors of the therapy centre, I can see that it's immaculate, like she got up in the middle of the night just to reapply it. I sit down next to her and she offers me a cigarette, which I take. She lights it with a silver Zippo lighter.

'I recognise you,' she says. I know for a fact that we aren't supposed to say things like this to each other, that it's in contravention of the strict Beaumont code of conduct. 'You're Alora Storm-Jones, the kid who tried to kill herself in the tub.'

I laugh, I can't help it. I wonder if this is what I'm known for now. If despite the two number one albums, sold-out stadium tours, Grammys, BRIT awards and countless front covers, my entire career has been relegated to the background by those few minutes lying in the bath at the Edinburgh Grand Hotel with a razor blade in my hand. 'Did you watch it live on z-pix?' I ask.

'Would you like it if I had?' I shoot her a quizzical glance but she just shrugs as though she's lost interest in the answer. I ask her name, which I know I shouldn't but considering she's breaking the rules... 'Vanessa,' she says. 'My name's Vanessa.' I remember now, how she had called herself 'V' in group therapy. 'But *they* know me as Vanessa Levine.'

'Who's *they*?'

'The world.' I assume she's joking at first but her face says otherwise. I ask her if she used to be famous and she laughs theatrically. 'Sure, doll,' she says. 'I used to be famous, all right. You might've even heard of me if you didn't think the whole fucking universe revolves around you.'

'Excuse me?'

'Jesus Christ almighty, if I have to sit through another day of your stroppy-teenager act, whining about how hard life is for you with all your talent and money and success, I'll slit my wrists as well.' She taps a little ash at our feet and seems to interpret my stunned silence as an invitation to continue. 'You're a world-famous recording artist, for fuck's sake. You've sold millions of albums, you've probably got more cash in the bank than some continents and it all landed on your lap when you were barely out of diapers. And yet here you are, not even able to manage a smile let alone feign interest in anybody else's far bigger problems.'

I'm not at all prepared for this onslaught and feel the impact of each and every blow. 'But we're in therapy,' I find myself saying. 'You don't . . . I don't—'

But she's already stood up. She throws her cigarette at the ground and without saying goodbye, struts away beneath the canopy. I watch her for a moment—I see now that her walk is that of a catwalk model, proud and aloof, but it also carries an air of broken resignation, like a caged tiger that still remembers freedom. I drop my cigarette next to hers and crush them both beneath my bare foot—they burn into my sole, a satisfying sear of pain. Then under David's watchful eye, I slowly limp back to my room.

ARTICLE FIRST PUBLISHED IN ISSUE 197 OF *RAW MODE MAGAZINE*, NYC (1970).

Vanessa Levine exploded onto the New York fashion scene last year and has taken the world by storm. We caught up with the model of the moment at her agency and shot her 10 quick-fire questions:

Favorite designer: Yves Saint Laurent
Favorite city: The Big Apple

Favorite food: I feast on life

Favorite club: Studio 54

Best compliment you've ever received: "You're the most breathtakingly beautiful girl in the world" (David Bowie)

What does it take to get you out of bed: A cup of Italian espresso or twenty thousand dollars

Favorite cocktail: Champagne and LSD

Age you first kissed a boy: Who says it was a boy?

Mick Jagger or Steven Tyler: Both at the same time

Best thing about modeling: The party never ends

EVA

ALORA CALLED HER DAD. BECAUSE SHE was still a minor, the lawyer we'd hastily appointed to review the record deal said she needed a parent or guardian to sign off on it too, and she wanted that person to be Billy. But the only number she had for him had gone out of service.

'He can be a bit flaky with paying his bills,' she said.

So that just left the mum. The MD arranged for a chauffeur-driven car to collect Julia from her home in Manchester and escort her to a boutique hotel in London's West End, where she'd be put up for the night, all expenses paid by the record label, with her daughter. Alora and I, now too excited to notice our hangovers, hurried down to H&M to buy outfits which might conceivably be suitable for a night out at Charlton Flamehouse, which is where the MD had arranged we'd meet for dinner and sign the deal. (It simply didn't occur to us back then to head down to Gucci or Prada or Vivienne Westwood, despite the flush of cash which was about to come our way.)

Alora walked out of the changing room wearing denim cutoffs, black over-the-knee socks and a cropped long-sleeved hoodie. With her platform DM boots she looked edgy and a little bit scary, like a warrior from a manga cartoon.

'Like it?' she said.

'You honestly look amazing.'

She turned to go back behind the curtain, but paused. 'Hey, don't mention to Julia that I called Dad, will you? The reaction won't be pretty. Things weren't exactly left in a good place between them.' I promised her that I wouldn't, I said her secret was safe with me.

The hostess behind the front desk at Charlton Flamehouse greeted us with the superior indifference of the truly beautiful. She was wearing a red jumpsuit which clung to her enviable figure like a second skin and left very little, if anything, to the imagination. She asked us if we had a reservation.

'We're meeting Doug Malone,' I said.

Recognition of the MD's name brought a disingenuous warmth to her face. She welcomed us inside and we followed her through the main restaurant with its clattering silverware and polite, self-entitled chatter, up a wide, sweeping staircase, through a set of double doors and into a private dining room. The room was opulent and grand, with oak-panelled walls and a marble fireplace, a long narrow table laid with starched white napkins folded into peacock's tails and many different sizes of wine glasses. Faintly throbbing dance music was playing over the sound system and trays of champagne swirled around us in the outstretched arms of provocatively dressed waitresses. Everybody from Low Slang was already there and suddenly the MD was by my side, pumping on my hand.

'Welcome, girls,' he said. 'Looking fabulous. Now let's get you both a glass of champagne.'

I turned towards Alora, intending to ask whether she'd ever tried champagne before, just as Roxanne slinked towards us and purred, 'Fancy a line? My guy gets the good stuff, he flies it in straight from Colombia on a private jet.'

And before I'd even had chance to contemplate my words and with zero regard for who I was talking to, I found myself saying, 'No thanks, I don't do drugs and Alora's *only sixteen*.' Then I linked my arm through Alora's and practically dragged her away.

'Whoa!' Alora said. 'You told her!'

'I did, didn't I,' I said, feeling slightly shocked. 'I really did.'

Everyone gathered round for the signing of the record deal. The Low Slang lawyer presented the contract—a hefty document filled with such complex legalities that you'd need a law degree just to read it, never mind understand it—and the MD gave a speech about how artists like Alora came along once in a lifetime, what a privilege it was to discover such raw talent. Then Alora picked up a pen and signed on the dotted line, just like that. Everyone cheered and Jason whistled and banged on the table with his palms, which sounded like heavy footfall running away from the scene of a crime. Then we all sat down and dinner was served, a gout-inducing three-course meal of pan-fried scallops served with a dollop of caviar, lobster thermidor and chocolate soufflé with Chantilly cream for dessert. But I couldn't relax enough to enjoy any of it. The MD had positioned himself between Alora and me at the table and I kept glancing at her anxiously to check if she was eating and having a good time, neither of which she appeared to be doing. Julia, meanwhile, who'd arrived late wearing a sparkly minidress which would've been more suitable for someone her daughter's age, was knocking back the champagne as though she'd entered a competitive-drinking contest, and with every mouthful she swallowed her voice seemed to get louder, at one point yelling across the table at no one in particular, 'She gets it all from me, you know!'

Then the dishes were cleared, the lights dimmed and the music turned up. It wasn't long before Julia was dancing on the table with Roxanne, Ray and one of the marketing guys. Ray's groin was grinding hopefully into Julia's buttocks. I scanned the room for Alora but couldn't see her. It was then that the MD asked if he could have a word in private.

I said, 'Of course,' and we made our way to the unoccupied lounge chairs in the corner of the room.

He sat down, sniffed hard and wiped a little white powder off one of his nostrils. 'The clothes,' he said, leaning in so close to me that I could feel his breath on my ear. 'We need to do something about them.' I asked him what he was talking about and he said, 'Don't tell me you haven't noticed? She's a pretty girl. She's hardly doing herself any favours. The mother dresses better than her, for fuck's sake!'

I glanced at Julia, still on the dining table, mid–slut drop. 'Do you think?'

'I'll introduce you to KAZY-K's stylist, Jean-George. Set up an appointment, ASAP.'

I stared at the MD and said nothing. Using KAZY-K's stylist for Alora felt like a wrong move. Okay, so that translucent dress KAZY-K had worn to the Grammys last year without underwear might've made the headlines but for all the wrong reasons. I loved Alora's style—it was quirky and distinctive. Why did we need to homogenise her into a teenage boy's wet dream? There were plenty of those kind of artists signed to Low Slang already, posting their jiggling asses all over social media, the music almost an afterthought to the sex. But I didn't say any of this to the MD, I was still very much intimidated by him back then; I admit that I didn't say much at all.

He placed his hand on my shoulder, gave it a light squeeze and said, 'Thanks, Eva. I knew you'd understand.'

I spent the next few hours smiling and nodding as various people from the label spewed out their coked-up monologues about Alora—she was just so beautiful and her music was just so incredible and they had all these brilliant ideas that they needed to tell me about and we'd have to hang out more often and we'd probably become BFFs. Eventually, I excused myself from Levi, who was singing his idea for a remix at me whilst simultaneously playing air guitar, by saying I needed the toilet. I stepped out into the corridor and took a deep breath, relieved to finally be alone. But my relief was short-lived when I saw Julia, bending over a large plant pot. Alora was holding back her mum's hair as she spewed into the soil.

'Oh God,' I said. 'What's happened?' Alora gave me a perplexed look like 'Isn't it obvious?' 'Let's take her back to the hotel,' I said.

Alora and I each hooked an arm through one of Julia's, heaved her to her feet and practically dragged her down the stairs. It took me a while to persuade a cab driver to take the ride, and I only succeeded by promising to pay the cleaning bill and tip an extra fifty if Julia threw up all over the seats. By the time we'd reached the traffic lights, Alora's mum was asleep, her head lolling on her daughter's shoulder, a patch of drool soaking into Alora's hoodie.

'Hey,' I whispered. 'You okay?'

Julia began to snore and both of us giggled. 'I'm hungry,' she said. 'That food was rank.'

I suggested we drop the mum off at the hotel, put her to bed and grab something to eat. 'Where do you fancy?' I asked. 'Anywhere you like.'

Fifteen minutes later we were sitting in McDonald's on Oxford Street, tucking into Big Macs and fries, Alora practically inhaling a vanilla milkshake. It was coming up to midnight and the place was rowdy, filled with waifs and strays, people laughing and fighting and drunkenly shouting their orders over the counter at the exhausted-looking staff.

'Did you have a good time tonight?' I asked her.

She took a sip of milkshake and wiped her mouth with the back of her hand. 'I'm happy about the record deal, obviously,' she said. 'It's amazing. And the money's basically insane. But that MD's a bit of a dick.'

I laughed, some food went down the wrong way and I ended up coughing. I banged hard on my chest until it dislodged. 'He wants you to meet with KAZY-K's stylist.'

'He doesn't like my clothes?'

'I think he just has certain ideas about how a woman should dress.'

She balked at that. 'Yeah, right. He probably thinks a woman's place is in the kitchen too. Well, no offence, but I'm not about to start taking fashion advice off a middle-aged chauvinist who very obviously dyes his hair and tucks his shirt into his jeans.'

I said that was fair. Just then a man yelled at the top of his voice, 'I love you, Rhea!' to which a woman (presumably Rhea) replied, 'Stop being a knob, Darren!'

We looked at each other and laughed. 'I'm sorry your dad didn't make it,' I said, and she lowered her eyes to the table and sat very still and quiet.

'I don't seriously expect my parents to be reliable people,' she said. 'But that's okay, because I've got you.'

ALORA

I LIE ON THE BED IN MY CHALET, daylight seeping ominously over the edge of the horizon, and think about what Vanessa said. Other people's perceptions of my personality have always fascinated me. I lose hours of my life reading what's been written about me online, entire articles dedicated to how I ignored some celebrity at a party I didn't go to, threw a hissy fit as I demanded to be upgraded to the penthouse suite in some hotel I've never stayed in, how I'm creatively controlling and a diva and unkind to my crew, and as I scroll on I feel a strange and not entirely unpleasant detachment from my own body. In many ways, it's liberating that the person you really are is largely irrelevant in the face of other people's opinions about you. And nobody knows the real me anyway. Nobody apart from *him*.

To say that I never aspired to fame sounds ridiculous now, because fame follows success like a bloodhound on the tail of a wounded fox. But I just wanted to live by my art. I wanted to spend my days reaching inside myself and pulling out these dark, twisted coils of song. I wanted to spend my nights on stages in every country of the world, performing my songs to thousands of people. I never stopped to ask myself why someone as insular and introverted as me dreamed about the publicly exposing aspect of a creative life. But ever since that day in the pub with Dad, when I sang 'London Calling' for him and his mates, I'd craved it like a junkie needs heroin.

When Dad left, Julia seemed to forget she had a daughter for a while. I ate cereal straight from the box for breakfast and dinner. I got myself ready for school whilst she lay in bed with the curtains drawn. Occasionally I ventured into her bedroom. It always smelled bad and was littered with dirty clothes, mugs and plates sprouting an assortment of new species of mould. She would invariably be asleep or perhaps more accurately, unconscious—I could tell from the empty pill bottles lying about that she was knocking back tranquilisers. And I would hold her makeup-compact mirror up to her lips to check that she was breathing. Then one day, I came home from school to see black smoke pluming out of the back of our building, swirling up into the sky like a flock of ravens. My first thought was that the café was on fire and I took out my phone to dial 999. But then I saw her, my mother, up on the flat roof, a bottle of wine in her hand. She beckoned for me to join her. She had, it transpired, acquired herself an oil drum from somewhere, the kind homeless people stand around wearing fingerless gloves in American movies. One by one she was feeding Dad's shoes to the flames, which gobbled them up greedily. All of his clothes were piled in a heap and she'd smashed his guitars, which were laid out on the concrete like dismembered bodies. All apart from one—his Gibson acoustic, his pride and joy.

She gestured towards it with a curt flick of the head. 'It's yours, if you want it,' she said.

I snatched it off the ground and sprinted back down to the flat, my school shoes clanging heavily on the metal stairwell, my body wracked with grief. That evening I sat on my bed, curtains drawn against the starless sky, and wrote my first song. I hadn't yet learnt how to play the guitar, I just plucked at the strings haphazardly with my index finger, but the words and melody still flowed without thought or effort and materialised as naturally as breath on my lips, like the song was always there inside me, just waiting to be found.

Within a year, I'd taught myself how to play properly and my writing was flourishing. Dad leaving seemed to have flicked a switch inside of me and music was literally pouring out of my body at an incredible pace. But it wasn't enough for me to sit up in my bedroom and sing to myself. So at thirteen years old, I snuck out of the house one evening and headed down to Ravello's. I walked up to the doorman and asked to see the manager, Nathan, an old friend of Dad's. Nathan was welcoming. He invited me into the back office and I sat down on a chair by the side of his desk whilst he fetched me a juice from the bar.

'What can I do for you, Alora?' he said.

I told him I wanted a gig. He removed a packet of tobacco from his top pocket and began rolling a cigarette. 'I'm afraid you're a bit young, babe. This is an over-eighteens venue.'

'But why do the performers need to be over eighteen?' I said. 'And I came here with Dad enough times, didn't I? I don't want to drink, I just want to sing.'

He asked me if I had a demo he could listen to and I said that I didn't but that I could do one better, I could perform for him, right now. 'Go on then,' he said. 'Show me what you've got.' He lit his cigarette and sat back with his legs crossed. I could tell he was just humouring me because I was Billy's kid. But I nestled the guitar into my lap and began to sing, and the atmosphere in the room shifted with Nathan's demeanour. He uncrossed his legs, stubbed out the cigarette and leaned forwards in his chair, suddenly all bright-eyed and eager. He offered me a gig the following Sunday, first on for a local band.

When Sunday came, I didn't invite anyone. I snuck out of the flat without telling Julia, and I had no friends to speak of. It was early doors and Ravello's was predominantly empty apart from a few sad punters dawdling at the back nursing half-drunk pints, a barman stacking glasses into the steaming dishwasher. The stage wasn't much more than a step, and I was so short that Nathan had to put a couple of plastic crates by the mic for my lips to reach it. I ran my fingers through my hair in the heavily graffitied toilets, splashed my face with cold water from the leaking tap. Then I picked up my guitar.

Up until that moment I'd been completely at ease with what I was about to do, so religiously had I rehearsed, so convinced was I that it was what I wanted. So it took me by surprise when my lungs suddenly constricted and my breath caught in my throat. I rested one hand on the sink and began to hyperventilate. I don't know how much time passed before Nathan found me there; panic attacks, a term now familiar to me, seem to suck you down a black hole where the laws of physics no longer apply. Nathan told me to sit on the floor and rest my head between my knees, to breathe deeply and focus. He fetched me a glass of water.

'You don't have to do this,' he said. 'You don't have to go onstage tonight, Alora.'

But the thing is, I wanted to. It made no sense and I can't explain it to this day. I was completely terrified, my body was telling me in no uncertain terms, 'NO, DON'T DO IT!!' And yet something deep within me, a stronger, more relentless force, was telling me to get out onto that stage and perform my songs in front of an audience, the very source of my terror. I reached into my pocket and felt for Dad's tooth. I carried it everywhere I went back then, before I had a Hatton Garden jeweller make it into a necklace. I rubbed my finger across the smooth surface of the molar and my heart rate began to slow. I stood up, steadying myself against Nathan's arm.

'I'm okay,' I said.

Nathan escorted me to the side of the stage, and then I walked out alone. My heart was pounding so hard it was sending earthquakes through my entire body. But through some feat of enormous willpower and determination, I stepped up onto the crates, strummed the first chord on my guitar and began to sing. And from that moment onwards, all the fear in my body dissolved and was replaced with nothing short of euphoria. There were six people in the venue, and five of them continued talking amongst themselves and didn't even seem to notice me there. But one guy set down his pint glass and stared. He never took his eyes off me, not once. And I knew that to him, I gave a secret part of myself that evening which only the two of us could ever understand.

EVA

THE VIRAL VIDEO ATTRACTED THE MUSIC industry's attention, but it didn't bring public recognition, notoriety, fame. Back then Alora could still sit in cafés in broad daylight without being mobbed by fans. We did a photo shoot in Piccadilly Circus, bumper-to-bumper traffic, hordes of people. Nobody even asked for a selfie. It's hard to imagine that ever happened.

She took a few months to record her debut album. She had a bunch of songs but they were pretty much sketches, just stripped-back vocals and acoustic guitar. The MD decided to A&R the project personally. He wanted the songs to sound as big as possible, he said we needed to turn them into 'hits'. I'd heard that word bandied about in the Low Slang office before by Jason and some of the others in A&R, the implication being that for a song to be a success it needed to have a forceful impact. The MD arranged recording sessions with a load of different producers, top-end guys, none of them charging less than thirty grand a track. And when he wasn't happy with the results, when he felt the production sounded try-hard and outdated and was ruining the intricacy of the melodies, he brought in the big gun—Silas Jax.

I'd heard of Silas from Ade, he was a celebrity super-producer from Los Angeles, hailed as the godfather of some new method of recording vocals, the technicalities of which were lost on me. I knew he'd worked with some of the most successful recording artists of the past ten years and had his own star on the Hollywood Walk of Fame. At the MD's suggestion—so that Silas and Alora could get to know each other and see if there was a vibe between them—I arranged a meeting. Alora groaned when I told her. She said she was sick of having her songs butchered to death by middle-aged white guys who didn't know a thing about how to relate to a teenage girl. But when I told her who Silas had previously worked with—Lizzie Ghost and Reckless Child and Jade LeRoy—she went quiet.

Silas suggested we meet in the bar at the Clarice, the hotel where he always stayed when he was in town. The place was fancy, all red-velvet drapes, gold-rimmed mirrors and art deco curves, with men in top hats and tails who opened the door for you so you didn't have to. Silas was already there when we arrived, sitting on a lounge chair in the corner drinking a long, turquoise cocktail. His dark hair was flecked with grey and tied in a little bun on top of his head, his skin was a deep shade of California tan and he was wearing Gucci sunglasses despite being indoors on an overcast British day. On his right index finger was a huge gold signet ring with an *S* mounted in the metal and on his left index finger was an exact replica, but with a *J*. I could imagine what Alora was thinking because I was thinking it too—what a *wanker*! I had no expectations that the meeting would go well. We pulled up two chairs and Silas extended his hand towards me in such a genteel manner I was unsure as to whether I was supposed to shake it or kiss it. He called the waitress over and ordered me a glass of champagne and Alora a fresh orange-and-ginger juice without asking either of us what we actually wanted to drink.

'I'll have champagne too,' Alora said.

'I don't think so, kid,' Silas said. 'Not on my watch.'

I bit down on my knuckles and waited for her to object, to insist that she'd drink whatever she liked and how dare he call her 'kid'. I was stunned when she sat there quietly, her features relaxing into an expression of placid calm. In that moment, I knew it was going to work out between them. They soon began discussing inspiration and ideas for the album, becoming increasingly animated, moving their chairs closer and closer together until I felt like I was no longer participating in the meeting. Silas said he wanted to take the production in a new direction—sparse electronic, understated and cool, to enhance rather than compete with the darkness of the lyrics. Alora said that sounded amazing, that she couldn't wait to start. Two hours later I said I needed to leave for dinner with a promoter.

'Sure thing,' Alora said. I could tell she wasn't really listening.

'Do you want to come with me? I can drop you off at Euston in my cab.' She was still living in Manchester with her mum at the time.

She glanced at Silas, who beckoned the waitress over with a brusque click of his fingers. 'No, it's cool. I'm going to hang out here for a bit longer.'

I left without her. I later found out they went back to Silas's recording studio—one of many he owned around the world—and wrote 'Underland' together:

I never wanted to tell you what I was thinking
I always worried 'bout what you would think 'bout me
I never wanted you to know that I was sinking
That I needed you to rescue me

I never dared to tell the truth cos deep down
We both knew the house was built on lies
I never wanted to show how hard I was trying
What I was willing to sacrifice

See you in the underland
See you in the underland
See you in the underland

I've been going round in circles ever since you left
I've been spiralling out of control
Even though my mama tells me that it's for the best
I know I've lost part of my soul

At 4.2 billion streams and counting, it became the most successful single off her debut album. It was the beginning of a creative partnership made in heaven.

ALORA

EVERYTHING CHANGED WHEN I MET SILAS. It was one of those rare, otherworldly connections which defies sense or logic because when I first saw him, I thought he looked like a complete wanker with his tiny topknot wearing sunglasses inside the bar, snapping his fingers at the waitresses. We'd met up for drinks in the Clarice Hotel in London. I was supposed to be catching the train back to Manchester that evening but Silas suggested we head over to his studio and do a writing session instead, then he'd pay for a taxi for me all the way home.

'But it'll cost hundreds of pounds,' I said, and he simply shrugged like hundreds of pounds was nothing to him.

I'd never written a song with anybody else before, I'd never collaborated that early on in the creative process. I'd endured some sessions with producers the MD had hooked me up with, guys who filled my own songs with synths and high hats and made them sound ridiculous, turning down my vocals to make space for their own penises. But writing comes from a place so deep inside it has no name, and the idea of exposing that open, honest part of myself to another human being felt utterly terrifying. But Silas had worked with some of my all-time favourite artists. I found myself saying that I was down.

Silas's recording studio was in a converted town house on a residential street in West London. Daily life was going about its mundane business outside—people walking small, fussy dogs, revving the engines of sports cars and yelling into mobile phones—but the house was completely soundproofed, as soon as we stepped inside and shut the front door the world beyond it disappeared. There were four floors, the lower three taken up by studio space and the upper one an apartment where Silas said he let artists he was working with crash if they needed a place to stay. He took me on a tour of the apartment first, which was kind of like a hotel. There was an open-plan lounge with a fancy chrome coffee machine in the kitchen and a Smeg fridge stocked full of food from Fortnum & Mason, with an entirely separate fridge for wine and beer. There was a games room with a Ping-Pong table and art all over the walls which was so abstract that it looked like a toddler had hurled paint at a few blank canvases unsupervised, but Silas said it was by some famous street artist and was worth millions. The bedroom was surprisingly feminine, with a white-cotton bedspread dotted with tiny rosebuds, a mirrored dresser with a hair dryer and selection of moisturisers on top, and fresh white lilies in a vase. Silas said that was because most of the artists he worked with were female and he liked them to feel at home. It was really nice, and I found myself imagining what it would be like to live there. I felt worlds away from the tiny flat in Salford with its peeling floral wallpaper and relentless stink of fried food emanating from the café downstairs.

The largest studio was in the basement. It was a dark, windowless room filled with an entire orchestra of musical instruments—guitars, violins, trumpets, keyboards, a drum kit, even a vintage Wurlitzer organ. A mixing desk with many switches and dials was running across one wall in front of a couple of leather swivel chairs, a vocal booth beyond the glass. Silas invited me to choose a guitar. After some deliberation I selected a vintage Fender, one I knew Dad would love. I plugged it into an amp whilst Silas dimmed the lights. I was nervous. I could feel a bead of sweat forming on my top lip, which I wiped away with the sleeve of my hoodie. To distract myself, I grabbed a plectrum and began to mess around on the guitar, strumming a few random chords. It had a rich, resonant timbre and as the notes vibrated through me, my jangling nerves began to steady.

'I should probably warn you,' I said, 'I've never written a song with anyone before, so don't expect too much.'

Silas sat down on the couch, leaned back and crossed his legs. 'I expect nothing less than perfection,' he said.

I couldn't tell if he was joking, so I rolled my eyes at him—a safe bet response to most things. He laughed and I was relieved. He said there was no pressure, no deadline, that before we got started we should just talk for a while, get to know each other and take our time. I propped the guitar against the mixing desk and sat down next to him.

'So,' he said. 'Where shall we begin?'

EVA

NOT LONG AFTER ALORA SIGNED THE record deal, I moved out of home and bought a flat in Dalston which quickly became *the* hangout destination, relegating Mimi and her pool house to second division. One Friday night I invited everyone round to watch the new stalker documentary on Netflix that everyone was chattering about online. I stocked up on crisps and guacamole, beers and frozen margarita mix and even gave the whole place a quick once-over with the Dyson vacuum cleaner my parents had bought me as a flat-warming gift and which I'd shoved in the cupboard and forgotten about. Petra turned up first, then Mimi and Mairead arrived together, gossiping about some girl in their spinning class who was apparently 'like, so annoying! She wears thongs over her leggings! I mean seriously, does she think she's in *Flashdance*?' Ade texted to say he was coming straight from football and he might be a bit late.

We got settled on my new couch in front of my new TV and I switched on the show, but after a few minutes Petra started talking about the guy she was seeing and the TV just became background noise with nobody paying attention. She'd met him in a bar in Hoxton. He was twenty-two and worked in the City.

'The sex is, like, incredible,' she said. 'So much better than Zane. He actually knows what to do with it.'

All of us laughed, me the loudest, but secretly I was deeply uncomfortable. Conversations like this were a regular occurrence between my girlfriends. Mimi, Petra and Mairead had all had numerous boyfriends and much experience sexually speaking. I, in comparison, was a novice. I'd only had sex a couple of times. I hadn't even lost my virginity until the second year of college and what happened there could hardly be called sex—a drunken fumble in the back seat of a car with some random I'd met at a house party who, thankfully, I hadn't encountered since. Occasion number two was with a guy I met on a dating app. He sent me a bunch of eager messages for weeks before we did it, then ghosted me afterwards. Boys simply didn't gravitate towards me with those kind of intentions unless they'd consumed large quantities of alcohol and the situation otherwise offered slim pickings. I got up to make more drinks and avoid any pressure to contribute to the conversation. It continued in full force without me, punctuated with hysterical shrieks and giggles. I was relieved when the buzzer rang and Ade showed up. He was still wearing his football gear and looked hot, both in the sexy and sweaty senses of the word.

He hugged me, then said, 'Shit, sorry, I probably stink.'

He asked whether he could take a shower and I fetched him a new towel from the matching set, a gift this time from my sister, delivered from John Lewis with a card which read:

> *You're a grown-up now, you need to own such things x*

I went back into the living room. Mairead asked how everything was going with Alora and I said, 'Yeah, good. She's started working with this amazing producer from LA, Silas Jax.'

Mimi's eyes widened and she leaned forwards in her seat, exposing her perfect cleavage. 'No way! I've heard of him. He's famous.'

'Yeah, he's a pretty big deal. They've been writing together. I haven't heard any of the songs yet. He's really secretive until everything's finished, apparently, but Alora seems really happy with them.'

Just then Ade walked into the room. He'd wrapped the towel around his waist, and his bare chest and shoulders were shimmering with droplets of water. He sat down beside me on the couch.

'Ade Oni, the one and only,' Mimi said, fluttering her eyelashes in his direction. 'How you doing?'

'Good. You?'

'I'm good, thanks. Were you playing football with Ali?'

'Yeah, and Warren and Zane and a few others.' Petra audibly huffed at the mention of her ex, who everyone knew had broken up with her despite the fact that she swore it was mutual.

'Who were you playing against?'

'Some guys from Brixton.'

'Who won?'

'Us, obvs.'

Mimi smiled and dipped her finger in the guacamole, which

I thought was very unhygienic but I didn't say so. After that we vaguely half watched a couple of episodes of the documentary but Mimi kept interrupting to ask Ade questions and Mairead and Petra started whispering and giggling to each other. When I excused myself to go to the bathroom, I came back to find Petra in the kitchen fixing herself another margarita.

'Hey,' she whispered. 'Someone's got an admirer.'

'What are you talking about?'

'Duh! How can you not have noticed? Ade is like, totally checking you out.'

I glanced behind me at the three beautiful people sitting on my couch. 'He is not.'

'Is too. And why the fuck is he sitting there in a towel?'

'His clothes are all sweaty from football and it's hot outside.'

'Yeah, right,' she said. 'Bit suspicious if you ask me.'

Just at that moment, Ade and Mimi exploded into fits of laughter. I knew that Petra was wrong. If the towel was meant for anyone, it wasn't meant for me.

ALORA

I DON'T THINK I EVER TALKED so much in my life than in that first session with Silas Jax. He asked a bunch of questions about me: where I grew up, how old I was when I learnt to play guitar, where I did my first live show. At first, I just gave him one-word answers: 'Manchester', 'twelve', 'Ravello's'. I wasn't used to that kind of scrutiny and felt all balled up like a hedgehog inside. But Silas was persistent. He emitted a soothing aura of acceptance and kindness and seemed so genuinely interested in me and what I wanted rather than imposing his own opinions like those other producers I'd worked with that as time passed I found myself starting to unfurl. He asked if I had a boyfriend or girlfriend and I said no, that I didn't do relationships, but that I occasionally hooked up with randoms at gigs.

'Ah,' he said. 'A free spirit. Noted.'

He said he needed me to tap into my pain because pain was the source of the most relatable, timeless songs. I said it was pretty much impossible for me to tap out of it and he laughed and said, 'Case in point, your songs are timeless.' We talked for three hours straight. Only when Silas said I was ready did we begin to make music. And it was then that I realised he was a creative genius.

We spent the next few months holed up in his studio together, talking, writing songs, barely pausing to piss. It was intense but amazing, one of the most incredible experiences of my life. I could sing a melody and Silas would immediately come in with the perfect beat or bassline. I could strum a few chords on the guitar and he would slot the keyboard's notes right in between them, like interlinking fingers or the missing pieces of a jigsaw puzzle. It sometimes felt like we could read each other's minds or, at least, like he could read mine. On paper, it made no sense. He was a forty-seven-year-old mega-producer from California. I was a sixteen-year-old nobody from Manchester. But on a creative level, we just clicked.

He went out of his way to look after me; he treated me like I was a somebody even before I was. He was always fussing over me, making sure I was eating enough, staying hydrated, tutting disapprovingly when I smoked. He'd order in food for me from expensive restaurants which didn't usually do delivery and they biked it straight to the door, then set it up in the studio with crockery and silverware. He never ate with me, he only watched. He was vegan and he showed me some videos on YouTube which meant I instantly became vegan too. My childhood wasn't exactly filled with physical affection—my parents didn't much go in for kisses or cuddles with their daughter. Dad and Julia were always either fighting or fucking, and I was largely ignored throughout both of these processes. But Silas would pull me into a big bear hug like it was the most natural thing in the world to do, and he held onto me like he couldn't let me go. I was never happier than in those moments.

Eva had warned me that he had a reputation for being a perfectionist, that the MD told her some artists hadn't been able to handle his methods, but for those who stuck it out it always paid off. I soon experienced this for myself. One evening he made me re-sing the same line at least five hundred times, the same four bars, over and over again. I heard that snippet of melody on loop in my brain for weeks to come, taunting me when I closed my eyes at night. I eventually removed the headphones and told him that my throat was sore and I needed a rest. He leaned back in his swivel chair and scratched his stomach beneath his T-shirt. It occurred to me that I sounded like a diva. It occurred to me that he might say no.

'Fine. I need to make a few calls so let's go back to my hotel, you can have your *rest* then we can come back and finish this off. I'm not letting you leave until it's perfection!' He kissed the tips of his fingers and made a *mwah* sound like a top chef sampling a sophisticated dish and finding it to his liking. This time, I didn't roll my eyes because I knew he wasn't joking.

Silas's hotel suite was like stepping into a palace. The doors swung open into a spacious lounge with an enormous chandelier and gold statues of half-naked women reclining on podiums, smiling bashfully at each other. Two sets of double doors led out onto a balcony where there was a hot tub and sauna. There was even a cinema room with a projector and popcorn machine!

'Make yourself at home,' he said. 'There's drinks in the fridge and if you press that button over there, a private butler will come running. Order anything you like.'

I said I needed to piss and he pointed to a door leading off the lounge, then wandered off with his phone pressed to his ear.

The bathroom had a black and white–tiled floor and a clawfoot bath, a heated rail laden with fluffy white towels which smelled like summer. One of the walls was covered in floor-to-ceiling mirrors. I approached my own reflection and peered at it critically. My skin had taken on a greyish hue and clung dramatically to my cheekbones, but when I stared deep into my eyes I noticed a slightly manic quality which I found strangely appealing. I could hear Silas out on the balcony, shouting at someone called Randy who I knew to be his long-standing manager.

'It's a scheduling nightmare, Randy!' he yelled. 'Are you seriously trying to kill me?'

The conversation didn't sound like it would be concluding anytime soon, so I ran myself a hot bath, flicked through the room service menu and pressed the button on the wall to summon the butler. I didn't know the names of any wines so when the butler asked me what I wanted to drink I just said, 'Silas's usual.'

When Silas finally finished his call he walked into the lounge to find me lying on the couch in a bathrobe, hair wrapped in a towel, eating French fries and drinking wine straight from the bottle.

He paused in the doorway and I braced myself for him telling me off for drinking alcohol 'on his watch'. But he smiled and said, 'What a sight to behold. My muse, eating junk food and washing it down with a five-thousand-pound bottle of wine as though it was soda.'

I bolted upright and spat the wine out all over the carpet.

'Are you kidding me?' I said. 'Five thousand quid?' But I was his muse—I smiled for the rest of the evening.

We didn't go back to the studio that night. We stayed up watching old movies in the cinema room, lying on daybeds eating popcorn and drinking wine which cost more than Julia's car. Silas chose *Rebel Without a Cause*—he said James Dean had a jawline that could slice steel. I chose *The Road* and Silas covered his face with a pillow for all the best bits.

'This is fucking bleak, kid,' he said, his voice muffled by the pillow.

I reached over for the popcorn. 'Really? I find it kind of comforting.'

He moved the pillow to the side, uncovering one eye which was staring at me quizzically. 'You find the end of the world as we know it *comforting*?'

'I mean, some people would argue that this isn't far off from reality. The environment's fucked. Our mental health and ability to communicate with each other in any kind of meaningful sense has been obliterated by our phones. This movie accurately depicts the hopelessness of society, how we'll soon be reduced to savages. It kind of calls a spade a spade.'

Silas shook his head and said, 'Wow, I can't wait to hear you in an interview, kid. You'll go down a treat.' Then he covered his face back over with the pillow.

When my eyelids started to close against my will Silas said that I should go to bed, that the suite had five bedrooms, I could take my pick.

As soon as I said it, I regretted it. 'Why don't you come with me?' The silence that engulfed us both felt cold and sharp, like stalactites dropping down from the ceiling.

Silas sighed. 'Kid,' he said. 'I'm old enough to be your daddy. We can be friends, but let's draw a line, huh?' The line was officially drawn.

After that night, he started inviting me to celebrity parties with him. Sometimes we'd get papped and a photo would appear online or in some gossip magazine, Silas always centre shot, me in the background, small and irrelevant, never mentioned by name. Once someone commented beneath a post of us together on z-pix:

Who's that little bitch he's with?

But then the comment was swiftly deleted. Eva, who it struck me must've been spending plenty of time scrolling, would call me immediately and say she'd seen me in the *Daily Mail* or *Heat* or on so-and-so's Instagram and why didn't she get an invite to the party. But it wasn't up to me. Silas didn't like hanging out with 'the business', he was all about 'the talent'.

He flew me over to Los Angeles in his private jet for Lesley Mirage's birthday. It was the first time that I'd ever been on a plane, never mind a private one, and I stared out of the porthole window the whole time, petrified that the thing was about to drop out of the sky. Silas laughed at me and said he hadn't had me down as one of the neurotic ones. I said I was riddled with neurosis and many other undesirable personality traits.

Lesley Mirage was one of Hollywood's heaviest-hitting PRs and her fiftieth birthday party was being hailed as the celebrity event of the decade. It was held in her mansion in the Hollywood Hills and if somebody had dropped a bomb on the place, it would have wiped out pretty much every successful musician and screen icon of the twenty-first century in one fell swoop. The terrace with infinity pool overlooked the city, which glittered enticingly with a thousand empty promises whilst actors and actresses sipped cocktails and talked about their latest movies and sacking their agents and who they suspected of having had 'work'. Silas introduced me to Sting and Mick Jagger—he said that they should remember my name, because I was about to achieve world domination and they both laughed like he was joking. Piper Spikes toppled over whilst re-enacting her dance routine from the 'Rule Me' music video in stilettos and Beyoncé belted out an impromptu duet of 'Drunk in Love' with Jay-Z which was next-level incredible and made me wonder whether I should just give up on trying to be an artist and apply to the local council like Julia had suggested. Some of the female guests were wearing so much makeup that they looked like cadavers in the morgue, heavily spray-painted and ready for their own funerals. Whilst Silas was talking to the self-proclaimed goddess of the dance floor, who in the flesh looked alarmingly like an ancient blow-up sex doll, I was left with her chaperone, who was either her son or boyfriend, I wasn't too sure, but he just looked over my shoulder as though scanning the room for someone more interesting and famous to talk to. I ended up excusing myself and wandered around the house alone. I did not fit in—the glitzy, glamorous life was never something I'd aspired to. Silas eventually came looking for me and found me sitting in one of the walk-in closets, slotted between a rack of fur coats and sequinned cocktail dresses.

'Budge up, kid,' he said. He crawled in beside me. His breath smelled of cigars and the miso tofu hors d'oeuvres the waitresses had been touting. He closed the closet door behind him and we sat side by side in the muted darkness.

'You hiding from someone?' he asked.

'Kinda everyone. Present company excepted of course.'

'Of course.'

'You?'

'You know I used to date Coco Cassidy, right?'

'The model?'

'Uh-hum.'

'She's mega-hot.'

'Yeah, well, between you and me, she's also mega-crazy. She's just showed up, high as a kite. I'm giving her a wide berth.'

'Nasty breakup?'

'More like impossible to actually break up. I'm a sucker for the wild ones. Every time we hang out we end up in bed, and that never ends well. So my new strategy is to avoid.'

'Cool. Well, I'm planning on spending the rest of the night in here.'

'Sounds like a smart idea. Mind if I join you?'

'That would be nice.' I rested my head on his shoulder. 'This isn't my scene,' I said.

He patted me on the knee. 'Don't worry about it, kid,' he said. 'Soon you'll *be* the scene.'

EVA

I UNFURLED THE ROLL OF PAPER on the MD's desk. Roxanne was standing next to him and they both peered at the sketches and collage of magazine cuttings—stills taken from Stanley Kubrick, Ridley Scott and George Miller movies, models in monochrome clothing, wearing face masks with cold metallic eyes.

The MD looked up and frowned. 'What's this?' he said.

'This,' I said, 'is Alora's treatment for the "Underland" music video.'

It would begin with a close-up of her face: pale skin, green eyes, blood-red lips. She would sing directly into the camera with a deadpan, listless expression, sitting cross-legged on the floor wearing a long-sleeved black leotard and heavy boots. As the camera panned out, it would be revealed that she was sitting in a white room, barely big enough for her to move, behind a layer of glass like an amphibian trapped in a tank, and that wrapped around her ankles and wrists were some kind of futuristic gold electronic devices. She would stand slowly, wrists first, as though being lifted up by the devices rather than her own free will, and begin to fling herself from wall to wall with violent, erratic movements, the implication being that her body was under the control of some external force. But as the camera continued to move backwards, the adjacent tank would come into shot, in which her clone was trapped. When the camera finally stopped panning out, the screen would be filled with twenty clones of Alora, all in separate tanks, all flinging themselves from wall to wall like girls possessed, lips parted as they screamed in rage. Then all of a sudden they would stop, sit down, cross their legs with almost yogic serenity and blink in unison, and the whites of their eyes would turn to gold, their red lips peeling back to reveal gold grills with UNDERLAND cast into the metal in capital letters. Then the shot would cut.

As I explained this to the MD he stared at me with an expression of mounting confusion. My voice was shaking—Alora had trusted me to sell her vision, to convince the record label that this was how they should spend their money, and until recently I'd been nothing but an intern, a dogsbody, fetching coffees and being bossed about by Jason.

When I'd finished my pitch the MD glanced at Roxanne and gave a curt nod which I misinterpreted as his approval. I was so relieved that I began to roll up the paper. 'Great,' I said. 'She can't wait to get started.'

The MD removed a toothpick from his desk drawer and started jabbing it in between his two front teeth. 'Eva,' he said, smiling in a way that didn't seem particularly friendly. 'I'm not one for gimmicks, and this feels rather gimmicky to me.'

'It's not a gimmick,' I said quickly, defensively. 'Alora wants the visual creative to represent her perspective on society, the sense of helplessness and isolation that a lot of young people feel even when in such close proximity to others. It's important to her.'

'Oh, I understand completely,' he said. It was clear to me that he didn't. 'But it's just not feasible, I'm afraid. Part of my job is to balance art with commercial appeal, and this is just *not* appealing. However, I appreciate that you're new to all this, so let me tell you what we'll do.' The record label would send out a brief to a few of the best production companies, the usual *guys*, the MD's *pals*, and would ask them to submit *their* ideas for treatments. Roxanne would filter them down to her favourite two or three, then Alora could take her pick. 'We'll need a dance routine, of course,' he said. 'Always best for virality to have something the kids can mimic and post on socials. Can she dance, or not really? Nothing that a few lessons and a body double won't fix. Jean-George can do the styling, something chic and sexy. How's she getting along with him, by the way?'

I fidgeted with the cord on my hoodie. 'Yeah, actually, she refused to meet him.'

The MD's eyes hardened. 'Why?'

And in the awkward silence which ensued, all I could think of to say was 'She doesn't want to take fashion advice from a middle-aged chauvinist who dyes his hair and tucks his shirt into his jeans.' But just as I parted my lips to speak those fateful words, Roxanne picked up the roll of paper, unfurled it again and held it out arm's length.

'Hang on a minute,' she said. 'This is *interesting*. Yes, it's kind of dark, but so's the music. We're never going to turn her into some kind of processed pop princess, it wouldn't be authentic, and authenticity is key for a project like this.'

'Exactly,' I said. 'Alora loves old dystopian movies and she wants that creative to run through everything: the videos, the artwork, the live shows. And you can already see on her socials how much these kids buy into what she's about.'

'I don't get it,' the MD said.

Roxanne winked at me. 'Well, I do,' she said. 'If we get this right, Alora won't just end up with a fan base. She could find herself with a cult following.'

ALORA

JUST BEFORE MY FIRST ALBUM CAME OUT, I played a show at The Oracle. It wasn't a massive venue—a thousand capacity—but it was for super-fans only, competition winners and people who'd raced against time to get their hands on tickets which had sold out in less than four minutes. I was nervous. I hadn't been gigging whilst I'd been recording with Silas and I felt out of practise, and that walk from the wings to the mic never got any easier, like making my way to my own execution.

Low Slang had released three singles which had all charted top ten and the album was, according to the online chatter, hotly anticipated. By the time we arrived for sound check, people were already queuing round the block. We drove past in a black cab and I peered out of the window. And what I saw not so much took my breath away as injected adrenaline straight into my heart. My fans looked like they'd just dropped straight out of one of my music videos: metallic face masks, gold contact lenses and grills, DM boots and white-blonde wigs—dystopian and dark. These weren't the kind of kids who wanted makeup tutorials and choreographed dance routines. They were the outsiders, the renegades, the lost children. And I had found my people.

The dressing room was four makeshift plywood walls precariously nailed together adjacent to the men's toilets, the acrid aroma of piss leaking out and saturating the air each time someone opened the door. Inside there were a few random mismatched chairs, a couple of grubby beanbags and a table with one missing leg which someone had balanced on a stack of boxes to keep it horizontal. I remember there was no mirror so I did my own makeup using the camera app on my phone, squished next to Eva on one of the beanbags. Glamorous it was not. But I was happy. And it felt like we were teetering on the edge of something big, of my dreams coming true.

When it was time for me to go on, Eva took hold of my hand and walked with me to the side of the stage. And when she let go and I walked out alone, I could still feel her with me, her grip moulded into mine. She stayed there for the entire set, mouthing all of the words, swaying in time to the music. She was inside it, she was inside the music with me. The crowd was like a gigantic unrehearsed choir. They held their phones above their heads, which lit up the darkness like stars in the sky. I was so overwhelmed that I very nearly cried onstage and I wished so badly that Dad was there to see it. And I realised in that moment that I had absolutely no control over it. My songs, my life, none of it was mine anymore. It was theirs.

The Truth—A Bold, Disturbing and Unapologetic Debut

★ ★ ★ ★ ★

Sixteen-year-old Alora crept straight from high school onto the music scene earlier this year and filled a gaping crater we never knew existed, defining a genre of music now widely referred to as Misery Pop.

Across the duration of *The Truth*, a forty-three-minute rhapsody of teenage angst, the young star removes a scalpel from her pocket, sharpens it on her teeth and dissects her life with startling ease and grace, singing of pain and anguish so sweet that it tastes like cherry pie.

The writing is bold, soaring cinematic choruses and snappy verses, whilst the production is electronic, lo-fi and understated, a stunning collaboration with legendary Los Angeles–based mega-producer Silas Jax, and the week-one sales and streams alone are guaranteed to secure her a place in *Guinness World Records*.

'Underland' is undoubtedly the biggest hit, and a hot topic on fan forums across the globe as the cryptic meaning of the lyrics is debated. Some believe 'Underland' is a reference to the dystopian concept of the end of humanity, the bleak desolate wasteland remaining on earth when society as we know it has been wiped out and we have drained the land and sea of all resources. Others are insisting it's the opposite—a metaphor for the truest versions of ourselves, an oasis of peace and happiness which exists in us all beneath the pain and suffering inflicted by the world.

Whilst her music videos may not be for the fainthearted *The Truth* is unquestioningly an astonishing debut album offering us the rare privilege of taking a trip inside the mind of a damaged but defiant teenage girl.

EVA

THE MEDIA BRANDED HER MUSIC MISERY POP. They said she'd invented her very own genre with her raw, bleak lyrics which tapped straight into the teenage soul. When the record label analysed the data, 98 percent of the streams originated from twelve- to twenty-five-year-olds. Within the bubble of youth culture, she became a phenomenon practically overnight and by the time she released her first album—*The Truth*—the press had already started hailing her as the voice of a generation. I remember one *VICE* journalist writing how she was articulating the thoughts and feelings of every miserable, depressed teenager in the country. Despite the MD's initial concerns about her style, her fans began to dress like her—they turned up to her shows like they were auditioning to be extras in her music videos. *Glamour, Marie Claire* and *Teen Vogue* ran features on how to emulate the 'Alora Look' and the clothes they featured would sell out in minutes. And then the album went to number one in fifteen markets and our worlds turned upside down.

We were at my flat when we found out, listening to the chart countdown on my digital radio which only picked up signal if you tilted it to the left and touched the aerial against the radiator. We both jumped up from the sofa and screamed. I hugged her and she whispered in my ear, 'We did it.' I can't tell you how much that one tiny word meant to me—*we*.

After that, she couldn't leave her mum's flat without being mobbed. She went out for dinner with her producer and the paparazzi stood outside the window of the restaurant photographing them through the glass. Somebody scaled the wall at the back of the café, just climbed up the drainpipe and knocked on her bedroom window in the middle of the night. She said she thought it was funny, but I could tell she was pretty freaked out. I suggested she move somewhere more secure with a high fence, electronic gates and a state-of-the-art security system. I assumed she'd want to stay up in Manchester with her mum. But she said she wanted to move to London, without Julia. I knew that the relationship between them was strained, but Alora was only sixteen and whilst I might've fantasised about it at times, I just couldn't imagine living alone at that age without Mum picking my dirty washing up off my bedroom floor, Dad reading me boring articles about the state of the economy at the breakfast table and bickering over the remote control together in the evening. I tried to talk to her about it but she just eye-rolled me and said, 'I'll be seventeen soon,' like that made all the difference. I couldn't tell her what to do, it wasn't my job to control her.

She chose the Hampstead house even before we'd viewed it. She stood outside on the private driveway, looked up at it and said, 'I want it.' Just like that, a multimillionaire child in a sweet shop of luxury real estate. It was raining hard and we were huddled under the golf umbrellas supplied by Edward, our estate agent at Savills, with his silver-spoon voice which occasionally slipped into cockney. The sky was a daunting slab of dark-grey cloud and I could feel fat droplets of water dripping down the back of my collar. But Alora's eyes were bright.

'This one's at the very top end of your budget,' Edward warned.

'Do you not want to look around it before you decide?' I said.

'I've already decided,' she said. 'We can look around, but I won't change my mind.'

I think it was the Gothic architecture with two turrets that did it. She said it looked like the love child of Dracula's castle and the My Little Pony palace. And inside it was just as impressive, with its high ceilings, polished parquet flooring and chandeliers in almost every room. It didn't have a pool, which was surprising for a place of its size and market value, but Alora said she didn't care because she hated water, she'd never learnt how to swim. We stood in the kitchen which was as big as a ballroom and looked out into the garden, designed by a team of horticulturalists who'd won at the Chelsea Flower Show and so saturated with colour it was like someone had just vomited a rainbow.

'I can't actually believe I'm buying a house!' she said.

'More like a mansion.'

'It's crazy!'

'Is it? Shit, maybe you shouldn't do it then.'

'I mean good crazy.'

'Oh, okay, cool.'

'I've just got one question.'

'What?'

'How do you work a washing machine?' That's when I suggested she hire a housekeeper. I got in touch with an agency which sent us a selection of candidates to interview. And out of all of them, Alora chose the frumpiest, most dowdy-looking woman you ever did see, in her midcalf-length woollen skirt, sandals and socks, and home-knitted cardigan with wooden toggle buttons. I was a bit surprised to be honest, I didn't think she seemed like a natural live-in companion for a sixteen-year-old girl. But I didn't say anything, it wasn't me who'd be sharing a home with her and Alora seemed happy, she seemed to think she was perfect for the job.

To celebrate the album charting at number one, I took Mimi, Petra, Mairead and Ade out for dinner at Click Club 77. It was very exclusive, almost impossible to get a reservation, but the MD had a contact there who he called up on my behalf and who managed to find a table immediately for 'Alora's manager'. The restaurant was 1930s glamour with fringed lampshades, a curved glass bar and a spectacular gold clock above the kitchen. The waiter seated us at a circular table in the corner on velvet tub chairs and I ordered a magnum of champagne.

'Are you kidding me?' Mimi hissed across the table. 'Have you seen the price?'

I said it was my treat, dinner too, and she exchanged looks with the other girls and said, 'Get you, Miss Fancy!' Then proceeded to encourage everyone to order the most expensive things on the menu.

We ate oysters and chateaubriand and sizzling garlic prawns served in their shells. Ade sat next to me and I found myself laughing giddily at nothing and playing with my newly cut and balayaged hair. Petra made a speech in which she said I officially had the coolest job in the world and everyone clapped and whooped so loudly that the people sitting at the adjacent tables all turned around and stared. But the attentive waiter kept topping up our glasses from the seemingly bottomless bottle of champagne and I drank too much too quickly. I stood up to go to the toilet and the earth tilted on its axis. I stumbled and Ade jumped up and steadied me.

'Whoa there,' he said.

'I should go home,' I slurred. 'I'm antisocially drunk.'

'Don't go home,' he said softly. His hand was holding mine. He didn't let go.

As we were collecting our coats, Mimi came up behind me and said, 'You and Ade are so obviously going to have sex tonight. And I just want you to know that I'm okay with it.'

I spun around to face her. Her eyes were filled with spite. 'Don't be ridiculous,' I said, and glanced anxiously behind us to check that Ade hadn't overheard.

Mimi took hold of her leather jacket from the cloakroom attendant and slipped it over her eternally fake-tanned shoulders. 'Oh, come on, Eva, don't make this weird. Me and Ade, we're ancient history. So if you want to help yourself to my sloppy seconds, honestly, be my guest. And in case you were wondering, yeah, he has got a massive dick.' And with that she flounced out of the door and hailed a cab.

I don't know how it happened exactly. But suddenly everyone else had left in taxis or on the Tube or had gone on to a club, and it was just me and Ade, standing alone in the street outside the restaurant, hugging each other for no apparent reason. I pulled away, and when our eyes met as they had done a million times before I somehow knew that the kiss was inevitable, a top-of-the-world feeling that I wish I could bottle and douse myself in each morning. We kissed all the way back to Dalston, sitting in the back of the Uber, pawing at each other's bodies through our clothes. But the prospect of actually being naked in front of him was a sobering thought, and by the time we pulled up outside my flat I was beginning to freak out, regretting not signing up to those yoga classes and eating an enormous slice of cheesecake for dessert. I rushed through the front door and into the bathroom where I locked myself in, sat down on the toilet seat and buried my head in my hands. I don't know how long I stayed there for, the room was mildly spinning.

But eventually, Ade knocked and said, 'Hey, you okay?'

I stood up, took a deep breath and flicked the latch. He was standing in the doorway holding a couple of bottles of beer. He asked me what was wrong and I just said it. 'I'm nervous.' Ade smiled, but not like he thought it was funny or stupid. He rested the bottles down on the sink and tilted my chin so I was looking straight into his eyes. He kissed me, flicking his tongue lightly against mine.

When he pulled away he said, 'We don't have to do anything, you know. We can just sit on the couch and talk.'

'No,' I said. 'I don't want to talk.' I took hold of his hand and led him to the bedroom.

I'd be lying if I said I hadn't dreamed about having sex with Ade, if I said my hand didn't slip inside my pyjama bottoms some nights thinking about his arms, his back, his kind, curious eyes. But in my dreams, I was never me—I was some lithe-limbed, extroverted creature who swished her lustrous hair over her pert, creamy tits and rode him into next Tuesday. This was different, this was reality. As soon as we were in my room I dropped Ade's hand, hooked my phone up to my speaker and began scrolling frantically through all my Spotify playlists, trying to find something 'sexy' in the midst of the potent silence before admitting defeat and settling on an Ibiza chill-out album which was soullessly inoffensive. Ade, as though tired of waiting for me to do so, had taken the liberty of removing his own T-shirt and was leaning against the wall, looking incredibly gorgeous and mildly bemused. I reached over and switched off the light. 'Hey,' he said. 'Don't. I want to see you.' He switched it back on again just as I noticed yesterday's pants had missed the linen basket and were lying in the middle of the carpet. I stepped towards Ade and hastily kicked them under the bed, hoping he hadn't noticed too. 'Eva,' he said. 'Chill.' And my name in his mouth sounded different somehow. I noticed it, and it was nice. But still, I began to babble.

'I *am* chilled. Okay, maybe not exactly *chilled*. But I mean, I *want* to do this, I don't *not* want to do this . . .' By this point Ade had me sitting on the side of my bed. He knelt down in front of me. 'It's just that I've met all of your exes, and let's face it . . .' He pushed me gently and I lay down, my legs dangling over the side of the mattress. 'I'm not exactly in the same league as them . . .' He lifted my skirt. 'I mean, that Swedish model, she was just the epitome of beautiful, she was a model, of course she was! And then there was Michelle . . .' He slid my pants down and took them off. 'Terrifying but so aesthetically perfect it was like she'd been grown in a lab. And how can we forget Mimi . . .' He parted my legs and nestled his body in between my knees. 'I mean we can't, she hangs around you all the time and—' Then he put his mouth on me and I lost the ability to speak altogether.

Later that night, as we lay entwined beneath the sheets, Ade smoking a joint and exhaling towards the open window, the sound of a police siren receding faintly in the distance, I said, 'I guess this is just a drunken-sex thing then.' He asked me what I was talking about and I said I knew it was a one-night stand and that he didn't actually like me.

He rolled onto his side and propped himself up on one elbow. 'Of course I like you, you're my best friend.'

My heart slumped morosely in my chest and I closed my eyes. 'Yeah, you like me as a friend.'

He began to stroke my shoulder, which made me feel weak all over. 'Eva, I'm in your bed, naked. I definitely like you as more than a friend.'

'But why now? After all this time? I've liked you for ages, surely you knew that.' I buried my face in the pillow to hide my burning cheeks.

He paused. 'I didn't, actually. I honestly had no idea.'

'Yeah, right.'

'It's true! I mean, I thought you were really cute when I first met you, but I was with Mimi then and by the time we broke up, you'd totally friend-zoned me.'

'No, I hadn't, *you* friend-zoned *me*! I kept you very firmly in the I-die-every-time-you-walk-in-the-room zone.'

He laughed and pulled me towards him. 'You *never* gave that impression. I mean, remember when we went to see Drake that time? I was so into you, even Warren noticed. Which is when I knew I had to call it a day with Mimi. But then nothing happened.'

'You got together with Astrid, like, ten seconds later.'

'I was single for six months. I don't think I could've been

more obvious about how I felt about you other than if I'd flown a blimp across London asking you out.'

I nuzzled into his neck. 'I *never* thought you were into me.'

'Yeah, because you spend so much time comparing yourself to other people, you don't seem to notice what's right under your nose. All my exes, they've got nothing on you. You're the best, Eva.' I knew it wasn't true, but it was kind of him to say it. I took hold of his joint, stubbed it out in the mug on my bedside cabinet and climbed on top of him.

The following morning, I left for Alora's first world tour.

ALORA

I ASKED SILAS TO COME WITH me on tour. I didn't expect him to say yes, and predictably he didn't. His manager had lumbered him with a schedule from hell, he said. He had boy bands coming out of his ears, seriously torturous. But he'd fly out to see me as often as he could. Everything had gotten pretty crazy by then. Life was whirring around me at a million miles an hour—airports, interviews, flashing cameras, my name in neon lights ten foot tall as the backdrop to my show—all I could do was hold on tight. I went from playing in pubs to thousand-capacity venues to venues which felt like Roman amphitheatres in less than a year, but I didn't feel like a gladiator, and the terror I experienced doing that short walk from the wings to the stage seemed to multiply tenfold with every show. Sometimes I felt like I was having an out-of-body experience, like I was floating above myself, watching this small blonde head bobbing about with a mic in front of a wild stampede of fans, all holding phones, all filming my every move. Mistakes no longer existed in the moment. If I forgot the words or sang one bum note or tripped and fell, the next day my embarrassment would be plastered all over the internet forever. I couldn't stand the thought of Dad seeing me like that.

The promoters weren't allowed to give me alcohol—I was still only sixteen—so I had my tour manager smuggle it into my dressing rooms and I developed a little pre-show routine, 'the ritual' as I called it: one shot of tequila followed by a double espresso to bring me up, a glass of red wine to add a little mellow to the mix, a vodka and Coke to even me out. If I timed the drinks exactly right, swallowing the last mouthful of vodka two minutes before I was about to go onstage and touching Dad's tooth just before I stepped out into the bright lights, I could move to the mic experiencing only a mild tremor of fear, my heart beating at a relatively regular pace instead of triple time like a petrified rabbit.

Each night I left the stage and rode the adrenaline high back to my dressing room where Eva would tell me how amazing the show was and how she couldn't believe the crowd's reaction, the way they were still chanting my name, demanding a second encore like a mutiny ready to revolt. A journalist for *Dazed* wrote that watching me perform was like watching someone peel off their own skin and bleed out onstage—deeply uncomfortable but irresistibly mesmerising. I ripped out the page, had it framed and hung it on my bedroom wall at home. I don't think I could quite describe the feeling of being out there—it's better than any drug I've tried, it's better than all the drugs combined. But when I got back to my hotel each evening, everything changed.

I'd been a loner since high school, I regarded it as part of my core identity. Yet each time I closed the door to my suite, my aloneness felt amplified and more acute, piercing and painful, and silence became intolerable. I'd switch on the TV and overlay its chatter with music playing full volume over the speakers. It didn't even need to be music that I liked, I just needed sound pounding against my eardrums to penetrate the emptiness. Sometimes I'd call Eva and she'd come round and watch a movie with me, but increasingly she'd lie on the bed answering emails or taking calls and that somehow made me feel even more lonely than when I was physically by myself. Other times I called Silas, but he was always in the studio and could rarely speak for more than a minute. Increasingly he didn't answer his phone at all. I began to wonder whether, now we had the number one album, he'd got what he wanted and had lost interest in me, if he'd moved on to the next new artist to win him another Grammy. One night when I was scrolling through z-pix, I saw a photo of him leaving a restaurant with a pretty redhead. She was tagged, so I clicked through to her page and there it was—a shot of her in the vocal booth at Silas's London studio, exactly where I'd been standing only months before. She was wearing a dress. It was short and green with thin straps and a gold belt. I knew it was from Chanel because it was exactly the same as the one he'd bought me. I threw my phone across the room as hard as I possibly could.

My seventeenth birthday fell on the night of the BRIT Awards. I was nominated in three categories—British Album of the Year, British Single of the Year and British Female Solo Artist of the Year—and Eva said I'd been tipped to win them all. For the occasion I flew back from Paris where I'd played a sold-out show the previous night. My record label arranged for a table right in front of the stage. Unknown to me, the MD had invited Silas.

'What the fuck?' I said to Eva when she told me. We were

already on our way in the car. I nearly told my driver to turn around.

Eva's face fell and I felt mildly guilty. 'I thought you'd be pleased,' she said. 'I thought you and Silas were friends.'

I tried to laugh but the sound which came out sounded more like I was choking. I turned away from her and looked out of the window at a homeless man slumped in a shop doorway with a boxer dog on his lap. 'Yeah, well, so did I,' I said. 'But seems like I've been replaced.'

'What are you on about?'

I opened up my phone and showed her the photo. She peered into the screen's blue glare. 'He *is* allowed to work with other artists, you know. That's his job. You can't get possessive over your producer.'

'I'm not getting possessive.'

'That's not what it sounds like to me. If you don't mind me saying, I think you're being a little bit childish.'

'Am not.' I stuck out my bottom lip and sulked. I asked to be seated on the opposite side of the table, as far away as possible from Silas.

We walked into the venue just as the show was beginning—a glitzy carnival of bright lights, music and flesh-revealing dresses. Silas was already sitting at the table and stood up as though about to greet me, but I sat straight down and allowed Eva to do the rounds on my behalf, exchanging a flurry of obligatory kisses and compliments. I could feel him looking at me whilst Rihanna and Drake were performing 'Work', pretty much simulating sex on the stage with their dance moves. But I didn't raise my eyes to his, I didn't relent. And when Mark Ronson read out my name and I stood up to receive British Album of the Year, I took hold of Eva's hand, my heart palpitating somewhere near my throat, and said, 'Come with me.'

I don't know how I managed to hold it together, remember my acceptance speech and stop my voice from trembling—sheer force of will, I guess. I thanked Eva, I said she was like a big sister to me and she let out a huge sob which the microphone amplified around the venue and someone later made into a meme which was widely circulated online. I thanked the record label—the MD, Roxanne and the rest of the team—for doing such a fantastic job with the campaign, for listening to all of my crazy ideas and executing them so flawlessly. I thanked my dad for introducing me to all the greats and being such an inspiration, and then I thanked Silas, I said I couldn't have made the album without him, but I couldn't bring myself to look at him.

People stopped by our table to congratulate me afterwards. I repeatedly said, 'Thank you, it means so much to me,' until I felt like a parrot, only able to repeat myself without my words meaning anything. When my cheeks began to ache from all the fake smiling I turned towards Eva, about to say I was going outside for a cigarette, and suddenly there he was—Noah Lamb.

I was aware of him, who wasn't? He was the breakout star of *Forgotten Midnights*, the arthouse film shot on an iPhone which had swept up at Cannes and had become a modern-day cult classic. The plot centred around a gang of teenagers who'd been kicked out of home and were squatting in a disused nightclub in downtown LA. The leader of the gang was a girl called Monique and Noah played her love interest. He wore a leather jacket and smoked a lot. He was edgy and cool. I remembered watching him skulk from behind the bar towards the camera with dead, ruthless eyes before he picked up the gun and pressed it to his skull. When he curled his finger around the trigger, I saw something in him which I recognised in me.

He introduced himself. 'I know who you are,' I said, and he smiled like, *Of course you do.*

He kissed me on the cheek and said it was a pleasure to meet me. He said he loved the album, that he listened to it every day. I knew he'd had a couple of run-ins with the paps, he'd given one a black eye and had done community service for it. He'd famously trashed his penthouse suite at the Gramercy Hotel in New York and one of his ex-girlfriends had publicly accused him of gaslighting. The guy clearly had some issues. I found him intriguing.

I knew Silas was watching us talking and as Noah walked away, saying hi to other celebrities as he passed by their tables, Silas leaned over the ice buckets of champagne and said, 'Hey, kid, stay away from that one.'

We hadn't spoken to each other all night, not even a distant hello. I raised my eyebrows and said as breezily as I could, 'How come?'

'Because he's trouble.'

By the end of the night, Noah's body was pressed up against mine in a toilet cubicle. We were kissing each other feverishly like our lives depended on it.

EVA

I INVITED MY FRIENDS AND ADE to fly out to see the Paris show. I had no idea where things stood with Ade, we hadn't had 'that' conversation, just one incredible night and then I was off jet-setting all over Europe whilst he stayed in London, studying for his diploma and DJing at weekends. At first, when I didn't hear from him for a few days, I began to convince myself it had been a mistake, that he regretted crossing the line or that I'd been terrible in bed, my sexual inexperience candidly revealing itself. I desperately wanted to message him and ask how he was feeling, but every text I composed sounded needy and pathetic so I forced myself not to press send. But then he messaged me with a photo of the two of us. Petra had apparently taken it in Click Club 77 when neither of us were looking. We were pretending to drink directly out of the magnum of champagne. We were laughing. We looked happy. We looked like a couple. His message said:

> What an amazing night!! Looking forward to more just like it 😊 xxx

I read it over and over again, unsure if I was reading too much into it. In the end I called Mairead and she indulged me with a few minutes of analysis and dissection before concluding that Ade was definitely saying that he wanted to have sex again.

'And since when did Ade Oni ever sign off with three kisses?' she said. 'It's unheard of. He's a strict one-kiss kind of guy. He clearly wants to marry you.'

He and I texted back and forth with our usual frequency after that, each of us becoming increasingly bold. And when he messaged to say he'd booked his flights to Paris, he said he couldn't wait to see me and added three more kisses. I texted back:

> Me tooooooo xxx

Everyone flew in the day before the performance. Alora was appearing on a French talk show that afternoon so I invited my girlfriends to sit in the audience and watch, but I got Ade an AAA pass so he could join me backstage in the green room. I met him at the guest entrance. It was the first time we'd seen each other since the morning after the night before and I went all shy and didn't know how to behave—hug him, kiss him on the cheek, pounce on top of him and rip his clothes off. But he made the decision for me. He picked me up, twirled me around and kissed me. And from that moment onwards, everything was just about perfect.

The talk show was being broadcast live which I always found more stressful than prerecorded because mistakes couldn't be edited out. But we'd seen the questions in advance and the producer had been given a list of topics which were strictly out of bounds, her childhood and parents being the main one. Alora hated interviews. She said they were 'too real', whatever that meant. She kept saying she didn't want to do it even though it had been booked for months and it was minutes before she was due to go on, and Shona, her PR lady, had to give her a stern pep talk in the dressing room. But Alora pulled herself together, walked out in front of the cameras and handled it like a true professional. The green room wasn't particularly swanky—three chesterfield sofas arranged around a table filled with bottles of booze and crisps in plastic bowls, a TV to watch the show. But having Ade next to me seemed to heighten my senses, like I'd taken some new and exciting hallucinogenic drug. Every salt and vinegar crisp tasted exquisite. My hair felt unbelievable soft and silky to touch. I couldn't stop smiling.

Later that evening, I went with Alora to a dress fitting before meeting up with Ade and the girls for dinner. I invited Alora to come with us but she said with the way the paps hounded her, eating out was more hassle than it was worth these days. We went to a fondue restaurant in the Montmartre district and sat on benches around a long, narrow table. The waiter was loud and gregarious with a thick moustache and striped sweater like a living, breathing cartoon Frenchman. The walls were covered in old newspaper clippings and they served wine in baby bottles, which we were told was something to do with tax avoidance by the owner but was definitely a novelty. Mimi made a real display of licking her tongue around the teat of her bottle in a provocative manner. I tried to ignore the feeling that she was doing it for Ade's benefit. We gorged on excessive quantities of toasted baguette and melted cheese, then headed on to a club. Alora's booking agent had put us on the guest list and the host walked us straight through to VIP. Peggy Gou was DJing and Ade immediately made his way onto the dance floor. He was an incredible dancer, he moved like he was somehow attached to the beat itself. I wanted to dance with him but found myself caught in a long and arduous conversation with Petra about her mum's new boyfriend who she said was trying to force her to pay rent.

'Since when is it his fucking house?' she shouted over the music. 'If anything, I should be charging him!' I nodded along and made sympathetic noises which she probably couldn't hear.

Mimi had been sitting at the table behind us with Mairead, but when I turned around she'd disappeared. I scanned the bar area, then the dance floor and suddenly there she was, wiggling her way through the crowd, cocktail in hand, making a beeline straight for Ade. Everything seemed to move in slow motion as she writhed up to him, pressed her hips against his and wrapped her arms around his neck, and in that moment, I felt like my heart might stop. But Ade simply removed her arms, shook his head and said something in her ear. Mimi looked pissed off, spun around and flounced off towards the toilets.

I didn't mention it until we got back to the hotel, I didn't want to risk ruining the night. I was staying at the five-star Le Beau Sommeil and as a special treat for Ade's trip, I'd upgraded to La Suite Royale with views of the Eiffel Tower. The place looked like it had been furnished for Marie Antoinette, lots of silk and frills and fussy drapes, over the top and opulent. But Ade didn't comment on the décor, he didn't even seem to notice it. As soon as I opened the door he rushed through the lounge and out onto the balcony.

'Wow!' he called. 'Check out this view! You can see the whole of Paris from here!'

I poured two glasses of champagne and followed him outside where the city was spread out before us in panoramic splendour like a gigantic electrical circuit board, the Eiffel Tower lit up and sparkling like a humungous postmodern Christmas tree. I handed Ade a glass and he touched it to mine. Then he leaned towards me and kissed me.

'I'm really happy,' he said.

I smiled and said, 'Me too.'

Later that evening as we lay in the king-sized bed, drinking champagne and eating the assortment of overpriced snacks that I'd ordered on room service, he said, 'Does any of this even feel real to you?'

I popped a smoked-salmon blini into my mouth and reached for another. 'What do you mean?'

'I mean, you're practically staying on the doorstep of the Eiffel Tower, you fly around the world on a private jet which, shameless carbon footprint aside, is kind of exciting, and people treat you like you're a celebrity, literally falling over themselves to usher you through to VIP and fetch you drinks and shit.'

I laughed. 'They do not.' He raised one eyebrow. 'Okay, maybe they do a bit.'

'Aren't you pinching yourself?'

'I mean, yes! Every day. I don't even know how this happened. I feel like I just followed your advice and faked it 'til I made it but I made it more than I ever thought possible and I still feel like I'm faking it! Like, sometimes I'm talking in a meeting at the label and all these really senior music-industry execs are listening and I'm like, hang on a minute, *I'm* actually talking, fuck, *I'm* talking here, and it kind of freaks me out.'

'I bet you're a badass in a meeting.'

'I don't know if I am, I'm just winging it. And ultimately, it's all about Alora. She's the star, I'm just her manager, I'm just tagging along for the ride.' I suddenly had an idea and grabbed hold of Ade's hand in my excitement. 'Hey, I know! I could help you release some of your music! Okay, so house isn't exactly my thing but I could ask around, put you in touch with the right people, and there's so much you can do yourself to build a bit of a buzz. You could start your own club night maybe, send your music out to other DJs to play in their sets, do remixes, that kind of thing.'

Ade rolled over and reached for his Rizlas. 'Nah, thanks, though.'

'Why not?'

'Nothing's really finished yet.'

'But all you need to do is finish one track, just one track, Ade, I know it might feel a bit daunting, the idea of actually putting your own music out, but everyone has to start somewhere.'

'I'll think about it,' he said, in a slightly dismissive way that indicated he probably wouldn't.

He began to skin up, intense concentration on his face, and he looked so cute and serious that I let it slide. Instead, I asked the question which had been bugging me all night. 'I saw you with Mimi earlier, in the club. What was that all about?'

Ade licked the edge of the Rizla paper and rolled the joint like a pro. 'It was nothing. You know what she's like when she's had a few. But I told her to back off, I said me and you are together now.'

I bit my lip. 'You serious?'

'Yeah.'

'So are we?'

'Are we what?'

'Together?'

'Aren't we? Shit, you haven't been seeing other people since you've been away, have you?' I rolled on top of him and kissed him all over. 'You're amazing,' he whispered, and for the first time in my life I allowed myself to believe that it might be true.

ALORA

AFTER THE BRITS, I TOOK NOAH back to my place. It was nearly two AM and I knew Gina, my live-in housekeeper, would already be in bed, but when we walked into the kitchen she'd left a plate of sandwiches out on the counter wrapped in cling film with a little note that read:

> In case you've got the munchies
> when you get home.

'That's nice,' Noah said. 'Does she always do stuff like that?' I said that come to think of it, she did. 'It's kind of like she's your mum.'

I laughed and said, 'You're kidding, right? Mums don't do that shit, do they?' He looked at me weirdly, opened up the fridge and helped himself to a beer.

I knew we were going to do it. I knew that people like Noah Lamb didn't come back to random girls' houses after nights out with the expectation of a nice cup of Earl Grey. I didn't see the point in skirting around the subject so I said to him, 'Let's go upstairs and get on with it, shall we?'

'Get on with what?'

'Sex.'

He looked amused and said, 'Don't you want to show me around first? It's a pretty amazing house, I'd love to see it.'

So I took him on a tour—the lounges, the study, the dining room, the recording studio in the basement, the games room in the turret, the seven bedrooms, nine bathrooms and attic room which Gina had named the Post Room.

'What's all this stuff?' Noah said, peering around the attic-room door. It was filled floor to ceiling with unopened parcels, tall, haphazard Jenga-like piles of them just gathering dust, much to Gina's irritation. I said that sometimes I went down a bit of a rabbit hole with online shopping. 'And what, you don't even open what you buy?'

'It seems the buzz is more in the buying than the owning for me.'

'I get it, sort of,' he said. 'I'm not sure owning anything ever makes anyone truly happy.'

As I walked past the final door on the landing, Noah said, 'Wait, what's in there?' Before I could tell him not to, he took hold of the handle and went into the room. He flicked on the light switch.

'It's another bedroom,' he said.

'Not really.'

'But there's a mattress on the floor.'

'Yeah, I just sleep in there occasionally.'

'Why? It's literally like a cupboard. Your room's massive and you've got a four-poster bed. These posters are cool, though.' The posters were of classic dystopian movies—*1984*, *Mad Max*, *Westworld*, *Battle Royale*. It was a replica of my old bedroom up in Manchester, but I didn't tell Noah that. I just said sleeping in there was something I liked to do sometimes and not to make a big deal out of it. Then I shut the door.

Sex with Noah was not like I'd expected. He kept asking me if I was okay and whether I liked what he was doing. His chest was smooth and hairless and he kissed my neck softly and whispered nice things about me in my ear. Afterwards, as he lay stretched out naked in my bed, I told him that he looked like a statue, his body and face were so perfectly sculpted, probably as a result of a painfully strict diet and intensive boot-camp-style workout regime.

'You're not my usual type,' I said, and he laughed like he knew he was everybody's type, like he'd been painted by the gods.

'How did you get this?' he asked, tracing his fingertip across the scar on the inside of my thigh, following the line of the curves.

'I did it.'

'On purpose?'

'Yeah.'

'Why?'

I shrugged and said I didn't know.

'It kind of looks like a snake.'

'Yeah, I guess it sort of is.'

We had sex again and afterwards, I took a photograph of the two of us together, only our hair, forehead and eyes visible above the sheets. I posted it on z-pix with the caption:

Guess who x

It pretty much broke the internet.

When I woke up, I was alone. The curtains were open and I squinted into the clean, cleansing sunlight, shielding my eyes with my hand. My mouth tasted like a dead thing had got lodged in my tonsils and my sheets smelled of his aftershave. I was due to fly back to Europe to play a show that evening, and when Eva couldn't get hold of me—I'd turned my phone on silent—she just showed up at my house. Gina let her in and she rampaged up the stairs and across the landing yelling that the private jet was booked to leave in an hour and that if we were even a minute late I'd be charged an extra twenty grand for taking up space on the runway. I was still in bed. I pulled the quilt over my head but Eva yanked it back and trilled, 'Wakey wakey, sleepyhead!' in an unbearably bright tone. I groaned and reluctantly heaved myself up off the mattress.

In the car on the way to the airport I remember looking out of the tinted windows at people riding bikes and pushing buggies down the street, hurrying home to husbands and wives and children with plastic carrier bags full of groceries, normal life passing by so close I could practically reach out and touch it and yet a million miles away.

'Do you not think it's a bit weird?' I said.

Eva was reading emails on her phone. 'What's a bit weird?' she said distractedly.

'How I can see all of them but they can't see me.'

'Who?'

'*Them*, out there, the normal people. It's like I'm living in a cage and they're all on the outside, peering in, or maybe it's the other way round, I'm not sure.'

'What cage? What are you on about?'

'I can't go anywhere these days without a bodyguard. I can't even walk to the supermarket.'

She looked up from her phone and frowned. 'Why do you need to walk to the supermarket? Your housekeeper does all of your shopping for you.' I felt like she was slightly missing the point.

When we arrived he was already there, two Louis Vuitton suitcases sitting on the tarmac. 'Oh, by the way,' I said to Eva. 'Noah's coming on tour with us. That's cool, isn't it?'

'It's your tour,' she said, and the three of us loaded into the private jet.

EVA

NOT LONG AFTER THE BRITS, ALORA got together with the actor Noah Lamb. His star had already risen so high—he'd appeared in some decent films, just edgy and arthouse enough to be cool, just successful enough to make him a household name. There's no denying he was objectively hot, he had the kind of face that ruined lives. But if Noah was a star then Alora was the whole fucking galaxy, and every time the tabloids or gossip magazines printed a photograph of them rushing to her car or leaning over the balcony in her hotel penthouse, their social media followings increased by thousands. We were inundated with requests for joint interviews by the likes of *OK!* and *Hello! Vogue* offered two million for a feature and front cover. But we turned them all down. Alora hated giving interviews and the Paris talk show had been touch and go. So the decision was made that she simply wouldn't do them. Shona's genius PR strategy was that she would be unattainable, aloof and alluring—the mystery would be an inherent part of her brand.

The MD called me just after the Vienna date. His exact words when I answered the phone were, 'Eva, we have a serious problem.'

I was lying on the bed in my hotel suite at the time and I sat up so quickly I very nearly toppled off the mattress. 'Go on,' I said, bracing myself for him telling me he didn't like the new Diplo remix of 'Underland' or that some horrific story about her was going to break.

'The boyfriend.'

'What about him?'

'Oh, come on, don't tell me I have to spell it out for you. She looks too fucking happy! Roxanne's working flat out to maintain the angst and misery of the brand across her socials, and then you've got her gallivanting all over town with this pretty boy, posting unscheduled selfies looking like she's about to self-combust with joy. It just won't do.'

'I mean, yeah. She's happy. I think he's good for her.'

The MD took a bite out of something and proceeded to chew down the phone line, the food squelching unappealingly as he worked his jaw. 'It makes the music look inauthentic, and like I've always said, authenticity is key for this kind of project. Do something about it.'

'Like what?'

'I don't know. Change her log-ins or confiscate her phone or pay him off to break up with her. Just get it sorted!' And with that, he hung up.

'Oh, just ignore the grumpy old bear,' Shona said. We were having lunch at her favourite Italian restaurant, Ciccone's. She reached for a breadstick and nibbled demurely on its tip. Shona was a force to be reckoned with, highly sought after in the music business and, as legend had it, she was one of the few women to have turned down the MD's advances and he seemed to respect her all the more for it. She wore her hair in sleek black waves and spoke in a syrupy-smooth voice which made any insult no matter how vulgar almost sound like a compliment. 'The world's been in desperate need of another rock-'n'-roll couple ever since Jonny Depp ditched Kate Moss in the nineties. The public's obsession with their relationship can only enhance the brand. Interviews with the glossies are a big no-no but the odd social media post does no harm.'

But it was clear to me that something was changing. She tried to hide it from me, she asked her tour manager to smuggle it into her dressing rooms in secret, but I knew full well that Alora was knocking back shots before she performed; I could smell the booze on her breath as I walked her to the stage. I told myself it was understandable given the circumstances: the size of the venues, the many thousands of people in the audiences, the pressure. I put it down to nerves. But with Noah it began to escalate, she took her drinking to a whole new level. The room service bill at the Skyler Oriental in Milan came to nearly five grand. I scanned my eyes down the lengthy list of wines and spirits—champagne, vodka, Jägermeister, three bottles of Merlot, Tanqueray, Patrón, an entire crate of beer.

'Jesus,' I said to the woman on reception. 'Was it just two of them up there last night?'

'I'm afraid I don't know, ma'am,' she said, in her seductive Italian accent, flashing a pink lipstick smile. 'I can call the concierge and ask if he saw anyone else heading up?'

'No, don't worry, it's all right.' I handed over the credit card for Alora's touring company and winced as the receptionist swiped it through the machine.

With Noah accompanying us on tour, the guest lists to Alora's shows drastically engorged. He seemed to have friends in every city in Europe and after a show, her dressing room would fill up with other actors and models and musicians, a rich buffet of youth and beauty. I tended to make myself scarce—I'd go back to my suite and call Ade or sit on the couch at the back of the room and answer emails whilst they partied around me. I was her manager, it was down to me to play the role of responsible adult. Yes there were sometimes drugs on offer but drugs weren't my scene, I always said no and went to bed. I trusted Alora not to join in. I knew she liked to get a bit stoned, she said it helped her relax after a show, but she promised me she'd never do anything harder. She said she'd been around 'real drugs' when she was a kid, that she'd seen what they did to people.

What I didn't know about was her addition to the guest list, that she personally telephoned through to the box office every night and gave them one name—Billy Storm-Jones. I was aware she'd had no real contact with her dad since she was twelve years old. But she went ahead and added his name to the list regardless, allocated him one of the best seats in the house in a VIP box to the side of the stage. She was certain that one day he'd come back for her, that he'd turn up unannounced, tearful with pride and that they would be reunited at last.

ALORA

NOAH AND ME NEVER REALLY DATED, we just locked eyes, held hands and flung ourselves into the eye of a media storm. We'd generally sleep in until an hour before sound check, do a couple of shots and head down to whatever venue I was playing that night. He'd read stories about himself online whilst I was prodded and preened by my glam team, then he'd watch my show from the wings. Afterwards he'd follow me back to my dressing room and we'd party with his friends before collapsing into bed and repeating it all the following evening. It was hedonistic and wild. I felt like I was pushing my body to the limits of its own capacity for sleep deprivation and consumption of alcohol. I began to feel pleasantly exhausted and too numb to notice my stage fright. When he appeared at the foot of the bed one morning in Prague with a bunch of red roses and told me he loved me less than seventy-two hours after we'd met, I found myself saying it back.

'You shouldn't post so many pictures of the two of you on your socials,' Eva said to me. 'You're just fanning the flames.' We were sitting at the back of the stadium in Amsterdam, watching my crew erect the ten-foot blue neon light of my name. Noah had gone to fetch us drinks from the bar.

'I like posting about us. The comments are really funny. Here, look at this one.' I opened up z-pix and angled my phone towards Eva.

> OMG your babies will be like, the most beautiful kids in the world!!! 😊 😊 😊 😊

She read it out loud, face aghast. 'You're not seriously thinking about having kids with him, are you? You're only seventeen! It'd be career suicide!'

I locked my phone and slipped it back into my pocket. 'Obviously not.' Eva seemed to relax and went back to checking her emails, so I didn't feel the need to elaborate and tell her that I'd already decided that I didn't want to be a mum, ever. Sometimes I found myself Googling search terms such as *uterus removal* and *female sterilisation*, then wiping my search history in case Noah saw and wanted to have a 'serious talk'. I craned my neck. 'Where's Noah got to with our drinks?'

Without looking up, Eva said, 'You've got yourself a handy little servant there.' I asked her what she was talking about and she said, 'Oh, come on, don't tell me you haven't noticed. He follows you around like a lovesick puppy.'

'No he doesn't.'

She rested her phone on her lap and gave me an accusatory stare. 'A couple of days ago I watched him follow you into the toilet.'

'Oh, he just does that sometimes.'

'And what, watches you piss?'

'He usually just looks at himself in the mirror, actually.'

'That's really weird, Alora.'

'Is it?' I don't think by that point in my life I had any bearing on what was or wasn't weird. Grown men with cameras stalked me everywhere I went. I had no grasp on normality whatsoever.

We were lying in bed in my hotel in Amsterdam when Noah announced that he wanted to take me out to dinner. I rubbed at my eyes with the heels of my hands. 'What, now?' It was five AM and we'd been awake for nearly twenty-four hours. I had no clothes on and Noah was wearing a hotel bathrobe, drinking a beer and flicking through the movie channels on TV.

'Don't be silly. Tomorrow night, or something. Because I've been thinking, all we do is party.'

I sat up in bed and positioned myself in the centre of the duck-down pillows before lighting a cigarette. I didn't care about the fine which would inevitably be added to the room bill, I was making enough money by then to be able to pay my way out of most situations. 'I thought you liked partying.'

'I do. But we do it every single day. I thought we could just, you know, eat some nice food and talk.'

I reached for the mug I'd been using as an ashtray, missed and tapped ash onto the carpet. 'We talk all the time.' Noah said he knew that but it was almost always during the early hours of the morning when we'd been up all night and neither of us could ever remember much of what had been said the next day. 'I remember everything you've ever told me,' I said.

'Okay then, where did I grow up?'

'This is stupid, Noah.'

'Where?'

I was forced to admit that I couldn't remember. He asked me

what his parents did for a living and I said I didn't see how that was relevant. He asked what his favourite film was and I said, 'That's easy. *Gold Tiger on Bleecker Street*.'

He shot me an exasperated look. 'Babe, just because I starred in it and it grossed millions at the box office doesn't make it my favourite film. Who do you think I am, some kind of narcissist?' He told me his favourite film was *Pulp Fiction*, that he loved Quentin Tarantino as a director, and that his second favourite was *Beauty and the Beast*. 'The Disney version,' he said, like that made it okay.

'Fine,' I said. 'Let's go out to dinner and *talk*.' I emphasised the word sarcastically. I texted Eva and asked her to make us a reservation somewhere vegan-friendly for the following evening.

Leaving the hotel together was like an undercover military operation involving decoys and back exits, wigs and disguises, but we made it into the car without a single pap or member of the public spotting or tailing us. I Snapchatted Eva: *It worked! Thanks so much for organising it all!*

She Snapchatted me back: *Amazing! Have a lovely time with Noah. Just relax and have a night off from the madness, you deserve it.*

We drove through the streets at a leisurely pace, watching the rows of Dutch houses pass us by like multicoloured sentinels, the barges on the canal with owners sitting out on deck surrounded by pots of tulips in glorious arrays of vivid colours. It was a mild evening and I wound down my window and allowed the fresh air to whip against my face. I felt free and alive. But Noah told me to wind it back up in case someone saw us.

We were stationary at a red light, had very nearly made it all the way to the restaurant, when I heard a tapping sound against the window. I glanced to my right and saw a motorbike. Its helmeted rider leaned over his own substantial gut and lifted his camera.

Noah pulled me close and shielded my face with his jacket. 'Just ignore him,' he said.

But within seconds there were more. They swarmed like angry hornets. As soon as the lights turned green my driver pressed his foot to the floor, swerved and took a left at the very last minute causing Noah and me to be flung sideways, but of course they followed. By the time we arrived we'd accepted the inevitable. Noah gripped my hand as we ran to the entrance, cameras inches away from our faces, their flashes leaving snowflakes of light falling across my eyes.

'How the fuck did they know?' he kept muttering. I didn't reply. But it was obvious to me that someone had tipped them off, someone who couldn't be trusted.

EVA

MY SISTER'S ENGAGEMENT PARTY INCONVENIENTLY FELL on the same day as the Madrid show. I thought about telling Katerina that I couldn't make it, but Alora said, 'Don't be silly. You're my sister from another mister but she's your *actual* sister. You've got to go.'

'But what about you?' I said. I'd held her hand and walked her to the stage at every single show. I didn't like the thought of not being there for her.

But she said she'd be fine. 'I've got Dad's tooth,' she said, and I glanced at the manky old molar she religiously wore on a chain round her neck and made a mental note to speak to her stylist about it.

The party was hosted by Arif's parents. Their house in Putney was a double-fronted Georgian affair with a long, thin garden, immaculate as a bowling green, which led to a quaint little summerhouse tucked in between the blossoming damson trees. I myself had just become the proud owner of a five-bedroom house in Clapton, and Ade came over to mine first to get ready.

But just as we were about to walk out of the front door he told me I looked really nice and I said he did too and we ended up kissing and soon our clothes were strewn all over the hallway as we toppled backwards onto my couch. I sat astride his beautiful body, which was now almost as familiar to me as my own, kissing my way down his neck, chest and stomach before taking him in my mouth. When he said he was close I climbed onto him. I shut my eyes. He took hold of my thighs and pulled me against him and within minutes explosions of colour were going off inside my eyelids and I was collapsing forwards, his breath hot in my ear. By the time we'd showered and made ourselves presentable again, we were over an hour late for the party.

'Shit!' I said, as I shot out of the drive in my new soft-top MG and very nearly collided with an inconveniently situated stationary vehicle.

Ade placed his hand on my knee. 'Chill, Eva,' he said. 'It's cool.' And I realised that it was. It was more than cool, everything was amazing. Alora was a global superstar with the world at her feet. I was managing one of the most talented, groundbreaking, iconic artists of modern times and to top it all off, I was dating my best friend, the hottest, kindest, most lovely guy I'd ever met. I felt so deliriously happy that I thought about killing the engine and dragging Ade back inside for another session on the couch. But I composed myself, checked my wing mirrors and manoeuvred the car safely into the road.

By the time we arrived the party was already in full swing—the house filled with family and friends and work colleagues of Katerina and Arif's, eating canapés off paper plates and drinking prosecco whilst a jazz band played out in the garden. In stark contrast to my high-school days, Katerina had been popular and remained close to her teenage friends as well as acquiring many more at university. I made my way through the house with Ade and out into the garden, saying our hellos to people I knew and making introductions. Every time I uttered the words, 'And this is my boyfriend, Ade' a tiny tremor of joy passed through my heart.

As soon as I laid eyes on her I could tell that she was pissed. Katerina tottered towards me in slingback court shoes and flung her arms around my neck. She was wearing a loose-fitting cream dress which on me would've looked as flattering as a hessian sack but on Katerina looked sophisticated and elegant.

'Little sis!' she cried. 'You *finally* made it!' She planted a big kiss on my cheek, then did the same to Ade, before immediately ushering me towards a young boy sitting cross-legged on the grass. She introduced him as Arif's cousin, Imad, who was in a band and wanted to know everything about the music business.

'You'll talk to him, won't you?' she slurred. 'Give him some advice?'

I mouthed, 'Sorry,' at Ade.

He smiled and said, 'It's cool. I'll fetch us some drinks.'

Imad was sweet. I could tell he was nervous, he seemed to find it hard to make eye contact and hid shyly behind his floppy fringe. He said he was a massive Alora fan, he said her music changed his life and I promised him free tickets to her next show. I was just explaining to him what record labels do when I heard my phone ping. Ade was over by the buffet seemingly engaged in a deep and meaningful with Arif, and Katerina was in the middle of a group of girlfriends, practically screaming with laughter. I smiled, then slipped my phone out of my bag and glanced down at the screen. It was an Instagram DM notification. And when

I saw the name, I thought I was going to throw up. I hastily excused myself from Imad without explanation and made my way down to the bottom of the garden for some privacy. I walked round the back of the summerhouse where I collapsed onto the grass.

Maddie Malkin—a name I hadn't seen since high school, and one I'd hoped I would never see again. She had been the ringleader. She had been the one who singled me out from a class of thirty-two as worthy of her undivided spite, gathered troops and led the charge. She was tall and athletic with hair that reached her bum. Her parents were both lawyers and she came top of class in almost every test. She rested her peachy ass on the sink and sneered as she instructed Laura and Jackie to hold my head down the toilet and pull the flush. She lobbed my school bag over the fence where it landed in dog shit. She spread a rumour that I ate ten boiled eggs for breakfast every day and people began to call me Egg-Breath Eva. When I think back on it now, it's almost too ridiculous to be offensive. But I remember crying when the boys yelled it behind my back, as I hurried home with my schoolbooks clutched protectively to my chest. Mum and Dad tried to intervene. They spoke to the school, the school spoke to Maddie and her parents. But Maddie's parents were governors and the headmaster seemed entirely unwilling expel his star pupil. My grades suffered. I did badly in my GCSEs. Then we moved house and I finally escaped my torturers. Egg-Breath Eva was in the past. But then here was Maddie Malkin, messaging me on a Saturday afternoon years later, and I was Egg-Breath Eva all over again.

With shaking hands I opened up the DM:

Hey, Eva. I don't know if you remember me. But I'm pretty positive you do, because I made your life hell. I've thought about you a lot over the years, about the way I treated you at high school, and I feel awful about it. It's not an excuse or anything (there is no excuse for what I did) but I was really unhappy. My parents put a load of pressure on me to do well at school and I felt angry and miserable all the time and I think I took it out on you. I've thought about trying to get in touch with you before now but never had the guts. Then I saw your picture in a magazine the other day. I couldn't believe it! I mean, you look pretty different with your hair blonde like that, but I recognised you. You were standing next to Alora Storm-Jones at some celebrity party and underneath the photo, the caption read, 'Alora with manager.' Well firstly, congratulations, that's obviously amazing! I can't actually believe that you manage Alora Storm-Jones, I'm a massive fan!! She's incredible, like, literally amazing. I'm really happy for you and also, if I'm honest, I'm relieved. I didn't know what happened to you after you left school. I heard your family moved away and you deleted all your social media accounts. I worried that you might have gone on to live a really unhappy life, that what I did messed you up for good. I even sometimes worried that you might've killed yourself, or something. But I guess you were stronger than I gave you credit for. I'm sorry Eva. I'm so so sorry, about everything. And I know that this is completely out of the blue, but I wondered if you'd be up for meeting for a drink sometime? I'd just really like to apologise in person. I totally understand if you don't want to, but I'd really appreciate it if you did.
Let me know.
Maddie x

I was still on the ground, back pressed up against the summerhouse, reading the message over and over again when Ade found me. 'Hey,' he said, rushing towards me. He crouched down beside me. 'What's the matter? Why are you crying?' I realised then that I was. I swiped at my tears with the sleeve of my dress. Ade pulled a paper napkin out of his pocket and handed it to me.

I took a huge gulp of air. 'There's something you don't know about me,' I said. And whilst the celebrations continued without us, I read out Maddie Malkin's message and I told Ade everything.

By the time I'd finished speaking, he was crying too. His arm was around me and he was holding me close. 'I'm so sorry,' he said. 'I wish you'd told me all this before. It's shit, and to be honest it explains a lot, about why you used to be so insecure. But she's right, Eva, you *are* strong, you didn't let them break you and look at you now.'

I sniffed hard. 'I guess.'

'Are you going to meet up with her, do you reckon?'

'Do you think I should?'

'I don't know, maybe. She's obviously sorry, and sounds like she had her own stuff going on at home. Maybe it would be good for both of you to see each other again, you know, clear the air.'

I slipped my phone into my pocket, and felt something inside of me subtly shift, a misaligned cog clicking into place. 'Do you seriously think she *is* sorry? She's had years to get in touch and apologise. Bit suspicious that she's only done it now she's found out I'm managing Alora.'

'You think she's got an ulterior motive?'

'Probably. She'll want tickets to a show, or a meet and greet with Alora, or something like that. No, actually, I'm not going to meet up with her. I'm not even going to reply. Why should I, after everything she did to me?'

Ade nodded. 'Sure, you do what's right for you.'

I kissed his cheek. 'Thank you,' I said.

'For what?'

'For listening, for being so kind and supportive.'

'Always. You can tell me anything, you know that. I love you, Eva.'

I pulled back from him in surprise. 'Do you?'

'Of course!'

'Well, that's a relief,' I said. 'Because I love you too.'

I honestly don't know if I've ever felt closer to anyone than in that moment. I had told Ade about my past, I had revealed the shame and humiliation of Egg-Breath Eva and he loved and accepted me regardless. So it felt like the perfect time to ask him to move in with me, and I began crying again, tears of happiness this time, when he said that obviously, he would.

ALORA

MY ONE-TO-ONE THERAPIST IN REHAB IS called Seren. She has honey-coloured hair and wears frameless glasses which are slightly opaque like slivers of ice. She flutters her eyelashes excessively and chews the tip of her pen in a contemplative way. Her office is on the second floor of the therapy centre. It faces south and buttery sunlight melts into the carpet at my feet. The window is slightly ajar and I can hear seagulls calling although I can't see the ocean. She asks if I understand the principles of the Method and I say a bit, though I was barely listening as Elijah explained. Seren says that since we were children, we've been conditioned to believe certain things about ourselves which are not necessarily true, that through a series of exercises, the Method will break down the internal barriers created by these false beliefs resulting in a deep connection with our real selves, thus seeing the world around us in a very different way. I nod like I'm interested and wonder how long it will be until I can go back to my chalet and lie down.

'You attempted to take your own life,' she says. 'In a very public manner.'

'Uh-hum.'

I'm staring out of the window and she's staring at me. I brace myself for her to ask me why I did it. But she doesn't, and I'm surprised that I feel disappointed even though I was intending to refuse to explain. She says that she'd like me to write down a memory from my childhood.

'What kind of memory?' I say.

'Any kind you like. I must leave it to you to interpret the exercise, I cannot lead you—otherwise it defeats the purpose.' She smiles so genuinely that it makes me want to scream. I smile back at her.

I go to my chalet. I sit down at the desk and tap the tip of my pen against the pad of paper which is embossed in gold with the Max Beaumont crest. Is this really why I'm paying thirty grand a month—to sit by myself staring at a blank page? I don't particularly want to be dissecting my mental health in front of a bunch of strangers either so none of it feels like good value for money. I feel anger writhing up inside me, bursting through my blood vessels. Why am I here? Why did I agree to this? I remind myself of the answer in Eva's words:

'You tried to kill yourself in front of millions of people. Even Shona can't sweep that one under the carpet.'

This is what I write:

It was Christmas, bobble hats and scarves weather. It hadn't yet snowed but you could tell it was going to, you could feel it in the way the air was crystallising against your skin. In the city centre, an enormous fir tree was lit up with fairy lights which flashed sporadically like they were dancing to the beat of an invisible marching band and the market stalls were selling mulled wine and mince pies dusted with icing sugar. I stared longingly at the mince pies as dad and me hurried past.

We set up in our usual spot, just by the main entrance to the shopping centre where the footfall was decent. Dad unfolded the camping stool and sat down. He pulled up his collar, positioned his guitar on his lap and took a swig from his silver flask. I removed his cap and laid it down in front of my feet. The cap was empty, but it wouldn't be for long.

'What do you reckon,' dad said. 'Begin with a classic?'

He began to play 'White Christmas', strumming the chords with laid-back nonchalance. Two bars in, I began to sing. I was only ten years old, but my voice was powerful and clear even without a mic, rising up hopefully into the afternoon sky. Soon a crowd started to gather. A fifty pence piece was tossed into the cap, followed by a couple of pound coins, followed by a shower of coppers. My hands were freezing, I'd forgotten to put on my gloves before we left the house, and I drew them up into the sleeves of my jacket. An old lady approached and pressed something into my palm. She smelled of lavender, I remember that about her.

'For you, dear,' she said. 'You keep this one for you.'

I looked down and to my surprise, I saw that she'd given me a twenty pound note. I'd never held so much money in my hand before! I knew that dad would be pleased and started fantasising about all the things we might spend it on—a trip to the fairground, hot chocolate, mince pies! By the time I snapped out of my daydream and remembered my manners, the old lady was walking away. I never even said thank you, it's one of my regrets in life, part of a long list.

We busked until the shopping centre locked its doors and the streets were practically deserted. And it was then that it began to snow; thick, soft, luscious flakes which drifted down from the dark satin sky and rested on my clothes. I lifted my eyes and I twirled, round and round, arms outstretched, head tipped back, mouth wide open catching the snowflakes on my tongue. Even when I felt dizzy and everything around me was spinning in a different direction I didn't stop twirling. And dad laughed and watched me at first, he watched me as though he was bewitched, and then he joined in. Both of us staring into the heavens, lost in the wonder of the world. When dad stumbled, I steadied him. He leaned on me and I stopped him from falling. The silver flask was empty by then.

He said we'd better get going, that it was late. He was heading over to Jonny's, he said, but he'd see me home first.

I handed him the twenty pound note and he smiled and said, 'You're an angel.' He slipped it into his pocket with the coins.

But I didn't want to go home to a cold flat and an even colder mother, and I loved it at Jonny's. I persuaded dad to let me go with him and we set off towards the bus stop. The snow was coming down heavily by then and my trainers were slipping on the icy pavement. But I held onto dad's hand and he held onto mine. We never let go of each other. As we passed by the market, a straggling trader was packing his wares into his van.

'Hey,' dad called across the street. 'Give me one of those mince pies will you? My little girl's hungry.'

The man looked at dad, then at me, and shook his head. But he opened up the back of the van, removed a mince pie and handed it to me. I bit into it and my mouth was flooded with Christmas. To this day, with all the fancy food I've eaten in all those expensive Michelin star restaurants, nothing has ever tasted so good.

EVA

THE MORNING AFTER MY SISTER'S ENGAGEMENT party, I helped Ade pack his stuff and he moved into mine. It took a few trips back and forth because the MG's boot was tiny and he had quite a lot of records and bags of clothes, one of which split on the pavement scattering his socks and boxers everywhere. But we gathered them up together. None of it felt like a hassle. We kept catching each other's eye and grinning like fools. My flight back to Madrid wasn't until nine that night, so we had time for a quick dinner together before I headed to Heathrow. Ade cooked an incredible chicken dish with yams, one of his mum's recipes, and we ate it out in the garden beneath the beech tree. He lit a fig-and-cherry-scented candle and somewhere in the distance kids were playing out in the street, the sound of their laughter rising up into the night sky, the soft repetitive thud of a football hitting a wall.

'Hey,' Ade said. 'This is our first dinner together as housemates.'

'Housemates? Wow, you make it sound so romantic.'

He laughed and scratched his arm. 'Well, what do you want me to call us? Cohabitees?'

'That's even worse!'

'Mum asked me if you were pregnant, you know.'

I nearly spat out my food. 'Seriously?'

'Yup. She couldn't understand why we needed to move in together in such a rush.'

'But we've known each other for ages.'

'Uh-hum.'

'And I'm on tour. If we don't do it now whilst I'm in London, we'd have to wait another month.'

'I explained all this to her.'

'And what did she say?'

Ade topped up my wine. 'The usual stuff. We're still young, we have our whole lives ahead of us, she wants to make sure I'm still focusing on my diploma, blah blah blah.'

'That sounds like the kind of thing *my* mum would say.'

He laughed. 'I know, right? Maybe Geraldine's rubbing off on her.'

'Oh God, I was hoping it would be the other way round.'

'She's right about the diploma thing, though, I do feel like I've been a bit slack lately.' I knew he'd handed in one of his coursework assignments late after we'd been in Paris together, that he'd been marked down because of it.

'Does she think I'm a bad influence?'

'Are you kidding me? She thinks you're an inspiration! She'd be happy if I had one-hundredth of the success in my career as you're having in yours. She'd be happy if I had a career, full stop.'

I reached across the table and took hold of his hand. 'You're going to be fine,' I said. 'You're so talented, the right door will open for you, you'll see. And my offer still stands about helping you with your own music.'

'I know, I know, that's really nice of you. I'll think about it, promise.'

I left Ade loading the dishwasher surrounded by stacks of boxes. I said I was sorry I couldn't help him clear up and unpack, but I didn't want to miss the flight. 'It's cool,' he said. 'I can handle a bit of unpacking and dish washing. It'll be all neat and tidy by the time you're home.'

Home—I loved that he'd called it that. 'You're quite the domestic goddess, Ade Oni,' I said, wrapping my arms around his neck and kissing him goodbye. 'I could get used to this.'

ALORA

DAD'S BANDMATE JONNY LIVED IN AN abandoned Victorian warehouse round the back of the Northern Quarter. From outside it looked gloomy and imposing with its soot-stained bricks and six storeys of boarded-up windows, standing alone and forgotten like an elderly gentleman accidentally time-travelled to another era. But inside it was magical. I'd never been to Disneyland, but I always imagined it to be just like Jonny's. There were colourful murals on the walls—the BAN THE BOMB sign made out of shiny plastic flowers, a pair of lips with a protruding silver tongue, blue snow-capped mountains framing the rising sun—fairy lights were woven around the bannisters, and there was a slide which spiralled from the top floor right to the bottom. By the time you shot out of it, you felt like you were travelling at the speed of light. The door was always unlocked and the place was always full of people, music and cigarette smoke so dense that it was like a cloud had descended from the sky. The crowd was eclectic and free—women wearing suits and smoking cigars, men wearing dresses and makeup with long, flowing hair. The parameters of the outside world's grey existence seemed to no longer apply. And everyone knew Dad.

I followed him up to the third floor where Jonny was sitting on one of the threadbare sofas. There was a beautiful man who looked like a movie star sitting on Jonny's lap. Jonny raised his hand when he saw Dad and Dad clasped it in his before dropping down next to him on the sofa. Dad said something in the movie-star guy's ear and he smiled coyly and pecked Dad on the cheek, then turned and fixed his slightly sleepy gaze on me.

'Hey, sweetie,' he slurred. 'Want to see some kittens?'

I looked at Dad, who was rolling a cigarette. 'Go see the kittens with Eddie,' he said without looking up from his hands. 'Me and Jonny need to talk.'

I pointed at the cigarette. 'Can I have one?' Dad shrugged and handed me the one he'd just rolled. I stuck it in the corner of my mouth and he lit it for me.

'Cute!' Eddie said. It was the first time I ever smoked.

The kittens were lying in a cardboard box in Jonny's bedroom, squirming around the mummy cat. I knelt on the rag-rug carpet which was pocked with rock burns and Eddie lifted a white one from the box and tucked it into my arms. He mewed sweetly and clung on to my sweater with his minuscule claws and I felt the most incredible rush of responsibility to hold him carefully and keep him safe.

'Can I take him home with me?' I asked. I could hear the yearning inside of me coming out in my voice. The idea of caring for this tiny creature was somehow wonderful to me.

Eddie tickled him behind the ear with a finger which was stacked with silver rings, one a ruby, one a skull. 'I don't know, honey, you'll have to ask your dad.'

I said I'd go back upstairs and find him and Eddie said it was probably better if we stayed down here. He said if I wanted, he'd plait my hair and tell me a story. He positioned himself behind me and started running his fingers through my hair, combing it, dividing it into sections. I remember the feeling so vividly, the way it sent shivers down my spine in stark contrast to Julia's painful yanking as she scraped my hair into a hasty ponytail, always late for school. The story was about a white kitten who lived in a cardboard box. It wasn't exactly a story, Eddie was just describing the situation we were actually in so nothing really happened, and he sometimes paused for a long time as though he'd forgotten he was supposed to be telling a story at all. So I started joining in, improvising, filling in the gaps, and soon it became me telling the story to Eddie whilst he stroked my hair, working it into plaits, the kitten soft and sleepy in my arms.

It was gone three AM when Dad and I tumbled through the front door of the flat, the kitten wrapped snugly in one of Jonny's old sweaters. Dad tripped on the first step and fell with a clatter. 'Shhh,' he hissed, finger to his lips, and we both giggled. But when a dark shadow passed across our bodies, our laughter abruptly ended. We looked up to see Julia standing at the top of the staircase in her nightdress, hands on hips. She glared at Dad, me and then the kitten, in that order.

'Absolutely no way,' she said. 'Not a chance in hell.'

She drove us back to Jonny's, still wearing her nightie, Dad and her screaming at each other in the front of the car and me wailing in the back with the kitten clutched to my chest. As I laid him down in the box with his brothers and sisters, sobbing so hard I was nearly retching, I promised him I'd come back for him, I swore it on Dad's life. But the next time I went round to

Jonny's there were no kittens and Jonny seemed to have no recollection of them ever having been there in the first place. The mummy cat was prowling round his bedroom. I tried to stroke her but she just arched her back and hissed.

EVA

ONE MONTH LATER I FLEW BACK to London for the Music Week Awards. Alora didn't come with me, she said she'd prefer to swerve it because on a moral level, all the money people who worked in the music business spent on congratulating themselves could just be donated to charity instead and actually do some good for the world. I think she noticed I looked slightly crestfallen because she went on to say that *obviously*, being nominated for Manager of the Year was a big deal, she was really happy for me and she hoped I'd win.

I caught an earlier flight than planned. I didn't tell Ade, I thought I'd surprise him. But the surprise was all on me.

I arrived home to find him in the living room with Warren. In my absence he'd set up his decks in the bay window, my new couch shoved to one side, and the music was so loud it was a small miracle that the neighbours hadn't called the police. Ade was mixing with headphones on and Warren was on the other side of the turntables, dancing like a gangly sunflower in the wind, all spindly limbs and big beaming face, occasionally shouting over the music, 'Nice one, mate!' or 'Yes! 'Avin' it!' My art deco coffee table was covered in empties and there was a wet patch in the middle of my cashmere rug, presumably a spillage which no one had bothered to clean up. I was standing in the doorway for quite a while before either of them even noticed me there, and when Ade finally did he looked so happy to see me that it temporarily stalled the velocity of my rising irritation. He turned the music down and bounded over to hug me.

'You're home! Look, I got you flowers.'

He lifted a limp bouquet of carnations off the mantelpiece and handed it to me. The carnations were an unnatural shade of blue and the price was still stuck to the plastic wrapper—£4.99. In the last hotel I'd stayed in with Alora, the manager had filled our suites with white roses, sprayed with some kind of special preservative which meant they'd last forever. I sniffed at Ade's flowers in an obligatory way. They smelled of nothing. 'Thanks,' I said. 'They're nice.' I placed them down on the coffee table next to the empty cans. Warren fist-bumped me and asked how I was doing. 'Tired,' I said. 'And hungry. The food in first class was like something a cat threw up. I'm going to make something to eat then take a shower. You guys carry on, but maybe turn it down a bit, yeah?'

A strange, slightly nervy look passed across Ade's face. 'Oh, erm...' he said. 'Eva, maybe you shouldn't go...' But I was already making my way towards the kitchen.

That's when I saw them. I stood in the doorway surveying the room in dismay—the unpacked boxes and bags, on the floor, on the table, all over the counter, exactly where they'd been when I left. Ade had followed behind me. I spun around to face him.

'What the fuck?'

He edged past me, hastily picked up a couple of the boxes and balanced them on one knee. 'I'm sorry, I wasn't expecting you home for another hour.'

'Another hour? You've had four weeks!'

'I've been busy.'

'Doing what? Playing superstar DJ for your only groupie?'

Ade laughed, which I found completely infuriating. 'Are we having our first domestic?' He tried to put his arms around me, but I shrugged them off.

'It's not funny. You don't know what it's like being on tour, on the move all the time, in different hotels practically every night—it's really disorientating. Sometimes you'd give anything for one night in your own bed. So when I finally come home I want to walk into a house which feels like my own, a tidy house, not a two-million-pound storage unit.'

'Look, I said I'm sorry, I just thought—'

'Thought what? That I'd put it all away for you? Typical man.'

'No, I—'

'I'm Alora's manager. I don't have time for... I just don't *do*...' I wafted my hands disdainfully at the mess before me, pulling a face as though it was emitting a putrid odour. 'My glam team's arriving in an hour, I need to get ready for these awards.'

'Okay, cool, I need to get ready too.'

It was a snap decision, made spitefully, and when I spoke I barely recognised my own voice, it sounded so superior and cruel. 'Actually, Ade, I'd prefer it if you just stayed here and sorted out this mess.'

His eyes widened. 'Really?'

'Yeah, really.'

Ade hung his head and nodded. 'Sure thing, Eva, whatever

makes you happy.' He was still carrying cardboard boxes up the stairs when the car arrived to whisk me away to West London without him.

The awards ceremony was in the ballroom of a beautiful old hotel in Mayfair. The MD had bought a table in my honour, which set him back a cool ten grand. Roxanne, Jason, Levi and a few others from the record label were already there with Shona when I arrived, professionally blow-dried and slathered in makeup, wearing Spanx pants and still sucking my stomach in for dear life in a skin-tight silver Versace dress. The MD had saved the seat to his left for me. The seat to my right, where Ade would've been sitting if I hadn't impulsively disinvited him, was empty and I felt a lump in my throat which I hastily swallowed.

Shona leaned across the table and purred, 'Ade not coming?' Her breath smelled of vodka and cigarettes.

'Last-minute change of plan.'

She touched the Tiffany pendant around her neck. 'Oh dear. Trouble in paradise?'

'Something like that. I think I might've been a bit of a cow to him.'

She grabbed a bottle of champagne from the ice bucket on the table and poured me a glass. 'Don't worry about it. It'll be easier for you to network if you don't have to babysit your other half, it's always a bit tedious when they don't work in the industry, isn't it? And we can have more fun together—girls' night!' She clinked her glass against mine.

I glanced around the ballroom. Everyone who was anyone in the business was there and the atmosphere was electric. I checked my phone to see if Ade had messaged but he hadn't. I thought about calling him, telling him to get in a cab, but then Roxanne came over to wish me luck and by the time we'd finished speaking and she'd sat back down again the ceremony was starting and it was too late. I felt surprisingly nervous considering I was convinced winning was an impossibility when I was up against such tough competition; the managers of Coldplay and Ed Sheeran had been nominated too. And when the presenter read out my name, I felt so light-headed I thought I might faint.

Shona nudged me and said, 'For God's sake, woman, get up and collect your award!'

I made my way through the tables, shaking hands and accepting congratulations from the heads of other record labels to famous recording artists to some of the most revered music critics in the world. My whole body was trembling and when I spoke into the microphone, my voice was horrifyingly loud. On the way over in the car I'd typed some hasty notes into my phone, thinking I'd never have to use them, but I have no idea if I stuck to them. I know I thanked the MD, Roxanne, Shona, I thanked my friends and family for their support, but most of all I thanked Alora. I dedicated the award to her. It was only when I was sitting back down, the MD refilling my glass with champagne, that I realised I hadn't thanked Ade.

We partied hard that night. The MD had booked a suite upstairs in the hotel and I found myself there until dawn. I somehow ended up in the bath with Jason, both of us sitting fully clothed, drinking champagne. He offered me a bump of coke. Ordinarily I would have said no, I didn't do drugs—it was a hard line I'd set for myself, probably something to do with the videos they made us watch in high school where the teenagers always ended up on life-support machines—but this night felt different, carefree, like nothing I did had any consequences. And I was drunk and giddy after the win. I found myself leaning forwards to sniff it off Jason's car key.

He proceeded to tell me about the first ever tape he'd bought as a kid—*Parklife* by Blur—how he'd copied it at home and sold the copies to his friends. 'I was basically a professional bootlegger,' he said. I threw my head back and laughed loudly for a very long time. He was suddenly far more hilarious than I'd ever previously thought he was. 'What's your social media following these days?' he said.

'Around one hundred and twenty thousand on z-pix, a hundred thousand or so on Twitter and Instagram, a bit less on Facebook. It's mainly just Alora's super-fans and journalists who follow me, though.'

'Do you use TikTok?'

'What's that again?'

'That app where people post videos of themselves dancing and doing other random stuff. I don't know if it'll catch on but the kids seem pretty into it.'

'I'll check it out.'

'You should do. Now you've got profile, you should actively manage your brand.'

'Yeah, you're right,' I said. 'Brand Eva. That has a nice ring to it, doesn't it? Maybe I should hire KAZY-K's choreographer to help me with a few dance routines. There's this move I do sometimes which I think's got potential to go viral.' I demonstrated the move by raising both my arms in the air and swinging them from side to side in unison with my head until I began to feel dizzy.

'Looks wicked, babe, you should totally post the shit out of that!'

When we eventually went back into the lounge area the party seemed to have tripled in size and the room was heaving. I was dragged into a conversation with a well-regarded live agent who was vying to work with Alora. Then the head of A&R at a competitor record label who was supposedly a mate of the MD's took me to one side and whispered in my ear, 'As soon as the deal with Low Slang's up, you come and talk to me. I'll make you an offer you can't refuse.' I'd never felt so popular in my life. A couple of male models introduced themselves. They were friends with Shona and had just flown in from walking the catwalk for Jean Paul Gaultier in Milan. They were sharp jawed and exquisitely attractive.

Every time I said I needed to go home, one of them, called Gabriel, grabbed hold of my wrist and said in a flirtatious manner, 'You're not allowed.'

At one point, he found an acoustic guitar from somewhere, sat on the bed and began to play. Someone turned the music down and the guests formed a circle around him. His voice was surprisingly rich and resonant for someone so dainty and his fingers flew over the strings like he was playing flamenco. It was mesmerising. I could tell the MD was impressed. Why is it, I thought to myself, that the beautiful people are always good at everything, leaving the less beautiful ones behind in the dirt? Once I'd been one of them, picked last for sports teams at school, staring at my trainers whilst everyone else's names were called out before mine, Egg-Breath Eva shoved up against the lockers whilst Maddie Malkin emptied out my bag. But not anymore—that person was dead to me. I pulled back the curtain and glanced out of the window. The street below was dark and empty. London was sleeping and oblivious. And here I was, high above it in an exclusive enclave of champagne, cocaine and dreams. Life felt like it was unfurling before me on an endless red carpet.

My phone buzzed in my pocket. I pulled it out and unlocked it—a message from Ade:

> How did it go? Did u win?? Hope u're not still mad with me, I've been tidying up like crazy all night. Don't leave me hanging!!! Love u xxx

Gabriel stopped playing the guitar. He picked up a bottle of champagne, meandered towards me with sultry eyes and filled my glass. I sent Ade the thumbs-up emoji, then I locked my phone and slipped it into my pocket.

I caught a cab back home around six AM. The party had descended into a few hardcore drug users—Jason and the MD included—snorting gear off a mirror and talking self-congratulatory nonsense and it had begun to give me the ick. Outside in my street, a dog was pissing against a flickering lamppost and someone had dumped an empty Domino's pizza box in my front garden. I didn't bother to pick it up. I found Ade in bed, motionless beneath the covers, and as much as part of me wanted to snuggle up next to him I knew I was still too wired to sleep. I jumped in the shower and rested my forehead against the glass door, wishing the water would cleanse me of all of my bad decisions. As soon as I got out, I dressed in a Balenciaga tracksuit, made a mug of instant hot chocolate and lay down on the sofa. I turned on the TV and flicked through the movie channels before turning it off again. I felt rough and wished I could crawl out of my skin and into somebody else's. Never again, I swore. Never again will I:

1. stay up past two AM
2. drink more than three glasses of champagne
3. consume drugs of any nature.

I told myself that as Alora's manager, I needed to be professional, that I should keep the lines clear.

I don't know what time it was when Ade came downstairs, I must've eventually nodded off because I opened my eyes to find myself drooling onto one of my Vera Wang cushions.

'Hey,' I croaked. He was wearing my dressing gown, the tie knotted round his waist. He sat down next to me and I rested my head on his lap. He began to stroke my hair and I closed my eyes again and focused on the soothing sensation of his fingertips massaging my scalp.

'Things got a bit messy last night then?' he said.

I smiled weakly. My lips were cracked and dry. 'Just a bit. Sorry I didn't call, just, you know . . .' I allowed my voice to trail off. I had no defensible explanation.

Ade said he wasn't sure what I'd meant by the thumbs-up emoji but he'd seen on z-pix that I'd won the award and it was fucking amazing. 'Are you happy?' he asked.

I said I was too hungover to be happy. 'Look, I'm really sorry about uninviting you, I overreacted big time. I wish you'd come with me, I wanted you there.'

'It's cool. I'm sorry I didn't put my stuff away, it's just . . . to be honest, all your things are so fancy and expensive these days. I started unpacking, but mine next to yours looked all wrong, like a jumble sale in Harrods, so I decided to wait until you got back and check with you where I should put it all.'

'You can put it wherever you like.'

'Really?'

'Course! This is your home too.'

'Okay, cool, thanks.'

'Actually, maybe not those decks, though, maybe stick them in the spare bedroom, they're kind of in the way there.'

'No probs.'

'And those *Star Wars* posters could go in the spare bedroom too. Oh, and that weird-shaped cactus thing.'

'You're not down with Spikey Dick? He was a housewarming gift from Warren.'

I pulled a face. 'Did you name him or Warren?'

'It was kind of a collaborative thing.'

'So gross. Spare bedroom, definitely.'

Ade said, 'You're the boss.' He suggested we go out to dinner that night to celebrate my win and I said I couldn't because I had to fly back to Hamburg. 'Some other time then?'

'Sure.'

'When?'

'I'll have to check my schedule.'

He seemed to give up on attempting to solicit any kind of enthusiasm from me for celebrating together and started telling me about some job he'd applied for. I found my mind drifting into my emails, making a mental list of the ones I needed to respond to urgently: a two-million-pound brand-deal offer from Puma which we'd turn down, a proposal from Vivienne Westwood for Alora to collaborate on a limited-edition clothing range which was definitely of interest. Those which were of moderate importance: a request from The Weeknd for Alora to feature on his next single and another for her to perform at the sweet-sixteenth of a wealthy movie producer's daughter. And those which were at the bottom of the pile: Alora's lawyer asking for the guest list to a show, Mum wanting to know if her and Dad could meet me for lunch when I was back off tour and my sister asking whether I could please call Mum and Dad a bit more often. Then my phone pinged with a WhatsApp. I opened it:

> Hey Eva so good to hang!! Let's grab a drink when we're next in the same city!!! Gabriel x

I had no recollection of even giving him my number. I swiftly deleted the message, relieved that Ade was still going on about something and didn't seem to have seen it. So when he eventually said, 'What do you reckon?' I very nearly replied, 'To what?' But caught myself just in time.

'Yeah, sounds cool. Hey, what time is it?' He said it had just gone nine. 'Shit! My flight leaves at half ten.' I jumped up from the sofa and as I did so caught sight of my reflection in the mirror above the fireplace. I looked thin. My cheeks were drawn and I finally had bone structure. With all the early-morning and late-night calls to various international teams at the record label, I was frequently skipping breakfast and dinner. I was slowly shrinking into Mimi-size proportions, into the person I'd always wanted to be.

ALORA

THE FOLLOWING DAY, MAUREEN TAKES ME to another one-to-one session with Seren. When I walk into her room she's holding a sheet of paper in her hand. I recognise the squat loops of my own handwriting. She smiles and lays the paper down on her lap.

'Sit, please,' she says, and gestures to the chair. She's wearing cream trousers and a green roll-neck sweater. Her poise is elegant and refined, even her fingers seem to move through the air with ballerina-like grace. 'How did you find the exercise?' she says.

'It was okay.'

'Only okay?'

'How did you want me to find it?'

She says that she wasn't looking for any particular response. 'I thought it was interesting, the memory you chose.'

'Why?'

'Do you remember the occasion fondly?'

'Yeah, I do.'

'I see.'

'What does that mean?' She smiles and says it means nothing at all. 'Do you enjoy performing, Alora?'

'Of course.'

'Why "of course"?'

'Because my fans are like my family. When I'm out onstage, it's probably the only time I feel truly loved. And in a weird way, it's the only time I feel like I actually exist.'

Seren nods as though what I've said is perfectly normal, rational and reasonable. 'And what's your greatest fear?'

I pause for a moment's thought. 'Being forgotten,' I say.

The next couple of weeks in rehab pass in a monotonous haze of talking, listening, eating, sleeping, traipsing behind Maureen from the therapy centre to the restaurant and back again. The dressings may have been removed but Maureen still comes to my chalet every morning to check there's no infection and that I haven't been trying to claw the wounds open again with my fingernails. She says I'm healing nicely and that I should even be able to go for a swim soon.

'It's a freshwater pool, so it shouldn't sting.'

I say that I can't swim. 'I'm surprised you didn't know that.'

'It wasn't in your notes.'

'But you would've read it somewhere, surely, it's common knowledge.'

'I read books and listen to the news. I don't pay attention to any of that other nonsense.'

'Okay,' I say. 'Well, I won't ask you to update me on what *they're* saying about me then.'

I try not to scoff when she says, 'This is a closed ecosystem of healing. But even if I could update you, I wouldn't. Seeing yourself as others see you, looking to *them*—whoever *they* may be—to validate who *you* are is toxic to the soul.'

But I'm not looking for them to validate me. I want them to tear me to pieces word by word. It feels like a dark void is swallowing me from the inside out, it's when I'm festering in the pit of its stomach that I do my best writing—I want to be swallowed whole.

That afternoon I arrive at the therapy centre to see a huge doll hanging from the rafters, dangling its ankles into the centre of the circle of chairs. It has no hair or features, like a crash dummy used to test new cars to see if they can withstand potentially fatal impact. I walk around it, staring up at it. It swings slightly from left to right. There's something macabre about it, like a dead cow hoisted on a meat hook after slaughter. Elijah bursts through the doors in a breezy manner and walks towards me smiling broadly. He doesn't acknowledge the presence of the doll. The others filter in.

'Please, take your seats,' Elijah says. He starts to talk about an exercise we did in the previous session and I raise my hand. 'Yes, Nobody?'

I point at the doll. 'Who's this?'

He claps his hands together in apparent delight. 'Ah, thank you,' he says. 'Great question.' He stands and using a pulley mechanism, lowers the doll, then he ties its ankles to a metal ring in the floorboards and pats it on the shoulder as if they're old pals. 'This can be anyone you need it to be.' When we all look confused he explains how the doll is what the Method calls a Fury Doll. That during the session we will take it in turns to visualise the face of someone who has caused us harm as the face of the doll, then we will lay into the doll in any way we see fit—we can yell insults, kick it, pummel it with our fists. Best Supporting Actress and Politician exchange a sceptical look.

Million-Dollar Smile, who I've internally categorised as a spoilt, rich brat, says, 'I'm not doing this, it's absolutely ludicrous.'

Elijah places his palms together in a prayer-like motion as though intending to convey his peaceful intentions. 'All that I ask is that you try. Right, who's up first?'

I slump down in my seat as Python raises his hand. He stands in front of the Fury Doll for a long time, staring into its face where its eyes should be like he's trying to psych it out. He swings a punch and his clenched fist meets with its stomach. The doll shudders on its harness. He swings a right hook, then a left, one for each cheek. The doll accepts the blows and I start to feel a bit sorry for it. Python punches the doll repeatedly until he's red in the face and sweating rivers. He turns to Elijah and his eyes ask a private question. Elijah nods and Python sits back down. Next up is Jane, Best Supporting Actress. I'm not expecting much of her but she takes me by surprise. She leaps into the air and delivers a high karate kick right on the doll's nose, then she spins and lifts her right leg and delivers three sharp, precise kicks which meet the doll where its bollocks would be hanging if it had any. I glance across the circle at Vanessa, who's watching her with obvious admiration. When she's finished, Vanessa claps and Elijah asks her to stop. When it's her turn, Vanessa slaps the doll and yells at it. She curses like a true professional, and the profanities sound particularly charming in her American accent. Rich Kid reluctantly takes his turn but after two punches says he's tired and sits back down. Next up is Politician. His punches, delivered with chubby fists, are pathetically soft at first, but as he continues they become increasingly fast and frenzied until he takes the doll in his arms, buries his head into its shoulder and sobs. I look away. Elijah approaches and touches him lightly on the back, guides him to his seat. And then it's my turn. I look at Elijah.

'Really?' I say.

'Over to you, Nobody,' he says.

I sigh dramatically, stand up and slouch towards the doll. I stare into its empty face and I try to visualise someone, anyone. I'm hailed as a creative genius and yet all I see is a blank oval of white cloth. I glance at Elijah. He looks so eager, so desperate to help me, to heal me, so to appease him if nothing else I lift my hand and slap the Fury Doll on the side of the face. It's a limp blow. The doll barely shudders. I glance at Politician, who is hanging his head towards his rotund belly, balancing his chin on his man-boobs as he continues to whimper. I lift my hand and deliver another slap, a little harder this time, and then another which is just about hard enough to make my palm sting. And I don't know where it comes from, but suddenly, I see *him*, and when I part my lips a great animalistic roar is released and I take a step backwards and lunge at the doll, pounding at it with my fists. I have never been in a real fight with a real human. My technique is clumsy and lacks finesse. But still here I am, yelling and screaming and pummelling as the Fury Doll willingly accepts my blows. And the voice which rises up inside me comes from nowhere but is as clear and audible as my own:

'Allow yourself to feel this. You have every right.'

EVA

IT WAS HER FINANCIAL ADVISOR AT Morgan Roth who told me about the money. George Callaghan managed the riches of many high-net-worth individuals: footballers and movie stars, members of the Royal Family, owners of exclusive department stores in London. He was nice enough if a little pompous, and he'd given Alora good advice about her property and investments. I'd called him to check in about the US tour dates, to ask whether it made sense for her to be paid by the promoter in dollars or pounds, and he said that in part depended on whether she still wanted to go ahead with the 'unconventional transaction'.

'Sorry, what?' I said.

The line went quiet. I could hear him breathing heavily. 'Oh dear. Maybe I've spoken out of turn.' I assured him that he hadn't, that he was allowed to discuss all of Alora's financial affairs with me as specified in his firm's contract which she'd signed. So George went on to explain how Alora had called him up personally to instruct him to deliver a substantial sum of money to a specified location the following week.

'How substantial?' I said. 'What location?'

'One million pounds cash to Golden Glow, a sunbed shop in Moss Side, which as far as I'm aware, is a rather unsavoury part of Manchester, not somewhere that either of us should be venturing after dark.'

'Sorry, George, what the fuck? That's a lot of money. Do you think somebody's blackmailing her? And why hasn't she mentioned this to me?'

George cleared his throat. 'I don't know about blackmail. Or why she hasn't told you, Eva. But it certainly is odd. If it's any help, she asked that the money be left on reception for the attention of someone called William.'

It took a moment for the penny to drop. William. Billy. Billy Storm-Jones. Alora's dad.

ALORA

I WAKE IN THE MIDDLE OF the night. I open my eyes and the darkness feels like it's pressing down on me, sitting on my chest, crushing my lungs. I want to scream, but I have no voice and I cannot move.

This isn't the first time this has happened. I told Silas about it once. We were walking along Venice Beach in LA. It was early morning, the day after Lesley Mirage's birthday party; we were both still wearing last night's clothes and neither of us had been to bed. Silas said he'd heard of it, that it was called sleep paralysis, that some people hallucinate too and see demons in their bedroom. I told him that sometimes happens to me but not when I'm asleep.

He smiled mildly and looked away. 'You won't be able to do this soon, you know?'

I squinted at the profile of his face against the bright, pristinely cloudless sky. He hadn't shaved and his chin was coarse with stubble. 'Do what?'

'Walk along the beach without being recognised, without being mobbed by fans.'

I laughed. 'Yeah, right.'

'I'm serious.'

'But no one's mobbing *you*.'

'I'm a producer, it's not the same. Public interest only goes so far. Your fame will have no limits.'

We stopped walking and turned towards the sea. The waves were small but joyful, racing each other towards the shoreline, and the salty air stung my eyes. I edged towards Silas and rested my head on his shoulder. He smelled like cedar, the expensive aftershave I'd seen in his en suite. He put his arm around me and I leaned into him.

'I don't want this to change, though,' I said.

He brought the tip of his nose to the crown of my head. 'I'm afraid that's unavoidable, kid. Soon you'll forget all about little old me, you'll leave me behind in the dust.'

'I'd never do that.'

'We'll see. Hey, where are you going?'

But I was already sprinting towards the ocean, the soles of my feet slapping hard against the wet sand, tar-lined lungs screaming for air, and when the water hit my ankles I didn't stop. I could hear Silas calling my name, shouting for me to come back. I knew the water was objectively cold but I couldn't feel it. I waded right in and when it reached my shoulders, I kept on going. Then the ocean bed dropped away and I found myself submerged. And it still surprises me now how in that moment, as I sank down towards the bottom, eyes wide open, arms raised above my head, last breath rising to the surface in a foray of gleeful bubbles, I experienced not one semblance of panic. Maybe I knew my life would always end in tragedy, or maybe I knew that Silas would dive into the waves and save me, maybe that was the point. And as I lay coughing on the beach, clothes sodden and stuck to my skin, spluttering salt water from the depths of my lungs, he rubbed my back and said, 'It's okay, kid, I'm with you, it's all going to be okay.'

The paralysis subsides and I force my body to sit, and what I need to do is suddenly clear, a bright blade of light piercing my thoughts. I climb out of bed and open my chalet door. David is sitting at his station but I see that his head is lolling forwards. It's three AM and he's working another night shift, dozing his way through his responsibilities. Barefooted, I pad out beneath the canopy and across the lawn. Above me the sky is black and studded with stars, diamond rings glittering across the fingers of a cruel unknown god, relaxing up there on his throne, laughing at us all. My footsteps are barely audible, damp and soft in the nighttime dew. I creep towards the restaurant, trail my fingertips across the circumference of its cool stone walls until I'm standing by the door which leads directly to the swimming pool. The overhead lights are off but the pool is lit by spotlights from under the water. And here it was all along, the solution to everything, the doorway to sweet nothingness which I so nearly made it through before they yanked me back against my will.

I hold my breath. I reach out and take hold of the door handle and pull. The door is locked. It doesn't budge. I have failed again and I crumple onto the grass. The dew soaks through the cotton of my pyjamas and after a while, I start to shiver. I hear footsteps, slow and steady. I do not move. I do not open my eyes. David takes me by the arm and lifts me to my feet.

'Come on now,' he says gently. 'Let's get you back to bed.'

EVA

I WAITED UNTIL THE EUROPEAN LEG of the tour was over before I tried to talk to her about it. I went over to her Hampstead house and we sat out on the terrace in her garden, drinking coffee. She looked exhausted but she insisted she felt fine. It was a bright, blue-skied day, but the garden walls were so high that they practically blocked out the sun. At one point a tiny white rat-like creature sprinted through the patio doors and circled my ankles, yapping like a lunatic on speed.

'Urgh,' I said, lifting my feet. 'What is it?'

Alora reached down and lifted the thing into her arms, cradling it to her body like she was nursing a small child. 'Not *it*,' she said. '*She*. Noah bought her for me. I told him about this pet kitten I'd had for, like, ten seconds as a kid, before Julia made me give him back. Noah said it was such a sad story that he went out and bought me a puppy. He says she's more versatile than a kitten because I can put her on a lead and take her on tour with me.'

'That was thoughtful of him. What's she called?'

'Carrie.'

'Carrie as in the Stephen King movie?'

'Uh-huh.'

'The kid who murdered everyone in her high-school class?'

'That's the one.' She tickled the rat-dog's tummy. I moved my chair backwards away from the dog.

I asked if everything was good between her and Noah. I knew he was about to start shooting some new billion-dollar-budget disaster movie in the Antarctic so wouldn't be coming with us on the US leg of the tour, and whilst I was worried she might get lonely and mopey without him, I also saw it as an opportunity for her to sleep more and party less.

'He wants me to meet his parents.' I said that was great, it showed he was serious about her. Little did I know as I uttered those words what was about to hit the newsroom.

When I finally brought up the subject of the money, she went quiet. 'What's going on?' I asked softly, coaxingly. 'You can tell me, you know.' After a long pause, she said that her dad had got back in touch with her on z-pix. 'That's great!' I said. *Carefully now*, I was saying to myself. *Show enthusiasm for the reunion, play it cool.* 'Have you spoken to him then?' She dropped her eyes and her eyelashes quivered against her cheeks like the dark wings of a moth.

'No,' she said. 'We just DM each other. But we do it a lot, like, every day.'

By this point a canyon of dread had begun to open up in my stomach. 'And he asked you to send him money, did he?' She nodded. 'Do you know why he needs it? It's quite a lot. Is he in some kind of trouble?'

'He's building a house,' she said softly. 'A big one. We're going to live there together when I'm back off tour.'

'What, in Melbourne?'

She looked puzzled. 'Why would he build a house in Melbourne?'

'Isn't that where he lives?'

She shifted in her seat and I noticed her cheeks colour slightly. 'Oh... uh... yeah, he used to live there, but he's back in Manchester now.'

At this point I admit that I completely lost it. I fired questions at her, my skin prickling, barely pausing for breath. 'Why would your dad need all that money and *in cash*, Alora? Sounds a bit dodgy, don't you think? And if he's back in the UK now, have you asked him why he still hasn't made it to a single show? And if you haven't actually spoken to him, how do you even know it's him?'

'Well, it's his photo,' she said defiantly. 'On his profile picture.' She opened up her phone and angled the screen at me. And sure enough there was a picture of an attractive if slightly dishevelled looking man, a cigarette dangling lazily from the corner of his lips. He was smiling into the camera with a small blonde child sitting on this lap—Alora. But I'd seen this photo before.

I ran my hands through my hair in exasperation. 'This is an old photo, it's on your mum's Facebook.'

'Yeah. So?'

'So this doesn't prove a thing! Anyone could've copied it. How could you—' I started to say. But I caught myself just in time. *How could you be so stupid?* I wanted to scream at my bewilderingly trusting seventeen-year-old artist, sitting in front of me, shoulders hunched with an unnecessarily small dog on her lap, unable to meet my eye. 'Look,' I finally said, as calmly as I could muster. 'Let me speak to George, he can do some digging and confirm that it's definitely your dad. We'll put a block on the payment until then. Okay?'

The dog growled. Alora closed her eyes. 'Okay,' she said, barely a whisper.

ALORA

THE FOLLOWING WEEK ELIJAH DELIVERS THE bombshell that we'll all be partnering up for a project. He passes a straw hat around the group and half of us draw names, and I know, I just know, even before I've dipped my hand in what my piece of paper will say. I stare at it in horror—the skinny old blonde. I look up and our eyes meet and she knows too and she sighs, loudly and rudely.

She raises her hand. 'Yes, V?' Elijah says.

'I'm not big on partnering up, as two of my three ex-husbands will tell you. I'd prefer to sit this one out.'

'This exercise is compulsory,' Elijah says. 'And what we resist in life is often what we need the most.' He hands her a sealed white envelope, then distributes the rest to the other couples. 'I want you to collaborate on your allocated assignments. You must not discuss your assignments with the others, each is specific to your pair alone. If you have any questions I would like you to work through them, solve them in honesty, humility and togetherness. I look forward to discussing the outcomes, and though it may be difficult at times, this exercise will leave you feeling lighter and more in tune with your inner child.'

There's much talk of our 'inner children' in this place. I feel like telling them that my inner child, if she ever existed, died the day my dad moved out and I was basically left to fend for myself.

I wait for Vanessa outside the door of the therapy centre, hovering apprehensively whilst she stays behind talking to Elijah. I can see her through the window scowling and waving her hands in a wild expressive way, presumably complaining about being partnered up with me. When she eventually strides through the double doors she almost sends me flying with the force of her exit. She leans against the wall and lights a cigarette.

'Well, this is fucking tedious,' she says.

I hold out my hand for the envelope and she passes it to me. We sit down on the steps of the therapy centre side by side but maintaining a safe distance. She blows cigarette smoke in my face as I slide my finger beneath the lip of the envelope and tear it open. I scan my eyes across the short, typed paragraph.

'What the fuck?'

'What?' I hand it back to her and she reads it for herself. 'Jesus,' she says. 'This is going to be a barrel of laughs.' She tosses the envelope back at me, says I'd better meet her at her place in ten, then walks away, leaving behind only the scent of her perfume.

Vanessa's chalet is a replica of mine: same bed, same desk, same sofa, same copper bathtub and bleak grey view. It stinks of cigarette smoke. I look up and see she's stuffed toilet tissue through the vents of the smoke alarm.

'That's dangerous, you know,' I say, and she shoots me a withering look.

'I hear you tried to break into the pool in the middle of the night.'

'Who told you that?'

'I can't reveal my sources. Fancied a three AM swim?'

No, actually, I was going to kill myself. I shrug the question off me like it's no big deal and sit down on the bed. 'Who's Wyatt?' I ask, knowing full well that I'm not supposed to. She'd been yelling the name at the Fury Doll in our previous session with Elijah.

She regards me coolly for a moment, as though weighing up her options by way of response—humour me or rip me to shreds. Eventually she says, 'Wyatt was my second husband.'

'Did he leave you or something?'

'Yes, he left me.'

'Younger woman?'

'No, colon cancer.'

I clear my throat before saying that I'm sorry. She lifts one bony shoulder then lets it fall. 'He was the love of my life. I married again but it wasn't the same.'

'Are you still with that husband?'

'Number three? No, I divorced him within a year. Complete bastard. He tried to get his hands on my money too. Good job my lawyer's prenups are legendary.'

I ask her why she's here, another taboo question. She cackles, then coughs. 'Can you not tell?' I stare at her blankly. 'The doctors say I shouldn't be alive. I tell them I'm a walking miracle.'

'Are you sick?'

'Only in here.' She taps the side of her skull with one fingertip. I'm stating the obvious when I say, 'You *are* extremely thin.'

She lights a cigarette and sucks on it like she's trying to draw blood. 'That was the look, back then. Twiggy kicked it off and the rest of us followed. The thinner you were the more you got booked, the happier you made your agent. When I shot the American *Vogue* cover I hadn't eaten a thing in four days. Then you get older and the work dries up but the mindset's already fixed. You look in the mirror and you know you're not fat but you always see room for improvement—a little off the hips, an inch off the thighs. The photographers and bookers would call you out on it to your face as well. I remember this French photographer turning to his assistant and proclaiming, "Get rid of this one! Zee legs are like zee legs of an elephant!" I mean, what complete wankers.' She laughs, so I allow myself to laugh too, and that feels strange. 'Anyway,' she says. 'We'd better get on with this before they throw us to the wolves.'

'I can't actually believe we've got to do it. Do you think it's some kind of sick joke? Do you think we're really on reality TV and there are hidden cameras in all the rooms and everyone sitting home watching is laughing at us?'

'Congratulations, you've achieved the peak paranoia of a serious drug user.'

'I don't use, actually.' That isn't strictly true.

'Do you want to go first or shall I?'

'I'll go, and you read this crap. Shit. Okay. I'm nervous.'

'You perform in front of stadiums full of people. How can you be nervous?'

'Actually, maybe you should go first.'

'Just do it, for Christ's sake!'

So I pick up my imaginary spade and I start to dig. And at first I'm in Vanessa's chalet and my hands are empty and I'm staring at the wooden floorboards, and this is ridiculous and embarrassing and what the fuck am I even doing here. But as she reads the words Elijah has written—the script to this bizarre role-play—my mind shifts, I feel it, and I start to see the soil, the edge of the spade as it parts the grass and slices into the ground, the weight of the earth as I throw it in a heap behind me. It's an overcast day and the church bell tolls sombrely once, then twice. A bullfinch perches on the gravestone to my right. It peers at me with its shining, inquisitive eye before resuming flight. And I dig, and dig, and dig, until I feel beads of sweat across my brow and trickling down my back. I stare into the grave. It is for me. This is the end. Is it not what I wanted? I climb into the trench of my own making and take my position. I cross my wrists at my chest. And a few minutes pass, and an hour and a day, a month then a year. I am less human now, more rotten flesh which falls away from bone and disintegrates into the earth around me. I am at one with the world I despised. I have escaped the life I rejected. And it is dark and it's too late. I was given a gift and I sent it back with sour, despicable words. It's too late, too late, too late.

'Hey, wake up.'

I open my eyes. Vanessa is crouched over me. I find myself scooped up in her jutting arms, being comforted against her wilted tits. I realise that I'm crying. I let out an almighty sob and she pats me on the back and we stay like that for a little while longer, until it becomes beyond awkward for both of us and she pulls away, brushes herself off as though I've left dirty particles of myself on her clothes and says, 'Well, I wasn't expecting *that*. Now get up off the floor, will you, and let me have a go.'

EVA

THEY SAY EVERYTHING HAPPENS IN THREES: bad, worse and disastrous. Well, this was number two. It all came out when we were in Mexico. Shona emailed me the photos the day before—one of her contacts at the *Daily Mail* had tipped her off but there was nothing we could do, the story was typed, the papers hot off the press. I'd eaten some fish tacos I'd bought at a stall in a bustling street market and they'd made me sick. I'd been up all night in my hotel bathroom, bent over the toilet bowl, sweating and puking and trying not to crap myself at the same time. So when I looked at my phone in the morning and saw them, I pressed my cheek against the cold tiles on the bathroom floor and cried like a baby.

You sometimes see a poor-quality shot taken on a phone from across a club which ends up in a mainstream publication, a famous actor or musician standing a little too close on the dance floor to a woman who is definitely not the girlfriend or mother of his children. Those ones can be explained away with a quick, clean statement to the press—*night out, close friend, nothing in it, et cetera, et cetera*. But this was undeniable. You could see Noah's tongue in her mouth, curling around her Hollywood smile. His hand was up her skirt, right between her long tanned legs, her body clearly sucking on his fingers. And even though they were in a dark nightclub the photo was bright, clear and precise. The fact that this was a British paper and we were in Mexico was of no comfort, they'd stick it online where it would get picked up by all the other tabloids and gossip magazines, then the pictures would be reposted across z-pix and Instagram and Facebook and Twitter and if she didn't stumble across it herself one of the fans would tag her, thinking they were doing her a favour, believing she should know about her boyfriend's cheating, and the haters would tag her again and tell her she deserved it, that he was too good for her anyway. I needed to get to her first.

I waited until I knew her tour manager would've woken her, when she'd be drinking coffee and picking at a fruit platter in her hotel suite. I knocked and she answered the door in a white towelling robe. She wasn't wearing any makeup and she looked much younger than seventeen, so fresh-faced and innocent. She stepped back from the door to allow me inside. The hotel was modern, all glass and angles. The floor was completely transparent and beneath it was the Underfloor Ocean, the only one of its kind in the world—shoals of tropical fish in fluorescent colours darting this way and that, seemingly oblivious to their captivity. The circular bed dropped down out of the ceiling at the push of a button and the bathroom was a dome of glass with an open archway for a door—an oversized igloo, trendy past the point of privacy or practicality. It was architecturally impressive. It was also a complete mess—drawers open, clothes and shoes strewn everywhere, empty bottles of champagne and tequila, overflowing ashtrays and an upturned pot of body lotion on the dresser. The mirror was balanced precariously on the edge of the coffee table, covered in a thin layer of fine white powder which definitely wasn't dust. With Noah on tour with us, she'd been a party animal. Without him, she seemed to have turned into a monster.

'I'm not even going to ask,' I said.

Alora flopped down onto the unmade bed. 'One of the girls who came back last night wanted to try on all my clothes.'

I asked her who the girl was and she said she didn't know but that she was hot. I perched tentatively on the edge of the mattress. I drew in a long, wavering breath, trying to prolong the before, dreading the after. I told her that there was no easy way of saying this, but that I was here for her and would help her get through it.

She sat up sharply. 'You're scaring me,' she said. 'What's happened? Is it Dad?'

I unlocked my phone and handed it to her. She stared at the screen. She said nothing for about ten seconds, and those ten seconds seemed to stretch the breadth of the universe, then contract into a singular atom.

'I know this must be hard to see,' I said. 'I know how much you love him.'

She dropped my phone on the floor where it landed with a heavy clunk. 'No,' she said. 'Actually, I don't. I'm in love with someone else.'

I was stunned, so much so that I didn't even retrieve my phone to check if the screen was cracked. 'What are you talking about? In love with who?'

She yanked on the cord of her bathrobe and the robe fell open. She tilted her right leg to one side. I'd seen her body many times before. I'd accompanied her to photo shoots, to fittings where she'd been stripped down to her underwear and sewn into her costumes. But I'd never seen her completely naked. So I'd never seen the scar, at the very top on the inside of her right thigh, and my skin went cold all over like my blood had frozen in my veins. I looked into her eyes. Her eyes were wide and hopeless. She pointed at the scar. '*Him*,' she said.

NOAH LAMB BUYS GROCERIES WITH NEW GIRLFRIEND!!!

Noah Lamb stepped out for a spot of grocery shopping on Thursday with a new lady on his arm. Since breaking up with internationally acclaimed recording artist Alora Storm-Jones, the bad-boy star of *Forgotten Midnights* has been spending time with twenty-year-old Brazilian beauty Lexi D'Silva.

Lexi is an up-and-coming recording artist who is signed to the same record label as Alora—ouch! Close friends say that Noah's smitten and we don't blame him. The two lovebirds held hands as they made their way around Waitrose in Victoria Park, London, stopping to sign a few autographs and pose for photographs with fans. They bought oat milk, a loaf of vegan bread, a bag of mixed salad, salted almonds, peanut butter and three bottles of white wine. At one point the couple paused by the frozen goods aisle and peered through the glass-fronted freezer cabinet at the selection of vegan ice creams but didn't make a purchase, no doubt to preserve their enviable figures.

Lexi looked stunning in hooped gold earrings, a Louis Vuitton dress and black Prada ankle boots. Noah was smouldering in Yves Saint Laurent trainers and a Gucci tracksuit, probably gifted by the fashion house when he modelled for them last season.

Alora and Noah split last month. A source close to the iconic recording artist reports that she's heartbroken and is hoping for a reunion with the actor. But if what we witnessed today is anything to go by, she shouldn't get her hopes up. Lexi is stunning and she and Noah make a truly beautiful couple.

ALORA

AFTER SHE GETS UP OFF THE floorboards, Vanessa says little. She arches her back and rubs at the base of her spine, stretches out her neck before sitting down at the dresser. She stares at herself in the mirror as though searching for imperfections where there are none, then applies more eyeliner to an already considerable layer.

'Should I go?' I ask. She begins to examine her pink talon fingernails as though they're suddenly fascinating. She nods wordlessly.

I walk outside and slip my hand in my tunic pocket, desperate for a cigarette. But finding the packet empty I head over to the shop for another. A wind chime jingles as I walk through the door. This place is more wellness hell than consumer paradise—shelves stocked with essential oils, hempseed lotions, turmeric-and-ginger shots in tiny glass bottles like I've fallen down the rabbit hole in *Alice in Wonderland*. Not a fizzy drink, bottle of vodka or even six-pack of beer in sight. There's also a no-magazines-or-newspapers policy, so adamant is Max Beaumont that his patients should be completely isolated from the goings-on of the outside world, but there are plenty of self-help books written by none other than, you guessed it, Max Beaumont. Jacob's sitting behind the till and we exchange small pleasantries. I ask for a twenty pack of Marlboro Gold and he reaches under the counter for them like I'm purchasing something illicit—tobacco, the one vice which isn't banned in here, which they don't seem intent on therapising out of you. I ask him if he fancies one and he says he shouldn't but I can tell he will. He flips the sign on the door to CLOSED and we walk behind the building and perch on a low brick wall. He lights my cigarette with a match before lighting his own, shaking it in the air to extinguish it.

'How are you finding it here?' he says. I say it's tedious and he laughs and says, 'But is it working?' Our eyes meet and he cocks his head, runs a hand through his hair, which is parted at the side, cut in a sensible style.

Just then I hear a whirring sound and look up to see a man driving a golf buggy down the walkway. He's wearing a grey suit with a paisley silk cravat, leather gloves, dark glasses and a French beret tilted at an angle. He's got a slightly Bond-villain, Karl Lagerfeld vibe going on but without the fluffy white cat. Jacob jumps to his feet, quickly tucks his shirt into his jeans and practically bows. The man raises one gloved hand and says, 'Greetings,' then drives on past, the buggy's electric motor whirring more insistently as it strains up the hill.

I frown in his direction. 'Who was that?'

'You honestly don't know?'

'Should I?'

Jacob sits back down on the wall looking mildly flustered. 'That was the big man himself, Max Beaumont.'

'Really? He kind of looks like a douchebag.'

'Oh no, not at all. He's a trailblazer in psychiatric care. He'll go down in history as one of the revolutionary greats. His success rate is coming up to ninety-nine percent, which is unheard of.'

'Wow, I hope I don't blight the statistic.'

He laughs. 'Which takes me back to my original question—is it working?'

Jacob isn't bad looking come to think about it, a slightly older, less chiselled Noah, and I can feel the fizz of chemistry between us, in the unnecessary brush of his arm against mine as he raises his cigarette to his lips, eye contact held for just a millisecond longer than platonic. But staff-patient relations are strictly forbidden, a sloppy, fast, meaningless fling could get Jacob fired, and besides, I need to learn my lesson. My track record's a testimony to my judgement, I'd be more likely to pick a murderer out of a lineup wearing a blindfold than select a remotely appropriate partner for myself.

Jacob's looking at me earnestly, still waiting for an answer. I close my eyes. 'I don't know whether it's fundamentally rewiring my brain, but maybe I'm having a few epiphanies.'

'That's great!' he says. 'Like what?'

I open my eyes and stub my cigarette out on the wall even though I've smoked less than half. 'Like, I really need to go.' He looks disappointed, a little confused maybe, but he says he'll see me round. And it feels good to walk away, to not pursue the temporary high and transient validation of losing myself in someone else's bed. I only wish I'd done the same with Noah before it ever began.

But the thing is, at first I thought that his heart was as dark as mine. But Noah is a gifted actor albeit heavily typecast and I was drawn to the role he played in his movies, the self-sabotaging fuckup who invariably met a violent end. Off-screen his PR expertly courted the image to keep the parts rolling in, she fed false titbits to the press about fights and trashed hotel rooms and the journalists lapped up her lies and turned them into the latest career-defining scandal. But the morning I woke up to find him standing at the end of the bed with a dozen red roses in his arms, saying he was in love with me only seventy-two hours after we'd met, I knew it was over between us. I could've ended it then. I could've blocked him on socials and shipped him straight back to the UK in a private jet. But I didn't. I said, 'I love you too,' and kissed him quickly so he wouldn't see the insincerity in my eyes. The press were already all over us and he was so undeniably, objectively hot, I wanted that exposure of us together. So I posted photos of us looking loved up and happy on all my socials. I even stooped so low as to anonymously tip off the paps about our romantic dinner in Amsterdam. I wanted the tabloid journalists to splash us all over the papers together, for global headlines in bold typographical font about how happy I was with someone else to be rammed down the throat of the only one who truly mattered to me, the one who'd crawled into my heart then cracked it in two, who'd snuck inside my soul with music.

Just before I set off on tour again, Noah and I drove over to Surrey in his Porsche with the soft-top down listening to BTS on the stereo (his choice). We pulled up outside his childhood home which was red brick with a picket fence. A black Labrador bounded towards Noah, jumped up and licked his face and Noah embraced the dog as though it was his long-lost brother. Noah's parents met us in the doorway. They were called Miriam and Nigel. Miriam was wearing a floral dress and Nigel a blue knitted vest over a shirt with silver cufflinks. They were holding hands, a vision of matrimonial bliss. It was all seriously wholesome. Miriam asked us to remove our shoes at the front door, then handed us both slippers 'so our tootsies wouldn't get cold'. The slippers were lined with fleece, soft and comforting. It was the slippers that finally tipped me over the edge, I just couldn't handle the slippers. I knew then that I had to do the right thing. The dog was called Mr Hawthorn, named after Noah's favourite teacher at primary school. Nigel told me this as he took my jacket.

'He's an old boy now,' he said. 'But we love him so much. They become part of the family, don't they?'

We sat in the conservatory, sunlight streaming through the glass, ecstatic Mr Hawthorn lying on top of Noah's slippered tootsies, as Miriam served a selection of crustless sandwiches and pastries filled with jam and custard, special vegan ones she'd made especially for me, which elevated my guilt to even greater heights.

'Noah says you grew up in Manchester,' Nigel said, dabbing at his lips with a napkin.

'Just outside, actually,' I said. 'Salford.'

'We used to go on hiking holidays in the Peak District when Noah was a lad. The Lamb family love a good hike, out in the fresh air.' Father and son exchanged a loving glance. 'That's not too far from there, is it?'

I'd never been to the Peak District. I'd never been on a hiking holiday or any kind of holiday with my parents. 'No,' I said. 'I don't think so.'

'Beautiful part of the country.'

The view from my childhood bedroom window was of the

café's overflowing industrial-sized bins, concrete paving slabs and coloured washing flapping on lines. 'Yeah,' I said. 'It is. Absolutely gorgeous.'

'It's such a pleasure to finally meet you,' Miriam said, leaning over the cake stand and squeezing my hand. 'Noah talks about you all the time. He's completely besotted.' Noah blushed violently and I willed the rug beneath my feet to whisk me away to a faraway land.

As we were driving home Noah said, 'They really liked you.'

'Noah,' I said. 'We need to talk.' I told him I was sorry, but that it was over between us. He cried all the way back to London.

A few days later I flew to Mexico. I'd expected the retaliation from his PR, rejection did not align with the Noah Lamb brand. And when I saw the photographs of him and Lexi D'Silva, so clearly staged, I felt absolutely nothing.

Eva had come to my hotel suite to break the news to me, thinking I'd be devastated. 'I know how much you love him,' she said, as she rested her hand on my forearm and looked at me with infuriating pity. I was so tired of pretending. So instead I told her the truth, about *him*.

Later that day I endure another one-to-one session with Seren. We talk a little about my home life, about Dad leaving and Julia's detached style of mothering before I say, 'I thought you had all my medical records, haven't you got access to my psychiatrist's notes? Dr Laurel. I was seeing him for a while.'

Seren says that she has, but that she finds it helpful to hear everything from the patient firsthand. I turn to look out of the window at the view but I'm distracted by a little smudge on the glass. I become fixated on the smudge, wondering why, if we're paying so much money to Max Beaumont, he can't use some of it to get the windows professionally cleaned. I consider getting up and wiping it off with my sleeve when Seren clears her throat and I realise that she's asked me a question.

'What was that?' I say.

She repeats, 'Can you see Billy through a stranger's eyes?'

I think about it for a moment. 'No,' I say.

Seemingly satisfied with my answer she nods and scribbles something down on her pad. She says she has a new exercise for me. I inwardly groan but outwardly smile. I must write two letters, she says. 'They will never be sent. In fact, after we've discussed them I suggest we rip them up or burn them, which can be cathartic in itself.'

'Who are the letters to?'

'Your mother and father.'

I've never written a letter before. 'Can't I just write a text?'

'The act of putting pen on paper can produce more fluent, honest results.'

'What if I can't think of anything to say?'

She smiles. 'You're a very creative person, Alora. I suggest you use your imagination.'

Maureen collects me and escorts me to dinner. She asks how my day's been and I say strange but not entirely bad. She deposits me in the restaurant which is the busiest I've seen it and I wonder if a fresh load of wealthy nutjobs have been dumped on the island to be pulled apart and fixed again. I notice Python and Best Supporting Actress. They're sitting together, opposite each other but unnecessarily close. One of his elbows is resting on the tabletop, his hand extended as though he's inviting her to arm wrestle. He flexes his bicep and she reaches out and squeezes it.

She laughs and her eyes sparkle. I glance across the room and see Vanessa watching them too, a bemused smile playing at her lips but not quite taking hold. I catch her eye and she maintains the shadow of the smile for a fraction of a second before she picks up her book. A plate of food sits in front of her, untouched. In a moment of boldness or stupidity or maybe both I make my way towards her. She looks up and notices me hovering.

'Okay if I sit here?' She seems mildly displeased but makes a gesture of resignation. I sit down. I ask what she's reading and she shows me the book's cover. *Connect with Your Inner Spirit Animal*.

'My nephew, Dylan, gave it to me. It's not really my bag, but I feel obliged to read it.'

'Are you close to your nephew?'

'Very. He's lived with me since he was eight years old.'

'Really, how come?'

'His daddy, Wyatt's brother, liked to use his fists. Wyatt and I intervened.'

'That was kind of you.'

'It didn't feel like a choice.'

I say it must've been nice for her kids, having their cousin around.

'What makes you think I've got kids?'

'Oh, I just thought—'

'You assumed.'

'Did you not want them then?'

Her eyes flare. 'That's none of your goddamn business.' The silence which ensues is uncomfortable. Jacob approaches with his usual cheerful demeanour, seemingly oblivious to the tense atmosphere. I order spiced lentil stew with coriander bread. He says he'll be working in the shop later if I want to stop by and I say maybe, whilst knowing that I won't. When he's left Vanessa says, 'Sorry, I didn't mean to snap. It's just a bit of a sore point for me. I wanted them but I couldn't. This body of mine wasn't up to the job.' I mumble something awkward. Across the room Python brushes his hand against Best Supporting Actress's and I notice Vanessa clock it too. 'Something's going on there,' she says. 'If they haven't fucked yet, mark my words they will. And I know for a fact they're both married.'

'Clearly not very happily.'

'You don't know that. Being in group therapy can give you a false sense of familiarity with others in the group. I've seen it happen before. They get drawn in and uproot their lives in the outside world only for it to all fall apart and they end up stuck in the middle of a messy divorce, miserable and alone.' I ask her how many times she's been in group therapy before and she says enough times to last her through this lifetime and the next, and if any of it was any good she'd be the most mentally stable person alive by now with an above-average BMI. My food arrives and Jacob sets it down in front of me. I tear off a small piece of coriander bread and dip it into the stew. It's delicious—the bread warm and fluffy, the stew dense and flavoursome.

Vanessa's watching me. 'It's so good,' I say, like I need to explain the look of incredulous rapture on my face. 'Want some?' She backs away as though I've offered her a taste of arsenic.

We fall silent. I find that I'm beyond hungry, ravenous, in fact, I feel like I haven't eaten a thing in years. I consider saying hell to dining-room etiquette, lifting the bowl to my lips and gobbling at my dinner like an animal. 'About that exercise we did in my room,' Vanessa says. 'That was pretty freaky stuff, huh?'

I set down my spoon. 'Yeah, I don't think I've quite got my head around it yet.'

'Same.' She shifts her eyes from side to side and lowers her voice to a whisper. 'I actually felt like I was there, lying in my own grave. I've been wondering whether they're using some kind of subliminal messaging on us, hypnosis, or something. Or pumping psychedelic drugs through the air vents.' I say I'm not sure, that I imagine we'd have to have consented to that kind of thing in advance and she says she sure as hell doesn't know what she's consented to, that it would've taken her days to read the small print in the contract and she just couldn't be bothered.

'Vanessa,' I say. 'Afterwards, when you'd got up off the floor, did you feel a tiny bit... you know.'

'What?' She raises her plucked-out, pencilled-back-in eyebrows. 'Relieved to be alive?'

'Well, yeah.'

She smiles, then reaches across the table and tears off a minuscule piece of coriander bread before pushing it between her overly plump pink lips.

EVA

THE DISCUSSION WHICH ENSUED STOPPED SHORT of a full-on argument between her and me, but only just. I couldn't believe what I was hearing—it was verging on insanity, and not in a cute, kooky, creative-genius kind of way. I left her then. I practically sprinted back down the corridor to my hotel room. I fumbled with my phone, dropped it on the floor, picked it up again, my vision blurring, certain I was about to throw up. I called the MD, I didn't know what else to do. He answered on the first ring and said he was delighted to hear from me, that my ears must've been burning because he'd just a few moments ago been singing my praises to another of the Low Slang artists who was looking for new management.

'Shall I give him your number?' he said. 'He's on all the ones-to-watch lists for this year.' I told him that I needed to speak to him about something urgently, that it was serious. 'Go on,' he said.

So I recounted the horrifying story, feeling a mounting sense of detachment from the scene in Alora's suite, almost like I was pitching a treatment for a new and disturbingly macabre series to Netflix. I told him about the scar. I told him why she said she did it, like she genuinely believed she had a perfectly rational justification for mutilating her own body. I ranted and babbled and swore down the phone line. 'She says she's in love with him,' I said, and he sighed deeply.

He recommended that she see a psychiatrist, some guy called Dr Laurel who he said kept half of the Low Slang Records roster on the right side of psychotic. I flew him out that day to meet us in Cancún. I didn't join the session, I left it to the professional. But after he'd left I drove down to the dispensing chemist and picked up the prescription—a large bottle of pills which looked like fluorescent Smarties. I watched helplessly as Alora knocked back two, then washed them down with a shot of tequila.

ALORA

AFTER DINNER I WALK BACK TOWARDS my chalet with Vanessa. She's smoking a cigarette—a Virginia Slim—and offers the packet to me. I take one and say that I'd love a shot of tequila to go with it.

'Sorry, doll, can't help you there,' she says.

But of course one shot would never be enough, I'd want the whole bottle and then another and then I'd want to throw a party in my hotel suite for twenty people I don't know and wake up in the morning with three of them in my bed. I'm trying to expel the niggling aftereffects of the grave-digging exercise from my mind, but each time I shrug them off they creep up behind me and jab me in the ribs. I start telling Vanessa about Seren's letter-writing exercise and ask her whether her one-to-one therapist has asked her to do the same. She says no, she has to help the chef bake bread in the kitchen.

'Why?'

'I think they probably want me to feel at one with the food.

You know, knead the dough, rub it all over my naked body, that kind of thing.'

'What are they trying to achieve with mine, do you reckon?'

'Not sure, but at a guess I'd say they think your issues are connected to your parents.'

Really groundbreaking stuff. 'Didn't Freud come up with that theory like, a hundred years ago?'

'Maybe there's something in it.'

I tell her I don't really see the point in them trying to make me normal when I'm never going to be able to live a normal life.

'Why not?' she says.

'Because I'm famous, and fame is a fucking prison. You can't go anywhere without being mobbed or filmed or photographed. Every little thing you do is scrutinised to the point when you wish you hadn't bothered in the first place, and that's never going to change.'

'But that's what you signed up to!'

'Did I? Because I don't remember that clause in my record deal. Why can't I just make music without having the paps camped outside my house, following me everywhere I go? I only ever wanted to be an icon.'

'What, like Jesus?'

'No, like Blondie.'

'Huh, I don't really get the distinction. Aren't being famous and being iconic the same thing?'

'No, because someone with zero creative integrity who doesn't even write their own songs and can barely sing but dances around half-naked in their music videos can be famous. Someone off a reality TV show who has sex on camera and sells their wedding photos to *OK!* magazine can be famous. And it's fleeting, the light shines bright for a short time, then burns out, it relies on the scandal not the art. Being iconic is about standing for something real that doesn't die when you do, that lives on in your art forever.'

'Yeah, well,' Vanessa says, glancing up at the sky as if checking for rain. 'No point being all purist about it now. Fame's just part of the deal.'

EVA

I'M NOT PROUD OF WHAT I DID. It was a slippery slope, and I slid to the very bottom.

ALORA

I PICK UP THE PEN AND I start to write. The first letter is to Dad, it has to be. I tell him that I love him and that I miss him. These are the words which rise up through my body, circulating on an eternal loop, which pass through my veins like blood to a heart which nods its recognition, then sends them on their way. These are the words which I refuse to question despite everything, which I cling to like a desperate sailor on a floating barrel in a stormy sea. I could tell him about the food in this place, I could tell him about the weather. But he will never receive this letter so instead, I tell him the truth.

EVA

'THE GUY'S A COMPLETE NUTTER.'

I was sitting in my hotel room in New York, phone pressed hard to one hot ear, as George from Morgan Roth recounted his findings with regards to the intended recipient of Alora's generous one-million-pound cash donation.

'He says he can't find his passport and that he has no other form of ID he could send us. He doesn't seem to have any fixed abode. He called me from a pay phone, I could hear the thing beeping when he was running out of change and he sounded drunk, the man could barely string a sentence together. If you ask me he isn't exactly what you'd call a fully functioning member of society.'

'This is crazy. She speaks so highly of her dad.' I opened up the minibar and removed a small bottle of gin and another of vermouth and with the phone cocked against my shoulder, started to mix myself a negroni. 'How can a grown man have no ID?'

'No idea,' George said. 'But I've told him we won't be sending the money until he sends us some form of official documentation, to prove he's who he says he is. And do you know what he had the nerve to say to me?'

I stabbed at the block of ice with the tip of a knife and dropped a few chunks into a glass. 'Go on.'

George cleared his throat. 'That I was a jumped-up posh twat and that the money was owed to him, that it *belonged* to him.'

'That's weird. What do you think he means by that?' I took a sip of my drink and the ice knocked against my two front teeth.

'No idea, but my advice would be that you speak to Alora and try to find out.' But with all the stress of the North American dates and the media attention surrounding the breakup with Noah, somehow speaking to her about it fell through the cracks. It was a chance call from her mum which brought it to a head, and swiftly led to number three in the triplet—the grand finale of all disasters.

I tried to keep contact with Julia to a minimum. Alora had blocked her number the day she moved out of the flat and as far as I knew, they hadn't spoken since. But Julia had somehow got hold of my number and occasionally sent me texts asking me to speak to Alora on her behalf, to 'try and patch things up between them', which I invariably declined to do. Alora had never invited Julia to a show and in a way, that suited me fine, because a pushy parent getting in the middle of the artist-manager relationship would be a pain in the ass. However, when Julia's number flashed up on my phone screen, thinking it might be something important I took the call.

'Eva?' she said. 'It's Julia.' It never ceased to amaze me how parents consistently forgot about the invention of caller ID.

'I know. What's up?' She said that she was worried about Alora.

That she'd seen pictures online of her looking thin even for her and that she was concerned. 'Do you think she's working too hard?'

I scoffed. 'Partying too hard more like.'

'Is she eating properly? Is she getting enough sleep? Do you think she's happy, Eva? Because she doesn't look very happy to me.' Alora's tour manager stuck his head round the door and said I was needed up front. I mouthed, *Okay*, and held up two fingers and he nodded.

'Not looking happy is part of her brand, Julia.' I made quotation marks in the air around the word *brand* even though Julia couldn't see me. 'Look, your concern is appreciated and everything but Alora's totally fine and I really need to go now.'

'I'm her mother, Eva,' she said in a curt, patronising tone which made me bristle.

'And *I'm* her manager,' I shot back. 'So if there's a problem, *I'll* deal with it.' I was just about to hang up when a thought occurred to me. 'Oh, Julia? One more thing, quickly. I don't suppose you've seen or spoken to Alora's dad recently by any chance?' The line went silent. 'Hello?' I said. 'Are you still there?'

'What are you talking about?' she said in a pointed tone. 'Of *course* I haven't spoken to him.'

'Okay, relax, it's just he's been in touch and it seems—' But she interrupted me. And what she said stopped me in my tracks.

I waited until after the show. Instead of walking with her back to her dressing room I pulled her into the production office and shut the door. I should've handled it differently, I know that now. I should've called her psychiatrist and had him supervise the intervention. I should've waited until she'd come down from the adrenaline high of performing in front of thousands of people. But I was confused and angry, and more than a little worried.

Her face was still flushed, her skin dewy. She smiled at me and said, 'What's the matter? Why are you acting weird?'

'Why have you been lying to me?' I said.

She furrowed her brow. 'What are you talking about? I haven't.'

'Yeah, you have.'

'About what?'

And when she continued to stare at me blankly, I said, 'Your dad, Alora.'

'What about him?'

'You've been adding his name to the guest list for all your shows.'

'So?'

'Just the other day were hell-bent on sending him a million quid.'

'He's building a house. I told you.'

'But he's not though, is he. Because he's dead, Alora. Your dad's dead. He died when you were twelve years old.'

And as I spoke her face remained perfectly still, eerily calm and serene. Then she smiled, she actually smiled, and it occurred to me that she'd completely lost her mind, that she'd vacated the premises and moved to la-la land. Then, quite without warning, she turned and ran.

She ran down the backstage corridors and straight through the fire exit. She ran around the side of the venue to the front entrance where paparazzi and fans were jostling against the metal barriers, vying for a sighting. She climbed up the mesh, teetered on the railing at the top for a brief, paralysing moment before flinging herself down into the middle of them all. With their arms outstretched and mouths gaping like bloodthirsty cannibals, they caught her. She yelled. She screamed. She cried hot, furious tears. They yanked at her hair. They tore at her clothes. They pointed their cameras and phones and recorded it all. Her security team arrived at the scene in seconds and pulled her from the chaos, dress torn, patches of hair missing, looking like a Victorian street urchin with a severe case of scabies. They carried her up to her hotel suite and Dr Laurel and his black bag of tricks arrived on the scene and administered a sedative. But by the following morning, the photos and footage were everywhere.

Some hailed it as a shameless publicity stunt. Others said she was clearly having a breakdown and called for her to be sectioned. Whichever way you looked at it, it looked bad. I took the very difficult decision to pull the rest of the tour. I needed to be seen to be helping her, to be doing something about it, not pushing her out onstage every night like a performing monkey. Shona suggested she go to rehab but she point-blank refused. So instead, I took her home.

She spent the next two months lying in bed in her Hampstead mansion, being cared for by her housekeeper with the paps congregated at her gates. I told her not to read the internet, but telling a seventeen-year-old girl not to look online is like telling her not to breathe. She wouldn't talk to me about Billy. Every time I brought him up she shut her eyes and rolled over in bed, turning her back towards me, so in the end I simply stopped trying. Shona scripted an upbeat message for her to post across her socials reassuring fans that she was okay, but no matter how many takes we did we couldn't get her to say it in a way which was even remotely convincing so we ended up scrapping the idea. It was stressful. And in the midst of it all, Ade suggested we go away for a mini break. I asked him if he was joking. I said there was no way I could leave Alora, absolutely no chance. But he was persistent. He said I needed a rest, that we needed to spend some 'quality time' together. He actually used those words even though we slept in the same bed every night and ate breakfast together every morning albeit with me usually checking my emails rather than talking to him, and we both laughed awkwardly.

I booked the executive suite in a country hotel in Bath, a former stately home with a heated outdoor swimming pool and Michelin-starred restaurant. Ade wanted to go further away, his idea was a remote cottage in the Scottish Highlands near to a beach where we could go wild swimming, but I didn't want to venture too far from London in case I needed to get back quickly and besides, I didn't think that kind of place would have decent Wi-Fi. So we drove over to Bath in my MG listening to James Blake and as soon as we got into the bedroom, Ade pushed me down on the bed and we started kissing, the intense face-consuming kind like two teenagers desperate to rid themselves of their virginities. I'd bought a new underwear set from Agent Provocateur especially for the occasion—it was lacy and slinky and there wasn't much of it. I reached for Ade's belt and undid the buckle just as he slid his hand up the inside of my T-shirt. Then my phone rang. Ade's hands didn't stop so I pushed him off me and sat up, grabbed my handbag from the bedside cabinet and rooted around inside it for my phone. It was the MD so I took the call, mouthing 'Sorry' to Ade as I wandered off into the bathroom for some privacy. I sat on the closed toilet seat whilst we talked, then I went back into the bedroom. Ade was lying on the bed smoking a joint. I went from zero to a hundred in less than a second.

'Ade, what the fuck are you doing? You can't smoke in here, it's a five-star hotel not the fucking Travelodge! Take it outside!'

Ade looked like I'd slapped him in the face. But he clambered up off the bed and opened up the double doors to the balcony whilst I perched on the edge of the mattress regretting my tone. Whilst he was gone I removed my jeans and T-shirt and attempted to arrange myself in a sexy pose, which by the time he walked back into the room just felt awkward and embarrassing. I waited for him to compliment my new underwear, but he didn't say anything about it. Instead, he lay down next to me, exhaled pungent weed breath all over me, then proceeded to kiss me in a determined manner. I tried to relax, tried to ignore the niggling feeling that he was forcing himself to do it, but when he grabbed hold of my left boob and yanked at the bra cup with such force the lace ripped, I said, 'For fuck's sake, Ade. That cost nearly two hundred quid.' He muttered something about buying me a new one as my phone rang again and I reached for it, covering myself with my other hand. I went back into the bathroom to take the call—it was Shona, just checking in. I told her I'd call her back, then I counted to three and returned to the bedroom. This time Ade was sitting propped up against the pillows. He'd switched on the TV and the volume was turned up loud. I asked him what he was watching and he just nodded towards the screen as if to say, 'You can see for yourself, I can't even be bothered to answer you.' It was a cookery show. The presenter was laughing because a contestant's sauce had turned lumpy. I pulled on my T-shirt and sat down on the bed next to him. We watched the show together in silence.

The following day we drove back to London. 'Was something wrong with the room, madam?' the receptionist asked when I told her we were checking out early.

No, just with my boyfriend, I felt like saying, but I managed to smile and said that everything was wonderful, something just came up back home.

In the car, I turned on the radio to avoid the need to attempt conversation and Ade just stared out of the window. As we were passing through Slough he said to me, 'I didn't get the job, by the way.' I asked him what he was talking about. 'The job at Low Slang Records, in A&R. I asked you if you'd put a word in for me with the MD, remember?' I started fiddling with the dial. 'You do, remember, don't you, Eva? You did put a word in for me, didn't you?'

'Of course I did.' I said it sharply. 'And I'm obviously sorry you didn't get it. But I'm sure it was tough competition so better luck next time.'

Now that I thought about it, I did have a vague memory of Ade mentioning some job he was applying for and asking me if I'd recommend him to the MD. I was tired at the time. I'd had a late night at the Music Week Awards, a flight to catch and a million things Alora-related I needed to think about. I slumped down in the driver's seat, wishing that I could turn on cruise control, slip beneath the steering wheel and crawl away from my boyfriend without being noticed.

When we got back home, I hurried inside and shut myself in the study with my MacBook, leaving Ade to unpack the car by himself. He eventually knocked on the study door.

'Yeah?' I said.

He said hey and I said hey back without moving my eyes away from the screen. 'Listen, I was thinking I might head to my parents' place for a couple of nights. Mum's really missing me and I feel like I'm neglecting them a bit.'

I rolled my eyes into nowhere. 'Sure, if you like. Tell them I said hi.' He kissed me on the cheek and said he'd see me soon. A few minutes later, I heard the front door slam.

Later that week I met the MD for lunch to discuss 'the situation' with Alora. He asked how she was and I answered honestly: not great. He asked whether she was still seeing Dr Laurel, whether she was still taking the medication and I said she was.

'Good,' he said. 'That's good. Because the fact is, we need to crack on with the second album.'

I was stunned. We had an artist on our hands who was seriously unwell, who needed rest, recuperation and daily psychotherapy. But when I said this to him, when I tried to explain, the MD simply smiled and said, 'Let me speak frankly here, Eva, if I may?'

'Go ahead.'

'The fact of the matter is, Alora's the real deal, the genuine article, a seriously messed-up kid. It's why she's so relatable to other teens. But believe me, we're up against the clock here. I know what I'm talking about when I say that with the broken ones, we need to get as much out of them whilst we still can.'

I shifted uneasily in my seat. 'And how exactly do you suggest we do that?'

He swilled his brandy around his glass, held it to his nose and inhaled deeply. 'She should make another album with Silas Jax.'

ALORA

THE LETTER TO MY MOTHER IS more difficult to write, the words harder to locate in the wishing for an entirely different mother altogether. Because I used to look at the other mums hugging their daughters by the school gate and wonder, what must that be like? What must it feel like to have your mum wrap her arms around you and squeeze you tight like she never wants to let you go? And I couldn't imagine it, I couldn't imagine that sensation of physical contact with her. And I know she must've touched me a thousand times, must have lifted me from my cot at night when I was a baby but still, I couldn't describe the smell of her skin, I couldn't imagine feeling the warmth of her body or the sound of her heart beating through her blouse. The life she imagined was not the life she was given. She met Dad, this talented, charismatic free spirit, and fell wildly in love, the passionate, intense, hedonistic kind. They were set to tour the world together. Then she got pregnant, at twenty-one. But she'd had a choice. I was just a bunch of cells growing helplessly in her body, she could have eliminated me before I acquired any semblance of consciousness, she could have saved us both all this pain. So the words I scrawl in the centre of the blank page in capital letters, with such fury that the paper tears beneath the tip of my pen are:

IT'S ALL YOUR FAULT!!!

Then I scrunch up the paper and throw it in the bin.

EVA

THE DAY AFTER I'D MET UP with the MD I drove over to her house. There were ten or eleven paparazzi standing at her gate and if I didn't think it might scratch the paintwork on my new bullet-grey Bentley I would've happily run them all over. They called my name as I stepped out onto the drive.

'How is she?' they yelled through the bars. 'Get her to come outside for an exclusive!'

I went round the back and the housekeeper flung open the door and said, 'She's up! She's out of bed!' I had to stop myself from hugging the woman. It felt like the dark clouds had finally parted and glorious celestial sunlight was streaming through direct from the heavens. The housekeeper said she was eating breakfast in the kitchen. I slipped off my boots and practically ran down the corridor. I remember the patio doors were open and Alora was crouched on the tiles next to the island. She was wearing short grey pyjamas with thin straps. Her body looked emaciated, like her muscles might collapse beneath the burden of bone. She didn't acknowledge me when I walked in but as I approached her she held up her hand without turning to face me.

I stopped. 'What are you doing?' I asked.

'Shhh, don't move.' She extended her index finger and pointed at a small pink-breasted bird with black-and-white wings hopping skittishly across the lawn. 'He's a bullfinch.'

'How do you know that?'

'I Googled him. He keeps coming so close, like he's inquisitive but isn't quite brave enough to do something about it. Here, pass me that bit of toast.' Slowly, so as not to scare the bird, I picked up the slice of toast and handed it to her. She tore off a tiny piece of crust and threw it towards him. He was startled at first and hopped backwards as if under attack, but after a few moments of contemplation he darted forwards, pecked at it and took it in his beak. 'He's beautiful,' she said. 'Look at the colour of his feathers, the way he puffs out his chest like he's proud to be alive. I bet it's amazing to have wings, to be able to fly away whenever you want, like the girl in your comic strips.'

I forgot I'd even told her about them. 'My comic strips were just babyish nonsense,' I said. 'Look, Alora, we need to talk.' I strode across the room and sat down at the island on one of the stools. The bullfinch flew away.

The first thing she said when I told her that we needed to get on with making the second album was 'But I thought you said I could take as much time off as I needed?'

Her tone of voice was a childish whine. I ground my teeth and tried to ignore it. 'I know, but I really think this would be good for you. It would get you up in the morning, give you a renewed sense of purpose.'

'But I don't feel like writing. Every time I pick up my guitar there's just nothing there.'

I nodded, I said that I understood. 'I've been reading about this. It could be the antidepressants.'

She snuck a glance towards the garden as if she might make a run for the patio doors. I stood up quickly and closed them. 'But they're helping,' she said. 'I like being numb. Feelings are just too hard.'

I took another slice of toast out of the rack, spread it with vegan butter and dropped it onto her plate. Then as lightly as I could muster, I said, 'The MD's blocked out some dates with Silas Jax and you know what his schedule's like, so we're kind of working to a deadline.'

All of a sudden, she reared up from her seat. The toast went flying and the plate smashed on the tiles. 'What? Why the fuck would I work with Silas again?'

I picked at a hangnail anxiously. 'Well, a few reasons I guess. You made a number one album together for one. He's a creative genius, two, you said so yourself. It's a recipe for success, guaranteed, that's three.'

'Because what, I couldn't be successful without him?'

'That's not what I'm saying—'

'It's what you're thinking though, isn't it? Go on, admit it!' She was screaming at the top of her voice, a lightbulb-shattering pitch, and I was feeling pretty panicked, my hand moving towards my phone in my pocket, wishing I had Dr Laurel on speed dial.

'Of course I don't think that,' I said, far more calmly than I felt. 'But you have to admit that the songs, your voice, became more . . .' I chose my words carefully. 'It all really came together, didn't it, with Silas involved. I could sit in all the sessions with you, make sure everything remains . . . professional.'

She sat down onto one of the stools, shoulders hunched, and closed her eyes. 'Maybe I don't even want to be an artist anymore. Maybe I just want to be normal.'

I ran my fingers through my hair, feeling increasingly exasperated. 'But you *aren't* normal. You could *never* be normal, Alora.'

She looked at me through narrowed eyes. 'What does *that* mean?'

'I mean, you have all this talent inside of you, it needs a release, an outlet, otherwise you'd explode.'

'I can write songs at home,' she shot back, like she'd got it all figured out. 'I can even write for other artists. I don't need to have a public profile anymore, I could basically live like a hermit.' She seemed bizarrely enamoured by this prospect.

'What are you *talking* about? You love the spotlight! You love your fans!'

'Do I? Or am I just seeking validation from millions of people who don't actually know me because of emotional neglect during childhood and some fucked-up need to feel adored?'

I was pacing the kitchen by this point, increasingly infuriated by this psychobabble bullshit that I suspected she was reading online. 'Don't do this to me, Alora. I've worked too fucking hard for you to just throw it all away on a whim. One more album, that's all I'm asking. Just one more, okay? For me. Then we can talk about this again.'

She sighed and sat back down. 'Promise?'

'I promise.'

Her head wilted forwards. 'Okay,' she said quietly. 'For you. But I'm not making it with *him*, so don't ask me again.'

She refused to attend a single session with Silas, and the MD was furious. So instead I set up a load of co-writing sessions with other big names known to churn out hits. The feedback was that she wasn't really contributing, that she was frequently showing up late or pissed and the other writers in the room were having to do all the legwork for her. Part of the process became actually locating her whereabouts, which generally involved me frantically driving around London, phoning up clubs and bars and ringing randoms' doorbells. She'd been recently inked—a tiny bird in flight behind her left ear—by some tattoo artist to the stars, Natalia Volkov, who Alora had now started dating. Then there was *that* photograph on the front page of *The Sun*—Alora emerging from a club in the early hours of the morning wearing practically nothing, makeup sliding down her face, eyes wide and crazed, clinging onto Natalia's hand. She was supposed to be in a session in less than an hour, but of course she didn't turn up and when I called her, her phone was off and she was nowhere to be found. It was a slog, like chipping away at a boulder with a teaspoon. But over the course of the next few months we managed to scrape together an album which, whilst a bit of a departure stylistically from her debut, the MD was happy with—he said it was bold, that the heavy pop production felt 'very now'. Alora seemed indifferent. When I asked her which was her favourite track, the one she felt we should lead with as the first single, she said she didn't care. And when one of the junior marketing managers at the label suggested in a planning meeting she get a 'new look' to go with the change in sound, we all grimaced. But she simply shrugged her shoulders and said, 'Sure, why not.'

She emerged from the stylist's dressing room wearing black leather trousers and a matching top, spike-heeled boots and large gold-hoop earrings. If I'd passed her in the street I don't think I would have recognised her, and with the hollow cheeks and general excruciating thinness, the outfit somehow worked. Her eyes shone brilliant green on the surface but something behind them was dull, like she'd closed a door inside herself and was refusing to open it again, even though she was standing right in front of it with the key in her hand.

Her eighteenth birthday was fast approaching. I was in the midst of planning the album campaign and working with her live agent to finalise arrangements for the second world tour, so I was far too busy to be organising a party. But I did it anyway, because even though she insisted that she didn't want one, I thought it might cheer her up. (It also, as an aside, gave us an opportunity to replace the widely circulated pictures of her writhing in the street being mauled with something more glamorous and controlled.) When I asked her who she wanted to invite she gave me a very short, uninspiring list, so I embellished it a little. I had the invites printed on cards shaped like diamonds covered with gold leaf. I sent one to Ade at his parents' house—he still hadn't come home and had been decidedly frosty with me over text. I kept meaning to call him but I'd been so crazy busy that I simply hadn't had the time and if I'm honest, part of me didn't want to pander to his churlish mood. I contemplated inviting Alora's mum but decided against it—her mental health was still so fragile the last thing she needed was Julia showing up and causing a scene. The thing was, I always knew what was best for Alora, even when she didn't.

ALORA

'WHEN DID YOU GET THAT TATTOO?' Vanessa asks. We're walking to group therapy side by side with slow, shuffling steps so as to prolong the journey.

'A few months ago,' I say. 'It's supposed to be a bullfinch but I don't think you can tell.' I pull back my hair to give her a better look.

'I mean, I like it. But I'd say more of a flying potato, from a distance.' She says she always wanted a star on her wrist but her agent had forbidden her from getting one because it 'would limit her high-end-fashion appeal.'

'It's never too late.'

'Maybe you can take me to where you got yours done, once we're out of his crazy place.'

'Hmm. Probably not a good idea. I kind of had a thing with the tattooist and it didn't exactly end well.'

Natalia Volkov was tall and sturdy with long black hair undercut at one side, numerous facial piercings and complex, intricate tattoos which covered every visible sliver of skin. She was a walking, talking work of art. I asked about each of her tattoos as I lay in her chair. She said that in every place she could reach, she'd done them herself. She warned me that behind the ear was a particularly sensitive area and that this was going to hurt. I didn't flinch once.

When she'd finished, she tilted her head to one side and said, 'You enjoyed the pain. A woman after my own heart.' She said if I waited whilst she shut up the shop, we could go back to hers and have a drink.

Natalia's house was in New Cross Gate. She'd described it to me as a 'party house' and when we arrived, I understood why. It was barely five PM and music was already pumping so loud that the windows were shuddering in their frames. As soon as she opened the front door the smell of weed hit me; I was sure I was going to get high just by breathing. Various model types were strewn about in the lounge, sylph-like limbs hanging off sofas and tangled on the rug. Two or three of them were gyrating in the corner, a couple were devouring each other's faces next to the speakers, all lips and tongues. It reminded me of Jonny's, but devoid of magic.

'Who are all these people?' I asked.

Natalia shrugged and said, 'Who cares?'

I followed her into the kitchen and smoked a cigarette leaning against the counter whilst she mixed us vodka cocktails which tasted primarily of vodka. 'Now I give you the tour,' she said. The tour consisted of me wandering around behind Natalia as she showed me all the signed photographs hanging on her walls of famous people she'd inked, and told me who was fierce and who was a pussy. I could tell she was impressed by the world of celebrity and it made me feel empty inside in a way that was not entirely unpleasant.

When she barked at me, 'You do coke, yes?' it sounded more like an order than a question.

I ignored the voice inside of me which told me to say no, because following in Dad's footsteps didn't seem quite so bad anymore. She rolled up a twenty-pound note and we snorted lines off a mirror in her bedroom. Then she grabbed hold of my hair and bit my lip. The next thing I knew, I was lying on my back on her mattress whilst she unbuttoned my jeans. I knew it was a bad idea. I knew I was supposed to be focusing on my album and getting my head straight and preparing for another world tour. But I didn't want to think about any of that stuff. I didn't want to think at all.

The following morning, she made me breakfast in bed—a bowl of fresh strawberries and a tumbler of neat vodka. 'Today, we party,' she said. I was supposed to be flying to LA to film *The Late Late Show with James Corden*. I didn't even text Eva to tell her I wouldn't be going.

It wasn't long before I was spending all my nights with Natalia and all my days sleeping off the nights. She decided what I wore, she decided what I ate, and when one day on the way to a warehouse party she instructed me to open wide and laid a blue pill on my tongue, I closed my mouth and swallowed. I don't remember the rest of the evening; it passed in a deliriously euphoric haze of Natalia's lips and hair and skin. I woke up on her bedroom floor. I was naked and my hair was matted with dried sick, presumably my own but I couldn't tell you for sure. Natalia was lying in bed, smoking a joint and scrolling on her phone.

A few weeks later I received an invitation to Drag's twenty-first birthday party. Drag was the controversial rapper whose violent lyrics and derogatory dance moves had young boys emulating him and young girls offering up their virginities to him on z-pix. When I showed Natalia the invite she said, 'We're going.' And that was that.

Drag's apartment dominated the top three floors of a modern high-rise tower block in South London. The concierge led us to the private lift, which shot up to the roof terrace so fast that I thought we might launch on into space. As soon as we stepped through the lift doors and into the party, Natalia lifted her arms in the air and writhed to the music with a look of pure ecstasy on her face. I felt jealous of her in that moment, that all it took to make her happy was a room full of celebrities and a monotonous beat. I followed her dully through the crowd, nodding and smiling insincerely as people said, 'Hey, Alora,' like we were old friends or 'Oh my God, I love your album!'

There was a swimming pool filled with beautiful people humping inflatable flamingos and squealing with laughter. Women dressed in pink latex served cocktails, and champagne flowed from a fountain into a pyramid of glasses shaped like the perfect breast. Natalia bumped into Lazy Lover, who she'd previously inked. I'd met her a couple of times before, she'd once asked me to feature on one of her tracks, but Eva turned it down because she said it wouldn't complement 'the brand'. Sometimes I wonder when I became a brand and stopped being a human. I stood next to them in silence, giving blunt, nondescript answers to any questions Lazy Lover directed towards me until she seemed to lose interest in trying to involve me in the conversation. I began to wonder if I'd be able to make it to the edge of the terrace and fling myself off without anybody noticing, how long it would take for me to make impact with the pavement and whether I would definitely die or just be paralysed for life. I eventually asked Natalia if I could go to the toilet.

'Don't be long,' she said.

I took the white-marble staircase to the floor below and wandered around the party aimlessly. Glitching images of bikini-clad models were being projected onto the walls and the music seemed to get more intense and frantic with every footstep. A well-known Hollywood actor who Shona told Eva pays young female actresses to pose as his wives and girlfriends in order to conceal his sexuality from the movie studios introduced himself, then disappeared into the bathroom with a male model. A reality-TV star famous for the size of her voluptuous lips stopped me and told me how much she loved my last music video.

'When you gouge your own eyes out at the end, it's like, super-realistic,' she said. 'I actually thought you must've done it for real.'

I assured her that I didn't and that special effects were very advanced these days. I pretended I'd seen someone else I knew to get away from her and ducked through a doorway and into a bedroom, where I leaned against the wall and inhaled deeply, grateful to be alone. It was when I heard the first groan that I realised I wasn't. I held my breath, my eyes slowly adjusting to the darkness. A male figure was perched on the edge of the bed. A woman was kneeling on the floor between his spread legs, his trousers ruched at his ankles. He held the back of her head as it bobbed up and down against his crotch.

When he roared, 'That's my girl!' I seized the moment of his obvious climax to exit. I took one tiny step, then another, and reached for the door handle just as the heel of one shoe—a ridiculous high-heeled strappy pair which Natalia had told me to wear—got caught in the strap of the other. I stumbled and fell, landing heavily on the carpet. With my face pressed into the thick woollen pile I heard the swift zip of a fly, then the light came on. I looked up, squinting, to see the MD of my record label standing next to the bed, doing up his belt. One of his other signings—an internationally successful but shamelessly manufactured pop product called KAZY-K—was clambering to her feet. A few seconds passed which seemed to echo around the room like thunder before the MD rearranged his facial expression into one of professional composure and boomed, 'Alora, darling! So good to see you!'

He strode towards me and I allowed him to take hold of my arm and help me up, and he and I made polite conversation about my new album and pretended that the situation was perfectly natural and not awkward at all. He ushered me towards the door, saying something about getting me a drink, but as he did so I glanced over my shoulder at KAZY-K. She was adjusting her bra top and pulling on her white faux-fur jacket.

'Are you okay?' I said.

'She's fine,' the MD replied, gripping onto my arm more tightly. But I shook him off. KAZY-K looked up and we stared at each other before she looked away.

'I'm fine,' she eventually said. With the gold-hoop earrings, pierced nose and tattoos across her knuckles, she looked tough and glamorous and intimidating, but I'd seen something else pass behind her eyes, something raw and vulnerable and broken, something I saw each time I looked in the mirror.

The following morning, Natalia and I split up. We'd gone

back to my place after the party and I woke to the sound of Carrie, my dog, yelping. I opened my eyes to see Natalia wrestling with the Teacup Chihuahua, one hand clamped around her jaw. The tattoo machine in Natalia's other hand was switched on and whirring.

'Hey!' I shouted, sitting bolt upright in bed. 'What the fuck are you doing?'

She looked up at me with sadistic eyes and smiled. 'Inking your dog,' she said. If I had woken from some drug-induced slumber to find Natalia tattooing my lips, my eyes, any part of my body however painful or intimate, I would've simply let her continue. But Carrie wasn't me, Carrie had done nothing wrong. I jumped out of bed and pushed Natalia hard. She fell backwards. Carrie scampered towards me and I scooped her up into my arms. I screamed at the top of my voice for Natalia to get the fuck out of my house. Gina appeared at the door and folded her arms across her chest—she looked surprisingly menacing despite the knitted cardigan, apron and sandals with socks. For a brief moment, I thought that Natalia might be about to cry. Then she grabbed her clothes and stormed out of the room.

'So yeah,' I say to Vanessa. 'It didn't exactly end well.'

'You can say that again! I'll be steering well clear of *that* lady. There's probably a decent tattoo parlour in Austin. You can come with me, if you like? Afterwards you could visit the ranch, have a holiday, meet my nephew and experience life in the middle of nowhere.' I say that I'd like that a lot.

EVA

I HIRED OUT THE WHOLE OF the Ritz. The idea was that the guests would simply roll from the party into the bedrooms, not that many of them would bother with sleep. Once word got out about it I was bombarded with calls from all the top designers wanting Alora to wear a piece from their latest collections. I arranged for her new stylist to meet me at her home with a rack of dresses he'd been sent for her, which he'd narrowed down to the most suitable options—sleek but not conservative, daring but not slutty.

He kissed the air above my cheeks. 'You should've seen what Lavonda Laing sent, darling! They wanted her to look like a giant pom-pom!' He stuck two fingers down his throat and made a barfing noise. Our laughter intermingled and echoed down the hallway. I couldn't distinguish mine from his.

The housekeeper helped him carry the rail up to her bedroom and I followed, checking emails on my phone. We burst through her bedroom door to find Alora still lying in bed. I strode across the room, flung back the curtains and opened up the window to cut the stale air whilst the stylist lifted one of the dresses off the rack and started plumping the chiffon beneath the skirt. Alora groaned from beneath the duvet.

'It lives,' I said, and the stylist giggled behind his hand. The housekeeper was loitering at the bedroom door, looking uncomfortable. 'What is it, Mrs er . . .' I said. I always forgot the damn woman's name.

'Gina.'

'Sure. What is it, Gina?'

'I could help her get showered and dressed first. She could meet you in the drawing room when she's ready.'

'No, thank you,' I said firmly. 'I can handle this. You can go now.' As she turned her back I pulled a face at the stylist and he giggled again.

It took nearly an hour to get Alora out of bed. With much cajoling and a bit of physical exertion in the form of me taking hold of her arms and the stylist taking hold of her legs, we finally succeeded, and she lay slumped on the chaise longue still wearing her pyjamas as the stylist paraded dress after dress in front of her.

'Are you sure she's feeling okay?' he said to me at one point. I assured him that she was fine.

We eventually chose a long black backless number—elegant and classy—which she'd wear with a simple gold pendant and matching earrings from Bulgari. I say we, it was really more the stylist and me who made the decision, Alora didn't seem too keen to contribute her thoughts, but when I asked if she liked the dress she waved her hand at me and groaned which I interpreted as a yes.

I'd sent out 1,500 invitations to the party and received 1,496 acceptances. It was disappointing that Taylor and her plus one couldn't make it but they were on holiday, and David and Victoria Beckham cancelled at the last minute. But everyone else who was anyone would be there. It was convenient timing, the day before the first single from the new album was about to be released, and I knew the press would be gathered outside on the red carpet. I'd made some vague promises to *Heat*, *Grazia* and *Closer* about on-the-night interviews because Shona said we could do with getting the trashy mags on side again.

'Just bear in mind that it's like inviting the foxes into the chicken coop,' Shona said. 'So we both need to keep an eye on them.'

'You keep an eye on them,' I said. 'I need to keep both my eyes on Alora.'

We arrived in a black SUV. Her head of security climbed out first and took hold of her hand. She stepped onto the pavement in heeled Chanel boots. The dress exposed a little leg but unless she fell, an up-the-skirt shot was totally avoidable. The cameras took aim and fired and she smiled into the explosion of light. She swung her hips as she moved down the red carpet and stopped to greet the regulars, the paparazzi who camped almost permanently outside her home. She asked them how they were doing. They thanked her for the cakes Gina baked them and the cups of coffee. They chatted like neighbours or old friends, like there was nothing remotely peculiar about their daily intrusion into her life. I followed her into the venue. Her eyes lit up with the wonder of a child as she stared into the chandelier above our heads, as the rows of smartly dressed waiters and waitresses bowed as though in the presence of royalty. The crowd cheered as she did a twirl. Her dress flared out. The cameras flashed. Alora smiled. I thought that everything was going to be okay.

ALORA

WHEN WE'RE TOLD IN GROUP THERAPY that we're going on a trip, Vanessa and I simultaneously smirk. 'Is everyone in the facility going?' Python asks.

'No, just you guys and gals,' Elijah says, in an embarrassingly bad American accent. 'We're leaving in half an hour. Your carers have already packed your bags for you so just collect them from your chalets and meet me out front. I'll be waiting in the minibus.'

'Minibus?' Vanessa says. 'For thirty grand a month? You've got to be kidding me.'

Elijah winks. 'It's going to be fun.'

I sit next to Vanessa on the bus. She goes in a mood when she asks how old I think she is and I guess at older than her actual age, then don't believe her when she swears she's only sixty-five, but I manage to get her out of it by asking about her ex-husbands and she goes through each of them in turn. Number one was the whirlwind romance, a famous photographer she married in a week and divorced within a year. Number three was the rebound, the sexy meathead she met in a dive bar when she was drowning her sorrows, trying to recover from the heartbreak of husband number two. And number two was Wyatt, the love of her life, the Texan horse breeder she met at a Shania Twain concert in New York City after she'd retired from modelling and was working as a booker at a top agency. She was there with some up-and-coming young models who were more interested in snorting coke in the toilets than watching the show. She found herself alone in the row of seats, and Wyatt—sitting behind—tapped her on the shoulder, invited her to sit with him and his friends. They struck up conversation. Six hours later, they were in a Lower East Side bar, still talking.

'Don't you want to get away from all this bullshit?' he said to her.

And she realised that she did, that she'd had enough of the drugs and sleaze and vacuous callousness of the fashion world. The very next day she packed her bags, booked a flight to Texas and moved in with him at his ranch.

'But damn thing couldn't carry to term,' she says, glancing down at her body with distain. 'That's when the obsession with surgery began, all I had left to give him was beauty.' She raises her eyes to the minibus roof and I see that they're glistening with tears. 'Jesus, I'm a mess. Ignore me.' She wafts at her face with her hand.

I'd like to hug her but I suspect she wouldn't welcome it. So instead I say rather clumsily, 'I'm never having babies either.'

'Oh? Bit young to be making those kind of big decisions aren't you?'

'Not really. I don't want to be responsible for inflicting existence on anyone else.'

'Jeez, Louise,' she says. 'Pretty gloomy perspective you've got there, doll. Well, at least enjoy the sex before the old menopause kicks in and you turn into a dried-up old prune down there.'

I sigh and fiddle with my ring. 'Sex. It's just so weird, isn't it? But I get that it's something you have to do.'

'What do you mean, *have* to?'

'People expect it.'

She looks puzzled and says, 'I mean, I guess, depending on the circumstances. But don't you enjoy it?'

I think about it for a moment. 'Honestly? Not that much. But I like it afterwards when they curl their body around yours and go to sleep. That's always the best bit for me.'

Vanessa looks sad and rubs the top of my arm. 'Oh, doll,' she says. 'Sounds like you've been having sex with the wrong people.'

I rest the side of my head on the damp window as we drive. I arrived on the island by helicopter and didn't venture out of the centre's grounds even once the one-month minimum stint in captivity drew to an end, so it's strange and slightly fascinating to see a forest of pine trees, a river flowing beneath a humpback bridge, a flock of swallows passing overhead in an arrow formation and a winding lane with many potholes which Elijah, as driver of the minibus, seems to be making no effort to avoid. We bump and bang forth.

'Do you miss modelling?' I ask her, and Vanessa seems to attempt a frown but her forehead barely moves.

'Sometimes, but it was different back then.'

'Different how?'

'It was the sixties and seventies. It was all so fast and there was so much coke and LSD flying around there wasn't time to ask yourself whether you were actually having a good time. I suppose

I was, in a way. But when I look back on it all now through the eyes of an adult I find it difficult to stomach the systemic abuse of young women.' I ask her what she means and she says, 'Well, put it this way. Do you think it's right that at seventeen years old I was fucking a forty-eight-year-old art director because he promised me the front cover of *Cosmo*? That I blew a famous rock star at a party because I had his poster on my bedroom wall at home and had idolised him since I was a kid?'

The minibus jolts and takes a left turn. 'But you wanted to,' I say. 'You wanted to be on the front cover of *Cosmo*. You idolised the rock star.'

'Exactly!' she says, with such vigour that a little spittle flies out from between her lips and lands on my arm. 'There was a very obvious power dynamic, and the men took full advantage of it.'

I reach for the scar on my left wrist and stroke it lightly with my thumb. 'But they didn't force you to do it.'

'Doll, you're missing the point. Consent isn't simply a question of yes or no, black or white, there are many different shades of grey.'

Just then the bus starts to slow. Elijah turns off the ignition and the engine slumps into silence. He swivels in his seat and claps his hands together.

'Right, everybody off!' he says.

'Where the hell are we going?' someone shouts from the back of the bus.

Elijah extends one finger towards the forest which looks thick and dense and devoid of light, an entirely unappealing destination. 'In there,' he says.

I don't know how long we've been walking. Python's striding on ahead next to Elijah as though we're competing in a race which he intends to win and Best Supporting Actress is lagging behind, complaining about her bunions and that she's being eaten alive by mosquitoes. We all carry the rucksacks on our shoulders which Elijah handed out as we stood by the roadside, whilst we huffed and complained and stubbed our toes into the dirt. I'm walking with Vanessa. Politician and Rich Kid are close behind, the four of us comprising an unenthusiastic cluster. Elijah doesn't hold a compass or a map and occasionally stops, rests his hands on his hips and stares at the sun as though it might point him in the right direction. The next time he stops and lifts his head I lift mine too, squinting to try to make sense of what he sees. But I'm no Bear Grylls. I'm still squinting when Elijah strides on.

It's surprising to reach water, but suddenly our feet meet sand and we're standing on a beach. The sand is sharp and pebbled, not the pretty package-holiday kind, and there are no coloured plastic buckets and spades, no sandcastles or ice cream vans. The beach winds around the side of the island before it meets jagged grey cliff on both sides—we're in a cove, completely isolated and alone apart from the insistent rush of waves as they greet the shoreline, then recoil demurely into the swell. Elijah wriggles out of his rucksack and drops it onto the sand, which prompts us all to do the same. There's a cool breeze which turns my skin to goose bumps, I rub at it with my palms. I don't know what time it is, how long we've been walking, but the sun has moved to the cliff on our left as though it's preparing to sink from the sky. Elijah instructs us to sit cross-legged in a circle. He walks around its circumference and connects each hand to another, then he asks us to close our eyes.

'Don't tell me we're about to chant,' Vanessa whispers, and I giggle.

We sit quietly in the darkness of our own minds and wait for instruction. I hear a bird calling from the trees. It repeats the same five high-pitched notes in close succession; nature's melody, sweeter than any man-made instrument. The sea whispers ancient secrets to itself and Vanessa's hand warms mine, her skin soft and paper-thin. Politician is sitting to my left and his skin is clammy but his palm is reassuringly large and I imagine him pressing it to the other in a crisis and restoring calm in the cabinet.

It's Python who eventually says, 'Hey guys, where's Elijah?'

I open my eyes. We're still holding hands but Best Supporting Actress breaks the circle so we all do the same and my hands are empty again, only my own. We look around us: forest, sea and sky. Definitely no Elijah. The sun has nearly submerged itself in the water. Elijah's rucksack is gone.

'Shit,' Rich Kid says. 'I can't believe it. He's only fucking left us here!'

EVA

AND AT FIRST IT *WAS* OKAY. Alora passed demurely through the crowd surrounded by her bodyguards. She smiled and kissed the air above perfumed cheeks, flawless skin, bejewelled necks. Waiters leapt around her bearing trays of champagne, hors d'oeuvres of smoked salmon and caviar, and 'the Alora'—a tall, lethal oil spill of a cocktail which the Ritz's head mixologist had designed especially for the occasion.

I'd arranged for a roped-off V-VIP area on a three-tiered podium in the centre of the ballroom. The idea was that the ice sculpture of Alora would be positioned on the third tier, like the decorative figurine on a wedding cake, but by the time the guests started to arrive its facial features had begun to melt and dribble down its body so I told the staff to take it away and stick it in a cupboard out back.

The bouncer unhooked the burgundy rope and I stood to one side to allow her to step up onto the podium in front of me. The microphone was on the second tier, ready for her performance. She'd been reluctant to give one but I'd insisted that her guests would expect it and she'd made some sulky remark about always having to do what people expected of her rather than what she actually wanted to do, which I ignored. Just as she was taking her seat her head of security approached and asked if he could have a word. He said that her ex—Noah Lamb—was outside, demanding to be let in and making a scene. He'd normally deal with it without bothering me, but Noah was insisting he needed to see Alora, that he was worried about her. I turned and glanced at her. She was standing alone, sipping on a personalised cocktail and surveying the room with a slightly startled expression.

'He's got no business being worried,' I practically spat. 'She's not his concern anymore. Get rid of him, now!'

The performance of the new single, 'Anybody', was simply stunning, the lyrics so honest and raw and distinctly Alora:

Wake up in the morning
Thought it might be different
It's exactly the same
I feel your body moving
I'd better get going
I can't remember your name

When I just need a body
It could be anybody
It don't matter to me
We were talking in the party
Doing it is easy
Forget how to breathe

I don't want you to say you love me oh no
Don't try to hold my hand or follow me home

The guests applauded and whistled until she agreed to do an encore. She chose one of her classics, 'Drowning in the Blue', the song from the original video, the video from which I'd discovered her. I felt quite overwhelmed with nostalgia, and if I'm completely honest, by the enormity of my own achievement in recognising the potential in this unsigned young artist when no one else did. And when the guests applauded this time, it felt as though their applause was, in part at least, for me.

As Alora was stepping away from the mic I spotted Ade by the bar, so I excused myself and made my way through the crowd towards him, squeezing past the white horse wearing a unicorn's horn and the topless male models serving shots. He didn't notice me as I approached, he was smiling as he chatted to a pretty brunette I recognised as one of the roving reporters on Channel 4's *Light Breakfast*. Her surgically enhanced breasts were barely concealed beneath her dusky-pink dress, and her unchallenging eyes were fixed on Ade. She flicked her long dark hair over one shoulder and lifted her chest a little as though offering it up to him to taste.

'Hey,' I said. He turned. His eyes passed over me without a glimmer of warmth. I drew a sharp breath and clenched the muscles in my jaw into a smile. I introduced myself to the brunette as Ade's girlfriend and watched as disappointment sank right through her demeanour. She lowered her chest and extended her hand.

'Layla,' she said, smiling valiantly. 'You manage Alora Storm-Jones, right?' I clamped her hand in mine as hard as I possibly could and held eye contact for longer than was entirely comfortable.

'That's right,' I said, my own considerably smaller chest lifting slightly of its own accord.

I released my hand and she began to massage hers. 'I'm a huge fan. I'd love to interview her sometime.'

'I'm sure you would,' I said. 'But she's very busy at the moment being interviewed by *real* journalists.'

I heard Ade mutter something under his breath. 'What's up with you?' I said. My boyfriend touched Layla's arm when he asked her whether he could have a word with me in private. His eyes followed the provocative sway of her ass as she sashayed into the crowd.

'You didn't need to be so rude to her,' he said. I leaned over the bar and wafted my empty champagne glass at one of the bar staff, who topped it up. 'Are you not even going to say thank you?'

'For what?'

'That bartender just filled up your glass.'

I stared at him in disbelief. 'Oh, sorry, Ade. Because you're so fucking polite perving over another woman in front of your girlfriend. When did you become such a sleaze?'

He looked embarrassed, but not of himself. 'When did you become such a bitch?'

His words winded me. I swallowed a huge gulp of champagne and the bubbles shot straight up my nose, but I refused to be so uncool as to sneeze. 'What did you just call me?' I was practically snarling, and he shook his head.

'You heard. I don't even know who you are anymore.'

'What? That's complete bullshit. Of course you do! You know me better than anyone.'

'No, I knew the old Eva. This new version, I don't know her at all. To be honest, I don't even like her.'

It suddenly occurred to me what this was all about, it was so obvious come to think of it. 'Hang on a minute. You're not still pissed off about the job at Low Slang, are you? I told you I was sorry, but I can't work miracles. If they didn't want to hire you they didn't want to hire you. We're not all cut out for the music business.'

Ade covered his face with his hands. 'Fuck, Eva, it's nothing to do with the job! It's to do with us, with ... *this*.' He gestured to the empty space between us as though that's where the concept of *us* had once existed but had now completely disintegrated. '*This* just doesn't work anymore. We hardly ever see each other, you're always working or away, and when we do see each other you spend the whole time on your phone and I spend the whole time wishing we hadn't bothered.'

I asked Ade if he was breaking up with me. He confirmed that he was. He said that whilst I'd been busy helping set up for the party, he'd gone back to the house with his parents and packed his stuff. He reached into his pocket and handed me his door key. By this point I was spiralling. I think I said something strident and sassy like, 'Your loss, honey,' and strutted away, desperate for Ade to run after me, devastatingly certain that he wouldn't.

The rest of the evening was a feat of endurance. Alora drank too much and so did I. She offered me a wrap of coke. I didn't ask where she'd got it from or when she'd started doing 'real drugs,' or insist that I didn't touch them, I simply waltzed off to the toilets and snorted a fat line. I said a fleeting hi to Shona. I had no idea where the gossip-mag journalists were lurking, nor did I care. I relinquished all sense of professionalism. I allowed myself to lose focus.

Jason, the head of A&R from Low Slang, appeared out of nowhere and told me that I looked sensational. He leaned in close when he said that he missed seeing my 'cute ass' on the fifth floor. In another universe, the one I should have been in, I would have laughed and walked away or maybe even slapped him in the face, hard. But instead, I found myself engaging in a shamelessly flirtatious display of heartbroken desperation with a man I historically loathed. He placed his hand on my hip as he complimented my dress whilst ogling my cleavage. I envisaged bundling him into the SUV, yanking his clothes off on the back seat, waking up next to him hungover and regretful in the bed I'd once shared with Ade, calling him a cab then avoiding him for the rest of eternity—the situation felt inevitable, I was drunk and high and powerless to prevent it.

I glanced up to see the bouncer unhooking the rope to Alora's podium and allowing a lithe young red-headed creature in a short green dress to pass through, closely followed by a man with shoulder-length hair and dark glasses who I didn't at first recognise. The creature greeted Alora. The man greeted Alora. Someone lifted their phone and took a photograph of the three of them with their arms around each other. Photographs were strictly forbidden—we had a room filled with celebrities wanting to let their hair down and have a good time without having to worry about the evidence being plastered all over the front pages the following day. I thought about having a word with our Mr Amateur Photographer, about having the bouncers confiscate his phone and throw him out of the fire exit, but I was distracted by

Jason asking me if I wanted to go for a cigarette. I didn't smoke but that clearly wasn't the point. I followed him out of the ballroom, the whole time scanning the crowd for Ade, hoping he was watching and seething with jealousy.

I flashed my access-all-areas pass at a member of the Ritz's security team and led Jason by the hand through a doorway marked PRIVATE. In the empty corridor next to a trolley full of dirty glasses, he pushed me against the wall and kissed me. His tongue was wet and thick. His kiss felt as though he was kissing himself, opening and closing a mechanical jaw without any regard for my movements. He reached under my dress between my legs and that's when all thoughts of Ade, which the alcohol, drugs and slobbery snogging of a chauvinist, self-entitled prick had momentarily held at bay, stormed through my mind on a wild rampage—our first kiss, our first time, Paris, my sister's engagement party, the moment our eyes met at the makeshift bar in a warehouse party all those years ago. I had wanted him for so long and now I'd lost him. I grabbed hold of Jason's groping hand and pushed him off me.

'Sorry, I just . . .' I left him standing in the corridor, pointing in protest at his cock straining against his trousers as though it was my nationalistic duty to serve it, and I ran back into the party.

But it was too late. It was too late that I walked towards the V-VIP area and realised that the man at her side who had now removed his sunglasses was none other than Silas Jax. I knew he hadn't been sent one of the diamond-shaped, gold-leaf embossed invitations; I'd had them printed and dispatched myself. But all of the guests had been allocated a plus-one. And the woman, or should I say girl, he was with was signed to Low Slang Records.

She was working with Silas; he was producing her debut album and I'd invited her at the MD's request. I shoved my way through the guests and hurdled the rope before the bouncer had a chance to lift it. I leapt up the steps two by two and grabbed hold of Alora's hand.

And she turned to me, smiled and said so calmly, with a look of such vacant serenity in her eyes, 'It's okay, Eva. It's okay. I don't care anymore. I just don't care about anything anymore.'

The picture appeared on the front page of *The Sun* the following morning. The headline was innocent, nothing racy or salacious or with any hint that the reporter knew the backstory. Because nobody knew the backstory. Nobody knew the truth about what had happened between Silas and Alora other than the MD, Silas, Alora and, of course, me.

ALORA

THE BLUE SKY DARKENS. MY STOMACH'S RUMBLING. Politician is trying unsuccessfully to coordinate the group into making a plan of action—some of us make a fire, some of us go looking for help, some of us wade out into the sea and try to catch a fish for supper with our bare hands, that kind of thing. Best Supporting Actress is crying and Python is consoling her with his overly muscular arm around her shoulders. Rich Kid is saying something about getting his father to sue Max Beaumont for all he's worth. Vanessa is sitting on the sand smoking a cigarette, saying very little. We have by this point realised that our backpacks are filled with nothing but blankets, thick woollen blankets. The wool is itchy and coarse. We have no food. We have no water other than the vast salty sea. We are not the kind of men and women who know how to make a fire by rubbing two sticks together.

'I can't believe this is happening,' Best Supporting Actress is wailing. I wonder if she means it or if she's performing the role of damsel in distress so that Python doesn't relinquish his comforting grip.

I start to think about *him*, the strange bulk of him. I stop when I realise that Vanessa's shivering. I take one of the blankets and wrap it around her emaciated body. She's the only person I've ever met who's thinner than me and with so little flesh covering bone she must be freezing right down to the marrow. She looks a little shocked when I touch her but she smiles and says thank you in a gentle voice. I ask her if she's hungry, then flinch at the stupidity of the question.

'I stopped being hungry in 1969,' she says.

'Vanessa,' I say. 'I can't stop thinking about what you said earlier.'

'Oh yeah? What about?'

'Those older guys you slept with when you were a model. Do you really think they did anything wrong?'

She purses her lips. 'Well, they would say no, but the world sees things differently now.'

'But just because someone's older, doesn't mean you can't have a connection.'

'True. It's not just about age. But it's definitely a factor in the power dynamic.'

'What power dynamic?'

'There's always a power dynamic in any relationship, to a degree. Money, age, socio-economic status. But those guys knew they had something on me or at least they should've known. Like I said, consent's a complicated concept.'

She asks me what this is about, whether something's happened. 'No, well, yeah, kind of. I was a bit obsessed with this guy once. He's a lot older than me.'

'How much older?'

'He's about to turn fifty.'

She makes a whistling sound through her teeth, a tone which starts high and ends low like a doomed aeroplane plummeting from the sky. 'And you're eighteen, right? That's quite the age gap. He's old enough to be your daddy, and then some.'

'Yeah, I know.'

'But nothing happened. I mean, you had a crush on him but it never went anywhere, right?'

I go quiet. And it's a betrayal of his trust to tell her, yet I find the words spilling from my lips, a waterfall of withheld truth.

EVA

IN THE HOTEL ROOM IN MEXICO she opened up her bathrobe and I saw the scar at the very top inside of her thigh, snaking into an S.

It looked like a cattle brand. '*Him,*' she said.

And at first I didn't get it. 'Who?' Then she said his name: Silas. And the word reverberated between my ears, clanging like a detuned church bell. 'Did he do that to you?'

'No, I did it to myself. With one of his signet rings. He's got this firepit at his house in the Hollywood Hills. I dropped it into the flames and—'

I cut her off. 'Enough already! Why the fuck would you do that?'

She shrugged dismissively. 'Because Coco did it.'

'Who's Coco?'

'His ex, Coco Cassidy.'

'The model?'

'Yeah.'

'Silas and Coco Cassidy dated?'

'For a while.'

'She looks about twelve years old.'

'She's twenty-two, actually. He said she was crazy, a total train wreck, but it was that wildness which drew him to her. He was always talking about her, I could tell that he still really loved her and I was jealous of that. I wanted to prove to him that I could be wild too.'

'But why would you need to *prove* anything to him?'

'Because I love him.'

My mouth went dry. I reached for the glass of water on her bedside cabinet but on taking a sip, discovered it was vodka. I spat it out. 'Stop saying you love him, will you? It's really freaking me out.'

'But I do love him!'

'But as a friend, right?' She shook her head. 'A father figure?' I said hopefully. She looked away. And then I exploded. 'You can't possibly love him like *that*, he's a middle-aged man!'

'So? We're soul mates.'

I almost laughed out loud. Almost, but I didn't. 'Soul mates? I've never heard anything so ridiculous! He's nearly fifty, you're seventeen! You were sixteen when you made the album!' And then I was falling, falling, falling, knowing I was about to hit the bottom but suspended in denial until that final earth-shattering moment. 'Oh God, please tell me nothing actually happened between the two of you.'

She looked me dead in the eye. '*Everything* happened,' she said.

ALORA

WE MIGHT'VE CLICKED FROM THAT VERY first session, but the more time Silas and I spent together, the more we wrote music together, the more deeply we merged. He had this way of making me feel like I was the most interesting person who'd ever lived, like he was hanging off my every word. I would tell him some irrelevant teenage drivel about my day and he would tilt his head and rest his chin on his fist and say, 'That's absolutely fascinating! Tell me more!'

Then he'd ask a million questions about how or why or what. He encouraged me to dig down into all of my most painful experiences and embrace them, allow them to infiltrate my art. He said shame as a concept did not exist—everything was simply raw material, a kind of emotional clay to be shaped and moulded into something beautiful. For the very first time in my life, I began to actually like myself. I felt like I could say anything to him and he wouldn't judge me for it. So one night, sitting in the studio, I told him the truth, something that I'd never told anyone before—that

Dad's death was my fault. And he listened so attentively, with such kindness and compassion, and when I cried he held me to his chest and comforted me. And it was liberating, to share the terrible secret I'd been carrying alone for so long. He took it from me and cradled it in his hands and I saw myself for the first time as he saw me—something dark and precious and rare.

After that, the music we were making together reached mind-blowing levels of incredible. At the end of every session, we'd listen to the finished track on the studio speakers and stare at each other in disbelief.

'You're on fire, kid,' he'd say.

Then he'd pull me towards him in one of his big bear hugs. But it wasn't me, it was the combination of the two of us that was magical. I knew we'd made a number one album even before we'd finished recording it.

One evening, we stayed up late in his suite at the Clarice Hotel, watching movies together and drinking wine. It was the first time he'd let me drink in front of him—he was usually really strict about that. He was a serious wine connoisseur and I loved him telling me about the places each bottle was from, which were just faraway dots on a map to me back then, and ordering different bottles on room service for me to taste. By two AM I was exhausted, falling asleep in my chair, but I was having such a nice time I didn't want the evening to end, and I didn't want to be apart from him. So I asked him to come to bed with me. I knew how it sounded as soon as I said the words out loud, but I honestly didn't mean it like that. I just wanted him to hug me as I closed my eyes. I didn't want to be alone. There was this excruciating, elongated silence and then he said no. He said he was old enough to be my daddy. He talked about crossing the line. But when I explained what I meant, flushing almost purple with embarrassment, practically pleading, he eventually agreed. I brushed my teeth and washed my face. Then we both lay down on the bed, fully clothed, and I fell asleep in his arms. His arms were still wrapped around me when I woke up in the morning, my cheek pressed up against his chest. And I felt so happy. I felt safe and I felt loved.

'Morning, kid,' he said, when I stirred. He kissed me gently on my forehead and I nuzzled closer to him. It was then, quite out of nowhere, that he started talking about Dad. I remember his exact words.

'Your daddy would be real proud of you,' he said. 'The album's incredible. It's just such a shame he's not here to hear it for himself.' I froze and he must've felt it, because he tightened his grip around me. 'You really loved him, didn't you?' I said that I did. I said that I missed him so much. 'But you killed him, right, didn't you, Alora? That's what you told me, and it's true, isn't it? You killed your own daddy.' I began to cry then, deep desperate tears which seemed to flow from my heart rather than my eyes. 'Shush, shush, little one,' Silas said, and began to stroke my hair and plant gentle kisses on my cheeks. So I guess when he kissed my lips, it didn't seem all that strange, an extension of his care and affection, just another part of his body pressed against mine. I didn't even think to ask him to stop, my body didn't feel like it belonged to me anymore. I tried to ignore his sour morning breath and sandpaper stubble. He slipped his hand under my vest, then worked it down towards my thighs. He knew I'd never done it before, that the guys and girls I'd hooked up with at gigs had never been more than a fleeting kiss. He knew that about me, because he knew everything—I had told him everything.

Afterwards, I stood in the shower for nearly an hour, trying to make sense of it or maybe not wanting to. And later that day in the studio, when I sang for him, standing in the vocal booth behind the glass, shivering for no apparent reason whilst he sat at the mixing desk like nothing had changed between us, I heard the new rawness in my voice, the sharp edge of pain which with it brought so much beauty—it's the quality the journalists always try to describe but never quite can.

I glance at Vanessa. She's biting her lip and looks very pale. I ask her if she's okay and she says not really. 'Alora,' she says. 'That's rape.'

My heart begins to thud very heavily in my chest, a cold stone repeatedly knocking against my rib cage. 'No, it's not. How can it be? I didn't say no, not out loud.'

'Doesn't matter. You were sixteen years old. You were a minor. In Texas and New York and many other US states for that matter, the age of consent's seventeen. And where he's from, California, it's even older—eighteen!'

'But we were in the UK, in London, the age of consent's sixteen. It was legal.' I can hear the panic rising in my own voice, the escalation of my tone up the octaves into practically a screech at the thought of that word, that label, applying for what happened between us.

'Was it? I don't know about that, we'd need to consult a lawyer to be sure. But what about when you were at that Hollywood party with him, the birthday of that PR woman you told me about. Did you do it then too?' I nod, swallow hard. 'Well, that sure wasn't legal, he was on home turf. And it doesn't sound to me like you ever even wanted to.'

'But I did! I mean, maybe not the first time, but after that I'd sometimes be the one to instigate it—in the studio, the apartment, back at his hotel.'

'And did you ever ask yourself why?'

'I...I...' I can barely bring myself to say it, to admit it even to myself. I drop my eyes, I can't look at her. For the same reason I took his signet ring and burned an *S* into my skin. 'Because I was scared he'd stop loving me if I didn't.'

EVA

THEY USED TO EAT DINNER TOGETHER in fancy restaurants. After a recording session she often went back to his hotel suite to watch movies with him. He took her to celebrity parties where he introduced her to the glitterati as his muse. I'd often hanker after an invite for myself but one was never forthcoming. 'He doesn't like hanging out with the business,' she used to tell me. 'He's all about the talent.'

I could've asked the question, I could've probed harder, delved deeper beneath the surface of her blossoming friendship with this much older, Grammy Award–winning mega-producer. But I didn't—why? And by this point I was clutching at my stomach, feeling sick in a way that I knew was nothing to do with the fish tacos. 'You won't tell anyone, will you?' she said. She looked afraid. 'Promise me you won't.' I said that I wouldn't, but I knew that I had to.

I practically sprinted back down the corridor to my hotel room. I fumbled with my phone, dropped it on the floor, picked it up again, my vision blurring, certain I was about to throw up.

I called the MD, and at first he harped on about some new artist signed to Low Slang who was looking for new management and I just wanted him to shut the fuck up so I could speak because I was really panicking, my breath short and shallow, my head spinning with his name, the image of a puckered red *S* seared into her pale skin. I recounted her story word for word and once I'd finished, I steeled myself for his response. I genuinely expected him to be horrified, to say we needed to call the police, to cancel all future sessions between Low Slang artists and Silas Jax and speak to every young female he'd ever worked with, of which there were so many, to ask them to speak their truths.

What actually happened was this. He laughed and said, 'What can I say? Silas likes the ladies.'

It took me a beat to compose myself. 'Did you just hear what I said?'

'Every word, Eva.'

'She's hardly a lady. She was sixteen when he . . .' I couldn't bring myself to say the word. 'A girl, a child.'

'A teenager. It's legal, isn't it?'

'I don't know, is it?'

'I'm sure. The age of consent's sixteen.'

'But would that make it okay, in the circumstances?'

'What circumstances?'

'He's in a position of power, authority.'

'He's not her teacher. Come on, Eva, lighten up. We're in show business. It's not the same as working in a fucking bank. She had sex with him—no big deal, he's a good-looking guy, beautiful women throw themselves at him all the time, he used to date Coco Cassidy, for fuck's sake. Silas Jax is an important part of this project, an important part of a lot of projects on the

Low Slang roster and what's more he's a close personal friend of mine, we holiday together in the Maldives every year. I can personally vouch for his good character. Alora clearly has no issue with what went on between them so let's not turn it into one.'

'I wouldn't say she has no issue. She's pretty messed up about it, she's saying she's in love with him.'

'Well, there you go then! She's in love, she's happy!'

'He's nearly fifty years old!'

'Age is but a number!'

'She branded herself, with his ring!'

'He didn't force her to do it! And how is it any different from getting a tattoo, really?'

'It should never have happened!'

'It's in the past!' He sighed, as though he was tiring of the conversation. 'Look, Eva, let's face facts. There's a lot at stake here. A second album is always . . . tricky, shall we say, and we need Silas on board to even have a shot at the same level of success as the first. Dragging his name through the mud will ultimately do the same to Alora's and could completely derail her career and, I'm sure it goes without saying, yours too. Do you really want to get all mixed up in a scandal? My advice is just call Dr Laurel and let him handle this.'

When I look back on it now, I almost can't believe how quickly the self-doubt began to seep into my mind—was I was overreacting, making a fuss, being too prudish? Then I began to think about the global news story which would ultimately be unleashed if we went to the police, the salacious headlines, how powerful men like the MD would side with Silas and attempt to silence Alora, one word against another, how stressful and damaging that could be to her mental health, to her career and, of course, to my own. The taunts of my high-school bullies ringing in my ears had finally begun to fade. Because I was a somebody—powerful, respected, revered. Everybody in the music business wanted to know me. Everybody took my calls. Every door had been kicked wide open and I was commanding all of the rooms. I couldn't give that up. I should've done the right thing. But instead, I kept my mouth shut.

ALORA

'OH, ALORA.' VANESSA'S VOICE IS THICK with pity. 'That bastard!' She reaches for me but I move away.

'And it was good between us, we were good. But then I went on tour and ruined everything. I started calling him up every night, begging him to fly out to see me. He always refused, he said he was too busy and a million other excuses, so in the end I said I'd just go to him, that I'd cancel the entire tour and give up my career to be with him. That's when he told me that he was with someone else, some new artist he was working with. He said he'd still love to work with me in future but just 'as friends'. I screamed at him. I called him a liar, a cheat, I told him I wished I'd never met him. But every night when I got back to my hotel room I felt so alone and missed him so much that I couldn't help phoning him, waiting for his voicemail to click in, leaving a grovelling, desperate, drunken message. He never called me back. So I started dating someone just to make him jealous—this actor, Noah Lamb. I should never have done it, he's a nice guy and I was just using him. And I drank myself into oblivion and took every drug I could get my hands on just to try and forget.'

'And did it work?'

'Obviously not. And the thing is, I tell myself I hate him, I refused to work with him on my second album even though I was terrified that I couldn't make it without him, like I wasn't talented enough by myself. But the line between love and hate is practically invisible, a hairline fracture, I learnt that from my parents' marriage. I met his new girlfriend at my eighteenth birthday party, she's so beautiful. He introduced her to me as his muse. It's what he used to call me.'

Vanessa takes hold of my hand and grips it so tightly, it actually hurts, and her voice when she speaks is filled with urgency and passion. 'Doll, listen to me. He's a monster. He groomed you and he manipulated you and he raped you. Those kind of guys, they prey on the vulnerable. Mark my words you won't be the first he's reeled in and you certainly won't be the last. You have to go to the police, Alora. You have to stop him from doing it again.'

'But—'

'Absolutely no buts. And what's all this nonsense about you killing your daddy?'

But just then Politician claps his hands and Vanessa and I stop talking. It's dark now and the moon has switched positions with the sun. I can just about make out the shape of him, the square jaw and rotund belly bulging through the white tunic. He says that as no consensus has been reached amongst the group as to a plan and night has fallen, the best we can do is wrap ourselves up in the blankets and huddle together for warmth. Then at dawn, he'll set out to find help.

'They'll come back for us before then,' Python says. 'Surely? We're paying them thirty grand a month.'

'Exactly,' Rich Kid says. 'They're trying to kill us off and get access to our bank accounts.'

'Don't be ridiculous,' Vanessa says. 'They'll never get access to mine, they're all offshore in Switzerland.' A squabble erupts and Best Supporting Actress starts to cry again. I allow my right hand to move towards my left wrist and search for the scar with my thumb. I press. It's still tender. The pain shoots up my arm and my eyes smart. Suddenly, Vanessa grabs hold of my hand. 'Don't,' she says.

'Don't what?'

'I know what you're doing and you don't need to do it.'

I snatch my hand away from her. 'You don't know what I need.'

'Yes,' she says. 'I do. You need unconditional love. You need to be told that you're enough. That whoever you want to be or don't want to be, that's okay. That you can be the biggest most successful recording artist of all time or you can be an absolute nobody who sits at home watching TV all day and doesn't even bother to put the trash out. And you will still be loved regardless. You will still be loved.'

I can see the whites of her eyes in the darkness, wide and wild and true. Rich Kid is squaring up to Politician and Politician is asking him to calm down. 'You need to live,' I say quietly. 'We both do.'

I wake up next to her. Our bodies are covered by the same woollen blanket, our arms touching at the elbow. I'm not shivering because she's next to me and her skin is emitting a mild, persistent warmth. The sky is morning grey with a smattering of gauze-like cloud. A gull swoops overhead and caws, moves on when it realises we have nothing to offer. The tide is out and the shore has reclaimed the seabed, which is dotted with shells, sheens of pearly white and pink. I take a deep breath, and then another and I am alive, I am alive, I am alive.

These words are still fluxing through my mind when Elijah appears from between the trees and greets us with a cheery, 'Hello, folks!' He walks towards us waving his arms in the air.

Best Supporting Actress gasps and exclaims in an almost sexily breathless voice, 'Thank God!'

Rich Kid jumps up, runs towards Elijah and punches him in the face.

EVA

THE DAY AFTER HER EIGHTEENTH BIRTHDAY PARTY, I drove over to her house and sat with her in the living room as she stared at the front page of *The Sun*, at the photograph of her standing next to Silas and his new project, smiling lightly with a personalised cocktail in her hand. She said nothing. She laid the paper down on the top of the coffee table and lit a cigarette.

I said I was sorry and she said I didn't need to be, that it was 'just one of those things'. I suggested that she talk it through with Dr Laurel. She said she'd decided to stop seeing him.

I looked up sharply. 'Since when?'

'Since last week. I'm sick of going over the same old shit.' I asked if she was still taking the antidepressants to which she responded, 'I don't need them. I'm totally fine.'

Her eyes emitted a joyless cheer, like she was a shop assistant in a department store telling me to 'have a nice day'. I glanced at her housekeeper who seemed to be loitering unnecessarily by the door and cleared my throat. The woman scurried away.

'Okay, if you say so. Now let's discuss this touring schedule.'

In the run-up to album release she spent the next few months making music videos, attending photo shoots, performing live sessions on mainstream radio stations and being asked the same questions over and over again by unimaginative journalists who were practically drooling at the opportunity to try to trick her into admitting something juicy, giving them the latest controversial scoop. When I look back on it now I can see that she wasn't herself. She wasn't happy or miserable or anything in between. There was a hollow numbness to her demeanour which I was, in all honesty, too busy to notice. And *busy* was my preferred state. I'd been unceremoniously dumped at Alora's eighteenth birthday party by the love of my life—I threw myself into my work with obsessive vigour. There was the album campaign to plan, the tour to oversee, a million brand deals amounting to millions of pounds in revenue to negotiate and invoice for. I didn't eat, I barely slept, I had my mobile phone practically glued to my ear. I hired an assistant, Marie, so that I could delegate the remedial tasks and take on more. I was an emailing, call-taking, deal-closing artist-management machine. I refused to allow myself the time to feel anything at all. Then the album shot straight to number one and we set off for Edinburgh, for the first date of the sold out *Beautiful Nightmare* world tour.

On the eve of the first show, I was woken in the middle of the night by someone banging on the door of my hotel suite, hammering at it like they were trying to break it down. I sat up, groggy in the darkness, and slung my legs over the side of the unfamiliar bed. My phone was vibrating against the bedside cabinet, a hard, unforgiving sound. I grappled for it and squinted into the screen. It was one o'clock in the morning and Marie was calling me. I answered.

'What the fuck? Do you know what time it is?'

She was screaming. And at first I couldn't make out the words, the pitch was so piercing, the speech so jumbled. And then I was running out of my hotel room in my pyjamas with the spare key card to Alora's suite in my sweating palm, sprinting down the corridors closely followed by Marie with my phone pressed to my ear and then I was the one who was screaming. To the woman at the end of the line in emergency services to 'send an ambulance to the Edinburgh Grand Hotel, the penthouse, right now!' And I was begging, please hurry, please, as I slotted the key card into the door, as I ran through the lounge beneath the chandelier, and flung open the French doors leading into the bathroom.

And there she was. And at first when I saw her I didn't believe it was real. It looked so much like any other scene from one of her music videos—the gown, the pale skin, the long blonde hair—life imitating art. But this time the blood wasn't fake. Her mobile phone was balanced on the taps, livestreaming it all on z-pix. Her Teacup Chihuahua was cowering in the corner of the room in a puddle of its own piss, whining like it knew. I ran towards her, hooked her beneath the arms and tried to pull her from the crimson water. Marie was standing behind me wailing and I ordered her to help me, to grab the phone and turn it off, but she didn't move. Alora murmured something incomprehensible. She was slipping in and out of consciousness and I was saying her name, saying please stay with me, please, when I realised that she was smiling—that she looked the happiest I'd seen her in years.

Beautiful Nightmare—A Disappointing Departure from the Darkest Heart in Pop

Beautiful Nightmare—the eagerly anticipated second album from international Misery Pop sensation Alora Storm-Jones—is her first foray away from legendary producer Silas Jax, and boy, does it show. Vocals aside, which are saturated with her trademark gut-wrenching blend of power, purity and grit, eight out of nine tracks are barely recognisable from its multiplatinum-selling, critically acclaimed predecessor, *The Truth*.

In contrast to Jax's subtle, minimalist production style, stepping demurely to the side to allow the thoughtful words and intricate melodies to the fore, every crevice of *Beautiful Nightmare* is jammed full of fast-paced pop electronica and pounding basslines which barge through the centre of the songs and demand to be let inside ahead of the queue. The result is certainly explosive if a little crass, and the list of Alora's co-writers and collaborators reads like the who's who of the music industry hot list, from Glitzy Gilbert to Danny 'Dans' Cosmos to Ellie M Lennox.

Lyrically, the album feels muddled and confused, talking of failed relationships and depression as though emotional pain is a commodity to be flaunted and exploited, and the messaging is barely recognisable in part and yet too obvious in others. 'Liar Liar' is a somewhat cringeworthy attempt to capitalise on the very public breakdown of her relationship with actor Noah Lamb, 'Gone' laments the loss of childhood as an anonymous sixteen-year-old girl (quite clearly Alora) is clamped between the jaws of fame and 'Dollar Signs' with the line 'Nah nah nah, all I see is green eyes / you only love me baby cos you want my dollar signs' sounds like it's been lifted straight off a KAZY-K B-sides album. Only lead single 'Anybody' gives us a glimpse of the old Alora we know and love, which according to the credits, she wrote alone.

But what *Beautiful Nightmare* may lack in authenticity and relatability for the everyday teen, it certainly makes up for in cinematic pop dynamite, and with the troubles in her private life filling more newspaper columns than reviews of her music and the streams still racking up in their billions, perhaps for Alora authenticity and relatability are no longer a concern. A disappointment on many levels, but predicted to dominate the number one spot globally for weeks on end as the loyal fan base—like feral cats around a saucer of cream—will lap it up regardless.

EVA

AFTER WE DROPPED HER OFF AT the Max Beaumont Centre for Wellness, I climbed back into the helicopter with her mother. I felt terrible. Leaving Alora on that remote Scottish island was like leaving an essential part of myself behind, a kidney or a lung.

'Fancy a drink?' Julia said. The propellers whirred and the helicopter lurched upwards. I said that I just wanted to go home. 'Fine,' she said. 'I'll come back to yours.' I didn't have the energy to object.

Julia walked around my house like she was an estate agent trying to make a sale, commenting on the abundance of storage space and the benefits of en suite bathrooms in all of the bedrooms. She asked me when I'd bought the place and I said it was just after *The Truth* went to number one. 'It's very big for just you,' she said.

'Yeah, well . . . my boyfriend moved in with me but then we broke up so . . .'

'I'm sorry to hear that. Men are such shits.'

'Actually, this one isn't.'

I went into the living room and flopped down on the sofa whilst Julia busied herself in the kitchen. She appeared at the door with a bottle of white wine, two glasses and a family-sized bag of peanut M&M's which she must have found at the back of a cupboard because I hadn't been shopping in months and Ade had cleared out all of his food when he left. The shutters were still closed and I hadn't switched on the lights.

'Shall I?' she said, gesturing to the bay window.

I told her to leave them. I wanted to sit in darkness, I couldn't face the day. I'd spent the past week making statements to the press, fielding questions and accusations with Shona by my side, dealing with the hellish logistics of cancelling a world tour and instructing lawyers as we played a constant game of whack-a-mole with the footage. Because every time we took it down from one place it sprang back up again somewhere else. The backlash against z-pix was fierce: marches in Trafalgar Square, emergency meetings at the White House and House of Commons, as celebrities and musicians and other people of profile shut their accounts and the public followed. Jared Brisk was last photographed climbing into his spacecraft, fleeing the planet.

The response from the fans was overwhelming. They congregated outside her homes with candles held up to the sky, tied letters and bouquets of flowers to her gates. The paparazzi were a small crowd in comparison, shunted to the side. And its impact on album sales was phenomenal. The critics may have slated it but *Beautiful Nightmare* was at number one in fourteen markets and the streaming figures were skyrocketing.

Julia handed me a glass of wine. I drained it and handed it back to her to refill. 'I feel so guilty,' I said.

'How do you think I feel? I'm her mum for God's sake. Everyone always blames the mother, that's where they point the finger first. But believe me when I say it wasn't easy. Having a young daughter and an addict for a husband was no joke. When she called her album *The Truth* I actually thought she was being ironic, because the truth was something my daughter always seemed to struggle with.'

I reached for the M&M's and tipped a generous handful into my mouth. 'It's so sad that she never came to terms with what happened, to Billy I mean.'

'But the thing is, I honestly thought she was over all that. She hadn't mentioned it for years, but I guess that was just wishful thinking on my part.' She laughed a little. 'I know it's not funny, but I guess delusions were something she and Billy had in common. I mean seriously, what kind of man changes his surname by deed poll to Storm-Jones? Someone who can't stand the thought that they're just ordinary old Mr Jones, that's what.'

'He was a talented musician, though, wasn't he?'

'Oh, he was incredible! I honestly thought I'd married the next Paul McCartney. Then he started using with the drummer after gigs, and when he was out of it the man could barely stand never mind sing. He got a reputation for being unreliable. Promoters stopped booking him after a run of no-shows. His own band kicked him out. That's when he began pedalling his kid around town, busking in the street and keeping the cash for himself to buy God knows what. She was quite the novelty, this beautiful little fairy-like thing with a huge power voice. It was sad really, she adored him and he was just using her. But I was still jealous, if you can believe it. I was jealous of my own daughter because of the attention she received from my husband. And he knew it as well. Whenever we fought and he stormed out, he always took her with him, just to get at me.' She took a sip of her wine and moved a strand of hair away from her face. 'You know, having a kid, you go into it with all these good intentions, thinking you're going to give them the best life, the life you never had. But you just can't help being you, you can't help fucking it all up with your own stupid issues.'

'You didn't fuck it all up.'

'Didn't I? My little girl's in rehab after trying to kill herself. I wouldn't say that's a sign that I did a brilliant job of motherhood.'

I reached over and took hold of Julia's hand. 'Hey, she's a good person. She's strong, she's determined, she'll get through this. And besides, you must've been practically a teenager yourself when you had her.'

'I was twenty-one, and before you ask, no, it wasn't planned. It was terrible timing, actually, I'd just signed my record deal with Hi-go Records and was about to go off on tour. Billy was coming with me, I'd persuaded my band to let him play guitar. We didn't need another guitarist, but I wanted him up onstage with me. I never wanted him out of my sight.'

I set down my glass on the coffee table. 'Hang on, *what? You* were the one signed to Hi-go?'

'Sure was. A three-album deal.'

'But . . . I always thought that was Billy?'

'Is that what she told you?' She shook her head sadly. 'No, it was me. I packed it all in, though, to have Alora. Even in times of supposed equality between the sexes it still tends to always be the women who make the big career sacrifices, doesn't it?'

I stared at Julia. She looked tired, her curls were hanging limp and her lipstick was smudged, but I looked into her eyes and for the first time, I saw that her eyes were green. I saw that her eyes were Alora's.

ALORA

THE CARERS ARE WAITING FOR US when we disembark from the minibus. Maureen wraps me up tight in a heated blanket. Rich Kid is bundled into the back of a car by two thickset men in heavy boots and the medics apply an ice pack to Elijah's nose and the ripe bruise circling his left eye.

'Looks like it was an eventful trip,' Maureen says.

'It was fucking awful and I stink and I'm starving and my shoes are filled with sand, but it was also amazing and I'd kind of like to do it all again.' I tell her I want to take a long hot bath, change into clean clothes, then eat a three-course dinner with second helpings of dessert. 'Where are we going?' I say, when I realise she's not actually leading me towards my chalet. I look around for Vanessa but she seems to have disappeared.

'You're going straight to a session with Seren,' Maureen says. She lifts her palm as I open my mouth. 'Don't waste your breath. This is all part of the Method. You can have a bath and stuff yourself senseless straight afterwards.'

Seren smiles. I smile back. I'm tired and my teeth feel furry.

My hair is unbrushed and unwashed and gritty with sand, a twig practically woven into my fringe. I make no effort to remove it. I cross my ankles and lean back in my chair.

'So,' I say. 'What do you want to talk about today?'

Seren adjusts her glasses and sniffs. 'Sometimes,' she says slowly, carefully, 'we have to ask ourselves whether the stories we tell ourselves are true.'

I ask her if she's read the letters to my parents and she says that she has. My vision starts to blur. I shut my eyes tightly and follow the pulsating blotches of violet and green which swirl and merge and part again. After a while, I open them. It's time to face the truth.

I was waiting for him outside the men's toilets in Ravello's. He'd just met with his dealer and had gone inside to shoot up. He'd promised to take me to see the sea at the weekend. I'd never seen the sea. But Dad always made promises which he rarely kept. I knew he was taking too long, that something wasn't right. I knocked on the door but he didn't answer. I called his name but there was no reply. I could've fetched someone, anyone, to help. I could've asked Nathan, the manager, or Leslie from behind the bar. But I didn't. I stood there, frozen in my fear, and I did nothing. The bouncers did a final sweep of the place before closing. They found him inside the locked cubicle, sitting on the toilet with a belt around his arm, me still standing sentinel outside the door.

I'm sobbing into my hands now as Seren comforts me. I'm twelve years old again, screaming hysterically as the paramedics try to prise me away from Dad's lifeless body.

'Listen to me, Alora,' Seren says, in such an authoritative tone that I sit up and stop crying. 'It was *not* your fault. *You* didn't buy the heroin. *You* didn't *make* your dad take it. *You* were a child. It was not your responsibility to look after your father. He was the parent. He should've been looking after *you*.'

EVA

MY SISTER MESSAGED ME AND SAID she wanted to meet for lunch. I said I couldn't, that I was far too busy and stressed. I watched as she typed her reply, the antagonising dots blinking, waiting for the guilt trip to come:

> I know you're having a hard time right now but
> please come, it's important . . . xx

We went to Pizza Express, the kind of corporate chain my sister and Arif favoured, usually because Arif had vouchers he'd cut off the back of a cereal box. Katerina ordered a Florentina pizza with extra cheese, I ordered Caesar salad, no anchovies, and a bottle of sauvignon blanc to share. She said I looked thin and I smiled grimly at her. She rubbed the top of my arm.

'She's going to be okay, you know. She's where she needs to be, getting professional help.' I said I knew this, that I'd done all I could. 'And what about you?' she said.

'What about me?'

'Are you seeing someone, a therapist, to talk? It must've been awful finding her like that. Are you having flashbacks? Nightmares? It's completely understandable if you are.' My phone pinged and I removed it from my bag. My sister looked a little irritated and dug into her pizza whilst I replied to the message. 'Something urgent?' she said.

'Just one of the marketing managers from the label. She wants to know if it's okay for her to post this shot of Alora on her socials.' I didn't look up whilst I was speaking, I carried on typing.

'You're still posting pictures of Alora on social media, even when she's in rehab?'

'Course. We can't neglect the brand.'

'Is that not a bit weird?'

I placed my phone down on the table and sighed. 'I don't tell you how to deliver babies, do I?'

Katerina raised her eyebrows. She opened her mouth, then closed it again as though she'd thought better of what she was about to say. 'Go on, spit it out,' I said.

'Nothing... it's just you're very different these days.' I asked her what she was talking about and she said that I was a little bit spiky. I told her it was disappointing that she, a self-professed feminist, was criticising a woman for being assertive.

'I'm not criticising anyone. I'm just saying that you used to be such a sweet little girl.'

'I am allowed to grow up, you know.'

'Oh I know, I'm not suggesting for one second that you're not. I'm just reminiscing, that's all. Oh my God, do you remember those lovely little comic strips you used to draw about the talking owl?'

'They were so stupid.'

'They were adorable! The main character was so obviously you, not that any of us would've ever said so. I felt so protective of you, Eva. When those girls did what they did to you, that awful name they used to call you, it absolutely broke my heart.'

I coughed into my napkin. 'Thanks, I appreciate you always looking out for me and everything, Kat, but no need to bring that up.'

'What was it again? Egg-Breath Eva?'

'I can't remember,' I lied. 'Anyway, I was such a loser back then, I probably deserved it.'

Katerina stopped eating and dropped a pizza crust onto her plate. 'What on earth are you talking about? You didn't deserve any of it! None of what happened was your fault! They singled you out because you weren't the same as them, because you were shy and gentle and kind. Even when they were making your life hell you were still trying to be nice to them. You invited them to your birthday party, do you remember?'

'Of course I remember!' I said snappily.

'And none of them came, not one person showed up. You sat at the kitchen table in front of all that food and tried to pretend that everything was fine. That's when Mum and Dad finally realised that it wasn't and went into the school.'

'Yeah, well, fat lot of good that did.'

'They moved house for you, Eva! Our parents uprooted their lives, left their jobs and their friends to get you away from them, so you'd never have to see any of them ever again! So I have to say we were all a little surprised when you went out of your way to make friends at college with a group of girls who were basically cut from the same cloth.'

I picked up my wine glass and drank deeply. 'That's unfair. Mimi, Petra, Mairead, they're nice people, they've been good friends to me.'

'They're *fake bitches*! They only started properly including you in their little gang when you started managing Alora and could get them on the guest list for all the best parties.' I said that wasn't true, but of course I knew it was. And in that moment I hated my sister for peeling away the tough, leathery skin I had so expertly cultivated which concealed so thinly the pink, tender person beneath. 'The only nice one out of the lot of them is Ade.'

'Yeah, well, we broke up so . . .'

'What? Why?' I was becoming weary, worn down by this line of honest talk. I skirted around the details and told her about the job he'd applied for at Low Slang. I said he was pissed off because he didn't get it, that I was supposed to have put a word in for him, 'like me having a word would've changed anything'.

I genuinely expected Katerina to agree with me, to take my side. Instead my sister said, 'Well, *did* you put a word in for him? *Did* you speak to the MD?'

'No, I didn't.'

'Why not?'

'I forgot. I was too busy.'

'Ade was a good friend to you, Eva. You going only slightly out of your way for him might've really changed the trajectory for him. I mean, when I had a word with Mrs Malone, you ended up getting the internship.'

My mouth hung open, exposing a swamp of mushed-up salad. '*What?*'

'You know about this, don't you? Or maybe Mum decided not to tell you in the end. The MD of Low Slang Records, Doug Malone, I delivered his twin girls. When Mum mentioned you'd applied for the internship I called his wife, Marianne, and asked whether she could pull some strings. She's a nice woman, we got on well, although I always thought her husband was a bit of a pig. She told me to leave it with her.' I said nothing. I stared at my sister. 'And whilst we're on the subject of Ade, wasn't it him who discovered Alora?'

'What are you talking about? That's insane! Why would you say that?'

'That's what he told Arif, at our engagement party. He said he'd sent you a video of her performing at her school concert, or something like that. Arif told him he should take the credit for it, particularly if he was keen to work in the music business himself. But Ade said no, he wanted all the credit to go to you, that men had been taking the credit for women's work for hundreds of years—the discovery of DNA and so on—and he wanted to do his bit to address the balance. I mean seriously, what a nice guy.'

I stood up. I threw my napkin onto the table. I picked up my sister's glass of wine which she didn't seem to have touched and downed it in one. I grabbed hold of my Prada handbag and marched out of the restaurant as my sister called out from behind me, 'By the way, in case you actually give a shit, I'm pregnant!'

ALORA

'AND WHAT NOW, ALORA?' SEREN SAYS. 'Where do you want this life to take you? You are the architect of your own destiny, after all.'

I think for a minute whilst she chews on the end of her pen. 'I know what I want,' I say. 'But I need to speak to someone first.'

EVA

AS SOON AS I GET HOME from lunch with my sister I run into my bedroom, fling myself down on the bed and pull the pillow over my head. It blocks out the light, but I can't hide from the truth. Katerina's right, about everything. Those girls did what they did and I transformed myself into a different person, a stereotypically 'cool girl', someone who would fit right in with the popular crowd and never get bullied again. I take out my phone to call Ade, knowing that he'll talk it through with me, comfort me and say the right thing, but then reality clobbers me over the head again—he's broken up with me, which is nothing less than I deserved. Instead I open up Instagram. I find the DM from Maddie Malkin, the ringleader of my high-school tormentors, and I write:

                                                      I forgive you x

Then before I have chance to reconsider, I press send. And as though the universe is miraculously responding with a delivery of instant karma, my phone rings in my hand. I recognise the number. It's Seren, Alora's therapist from the Beaumont Centre. After just over a month of no contact, a month, one week and two days of the total seclusion from society which Max Beaumont insists is necessary to achieve complete emotional and psychological healing, Alora wants to talk.

ALORA

I WAIT FOR HER IN THE therapy room. I'm alone with the six wooden chairs arranged in a circle, but I can almost feel Vanessa sitting by my side and that's reassuring. I hear the door open behind me but I do not turn. I hear heeled footsteps tapping across the wooden floorboards but still, I do not turn. I don't look up until she's standing right in front of me wearing a Gucci suit and an expression of gallant concern. She opens up her arms. I stand. We embrace stiffly. I sit back down. She takes a seat opposite me on the other side of the circle in Python's place.

'You look amazing,' she says. 'You look really . . . *amazing*.' I lift a smile and let it drop. It shatters on the ground into a million little pieces. 'I was so relieved when your therapist, Seren, am I saying her name right?' I nod. 'When she called and said that you wanted to see me. I've been so worried about you, I mean, I haven't been sleeping, not much anyway, sometimes less than an hour a night. I know I look terrible! I've aged about twenty years in a month. But enough about me. The album's still at number one in the UK, USA, Japan, France and Germany. Can you believe it? It's gone triple platinum in the UK already—it's crazy! You won't have enough walls for all the plaques! The MD's thrilled as you can imagine. He sends his love. He wants to extend the record deal, get you locked in—maybe not locked in, that's the wrong expression, secured—for another two albums but we can talk about all that once you're out of this place. When do you think that will be, by the way? No pressure, no pressure at all. Anyway, you do look really good. They say the food's amazing here. Have you been exercising? You look a lot stronger. You look like—'

I raise my hand and she stops talking. She shifts a little in her seat and I notice that her hands are shaking. Her cheeks and neck are blotching up. She's nervous. Because deep down, she knows what I'm about to say.

EVA

AND IT'S EMBARRASSING THAT I AM sitting in front of *her* a blubbering mess when *she's* the patient, the one in rehab. That all I can do is cry my way through the guilt, shame, disintegration of self into a person I don't recognise.

'It's all my fault!' I wail. And she doesn't tell me I'm wrong. My words are feeble, totally inadequate, but still I attempt an apology. For placing her in the jaws of a wolf. For not seeking the truth and when it sought me, burying it with pills, turning up the music to silence her screams. For pushing her into the spotlight when she wanted to step back into the shadows. For wearing the glittering cape of her success as though it belonged to me. For colluding with a monster and in doing so becoming a monster myself. I know and admit these things to her through my tears and she watches me, not coldly, but with an expression of alert intelligence, like the bullfinch in her garden, observing from a distance, weighing up the risks before deciding what to do. Then suddenly, without warning, she stands. She strides towards the door.

I stop crying, stunned into silence. 'Where are you going?' I ask.

She rests one hand on the doorframe and turns towards me and the light is low but she's still shining, just like the day I met her. 'To Texas,' she says.

ALORA

I BURST INTO VANESSA'S CHALET. SHE'S lying in the bathtub, suds up to her chin, reading a magazine which she must've smuggled in somehow and which she drops into the water when she startles.

'Jesus, is it not customary to knock in Scotland?'

'You know when you invited me to stay with you in Texas, did you mean it?'

She fishes the sodden magazine out of the water and places it on the bath mat. 'Doll, I *never* say things I don't mean.'

'Cool. Well, how would you feel if I took you up on the invite, like, right now?'

Vanessa stares at me for a long solemn moment, and her face is so unnaturally smooth that there's no hint of an expression to read. But then her lips curl into a smile. 'I'd feel pretty goddamn jubilant. Let's get the hell out of this loony bin, I say!'

I rush out of her chalet with not so much spring in my step as a bound, a positive leap. And smack straight into none other than Max Beaumont himself, disembarked from his golf buggy and deep in conversation with Maureen. Maureen doesn't look entirely comfortable. She's fiddling with the hem of her tunic, her usually sparkling eyes creased into mild anxiety. But when she sees me she smiles. 'There you are! I was just looking for you. I—'

'I'm leaving!' I announce before she can even finish the sentence, aware that I'm almost shouting, one step away from punching the air with my fist.

Maureen opens her mouth just as Max Beaumont steps forwards and says in a hypnotically charming voice, 'Ah, Alora Storm-Jones, I've been reading your notes, a fascinating case. Let's step inside for a moment, shall we?'

Soon I'm sitting in my chalet on the edge of my bed as Max Beaumont talks to me about 'support networks' and 'relapses' and 'risk', each word a pellet fired from between his lips which chips away at the fragile porcelain of my plan. Perhaps, he suggests, I should stay for a few more days, maybe a week, have a few more sessions with Seren, to be certain I'm 'ready' for the outside world. I feel like a deflating helium balloon. Resignation seeps into my bones—maybe I should just stay here forever? But just then someone bangs on my chalet door with the force of a battering ram. Maureen answers it and Vanessa blows into the room like a hurricane. She's still wearing the compulsory white tunic but it's now paired with black leather cowboy boots and she's lugging two gigantic suitcases behind her, heels clomping determinedly across the floorboards.

'Step away from the celebrity!' she orders. She barges past Max, takes hold of my hand and pulls me up from the bed. 'Come on, doll, your carriage awaits. And by carriage, I mean helicopter.'

Max raises his hand. 'One moment, please. I was just saying that it might be best for Alora to stay—'

Vanessa turns to him, teeth bared. 'Best for your bank balance more like! We've done the minimum stint, we're here of our own free will. So fetch our personal belongings now or believe me, this ain't going to be pretty.'

We take the helicopter to Heathrow where we board a private jet. Vanessa sits by the window and runs her hand across the polished mahogany interior. 'Very fancy. I haven't flown private since the nineties.'

'Really? I kind of hate it. I fly everywhere like this and I feel like a dick and it's terrible for the environment.'

'If the environment's your concern then maybe you should travel the world in a horse and cart for your next tour.'

I pull down the blind. 'Who says there'll be a next tour?'

The journey is long and turbulent. I gasp with every drop, the flight attendant occasionally stumbling down the aisle to offer us drinks and snacks which slide off the table the moment they're set down, the FASTEN SEATBELT sign glaring at us like an angry eye. Vanessa takes hold of my hand and squeezes it. With the other she grips the armrest with white knuckles. I feel afraid, but my fear feels strangely validating, comforting almost, like I'm valuing life enough to care whether we fall from the sky and plummet to our deaths. We don't, and eventually we reach Austin. Before we disembark Vanessa unzips one of her cases and hands me a cowboy hat. 'For you,' she says, with a perfectly straight face so I suppress the urge to laugh. I put it on, tucking my hair up inside it. The hat is white and studded with rhinestones. I feel like Dolly Parton but without the gigantic tits. Our passports are checked on board the plane and the cabbie collects us directly off the runway. He glances at me a couple of times as he lugs my case into the boot as though wondering where he's met me before, trying to place me, but if he figures it out he doesn't say so. It's unbelievably humid here, like the air is sweat which mingles with your own to form a slick, sticky layer beneath your clothes. Vanessa says she can't wait to strip off and swim in the creek.

'It's kind of crazy you can't swim,' she says. 'Don't they teach kids in England, or something?'

'Yeah they do, in school. But Julia wrote me sick notes so I could skip it.'

'Why would she do that?'

'Because I was scared of water.'

'Hmm, mollycoddling the kid never does anyone any favours in the long run.' I'd never thought of Julia as a mollycoddler, I had thought of her as a cold, distant stranger with whom I happened to share a flat. But as Seren said, we should question the stories we tell ourselves.

Julia once told me about the day she met Dad. It was after he'd gone and I think she thought hearing about the past might help me come to terms with the present. He apparently stuck his head round the door of the rehearsal room and said he could hear her from Studio C, that he had to meet the woman with *that voice*. He kissed her hand, acted all chivalrous. He asked her if she'd sing backing vocals for his band and she laughed at him and said, 'Sweetie, I'm signed to Hi-go Records. I'm making my own album. I don't sing backing vocals for nobody.'

He asked for her number and she refused to give it to him. But the following day, he just showed up at her house—he'd asked around at the studio and somehow got hold of her address. He stood outside in the street with his guitar and sang a song he'd written about her whilst she stood in the doorway laughing. And he didn't stop singing until she agreed to go on a date with him. But all that was before I was born. She used to sing around the flat sometimes. I would hear her whilst she was making dinner or vacuuming, when she thought no one was listening. But as I grew older and Dad's addictions took their hold she stopped singing altogether. Her voice was like nothing I'd ever heard. She had a voice which could entice the stars out of the sky.

I still haven't switched on my phone. Not so long ago I would've dived straight into the vicious comments, gorged on them until I was stuffed to the gills with hate. But as soon as the Beaumont Centre handed it back to me I packed it away in my suitcase, right at the bottom, swaddled in a sock. I know that I'll have to face it sometime, to face *them*, that I'll be sucked back in and dragged back down into the whirling vortex of public opinion. But for now I just want to exist in this blissful bubble of ignorance, to pretend that this could be my life.

We drive for hours, through desolate towns with a single rusting petrol pump beneath a creaking sign, where children on bicycles congregate in dusty streets eating ripe peaches, through barren red terrain where there is nothing more than sun and soil.

As though she can read my mind Vanessa says, 'I did tell you it's remote. And we live in a valley so you probably won't even get cell reception.'

I say that suits me fine. I take a sip of now-tepid water, then I close my eyes. For the rest of the journey I remain somewhere between sleep and wake, dream and reality, lulled by the movement of the car, the warm jets of humidity occasionally breaking through the air-conditioning. I open my eyes when I feel we're slowing to see a dirt track which twists and winds through pasture, a herd of horses, their heads buried in tall dry grasses. I see a magnificent ranch house built from wood with a pitched roof and a veranda, a rocking chair positioned on each side of the door as though ready for lazy Sunday afternoons with the day's paper and good strong coffee. I see a guy sitting out on the veranda, maybe older than me but not by much. He lifts his head, followed by his hand—I'm guessing this must be Dylan. Then a tiny head pops up at his feet.

'Who's that?' I say.

'Oh, that's Evelyn,' Vanessa says. 'Dylan's daughter, the sweetest child who ever walked this earth.'

Dylan swings the little girl up into his arms. He walks towards the cab, jiggling her as she giggles and squirms. He's tall with broad shoulders, dark hair, tanned skin and the rosy glow of good home-cooked food and a life spent outdoors far away from laptops and violent video games. The child is fair—blonde with red-berry lips, Disney-blue eyes, adorably chubby cheeks. She wears her hair in two long braids, tied at the ends with yellow ribbon. Vanessa climbs out of the cab first and I hang back as the three of them reunite, not wanting to intrude. Dylan hugs his aunt and the kid reaches out and pats her cheek, takes hold of a strand of her hair and tugs on it gently. I hear Dylan say that Vanessa looks well, I hear Vanessa call Evelyn her little pumpkin. I notice that Dylan's hair is shorter on one side than the other as though he's cut it himself with the kitchen scissors. His jawline is covered in stubble like he hasn't been near a razor in days. I wonder if there are any at the house, hiding at the back of the bathroom cabinet. I crowbar the thought from my mind.

Dylan looks up and smiles. 'Hey, howdy,' he says. 'Aren't you going to introduce us, Aunty V?'

Vanessa clears her throat theatrically as though about to make a grand announcement. 'Dylan, please meet our guest of honour, Alora Storm-Jones.'

And I wait for the recognition. I wait for him to tell me how much he loved my last album followed by an in-depth explanation of what track was his favourite and why. I wait for him to pull out his phone and take a selfie of us together. I wait for him to say he watched it live on z-pix and ask me why I did it, why, when I had everything anyone could possibly dream of, was it not enough. And when he does none of these things initially, I'm a little bit stunned. He transfers Evelyn to Vanessa's arms, walks towards me and extends his hand. I slot mine into it where it fits snugly like a nail into wood, tongue into groove, and meet his eyes, which are hazel and kind. He says it's good to meet me or some other generic politeness and I find myself reaching up and removing the cowboy hat, but it makes no difference, it instigates no further reaction from him.

'And this,' he says, turning to gesture behind him, 'is my little girl, Evelyn.'

The child observes me with sceptical curiosity. I've got no idea how old she is, two, maybe three. But she's small, a miniature human. She's wearing a white smock dress with a frilly collar and red leather sandals. Her fingers are tiny, her nails like specks of mother-of-pearl.

'Say howdy, Evelyn,' Dylan instructs, and the child buries her head in her great-aunt's shoulder.

It's not a response I'm used to. Dylan laughs and says that she's shy with strangers. He picks up our suitcases as though they're filled with cotton candy and we follow him into the house.

And as soon as I step through the front door, I feel it, the peace—like stepping into the glade of a forest. This house is a living creature, welcoming me, drawing me inside. There are three large slouchy sofas in front of a stone fireplace, a tasselled rug interwoven with a symmetrical design. A ceiling fan whips at the air overhead like a ship's propeller. I half expect to see pictures of Vanessa in her modelling days all over the walls but there aren't any, only photos of family—a small child dressed in cowboy boots with his shirt tucked into belted jeans, a handsome dark-haired teenager shying away from the camera or racing round a barrel on the back of a chestnut horse, the animal's heels turfing up huge gusts of sand in its haste—Dylan.

Vanessa lowers Evelyn to the floor and the child scoots away. She flops backwards onto one of the sofas, eases the cowboy boots from her feet and massages her toes.

'Ahh, it's so good to be home,' she says. 'My ass is going to be welded to this couch for a week.'

'Your place is amazing,' I say.

'Thanks, doll, we like it here. Say, let's get you settled in. Dylan, be a sweetheart and show Alora to her room, will you?' He says no problem and picks up my case.

So I follow Dylan up a wide wooden staircase which leads first to a mezzanine with numerous doors leading off it, then narrowly spirals to the very top of the house. At the summit there is only one door. Dylan opens it and steps back to allow me through first. He ducks slightly before he follows. The attic bedroom is large and bright, the ceiling sloping on each side towards a triangular peak with windows on opposite walls, looking out onto pasture which seems to stretch out into forever like a clean slate.

'Bathroom's just through that door,' Dylan says. 'This room's my favourite, my uncle Wyatt put that window there to capture the sunrise, and that one there captures the sunset.'

'It's lovely,' I say.

He asks me where I'd like my case and I gesture to the bed. The sheets are tucked tight beneath a knitted patchwork quilt and there's a vase of flowers on the dresser. The flowers' petals are startlingly blue, like tiny pieces of sky. I reach out and touch one.

'Texas bluebonnets,' Dylan says, 'Aunty V's favourite.'

I'm aware that Dylan's watching me and suddenly, out of nowhere, I think of Silas—the way he'd observe me with intrigue through the glass of the vocal booth like I was a rare butterfly he'd trapped in a jar—and my body tenses, my hand frozen around the petal.

As though he can sense my discomfort Dylan clears his throat and says, 'I'll leave you to it. Holler if you need anything.'

He closes the door behind him and I relax again, my arm falling limply to my side. I listen to his footsteps fading down the staircase and even though I'm relieved to be alone, the room feels different without him in it, empty somehow, like a cathedral devoid of song.

We eat lunch out on the veranda. Vanessa clearly hasn't told Dylan I'm vegan and he seems confused when I ignore my steak and load my plate with salad. Vanessa cuts her meat into minuscule slivers and Dylan smiles encouragingly each time she lifts one to her mouth. Evelyn's sitting in a high chair. She's insisting on eating unassisted, some kind of mush in a plastic bowl which she spreads all over her face. I wonder where her mum is, whether she'll come home soon and yell at her for making a mess. But Dylan just laughs and wipes her mouth with the sleeve of his shirt. I'm a passive spectator, a passenger floating gently downstream on the current of familiar chatter between aunty and nephew. Vanessa's telling Dylan about the Beaumont Centre, breaching every clause of the confidentiality agreements we signed. She goes into elaborate detail about the Fury Doll, digging her own grave and being abandoned on the coast for a night without shelter, food or water. She really embellishes the story. She makes it sound like we nearly died and Dylan looks alarmed. I tell him that actually it was quite grounding being left alone with nature and all of us felt better for it, apart from Rich Kid who got kicked out. A wasp hovers over my lemonade and lands on the rim of the glass. I'm struck by the vibrancy of his hairy stripes and wonder how the world appears to him through those glossy black eyes. Vanessa shoos it away with her hand.

At one point Dylan asks, 'What do you do for work, Alora?'

Vanessa tuts. 'I told you, she's a musician.'

'Oh, yeah, right. What kind of music?'

I glance at Vanessa to check if he's joking but she's examining the meat on her fork. 'The critics call it Misery Pop,' I say. 'That's the genre I basically created. Sorry, Dylan, I can't tell if you're messing with me. Have you seriously never heard of me?'

Vanessa coughs and covers her mouth with her hand. Dylan seems to be suppressing a smile. 'I only really listen to country music,' he says.

I feel tired after lunch and go back to my room to lie down. After staring at each other with heart-shaped eyes all afternoon, Vanessa and Dylan argue. I hear the fight unfold through the house, a slow escalation of anger contained on his part for longer than hers, but it still invokes memories of Dad and Julia, of all those times I crawled under the duvet with my headphones on and turned my music up loud. And I think of Julia and realise that unless Eva's told her she'll think I'm still at the Beaumont Centre, not in the middle of the Texan outback. I need to call her, we have to talk. I climb off the bed and tug my suitcase out from underneath the frame. I open it, rummage around for the sock and take out my phone. I switch it on and the screen lights up and I wait impatiently as it searches for signal. And when it doesn't find it, not even a glimmer of Wi-Fi, I'm equal parts frustrated and relieved. I shove it back in the sock and go downstairs.

Vanessa's sitting on the couch staring into nowhere with Evelyn on her lap. The kid is leafing through a picture book, making happy little noises which don't quite sound like words. I ask Vanessa if she's okay and she nods and sniffs. I ask after Dylan and she says that he's gone outside in a huff.

'What were you two arguing about?'

'The usual.'

'Which is?'

'Me.' She says Dylan caught her puking up in the bathroom after lunch. 'Damn lock,' she said. 'He keeps saying he'll fix it but I'm sure he doesn't on purpose. Don't you look at me like that!' I avert my eyes. I ask if she wants to talk about it. She says definitely not. So I allow her to sidestep the obvious fact that five weeks in the Max Beaumont Centre for Wellness have clearly not fixed her, and this fills me with a sense of foreboding and dread deeper than I ever thought possible—that Vanessa might be in the 1 percent that Max Beaumont couldn't cure. There's still no sign of Evelyn's mum, but I notice a photograph on the mantelpiece of Dylan with a slender blonde. She's got daisies woven into her hair, a wistful, faraway expression in her eyes and she's wearing a wedding dress with one hand resting lightly on her pregnant belly. I force myself not to stare. There's a photograph of Vanessa too, a much less plastic version. She's holding hands with a man in a blue shirt with a silver toggle at the collar and they're staring at each other like they've just won the lottery.

'This Wyatt?' I ask.

'Yup.'

'You look really happy together.'

'We were. Every morning when I woke up next to him I pretty much pinched myself. He was a good man, an incredible father to Dylan. He taught that boy what it means to be loved.' The kid squirms and Vanessa releases her. I watch as she shuffles her bum across the floor to a wooden box filled with toys. She begins to remove the toys one by one, examining each before placing it down on the rug. 'She'll spend hours doing that,' Vanessa says. 'It's like she's doing a stock check. She'll make a huge mess then she'll put them all back again. I mean, what two-and-a-half-year-old tidies up after themselves? She definitely doesn't get that from Dylan.'

'Does Evelyn's mum live here too?' I say. Vanessa places a finger to her lips and shakes her head.

I wake the following morning to the smell of freshly ground coffee and fried eggs drifting beneath the door. I stretch out luxuriously in bed, reluctant to leave the snug patch of warmth my body's impressed into the mattress. I didn't close the curtains last night and through the opposite window, the sun is peeking demurely above the horizon, its rays fluttering across the landscape like golden feathers. I allow myself to bask in this blissful pause. But when Dylan calls my name, in an enormous feat of willpower I push back the sheets and fling myself out of bed.

I find him in the kitchen, standing at the stove tending to various pots and pans with the enthusiasm of a great conductor before his symphony orchestra. All the appliances are supersized—the fridge could accommodate the bodies of at least four fully grown men. The table is set for three with a high chair for Evelyn. There's a jug of freshly squeezed orange juice, folded gingham napkins and another vase of Texas bluebonnets. Vanessa hasn't yet made an entrance but Dylan tells me to sit, then rushes towards me with pan in hand. He ladles some kind of beige, vomitous slop into a bowl and I look up at him like, 'Are you fucking kidding me?' and he says, 'Just try it.'

'What is it?'

'Grits. Kind of like what you Brits call porridge but made of corn. Aunty V tells me you're vegan so I cooked it especially. Shame she didn't say before I served y'all steak for lunch.'

So I pick up a spoon and, if only to be polite, insert a minuscule amount of slop into my mouth. And it's delicious, seriously good, creamy and buttery and perhaps with even a hint of garlic.

'Wow,' I say, in between mouthfuls, restraining myself from making weird, inappropriate noises. 'You're an amazing cook.'

'Thanks. It's nice to have someone to cook for. Aunty V's not exactly a foodie as you know and Evelyn only really ever wants to eat mashed banana.'

I look around at the empty kitchen. 'Where is Evelyn, by the way?'

'Day care, she goes every weekday morning. If it was up to me I'd have her here all the time until she has to start school, but Aunty V says being an only child, she needs to socialise with other kids her own age. And I get it, I mean, horses are the same. If you hand-rear a foal in isolation it grows up to be a complete lunatic.' I already know from Vanessa that Dylan trains horses for a living and apparently he's pretty good at it; he's got a reputation locally for being a bit of a horse whisperer. I say that I'm scared of horses. 'We can soon fix that,' he says, and smiles.

I look at him and he looks at me and something subtle but real passes between us. And I don't know what it is, but it feels nice, and this time my body doesn't freeze. But then Vanessa walks in and Dylan and I simultaneously look away. He busies himself with rinsing a pan in the sink whilst I sit staring into my empty bowl, feeling confusingly guilty. Vanessa goes up behind him, wraps her arms around his waist and kisses his cheek, and that's all it takes for yesterday's words spoken in anger to be forgotten entirely. She's wearing flared blue jeans and a red shirt with a pointed collar, a pair of tan cowboy boots with an elaborate swirling pattern embroidered in the leather. She says she's going to take her horse out for a ride down to the creek and asks me if I'd like to join her. I say absolutely not, that there's no way anyone's getting me on the back of a horse.

Less than an hour later I'm wearing a pair of suede chaps and the white cowboy hat, sitting in a Western saddle, banging about in every possible direction as Dylan shouts instructions from the centre of the corral. The horse's name is Chad and he's surprisingly tolerant. His coat is black and white in patches like an English cow. Dylan says he's a pony which means he's smaller than a horse but from up here, he doesn't feel small and the ground seems pretty far away. Vanessa is leaning against the fence, yelling at me to relax, which isn't particularly helpful.

Dylan strides towards me and says, 'Whoa,' in a low soft voice and Chad grinds to a halt, which very nearly sends me flying between his ears. I grab onto a clump of mane and try to right myself in a dignified manner. Dylan places one hand on my thigh and the other at the small of my back. 'You need to move with him,' he says. 'Here, and here. The more you tense up the harder it'll be.' He tells me to close my eyes. 'I'll handle Chad. You focus on you.' I close my eyes if only to appease him. I'm conscious of his big practical hands on my body and although I find this aspect of the exercise more thrilling than I'd like to admit, I've already decided that I'll endure one last lap of the corral then tell him thank you very much but no, not for me. But as Chad takes one step and then another I feel my hips move with him, not quite in unison but almost, following the gentle shrug of his shoulders from left to right. 'That's it,' Dylan says. 'That's much better.' His hand is still on my thigh. The three of us move forwards together. Then Dylan takes his hand away and I open my eyes and he's gone, and it's just Chad and me, ambling towards the fence together like we don't have a care in the world.

The creek meanders through trees and over smooth grey rocks like a strip of blue ribbon before pooling into a lake. The water is so clear that I can see shoals of fish darting across the sandy bottom and a slick, keen-eyed beaver diving for his dinner. The sunlight turns to silver as soon as it strikes the surface of the water and ripples with it like tiny mirrors reflecting my hopes and fears. We jump off the horses—Vanessa more gracefully than me—and tie the reins to the branch of an enormous tree which Vanessa says is a red cedar. Its trunk is so wide that it would take five or six of me to wrap my arms around it. I say it must be hundreds of years old and she says more like thousands.

'Think of all the things this tree must've seen,' I say. She says it's definitely seen her and Wyatt at it a few times.

Vanessa strips down to her swimsuit. It's yellow and stylish with a halterneck but there's so little of her to fill it that it hangs slack against her torso. She slips down gracefully into the water and begins to front crawl to the other side of the river. I remove my boots and chaps, roll up my jeans and dip my feet in. It's cool and refreshing but there's a current which, despite her skeletal frame, Vanessa appears strong enough to pull against. I ball my fist around a clump of grass in an attempt to feel rooted to the earth. Vanessa reaches the bank on the other side, then lies on her back and allows the water to carry her downstream into the lake, and the realisation that I'm content pulls everything around me into sharp focus, like a pair of cracked, fogged-up glasses have been removed from my eyes and I've discovered that behind them, my vision was okay all along. I lie down on the bank and think about Dylan's palm on my thigh before telling myself that this pathetic schoolgirl crushing has to end right now, that looking to someone else to fix me is the last thing I should be doing and that he never could anyway, even with those big practical hands. My phone's switched off in my pocket. I went back to my room and fetched it before we set out thinking I might pick up some reception. But now that I'm here, I don't want to look.

Vanessa tells me about Evelyn's mum, and it's a heartbreaker of a story. Dylan met her in high school, she was an amazing horse woman, everyone said they were perfect for each other, not so much yin and yang but yin and yin. But the baby was an accident and they were so young—seventeen. Her parents were religious and the pressure to marry was strongly insinuated if not outright expressed—impromptu visits from the local pastor when Dylan just happened to be at their house, passages underlined in the Bible left open on the breakfast table. So Dylan proposed and she said yes, without either of them really knowing if it was what they wanted, and they tied the knot as soon as they turned eighteen, her mother's bridal gown straining across her belly because by then she was nearly due. She moved into the ranch and then one day, she was gone, leaving behind nothing but a note—she was sorry, but she needed to be free. Evelyn was six months old. 'And in a funny way, I can't begrudge her for it,' Vanessa says. 'She was a teenager, far too immature for all that responsibility. Although obviously I was furious at the time and felt terrible for poor Dylan, because he was left carrying the load. He put on a brave face but he barely slept for months. He drove all over the place trying to find her but it was like she'd disappeared in a puff of smoke. His job now, and mine too, of course, is to make sure that little girl never wants for anything, and that she doesn't feel like there's a mommy-shaped hole in her life.'

'That's so sad,' I say, and Vanessa shrugs and says, 'That's life.'

'Does Dylan still talk about his wife?' I ask, in what I hope sounds like a vague and disinterested tone.

'Rarely. But he won't hear of me taking down their wedding photo. I think deep down he believes she'll come back, one day.' I try to ignore the ludicrous twinge of self-absorbed disappointment.

'Evelyn's so lucky to have you both,' I say.

Vanessa smiles a little sadly. 'Oh, I don't know about that. But we try our best, and that's all anyone can do.'

We spend a week like this—waking with the sun, eating breakfast together in the kitchen or in Vanessa's case chopping it into tiny pieces and pushing it around her plate. Dylan spends most of his time playing with Evelyn or outside with the horses. I watch him out of my bedroom window, how the horses follow him around the corral unbridled, mirroring his movements. When he rides he gives no visible commands, there are no whips or spurs, he simply sits deep in the saddle, reins held loose in one hand, and zigzags this way and that, changing gait, sliding to a halt, as though both man and animal are one and the same.

When daylight starts to fade Vanessa and I sit out on the veranda, drinking coffee and talking about small things. I help Dylan cook dinner one evening—I peel carrots and scoop out the soft flesh of a pumpkin, homegrown in his pristinely tended vegetable patch, with which he makes a delicious pie spiced with cinnamon and nutmeg. We say little and it feels like there's a sense of familiar ease between us. In bed at night I try not to think about him, try to shove my stubborn thoughts towards less dangerous terrain than the quicksand of relationships. But they always snap back at me like an elastic band and I find myself imagining him lying behind me, curled around my body, then I feel mortified when I see him at breakfast like he somehow knows and I can barely bring myself to look at him. The house groans as the wood expands and contracts with the changes in the weather, the long hot days and cooler nights. I'm by no means competent on horseback but I can steer and stay on. More than anything I like grooming Chad, dragging the brush across his round belly, inhaling his sweet meadow breath, staring into his eyes, which are clear and wise and definitely something close to magical. The days are indistinguishable from each other. There's only sun and moon. I still haven't switched on my phone, haven't gone online, and I still haven't called Eva or Julia.

The following Monday Vanessa doesn't come downstairs for breakfast. Dylan says he'll go check on her but I say, 'It's okay, I can go.' I make her a mug of black coffee, thick as treacle, just how she likes it, and carry it upstairs to her room. I knock. There's no answer. So I try the door. And there she is, splayed out next to the bed, all jagged limbs at awkward angles like a broken insect, eyes closed, her cheek pressed into the rug. I rush towards her and kneel by her side, yelling for Dylan, who appears in seconds. We help her stand and she lies on the mattress, covering her face with her hands. 'Sorry,' she mumbles. 'I'm sorry.' Dylan checks her over, asks her to move her arms, legs, fingers one by one and she obliges like a compliant child. She seems disorientated, her eyes unable to focus. And it's horrible seeing her like this, my strong defiant '*Fuck you all*' friend, so weak and confused. Dylan wants to call the doctor but she whispers, 'Don't you dare.' She spends the day on the sofa beneath a blanket. Dylan heats her a can of chicken soup which she refuses to eat.

'This happens sometimes,' he says to me quietly as he carries the bowl of soup back into the kitchen. 'She gets dizzy. She's been eating more since she got back from the centre, but it's impossible to know how much of it actually stays down.' He should be taking Evelyn to nursery soon, then trailering a horse for a client. He says he'll call and rearrange but I say he doesn't need to, that I'll stay here with Vanessa.

I sit quietly by her side. I feel like crying but what good would wallowing in my own self-pity do? I don't know how much time has passed when, with her eyes still closed, Vanessa croaks,

'Would you read to me? There's a few books up there in Wyatt's study—second door on your right.' I say yes of course. I ask her what she'd like me to read and she says something romantic and not too complicated, that her brain needs an easy ride today.

The 'study' with 'a few books' is more like a library; a large rectangular room lined with wooden shelving from floor to ceiling, a sliding ladder, the comforting scent of dusty paper, leather and a simpler time gone by. In one corner there's a desk and a wooden chair, a reading lamp and a window which looks out onto Dylan's vegetable patch. There's a fountain pen on the desk and a pad of yellowing paper with a note scrawled at the very top, next to a photograph in a silver frame. I read the note. It's an address with a set of directions—left at the general store, past the pecan farm and so on. It's signed off, WYATT. I pick up the frame. It's a photo of Vanessa, smiling with vulnerable adoration at whoever's behind the camera. She's wearing no makeup and her skin and eyes are gleaming, and I imagine that despite all her phobias, this is how Wyatt loved her the most. I replace the photo, taking care not to alter this small, simple shrine to the past, and back away from the desk, then set my mind to finding the perfect book to read to my friend. I see some of my all-time favourites on the shelves—*Bad Behavior* by Mary Gaitskill, *Norwegian Wood* by Haruki Murakami, *The Bell Jar* by Sylvia Plath, *The Night Circus* by Erin Morgenstern—but in the end, to fit the brief, I settle on a cheesy romance novel which, when I present it to Vanessa, she insists belonged to Wyatt's mother but I suspect is secretly hers. I sit next to her on the sofa and read. And it's obvious from the start who's the hero and who's the baddie, that the good guy is going to get the girl and they'll both be deliriously happy by the ending. I initially hate the protagonists for portraying such an unrealistic depiction of love, but then I realise that I'm jealous. Because I have no idea how that feels and probably never will. Eventually Vanessa dozes off.

She's still dozing when Dylan arrives home later that afternoon with Evelyn. He asks how his aunty V is doing and I say a little better, I think. 'That's a relief,' he says. 'Thanks for looking after her.' I say it's no problem. 'Hey, Alora, sorry, I know you're the guest of honour an' all, but would you mind if I leave a little one with you for an hour? I've got the vet coming out and this particular horse ain't too trusting of humans. I don't want Evelyn around in case she gets kicked.' I say of course I don't mind whilst thinking, 'Oh fuck!' and stand up to receive her, almost buckling under the weight of her—she's surprisingly heavy for someone so little. She grumbles when her daddy says she can't go with him but stops when he promises her a treat if she's good.

'Lollipop,' she says, or a noise which sounds similar.

So here I am, left holding the baby, literally. Vanessa's snoring on the couch and Evelyn reaches out and touches one of my gold hoop earrings. I jolt my head away and the kid looks annoyed. We lock eyes and stare each other out. 'Not a toy,' I say, and she frowns. She may as well be an alien, I think, such is my inability to communicate with her in any meaningful way. I remember the wooden toy box in the corner of the room and say in a pantomime voice, 'I know what we can do!' I deposit her on the carpet and crouch down next to her. I'm relieved when, without encouragement, she begins another stock check—lifting out each toy and examining it before lining it up in an orderly row with the others. She's methodical, meticulous, and half an hour later, I'm still watching her without even an inkling of boredom. I wonder if she remembers her mum, if she, like me, understands the hollowness of abandonment even if she can't yet put it into words. Her long blonde hair is loose today and a strand falls across her eyes. I reach out and tuck it behind one ear, and I'm struck by her trust as she sits with me, an almost stranger, allowing me to share her world. She's just a child, I think. A sweet, innocent little girl. And so was I. It wasn't my fault—I need to start believing that now. Evelyn reaches up and with clammy hands swipes at the tears dribbling down my cheeks, then licks them off her tiny fingers.

The next morning Dylan asks if I'd like to ride out with him and help him move the horses. I think it's obvious to both of us that I'll be no help whatsoever, but I change into my borrowed chaps and grab my cowboy hat, pausing in front of the full-length mirror to marvel at how ridiculous I look. I hang back on Chad and watch as Dylan moves his horse, skilfully anticipating the herd's every movement like a matador in the ring but without the gory intentions. After the other horses are safely grazing in their new pasture, the gate secured with rope, Dylan suggests we ride to the creek.

'You don't need to babysit me,' I say.

He shields his eyes from the sun with one hand and squints at me. 'I know that. I just fancy a swim. If you don't want to come, don't.'

I sit on the grass beneath the red cedar tree and focus on my toes as Dylan strips down to his boxers, refusing to acknowledge that his body—which I piece together in fragments of sly glimpses—is better than Noah's, my ex-boyfriend who spent half of his life in the gym. And I don't know why I choose this moment to do it, maybe everything's just too perfect and I can't resist pressing the self-destruct button. But as Dylan swims away, his broad shoulders just above water, his muscles moving smoothly beneath his skin, I remove my phone from my pocket and switch it on. And in the elevated position of the creek it finds a signal. It pings repeatedly as Eva's texts and missed-call alerts arrive in their hundreds:

Where are u?
Please can u call me??
Can you at least let me know if u're ok???

I scan a longer message before it slides up off the screen, something about a televised BBC event with various acts on the bill which they want me to headline:

It would be a great look, a strong comeback from . . .

The message disappears. I hold my finger over the app for less than a second and then I click on it. I type my own name into the search bar and wait for the results to load.

And of course, no matter how many lawyers you have working for you round the clock at an extortionate hourly rate, once these things surface they can never be forced back under and everything ultimately lives on the internet forever. And sure enough, there it is, right at the top of the search. I press play. And watch as I climb into the bath in all my finery and smile into the camera as though I'm genuinely happy at the prospect of leaving this life. And I'm aware that it's me but at the same time I feel entirely detached, as though the girl is someone I once encountered in a dream. I scroll down to the comments. I'm still reading them, taking each judgement into my body, sucking them into my heart and making them true when Dylan sits beside me and shakes his hair like a dog, sending droplets of ice-cold water flying all over me. He peers into my face which, beneath the shadow of the tree, is lit up by the mechanical glow of the phone screen.

'Hey,' he says softly. 'Why are you crying?'

And the kindness in his voice makes me cry even harder, huge gasping sobs which wrack my shoulders and tremor to my fingertips. I tilt the phone towards him. He takes it from my shaking hand. His thumb moves down, his hazel eyes flit from left to right. He says nothing. Then suddenly, he rises up, lurching forwards and springing towards the creek with great manly leaps. He lifts his arm and flings my phone up into the sky like a professional baseball player. It swoops into an impressive arc, before falling and plopping into the water. I stop crying. I'm shocked. He turns to face me and his eyes flare with something like anger but more at the world than with me. 'Why would you read that stuff about yourself?'

I wipe my face with the back of my hand, certain that I look like a beef tomato again. 'Dylan,' I say. 'I'd find it very difficult to answer that in a way that doesn't make me sound completely insane.'

He takes hold of both my hands in his and turns them over so my palms are facing the sky. Very gently, he eases up my right sleeve, then my left. I look away, not wanting to witness his face when he sees the ugly scars, the eternal reminders of what a fuckup I am. He exhales. 'I'm sorry, I know what it's like to feel trapped in the darkness, like there's no way out.'

I turn to face him. 'Do you?'

'Yeah, I do. But there always is. There's always a way out, Alora.'

Over the next few days Vanessa regains her strength. She eats a bowl of grits, sits out on the veranda smoking a cigarette, finishes off the cheesy romance novel and pretends she's got something in her eye when I catch her crying over the ending. I, on the other hand, have started to sink. Reality has caught up with me. It's grabbed me by the shoulders and violently shaken me and I'm no longer floating through this fantasy land of ponies and pastures on a raft of make-believe. I'm back there, trapped in my house in London with the paparazzi camped outside my gate, tangled amongst snatching hands which tear at my hair and skin and clothes with the truth about Dad ringing in my ears, I'm at my eighteenth birthday party, which is filled with people I recognise from TV and social media but have never spoken to in my life, with Silas's hand on my waist as he kisses my cheek with cold, wet lips and says, 'Wow, haven't you grown up since I last saw you?' Someone had written beneath the video:

> Everything she ever does is for attention, it's probably not even real.

The comment had been liked over five hundred thousand times. Other comments were filled with declarations of love—fans saying how much they missed me, begging me to come back, to release another album. One wrote:

> I can't live without you 😨 😨 😨

A girl—maybe ten or eleven years old—held her wrists up to the camera where she'd drawn on copycat cuts in red felt-tip pen. I shudder.

'What's up with you?' Vanessa says. We're eating lunch in the kitchen, sandwiches which Dylan prepared before going back outside to fix a loose fence post. He's cut the sandwiches into small triangles and removed the crusts, just like Gina does, the woman I hired to be my surrogate mum. I tell Vanessa that I switched on my phone. 'Was that a good idea?'

'I had to find out sometime.'

'And?'

'And what?'

'What are you going to do about it now you know what *they're* saying?'

I take a bite out of my sandwich but can't swallow. I spit it out into a napkin. 'I don't know yet.' But the truth is, I do.

After lunch I sit alone at the kitchen table, allowing my irrational thoughts full access to every rational part of me. Dylan walks in. He looks flushed, perspiration glistening across his brow, dark patches at his underarms. He smells of sweat, I can actually smell him from across the room and I don't know why but it's totally hot. I inhale deeply. I ask him where I can find a postbox which sends international mail and he says in town, about a forty-minute drive away. I ask what else is there and he says, 'Not much: a gas station, a grocery store, a cowboy bar.' He says he'll take me, if I like. I come downstairs wearing my disguise—a checked shirt which I've borrowed off Vanessa, jeans, sunglasses and my hair tucked up in the white cowboy hat. We climb into Dylan's truck.

The air is muggy and close. Dylan winds down all the windows and I grip onto the hat to stop it flying off as he speeds along the dusty track. He switches the radio on and country and western music blares out of the speakers at full volume. The song is sad and melodic, about love lost and loneliness in the mountains, and the woman's voice carries the twang of genuine heartbreak. Dylan hums along to the tune and I realise then that I haven't written in months. I haven't picked up a guitar or heard music in my mind since long before what happened. My entire second album, which has my face on the cover, my name on the artwork in bold, luminous font, is the work of other people—their words, their thoughts replicating mine, a faint carbon copy of the concept of real emotion. I wonder if my creativity is lost forever, and who I am without it.

We park in the town, which is really nothing more than a cluster of wooden prairie houses; potted plants neatly arranged on porches, a rope swing hanging from a tree, the occasional poster for a local political candidate tacked in a front window. Dylan points out the postbox and I jump out of the truck with the envelope in my hand and before I can give myself a chance to chicken out, I shove it into the postbox's gaping mouth. Then I stride away. Dylan gets out of the truck just as I reach the bar's swinging saloon doors and step forwards into the rusty music spilling out into the street. People turn and stare at me and their stares are almost reassuring. But these stares aren't the usual kind, hankering after a little fame. They're predatory hunger stares, because other than the bartender I'm the only woman in this place. Dylan appears by my side just as she's asking me what I want to drink.

I point at the top shelf. 'A bottle of that.'

'Which one, darlin'?'

'Any of them,' I say.

'Listen, Alora,' Dylan says quietly, tentatively. 'It's none of my business but Aunty V said you're sober. Are you sure you want to do this?'

'Yes.'

We take a seat at the back of the bar. The music seems to get louder and more intense with every inch of whisky I swallow. This stuff is strong, it burns the back of my throat. Dylan sips it with obvious reluctance. I fill his glass so full that the next time he raises it to his lips he spills some on the table. I pull my chair closer to his.

'You've got beautiful eyes,' I say, although I'm not sure the words come out quite that way and his eyes seem to be moving around his face in a confusing hazel blur. He slides his chair backwards, away from me.

'We should go soon, I need to collect Evelyn from day care and Aunty V'll be wanting some food.'

'I doubt that very much.' I reach forwards and sweep his hair off his forehead, his adorable wonky haircut. He visibly flinches. So when I try to kiss him I can't realistically expect him to kiss me back and sure enough, he doesn't.

'Why not?' I slur. 'It's just sex, I don't want to marry you or anything.' Although that feels like a lie.

'Okay, glad we got that one cleared up.' He stands.

'Where are you going?'

'I'm taking you home.'

I stand up too and in the process knock my chair over. It clatters to the floor and the music suddenly seems quieter and no one seems to be talking anymore.

'It's not my home!' I'm practically shouting now. 'It's yours! And I don't want to go back there! I want to hang out here and have a good time so if you're not interested in me, I'll find someone else who is!'

I turn to walk away but he grabs hold of my arm and

suddenly, I'm being lifted through the air and flung over his shoulder. And at first I'm so shocked that I go all floppy like a rag doll, I put up no fight whatsoever. The cowboy hat falls off and lands on the wooden floorboards and my hair sweeps through the sawdust. The stares are upside down now. I kick and scream and nobody moves, not one person retrieves a phone from their pocket, points it at me and starts to film. The bartender polishes glasses and the men sup their whisky like this kind of thing happens every day in this town. I'm carried out of the bar on Dylan's shoulder, across the road and lowered into the passenger seat of his truck. We drive home in silence, Dylan doesn't even turn on the radio.

When we get back to the ranch I climb out of the passenger seat and slam the door with such force that the truck shudders. Dylan accelerates back out onto the track as I stomp my way towards the pasture where Chad's grazing with the herd. I lean against the gate for a while and sulk. I consider catching Chad, tacking him up and riding down to the creek by myself but think better of it considering I can barely stay on a horse sober and I'm not entirely sure how to tack up. I'm still sulking when Dylan returns in the truck with Evelyn and I watch from my lonely distance as they go into the house and eventually, I accept the need to get over myself and follow.

I'm greeted by the scene of Vanessa sitting in the living room with Evelyn on her lap. Vanessa's reading to the child, a blanket covering them both. They look cosy and snug, a gut-wrenching certainty in Evelyn's eyes that the world is a wonderful place where nothing bad could ever happen to her. Vanessa looks up from the book, she asks me if I'm okay in a kind voice with no judgement whatsoever which is completely infuriating. I say I'm fine, that I just need to make a call.

'Sure,' she says. 'Phone's in the kitchen.'

My phone may be dead at the bottom of the lake but I know Eva's number off by heart. I punch in the numbers, leaning against the kitchen wall, twisting the cord around my index finger. It rings once, twice. The room is pulsating and I feel a little sick. Eva answers with a tentative 'Hello?'

'I'll do it,' I say. 'I'll do the show.'

I read out Vanessa's address from a letter stuck to the fridge door by a magnet in the shape of an ear of corn, I make arrangements for my imminent departure. Then I storm upstairs like a whirling dervish and begin flinging my clothes into my suitcase, making no attempt to fold them neatly. I'm furious, like this whole situation is somehow Dylan's fault. There's a fresh vase of Texas bluebonnets on the dresser and I feel like picking it up and hurling it against the wall. My fingers itch. I resist. I slide down to the floor and drop my head into my hands.

When I wake up I'm drooling, my tongue thick and heavy in my mouth. The drunkenness has worn off and has been replaced by crippling shame. I clamber to my feet and stumble downstairs, where I stand outside the kitchen, trying to muster sufficient courage to go in. I know Dylan and Vanessa are in there because I can hear the low rumble of their muffled voices through the closed door, but when I finally open it, they stop talking so it's obvious they were talking about me. Dylan lowers his eyes to the table, avoiding mine.

'Sit down, doll,' Vanessa says warmly. 'There's some stew in the pot if you're hungry.' I say that I'm not hungry. I don't sit down. I loiter in the doorway, crossing one ankle in front of the other. The hangover is really kicking in now and my head's pounding like it's become its own bass drum. I'm cringing at my behaviour, boiling with embarrassment over the things I did and said to Dylan, Vanessa's nephew, Evelyn's dad, in that bar.

I clear my throat. 'I'm going back to London. There's this live show my manager wants me to do. It'll be broadcast on TV and it's kind of a comeback thing to prove to everyone I'm well again.'

Vanessa glances at Dylan. He reaches for his tin of tobacco and starts to roll a cigarette and I see Dad's hands, the pointed tip of his tongue extending from between his lips as he looks up seductively into the eyes of some woman he's just met and asks if he can buy her a drink with money I know that his wife, my mum, earned from working a double shift.

'You know you're welcome to stay as long as you like, don't you?' Vanessa says.

'I just think it's for the best.'

'If you say so.'

Dylan stands. He mutters, 'Excuse me,' as he walks past me and his extreme politeness makes me feel even more wretched.

'Dylan, wait.' But he doesn't, and I don't follow.

Evelyn bangs her plastic spoon against the high chair. 'No!' she wails. 'No!' She's staring at me with fiery, defiant eyes. I wonder if one day she will look in the mirror and see her own mother there in the way that I see mine. Vanessa smooths her hair, tells her to hush. I turn and walk away, closing the door behind me.

My dreams that night are filled with distorted incoherent flashes of false memory: Julia tucking me into bed at night and reading me a story wearing Dad's clothes, Dad standing at the hob stirring gravy for the Sunday roast, Julia and Dad in front of the electric fireplace in the flat, the Christmas tree plump with homemade decorations, the scent of freshly baked gingerbread, the sound of carols and laughter whilst I wriggle merrily in my cot, Dad lying drunk on the carpet in front of the stage at Ravello's whilst Julia lifts me up with tears in her eyes, carries me outside and straps me into my car seat. In each of these scenes I'm fully grown but dressed like a child in blue T-bar shoes and a matching woollen cape, and I am both actress, centre stage in the production of my life, and audience, silently observing from the gallery, critiquing my own performance.

'See, I tried my best, but I never wanted to be a mother,' Julia explains.

I wake up. The curtains are drawn and though it's dark, I can make out the shape of objects in the room; people from my past crouching in the shadows, my own shaking hands as I hold them out in front of my eyes. I climb out of bed and slip on my bathrobe. I pad across the creaking floorboards and step out into the corridor, make my way downstairs. The house is quiet. I don't know where I'm going but I need to move, to walk forwards into the physicality of my body and escape my broken mind. But when I step out onto the veranda Dylan's there, sitting in one of the rocking chairs smoking a cigarette. The early morning air carries all the freshness of a new day which promises forgiveness and second chances. He gestures quietly to the other chair. I sit down and wrap my arms around myself even though it's not cold.

'I'm sorry,' I say. He says I don't need to be. 'Yeah, I do. What I said yesterday was... I shouldn't have...'

He shakes his head. 'I'm sorry I got mad but, how can I put this... Some guys, especially the kind who hang out in bars like that, they don't treat women with respect, they just use 'em and throw 'em away like yesterday's paper.'

'They use them for sex, you mean?'

'Well, yeah.'

'But what if I just wanted sex too?'

'And that's fine if you did, no judgement. But I'm not sure that's what all that was about.'

Full credit to Dylan, he's more insightful than Dr Laurel, my five-hundred-quid-an-hour shrink. 'No, it wasn't, I guess.' I feel exposed, vulnerable, deeply uncomfortable, but instead of pulling back, of resisting with all my might, I decide to be honest, to reveal the real me.

'I've got a few issues, Dylan. I'm sure you already know that. But the thing is, I like you.'

There, I've said it. Two weeks of schoolgirl crushing and late-night fantasising, confusion and guilt finally coming to a head. But he looks away, and I know, I just know. He says he's flattered, honestly he is, I'm a beautiful girl and a very special person. But as his Aunty V may have told me, he's married. He's got no idea where his wife is, which he appreciates is an unconventional arrangement, but he wants to stay true to his vows. 'So I don't think it would be fair on you for me to, you know...' I exhale slowly. Rejection hurts like hell, but I also feel alive. I've taken a risk and it hasn't paid off but maybe in some ways, it has. 'So... you're heading back to London.'

'Apparently so.'

'Good idea?'

'We'll see, I suppose.'

'Well, don't forget about us out here. Maybe we'll all come to a show one day.' I say I won't forget about them, ever, that they're welcome to come to all of my shows, that Vanessa, Evelyn and he would be *my* guests of honour. 'And just remember,' he says. 'It's your choice how you live your life, no one else's. And if things get bad, there's always a way out.'

'You make it sound so simple.'

'Isn't it?'

He reaches down and stubs out his cigarette on the heel of his boot. And I know he's going to leave. He'll say he needs to move the horses or fix a fence or do some other practical task which all other men I know would be totally useless at even following a step-by-step instruction video on YouTube. And I tell myself to remember this moment, to hold it on my tongue and savour it forever, but like everything which tastes too sweet the sugar rush recedes and only leaves you wanting more. I want to leave before he does, want to walk away from this unsatisfactory ending to the failed rom-com with a milligram of dignity, so I stand up quickly but Dylan does the same at exactly the same moment and our bodies collide. He reaches out and holds onto my arm to steady me. I look up at him and he looks down at me and our faces are inches away from each other's and I admit that I contemplate kissing him, despite everything that's happened and everything he's said. I part my lips slightly. But he shakes his head.

'Believe me,' he says. 'I want to.' And I can see from the restraint in his eyes that he does. And life's confusing and unfair but also sometimes wonderful.

I don't cry until I'm in the car, driving away down the dirt track. Vanessa and Dylan are standing outside, squinting into the cascades of dust. Evelyn is in Dylan's arms, waving one pudgy hand. I wave back, knowing that she'll probably have forgotten me by tomorrow. I kneel on the back seat until they become vague smudges on a vast horizon. Vanessa said that I can come back whenever I like, that her door will always be open and my bed made up in the attic. But these are just words and as time passes, they'll empty themselves of meaning just like everything else always does. I remember the letter I posted in town and groan.

'You okay, miss?' the driver says. 'Do you need me to pull over?'

'No,' I say. 'I'm fine.' And wonder if I'm convincing anyone.

I can't sleep on the flight back to London. I drink a double espresso just before we land and it makes me feel wired and manic with a nagging undercurrent of fatigue. I'm ushered from the private runway behind dark glasses and the burly bodies of my security team. Eva's waiting for me in my Range Rover. She makes strained declarations about how good it is to see me, how great I look even though we both know full well that I've been crying and look like shit. She looks exactly the same as she always does, and yet like a stranger. There aren't any paparazzi at my gate, they must think I'm still in rehab. But it's only a matter of time before someone lets slip that I've left—Maureen, David, Jacob, Elijah. One of them will be tempted by a little cash, it's always the way.

Gina opens the back door with a warm, dimple-cheeked smile, delicious cooking smells wafting out from the kitchen behind her. She hugs me with her one free arm, because in the other she's holding Carrie. Carrie's wearing a huge pink bow around her neck and a frilly ballet tutu. Her toenails are painted hot pink. I burst out laughing. 'What the hell happened to you?' I ask my dog, as I take her from Gina, tip her upside down and tickle her tummy. She smells like a French perfumery. She stares at me with bulging Chihuahua eyes, looking unimpressed. Gina says she took her to the grooming parlour and booked her in for a 'Princess Package'. We both agree that they went a little over the top.

'I've missed you, sweetie,' Gina says. I say that I've missed her too. She takes my suitcase and I follow her into the house, and all I can do now is wait.

For the next few days Gina keeps the curtains drawn. Carrie sleeps in my bed and trots at my heels as I move aimlessly from room to room, conscious of just how many rooms there are. I miss the ranch. My house and all of my belongings with it seem grotesquely opulent and excessive. I could accommodate multiple families here and yet there's only me. And I own four more homes—in Los Angeles, New York, Cannes, Florence—that I rarely even visit. I call my financial advisor, George, and tell him I want to sell up.

'What . . . everything?' he asks, in his pompous nasal tone.

'Yup. The whole damn lot.'

'But where do you plan on residing?'

'Minor detail, George, don't worry about that for now. Oh, and while we're at it, I want to make a will. Can you help with that too?'

'Of course.'

'I want a generous provision left for Gina, my housekeeper. Then I want my estate divided equally between the following causes.' I reel off the list—animal rights, climate change, mental health, asylum seekers, orphaned children.

'Miss Storm-Jones,' he says, lowering his voice. 'Pardon the intrusion, but there's nothing I need to be worried about here, is there?'

I smile down the phone line. 'Nothing at all, George. Everything is, as you would put it, tickety-boo.'

I miss Vanessa, her quick wit and reassuring glances, the pressure of her hand in mine. I Google 'Vanessa Levine' and find hundreds of photographs of my friend in her modelling days, a young, skinny antelope with thick eyelashes and sultry, kohl-lined eyes surrounded by salivating actors and rock stars with wide, lecherous smiles. She was beautiful, that rare, innocent kind of beauty which has nothing to do with makeup. I tell myself that I don't miss Dylan, that I don't feel the loss of what could have been in another lifetime if everything was different, if he hadn't got his high-school girlfriend pregnant at seventeen and I wasn't such a messed-up disaster of a human. I touch my cheek where Evelyn once wiped away my tears. One morning when I'm in the shower, I find myself singing 'I Will Always Love You' by Dolly Parton. I try to write a new song but the words cower at the edges, refusing to reveal themselves. I spend a long time lying in bed scrolling through old messages, trying to work out who I was before the Max Beaumont Centre for Wellness, whether I'm still the same person now. One exchange between Noah and me reads:

Noah
Where u gone?

In the bath. Come.

Noah
In a bit. Ordering room service. Want anything?

U

Noah

I used him, then I discarded him like the spit-sodden butt of a joint. After I broke up with him, he sent me a long email:

Hey.

Look, I've been thinking about everything you said and you're right. We aren't the same. My parents are rich. I went to private school. The worst thing that ever happened to me during childhood was my pet rabbit dying. I didn't sleep rough in bus stations or busk in the street with my dad so he could buy drugs. But one thing we have in common is this—we both pretend for a living. Okay so I'm officially a professional pretender but don't tell me you don't do it too. I've seen how you shake before you walk out onstage, the hopeless look in your eyes before you down the first shot. People love your music but I don't think they ever think too deeply about the fact that it's your life, that those words are real to you, because it suits them not to as long as you carry on churning out hits. I love you, Alora. But I love the real you, the scared little kid beneath the act. I feel like I'm being punished for saying that and meaning it. But I respect your decision, I'm not going to try and change your mind, it's pretty clear that I couldn't even if I tried. Ignore everything you read in the papers about me, it's all a load of bullshit, but you know that anyway. I'm always here if you want to talk.

Love,
Noah x

At the time I read it and moved it straight into junk. Now, I drag it back into my inbox and press reply:

I'm sorry about the way I treated you. You're right, we're both pretenders. And if you aren't happy pretending anymore, you should just stop xx

Vanessa calls me every day. We talk for hours about pleasantly unimportant things—the weather in London, the bird feeder Gina's hung in the oak tree for the blue tits and greenfinches and robins, Evelyn's painting of a three-legged purple zebra with a yellow mane. Each time I ask after Dylan. Vanessa usually says he's out with the horses but one day she says, 'He's just here, I'll put him on.'

'No, don't, I—'

'Hey, Alora. How's things going in the Big Smoke?' I blush violently, relieved we're not on FaceTime. 'You ready for your show?'

'You could say that.'

When he hands the phone back to Vanessa, she says nothing for a while and I start to think she's forgotten I'm there.

'Hello?' I say into the silence.

'One second,' she whispers. 'I'm waiting 'til he's out of earshot.' She tells me that Dylan received a letter in the post that week. 'From his wife, if you can believe it. Two years and not a peep, then out of the blue she writes to him. I watched him read it, his face all serious and still, then he set fire to it and dropped it in the grate. So I'll never know exactly what she said, and why should I, that's between him and her. But the crux of it is this: she's divorcing him. She's living in a commune in India, wants to marry the sun, or some other hippie baloney. I asked him if she enquired after Evelyn. He said not.'

'That's awful,' I say. 'For Evelyn, and for Dylan.' And I can feel the heat of his body as he holds on to my arm and we gaze into each other's eyes and my pulse begins to bound. 'Is he upset?' But Vanessa says that actually, he seems lighter somehow, like he's finally been set free.

It doesn't take me long to work out that Eva's cleared the whole house of drink and drugs, which means she's been rummaging through my stuff, and there are no sharp knives to be seen in any of the kitchen drawers. I could get mad. I could call her up and yell. But I don't. Because I have far bigger plans.

Julia arrives on a drizzly Thursday afternoon. I'm waiting for her in the kitchen. Gina's laid out plates of sandwiches and home-baked scones with jam and clotted cream, a pot of tea and matching cups from a set she tells me I bought from Harrods during one of my online shopping splurges and left in the Post Room unopened. I'm anxious. Right now I could go on a real bender, I could down a whole bottle of tequila and smoke ten million cigarettes and snort the whole of Colombia. Seren told me to burn the letters or rip them into shreds. I flushed the letter to Dad down the toilet at the Beaumont Centre. But the letter to Julia I carried in my suitcase to Texas and I posted it.

I can hear Gina welcoming her now, saying how wonderful it is to meet her, how excited I've been about her visit, which isn't strictly true, I barely slept last night and very nearly messaged her and told her not to come. But she walks into the kitchen, concertina-ing her red umbrella, and the first thing that strikes me about my mother is that she is small. It's as though she's shrunk. The dark curls which once seemed so overbearingly flamboyant and domineering are withered and lank and streaked with grey. Her huge boobs which she's always flaunted so proudly are concealed beneath a frumpy roll-neck jumper which is tucked into high-waisted jeans. She wears no makeup, no false lashes or painted talons. She has come as a mother, stripped bare of everything else. She clutches the Mulberry handbag to her chest as though it's a shield—it's a handbag I bought for her, one of many. Inside each I slipped a cheque for fifty grand which she always banked. Her eyes meet mine, both of us uncertain, unsure. She glances up at the copper pans, the double fridge complete with water cooler and ice machine, the landscaped garden visible in a collage of colour through the rain-streaked glass. She's never visited my home before and it's clear that it intimidates her—neither of us are from this world of riches. I take a step towards her and she falters, looks away. And I know how dangerous it is to relinquish control like this, but that's what it means to be alive. So I rush towards her and she opens her arms. I collapse into them and bury my head in her curls.

EVA

AT THE BAR I ORDER TWO pints of lager and take a seat by the slot machine. It feels like I've lived a life ten times over since I last stepped foot in a place like this—a chain pub with chart music playing over the speakers and laminated posters on the walls advertising pitchers of blue slushy cocktails which look radioactive. For the past couple of years I've been all about five-star hotels, private members clubs and bottles of the finest champagne. But I was so relieved that he actually agreed to meet me that I wasn't exactly going to kick off about his choice of venue. I sit down on a sticky pleather couch and trace my fingertip around the love heart scratched into the table in which someone called Rod once pledged allegiance to BEV 4EVA.

I see him before he sees me. He steps through the doorway and lowers his hood and my body feels weak and my heart's pounding, just like when I first saw him at that warehouse party, just like every time he touched me or sent me a message or his name flashed up on my phone when he called. We haven't spoken to each other since Alora's eighteenth birthday party. When her suicide attempt hit the headlines he sent me an email saying he hoped we were both okay, but it was succinct, reserved, with a distant formality I found upsetting, no kisses or heart emojis. With the secret performance happening tomorrow my phone's on fire. But I know that everything's under control, that I'm just one cog in a very big machine, that this is important too and should've always been.

Ade nods when he sees me. He makes his way towards the table where he sits down opposite me, not by my side. I gesture to his pint and he says thanks but he's not drinking, if he's not careful with all the DJing he finds himself pissed every night and hungover every day.

'I hear it's going really well,' I say. I know he's been taken on by a big agent, that he's been booked to warm up for Black Coffee at Fabric at the end of the month, I've seen his name on fly-posters around London.

'Yeah, really well, thanks. When I didn't get that job at Low Slang Records I decided to get my head down and properly try to make a go of it. I started producing a lot more music and actually finishing the tracks, sending mixtapes out to promoters, that kind of thing. The rejection gave me the kick up the arse I needed, I think.'

I know he's trying to be nice, to let me off the hook. But I'm ashamed and sorry and I tell him so. He says it's cool, that it's all worked out for the best.

I look up from my pint. 'Has it?' We both know that I'm no longer talking about the job and he sighs.

'I don't know. Maybe, yeah?'

I already thought my heart was broken, but I feel it break

just a little bit more. I've practised this speech many times in the privacy of my beautiful, empty, too-massive-for-one home, and I find myself reciting it without pausing for breath. I tell Ade that I should never have prioritised work over him, that I should never have taken the credit for finding Alora, I didn't realise how much I wanted to impress people, to feel like I was a 'significant person', how susceptible to all the bullshit I became. I told him I wished that I could turn back time and do everything differently.

'I lost myself. But I'm back now, I'm back to being the old Eva.'

I try to smile when I ask him for a second chance. And when he closes his eyes I have my answer, right there. I can barely hear him as he speaks, because the white noise between my ears is deafening, the rushing current of loss. He's met someone else, a DJ signed to the same agency as him—Jia. It's early days but it feels good. He says he's sorry, that he'll always be here for me, that he'll always love me as a friend.

ALORA

ON THE DAY OF THE SHOW, I'm smuggled into the venue in a custom-made tunnel. From the outside it looks inconspicuous but inside, it's draped with cream silk, lit with fairy lights, comically bridal. I sit in my dressing room whilst Eva fusses—am I too hot, too cold, hungry, thirsty—flapping around me like a trapped starling with a broken wing.

'Are you sure you want to do this?' she says for the millionth time that day. I say that I'm sure.

I've insisted on doing my own makeup, I don't want any fuss or fanfare. I turn towards the mirror and apply red lipstick, electric-green eyeliner, mascara, a little blush, painting myself into the person they expect me to be. I'm looking up at myself through deep water, buried at the bottom of the ocean watching a distorted reflection of real life pass by above me with the clouds. The sensation is familiar, I've been here before—in the bathroom of the Edinburgh Grand Hotel. Someone knocks at the dressing room door and Eva leaps up and grabs the handle even though it's double-locked from the inside.

'Who is it?' she calls.

And when I hear Julia's voice I stare at myself in the mirror, look deep into my own eyes and for the final time, I see her there.

'Come in, Mum,' I say, a word I haven't used since the day he died, and it feels soft and comforting in my mouth.

She stands in the doorway, teetering in patent high heels, a nervous smile twitching at her lips. I stand and walk towards her and she opens up her arms and draws me close.

I love you, I think but do not say.

With her body still pressed against mine, in a cloud of her perfume, I glance at the clock on the wall. And I know it's time.

The crowd is huge—twenty thousand people. They surge and shift, pushing and pulling against each other like deadly riptides which could drag me down to the very bottom. I'm announced as the mystery guest, they have no idea it's me. And after everything that's happened, I know how this could end—booed off stage in a hailstorm of aluminium cans and plastic cups and shame. My hand is simultaneously trembling and sweating at the neck of my guitar, my bottom lip quivering. I begin to hyperventilate and try to focus on my breath, the sensation of it entering my body, passing coolly into my lungs and out through my nostrils. I reach for Dad's tooth, run my fingertip across it, then I grasp hold of it and yank. The chain snaps. I drop it on the floor and crush it beneath my heel. Then I step out onto that stage. And when I do the audience erupts. And I can do this, I can come alive beneath the bright lights, get high off it and let it validate my existence one last time. I walk towards the mic with my guitar in my arms.

'Hey,' I say. I can barely hear my own voice in my earpiece over the crowd. They're whistling and cheering and screaming my name. On the front row, girls are hugging and sobbing into each other's shoulders. It's nothing short of hysteria. I continue regardless. 'Sorry that I've been away for a little while. I guess most of you probably know why. And I just want to say that what I did, and the way I did it, so publicly like that, it wasn't cool. We all have our shit going on, pain that sits so deep inside it feels like there's no other way to escape it. But there's always a way out, and it's not that.' I pull back the sleeves of my leotard and hold my wrists out to the crowd. 'These are my scars, the ones you can see on the outside anyway. They'll fade with time, but they'll be part of me forever. And there's one more.' I angle my thigh towards the closest TV camera and it appears on the huge screens on either side of the stage. 'I did this for *him*, under some misguided delusion that I needed to earn his love. And the song I'm going to sing for you, I wrote for *him* too. It's called 'Piece of Me'.

I allow my eyes to lose their focus, I pick lightly at the strings beneath my fingers, and the words are there when I need them most:

I always thought I would die for you
But now I've changed my mind
So blinded by your bright white lies
I missed all of the warning signs

You made me think I was somebody
Put your cold hands on my body
Worshipped you like a fool
You played my life like a video game
But you made up the goddamn rules

All those nights you lay by my side whispering into my heart
Now each time I close my eyes I feel you creeping in the dark

Hold me just a little bit closer
Take a little piece of me
It's the last you'll ever see
Cut me just a little bit deeper
Take a little piece of me
It's the last you'll ever see

The song draws to a close. I lower my guitar. There's no applause, just a deathly eerie silence. A TV camera zooms in on my face. I look into the lens and see my own reflection, the tears streaming down my cheeks. And time is motionless and neverending and I'm not even sure I'm breathing. Then a lone voice hollers, echoing across the stadium.

'We love you, Alora!' Another follows, then another. Soon the entire crowd is chanting in unison, 'We love you, Alora! We love you! We love you!'

And I've risen from the ashes on wings of flame. And their love means everything to me. And at the same time, it means nothing at all. Because none of it's real and all I ever wanted was a family. I lean into the mic and mumble, 'Goodbye,' before I run into the wings, leaving behind me only a shadow in time, a dark silhouette on a television screen which fuzzes and crackles before turning off completely. Eva and Julia are waiting for me there. I hand the guitar to one of my techs and we hurry down the narrow corridors, bursting through the exit into the dusky street where my bodyguards bulldoze the photographers to one side and bundle us into my Range Rover. The engine's running.

The door is slammed, the handbrake released and tyres scream against tarmac. We speed towards the port, paparazzi hot on our heels. My driver swerves around the bends like he's become his own stunt double. We lurch wordlessly from side to side on the back seat. Eva's phone is ringing repeatedly—she cancels the calls.

'It's begun,' she says.

I open up Twitter on my phone and I see the comments, and those comments are multiplying fast, hundreds into thousands like cells dividing and replicating beneath a time-lapse camera— the press, the fans, the lovers, the haters, everybody wants to know who *he* is, who the song's about. Lizzie Ghost posts something cryptic about having a lot in common with certain other teenage female artists and tags me in a photograph of a faded scar, on the inside of her thigh: *S*.

Someone joins the dots and posts his name in the thread— Silas Jax—and it spreads like a deadly virus which will eliminate his career, his reputation, his freedom. Reckless Child posts a photo, then Jade LeRoy, then another artist, then another, and soon the internet's a havoc of horror stories as more young female starlets reveal their hidden scars and with them, their truths. Silas's lawyers immediately fire out a cease-and-desist letter to my lawyers, demanding we make a public statement denying the accusations. But we're prepared. Eva emails my statement directly to the chief of the Metropolitan Police. He replies in an instant—the power of fame—an investigation has been opened.

The yacht is already waiting in the port, the captain standing out on deck wearing a pristine white shirt, surrounded by his crew. He lowers his hat and salutes as the car pulls up and slows to a halt. I salute back at him even though from behind the blacked-out windows I'm invisible.

Eva takes hold of my hand. Hers is clammy, her grip desperate. 'Are you sure?' she says again, her mantra of the day. And I see in her eyes that she wants me to stay, to weather the storm by her side. But this isn't about what she or anyone else wants, not anymore. My driver unloads my bag—one small case. I tuck Carrie beneath my arm. With the other, I hug Eva.

'Thank you,' I whisper. 'For everything.'

She shakes her head, blinks the tears from her eyes. 'I'll miss you,' she says. And when I hug Mum, I feel her heart beneath her blouse, beating slightly out of kilter with mine.

Front page column of *The New York Times*.

The prolific recording artist Alora Storm-Jones has drowned. Alora catapulted into the stratosphere of fame at the tender age of sixteen years old with her record-breaking album *The Truth*, closely followed by the critically massacred but commercially explosive *Beautiful Nightmare*. The star valued her privacy and increasingly refused to give interviews; however, through her lyrics she spoke openly about her personal struggles with mental health and had previously made a very public attempt to take her own life, resulting in the closure of z-pix and prompting a global backlash against social media. After a stint in rehab, Alora was believed to be fit and well and looking forward to the future. But only three days ago, after a rousing speech encouraging her fans to embrace life, she debuted a new song, "Piece of Me," revealing allegations of sexual abuse at the hands of legendary music producer Silas Jax. As more young victims come forward, Jax is under house arrest at his multi-million dollar estate in Los Angeles, awaiting trial. On Friday evening, Alora boarded a luxury yacht manned by a crew of fifteen and set sail for the Mediterranean. The last known sighting in the flesh of the talented but troubled teen was on Sunday when she took her evening meal out on deck, her beloved Teacup Chihuahua sitting on her lap. However, CCTV footage from around 2 a.m. shows a young woman, believed to be Alora, out on deck in the rain. Her head is tipped back and she is twirling erratically with her mouth wide open as though catching the droplets on her tongue, the dog in her arms. Then suddenly she appears to lose her balance and topple overboard with the dog. For reasons unknown, Alora could not swim. Deep-sea divers are continuing the search for the bodies of the iconic starlet and her beloved pet. As the world's youth mourns, Alora's albums dominate the top of the charts once more. Our thoughts are with her family during this tragic time.

EVA

THE MEMORIAL SERVICE IS HELD IN St Paul's Cathedral. Flower arrangements line the aisles, huge bouquets of larkspur and lilies, daisies and dahlias. The Royal Philharmonic Orchestra are playing a classical arrangement of 'Faker' as the congregation file inside—actors, musicians, movie directors, TV presenters. The glitterati have turned up in force to pay their respects to someone they barely knew, wearing their finest regalia for the cameras outside.

I'm sitting in the front row staring at her photograph, blown up and framed in gold, bordered by an intricate wreath of roses, snowdrops and ivy. In the photo, she's standing onstage looking out into the crowd with an expression of pure astonishment, as if she can barely believe that they're all there for her, eyes wide and shining and filled with wonder. The image is static but she looks so heartbreakingly alive, like she could very well just step out of it at any moment and break into song. The seat to my right is reserved for Shona but the service is due to begin in three minutes and she still hasn't arrived—she's probably outside, courting the journalists. To my left is my sister and Arif, Mum and Dad. Arif lays his palm flat against the bump, whispers something in Katerina's ear. She smiles and kisses his cheek. One life ending, another just beginning. I glance at Julia and Gina, sitting together on the opposite side of the aisle. Julia looks up and our eyes meet. We nod to each other in mutual understanding.

I crane my neck and see Roxanne, the head of marketing at Low Slang Records, sitting with Jason and Ray a few rows back. She looks bored. Jason's staring at his phone. The MD is notably absent, currently on bail and avoiding the press, lying low at his good friend Harvey's condo after KAZY-K went public with the things he made her do in private—the price she paid for fame. They're saying that the music business is riddled with misogyny, that the men close ranks and look after their own. But the mutating forces of ego, power and greed don't discriminate by gender, I should know. When she notices me, Roxanne hauls her expression into the most insincere of smiles. Without Alora, my superstar client, it's almost comical how swiftly my popularity has waned. Phone calls aren't returned, messages are marked read but left unanswered. I'm a nobody again, and it's strangely liberating.

Just then Shona walks in. Her arm is linked with that of a fashionably dressed man who I recognise as Bob Lamont, a hotshot artist manager who must be well into his sixties but the extensive work makes it impossible to tell for sure. Bob's followed by a young girl. She's wearing a white leather dress, prancing rather than walking, swishing her lustrous auburn hair from left to right. Kennedy Maxwell—all the record labels are trying to sign her. Last I heard the deal had reached a million but Bob's holding out for more. Kennedy's just turned fourteen. I watch

Roxanne, Jason and Ray leap out of their seats, practically salivating as Shona introduces them to Kennedy. You have to hand it to the woman, she's turned a memorial service for one deceased client into a networking opportunity for another. Kennedy struts towards the altar, angles her phone at herself and pouts, snaps a selfie with Alora's photograph. I raise my hand, gesturing for Shona to come join me. I watch her quite obviously see me and pretend that she hasn't. She sits down next to Kennedy and Bob four rows behind.

Right at the back, I see Ade. He's wearing a dark suit with a slim tie. Attached to his hand is an elegantly dressed Korean woman with a shaved head—his DJ girlfriend, Jia—and I inhale sharply at the very definite stab of pain in my chest, tumbling forwards into the black hole of my aloneness. I've looked her up online before, I've seen her picture in *Mixmag*. But this is the first time I've actually seen them together as a couple and the combination is almost blinding, like staring straight into an eclipse. Ade notices me and smiles, and in that smile I know he's saying that he hopes I'm okay, that he's here for me. I manage to smile back, mouthing, 'Thank you.' And I wonder what I'm supposed to do with all this unrequited feeling. Pack it away in a box maybe, hope that someone else comes along one day who'll take it off my hands, make sure I never prioritise work over love again.

I don't cry during the service. I stare straight ahead into the vacuum of stale, floral-scented air whilst the priest drones on about the forgiveness of sins. Noah Lamb reads 'New York Address', a poem by Linda Gregg which was one of Alora's favourites. Noah says that Alora was a precious gift to the world, that her music changed lives. He sheds a few tears which are either genuine or the performance of a lifetime. Lazy Lover performs a cover of 'Underland' with three backing singers. She writhes around on the altar during the final verse whilst the A&R executive who signed her beams with something oddly close to parental pride. The priest looks horrified. She receives a standing ovation.

When the service is over the congregation trickle out, adopting appropriately mournful expressions before stepping into the flashing lights, each of them secretly vying for front page. My sister excuses herself, she says the baby's pressing on her bladder and she's seconds away from pissing herself, that she'll wait for me in the car. It's only when the cathedral's completely empty that Julia crosses the aisle. She sits down next to me and touches her left shoulder lightly to mine. She dabs at her eyes with a handkerchief. For a moment, we sit in silence, motionless in this strange new reality without Alora in it.

'Well?' I eventually croak.

Julia slips the handkerchief into her bag and snaps the clasp shut. 'It was beautiful, really authentic.'

'There's a total shitstorm going down online, you know.'

'I know, I've seen it.'

'Some people are calling her out as a hypocrite, saying that after everything she preached at that televised gig she still went ahead and took her own life. Others are saying it's all a hoax, that it wasn't her in the CCTV footage.'

'Well, that's just ridiculous, it's so obviously her.'

'The whole "see you in the underland" thing she posted on Instagram the night before has really got them fired up—I don't know what she was thinking.'

'She never publicly confirmed what *underland* means, though.'

'Maybe not, but some of the super-fans get it.'

'It'll simmer down soon. The police aren't listening to a bunch of teenagers, bureaucratic incompetency is on our side.'

We fall silent. We breathe. A door slams behind us and the sound echoes around the cathedral. 'Do you think people will think it's weird if I take some of the flowers home with me?' Julia says.

'After everything that's happened, do you honestly care what people think?'

She stands and walks to the front. Frivolous shafts of afternoon light catch the streaks of grey in her hair and they glint like silver. She pauses for a moment before the photograph of her daughter, reaches out and strokes her face, like a mother tenderly soothing an infant to sleep in her crib. Then out of the abundance of extravagant bouquets from top-end florists she chooses the most modest bunch—blue flowers, a simple arrangement tied with string. Texas bluebonnets. An anonymous delivery.

VANESSA

WAKE AND SLEEP ARE BECOMING LESS DISTINCT. My nights are filled with pale morning light, buttercup confetti raining through my dreams. Memories infiltrate my days, layered on top of my thoughts like touch—a held hand, a gentle kiss, a gust of wind which steals the breath. He was always here in the ranch with me, but I feel him now more than ever before. And I know that I will join him soon. But every day before I leave, I will live like it's my last.

She arrived in the depths of night; the moon a luscious pool of spilled cream, the stars like tiny pinpricks of hope. Shivering, frightened, clutching the dog. Dylan lifted her from the seat of his truck and carried her inside. She'd asked me to teach her how to swim. I stood on the banks of the creek and watched as she transformed from fearful teen into water baby. The plan she concocted was not without risk. But determination burns bright in those emerald eyes.

Dylan cooked. She slept and grew stronger. And I watched as they slipped into each other's arms. They thought they were being discreet I'm sure, but nothing gets past this wily old fox: the twilight walks, the shy smiles, the click of the latch on her bedroom door as he left at dawn. So when one day at dinner he took her hand, Evelyn bouncing on her lap, and said, 'There's something we need to tell you,' I played the fool, expressed my surprise and delight, hugged them both and gave them my blessing.

And I'm thankful for all my blessings. The warmth of a steaming mug between two cold hands. The leisurely unfurl of a rosebud in spring. A line of a book which pierces your heart. These are the things that matter in life. Not Bentleys or Balenciaga, mansions or millions of followers online—strangers envious of the person you pretend to be.

My saddle days are over now, these creaking joints just won't oblige. But the three of them ride out together, early morning when the wider world is a charade of peace and mist coats the valley like thought. Evelyn will sometimes ask her to sing and her voice will echo around the canyon, a whirlwind of beauty. And while the horses graze in the distance, she lays one palm on the swell of her belly. When the breeze is pulling in the right direction, I can hear her from the ranch. She sings for herself and her family alone.

ALORA'S SONGS

DROWNING IN THE BLUE

I've forgotten how to live
Or maybe I just never knew
Convince the shrink I'm doing fine
When I'm drowning in the blue

Kill me with your kindness
Suffocate me in belief
Don't know how to love myself
So how could he love me

His eyes are gold and he tastes like fire
He swears he's mine he's a beautiful liar
He's burned his body into my bones
I fall asleep in his arms but I wake up alone
Sleep in his arms but I wake up alone

All the money in the world
Won't buy you into paradise
When you wake up screaming to
The nightmare of this life

Take the meds so you forget
No one really gives a damn
When you're drowning in the blue
Only you can swim to land

His eyes are gold and he tastes like fire
He swears he's mine he's a beautiful liar
He's burned his body into my bones
I fall asleep in his arms but I wake up alone
Sleep in his arms but I wake up alone

FAKER

I'm just a faker just a pretender
Been like this so long don't know who I am
I'm just a faker just a pretender
Been like this so long don't know who I am

Got to peel back the layers and start again
But how do I do that where do I begin?
Would you still like me would you recognise me
If I lose this disguise I've been wearing to hide me?

Cos I'm just a faker just a pretender
Been like this so long don't know who I am
I'm just a faker just a pretender
Been like this so long don't know who I am

I want to be happy with the tiniest things
A walk in the park with morning sun on my skin
Want to know on my last breath that I have been real
That I've given myself permission to feel

I'm just a faker just a pretender
Been like this so long don't know who I am
I'm just a faker just a pretender
Been like this so long don't know who I am

UNDERLAND

I never wanted to tell you what I was thinking
I always worried 'bout what you would think 'bout me
I never wanted you to know that I was sinking
That I needed you to rescue me

I never dared to tell the truth cos deep down
We both knew the house was built on lies
I never wanted to show how hard I was trying
What I was willing to sacrifice

See you in the underland
See you in the underland
See you in the underland

I've been going round in circles ever since you left
I've been spiralling out of control
Even though my mama tells me that it's for the best
I know I've lost part of my soul
I've been going round in circles ever since you left
I've been spiralling out of control
Even though my mama tells me that it's for the best
I know I've lost part of my soul

I never wanted you to see that I was vulnerable
That I wasn't made of steel

Always trying to pretend that I was perfect
But nothing perfect is ever real

Maybe in the underland I'll understand how
You could close your eyes and let me go
Hiding in between the smoke and mirrors are
The answers that I guess I'll never know

Five four three two one go
See you in the underland
See you in the underland
See you in the underland

I've been going round in circles ever since you left
I've been spiralling out of control
Even though my mama tells me that it's for the best
I know I've lost part of my soul
I've been going round in circles ever since you left
I've been spiralling out of control
Even though my mama tells me that it's for the best
I know I've lost part of my soul

ANYBODY

Wake up in the morning
Thought it might be different
It's exactly the same
I feel your body moving
I'd better get going
I can't remember your name

When I just need a body
It could be anybody
It don't matter to me
We were talking in the party
Doing it is easy
Forget how to breathe

I don't want you to say you love me oh no
Don't try to hold my hand or follow me home
I don't want you to say you love me oh no
Don't try to hold my hand or follow me home

Wonder what he's doing
If he's ever thinking
Of who I am with
I'm trying to forget though
There isn't any new low
I wouldn't forgive

I block unblock his number
Tell my heart we're done there
It's not listening
I'm dancing on my own now
Never fell so low down
Cos you're never him

I don't want you to say you love me oh no
Don't try to hold my hand or follow me home
I don't want you to say you love me oh no
Don't try to hold my hand or follow me home

I can't forget the way that it felt when he held me close
So I get in your bed meaningless sex and it never comes close
And then you want me but I don't want you back cos I only want him
And so I turn my back move on to the next the cycle continuing

Wake up in the morning
Thought it might be different
It's exactly the same
I feel your body moving
I'd better get going
I can't remember your name

When I just need a body
It could be anybody
It don't matter to me
We were talking in the party
Doing it is easy
Forget how to breathe

I don't want you to say you love me oh no
Don't try to hold my hand or follow me home
I don't want you to say you love me oh no
Don't try to hold my hand or follow me home

PIECE OF ME

I always thought I would die for you
But now I've changed my mind
So blinded by your bright white lies
I missed all of the warning signs

You made me think I was somebody
Put your cold hands on my body
Worshipped you like a fool
You played my life like a video game
But you made up the goddamn rules

All those nights you lay by my side whispering into my heart
Now each time I close my eyes I feel you creeping in the dark

Hold me just a little bit closer
Take a little piece of me
It's the last you'll ever see
Cut me just a little bit deeper
Take a little piece of me
It's the last you'll ever see

All those nights you lay by my side whispering into my heart
Now each time I close my eyes I feel you creeping in the dark

I sold all of my power for
The silver of your tongue
Sucked inside the melody
My world became a darker song

Let's rewrite the fairy tale
If you're the coffin I'm the nail
Ending's gonna come true
Thought I was the faker but
The biggest fake of all is you

All those nights you lay by my side whispering into my heart
Now each time I close my eyes I feel you creeping in the dark

Hold me just a little bit closer
Take a little piece of me
It's the last you'll ever see
Cut me just a little bit deeper
Take a little piece of me
It's the last you'll ever see

Just a little bit closer
Just a little bit deeper
Just a little bit

ACKNOWLEDGEMENTS

Putting a book out into the world is a wonderful and terrifying process, but step one was mustering sufficient self-belief to write a book in the first place, to accept that the voice of the inner critic would always be present in various degrees of volume as I typed the words, as I drafted emails to agents and as I went out on submission to publishers. I would like to thank everyone who, even if they didn't even realise it, contributed to me thinking that this was ever a possibility for me.

I'd like to thank all of my classmates at Faber Academy, the first people who ever read any of my fiction and whose feedback encouraged me, thickened my skin and made me a better writer. In particular I'd like to thank my classmate and fellow author Tanya Cornish for taking me by the shoulders one day, looking me in the eye and saying, 'Delphine, you *are* a writer!'

I'd like to thank Rachel Petty at The Blair Partnership for believing in me, for taking a chance on a book which was far less accomplished until she set her keen editorial eye to it—I'm eternally grateful to you, Rachel. I'd also like to thank

Rory Scarfe at The Blair Partnership for being so brilliant, my wonderful lawyer Sebastian Davey at Russells for all his help and support, and Kitty Walker for her insightful feedback on an early draft of the manuscript.

I'd like to thank my editor, Sara Goodman, a very special human who climbed inside *Darkening Song* with me and bedded down next to me, and has remained there ever since. I couldn't wish for a more wonderful literary comrade; everything about the book is better because of you, Sara—thank you for making my dreams come true. Huge thank-you also to the entire UK team—Taylor, Tommy, Aaron and everyone at Round, Eve, Amy, Amelia, Nan, Charlie and everyone at Blue Neon Books - you are all an absolute joy to work with.

I'd like to thank my cousin Anne, a nurse in the prison service for many years, for ensuring I made no medical blunders with regards to Alora's recovery. I'd like to thank SK for checking my descriptions of Ade's parents' home to ensure they rang true for their Nigerian culture.

I'd like to thank Amelia Scivier for being one of the most supportive, impressive and downright lovely people you could ever hope to meet, one of *Darkening Song*'s early readers and advocates. I'd like to thank my long-standing friend Nan Davies for all the same reasons and my newer but no less dear friend Carol Nixon for being so kind and encouraging and making such a profound impact on my understanding of life.

I'd like to thank my sister Yolande for giving me a serious talking-to and preventing me from sending an email to agents essentially apologising for my book. I'd like to thank my parents, Marjorie and John, for placing such importance on reading from a young age—our bookshelves at home were always overflowing (and messy).

I'd like to thank everyone who took the time to read *Darkening Song* in advance and provide a blurb—what incredible kindness and generosity: Dave Bayley, John Niven, Isabel Banta, Rachel Dawson, Bexy Cameron and Honor Teideman. I hope one day I'll be able to return the favour tenfold.

I'd like to thank Darren Woodford for his incredible musical ear and talent for polishing vocals. I'd like to thank Ellie Mason, producer and mixer extraordinaire, who worked her magic on Alora's songs and made them sound far better than I could have ever imagined. You can find her on IG: @msn_ellie. I'd like to thank Syd Michaud who lent her stunning vocals to be the voice of Alora; the line in the book about meeting an artist and seeing their talent shining through their skin was easy to write because I experienced it firsthand when I met you. If you want to be blown away, listen to more of Syd's music—you can find her at S.Michaud on Spotify—and the gorgeous bonus track at the end of the audiobook is one of Syd's own.

A&J—thank you for everything.

And last but not least, P—you are always behind me with your rambunctious energy; thank you for your unwavering support.

ABOUT THE AUTHOR

DELPHINE SEDDON writes female-driven contemporary fiction. For the past twenty years, she has worked in the music industry. *Darkening Song* is her debut novel.

Connect with her on:

 www.delphineseddon.com

 @delphineseddon

 @delphineseddon

 https://drivingblindlyintothemist.substack.com